Message from
Hidenori Kusaka

I was surprised to see Magearna's description added to Pokémon HOME. It was so nice to be able to get hold of Magearna in its true original color (from 500 years ago) and use it. I've always loved how Magearna is able to transform into a Poké Ball shape, and I would create paper crafts that were capable of transforming. So I was very happy to have Magearna appear in the manga. I hope you enjoy the new Kalos episode.

Message from
Satoshi Yamamoto

It's been eight years since the *X•Y* arc started and five years since it ended. In Volume 6 of *Pokémon Adventures: X•Y*, we were finally able to complete the *X•Y* arc. Scenes that I was unable to fully depict in the mini-volumes, scenes that needed more details, scenes that I wanted to fix...I think I managed to make improvements on all of that. I hope I will be able to work on the following *Omega Ruby Alpha Sapphire* arc in an equally satisfying manner for both the creators and the readers of the series.

Hidenori Kusaka is the writer for *Pokémon Adventures*. Running continuously for over 25 years, *Pokémon Adventures* is the only manga series to completely cover all the *Pokémon* games and has become one of the most popular series of all time. In addition to writing manga, he also edits children's books and plans mixed-media projects for Shogakukan's children's magazines. He uses the Pokémon Electrode as his author portrait.

Satoshi Yamamoto is the artist for *Pokémon Adventures*, which he began working on in 2001, starting with volume 10. Yamamoto launched his manga career in 1993 with the horror-action title *Kimen Senshi*, which ran in Shogakukan's *Weekly Shonen Sunday* magazine, followed by the series *Kaze no Denshosha*. Yamamoto's favorite manga creators/artists include FUJIKO F FUJIO (*Doraemon*), Yukinobu Hoshino (*2001 Nights*), and Katsuhiro Otomo (*Akira*). He loves films, monsters, detective novels, and punk rock music. He uses the Pokémon Swalot as his artist portrait.

What if you knew
that in ten days' time,
your planet would
be vaporized—
destroyed in the
blink of an eye?

What would you do
during those ten
days, and who
would you spend
them with...?

POKÉMON™
ADVENTURES
OMEGA RUBY • ALPHA SAPPHIRE

POKÉMON ADVENTURES

the 13th Chapter

thirteenth

Ω·α

1

VOLUME ONE

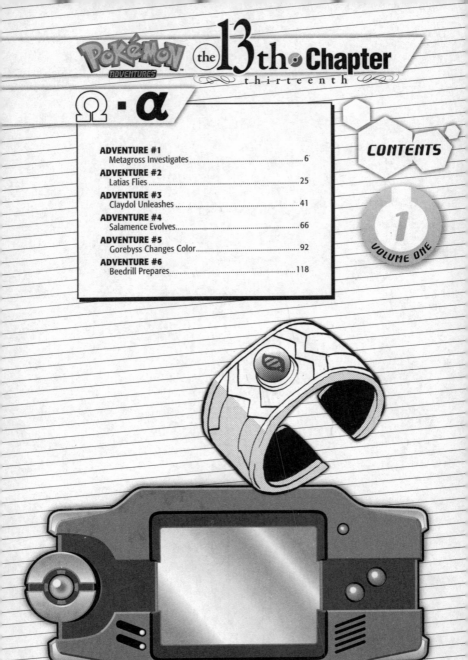

POKÉMON™
ADVENTURES
Ω RUBY α SAPPHIRE

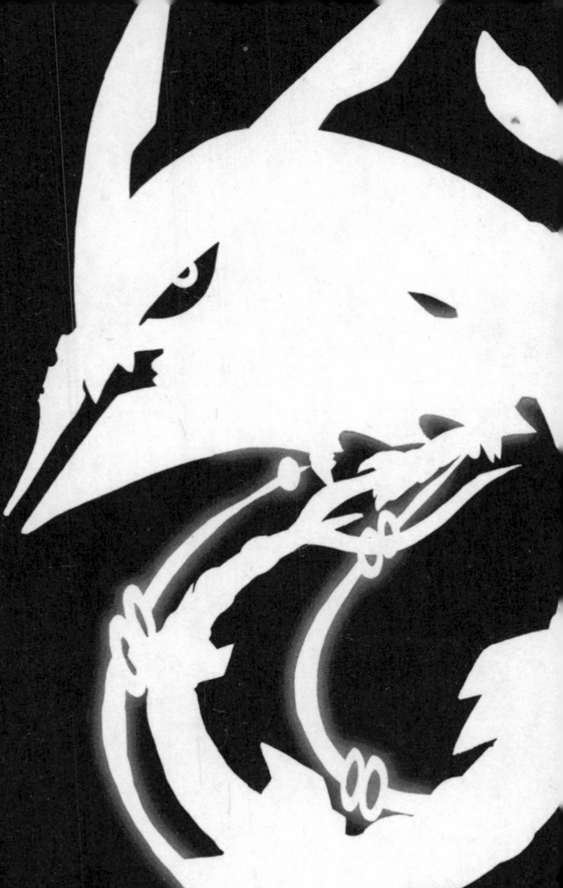

ADVENTURE #1

Metagross Investigates

Pokémon™ Adventures Omega Ruby • Alpha Sapphire

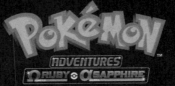

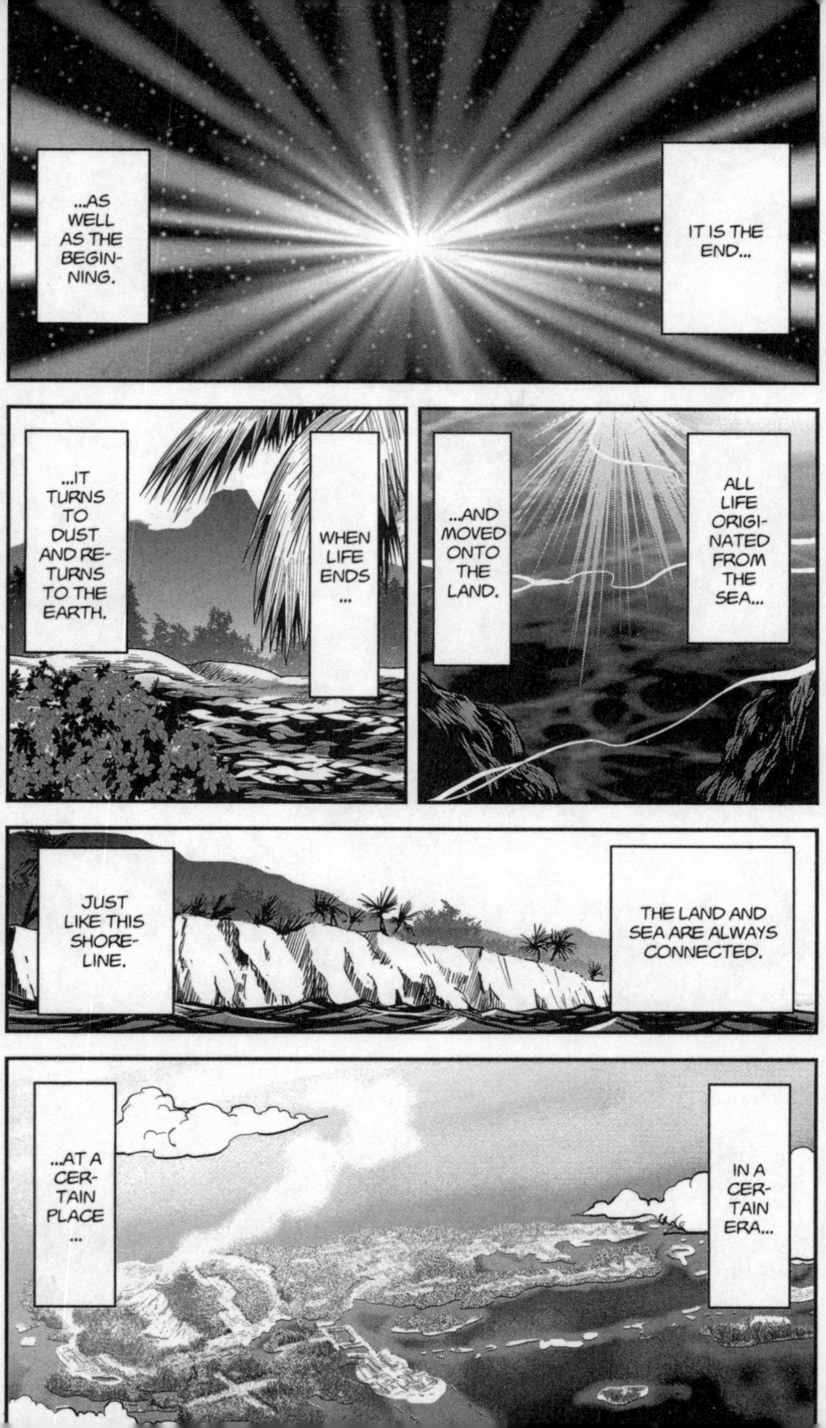
IT IS THE END...
...AS WELL AS THE BEGIN-NING.
ALL LIFE ORIGI-NATED FROM THE SEA...
...AND MOVED ONTO THE LAND.
WHEN LIFE ENDS ...
...IT TURNS TO DUST AND RE-TURNS TO THE EARTH.
THE LAND AND SEA ARE ALWAYS CONNECTED.
JUST LIKE THIS SHORE-LINE.
IN A CER-TAIN ERA...
...AT A CER-TAIN PLACE ...

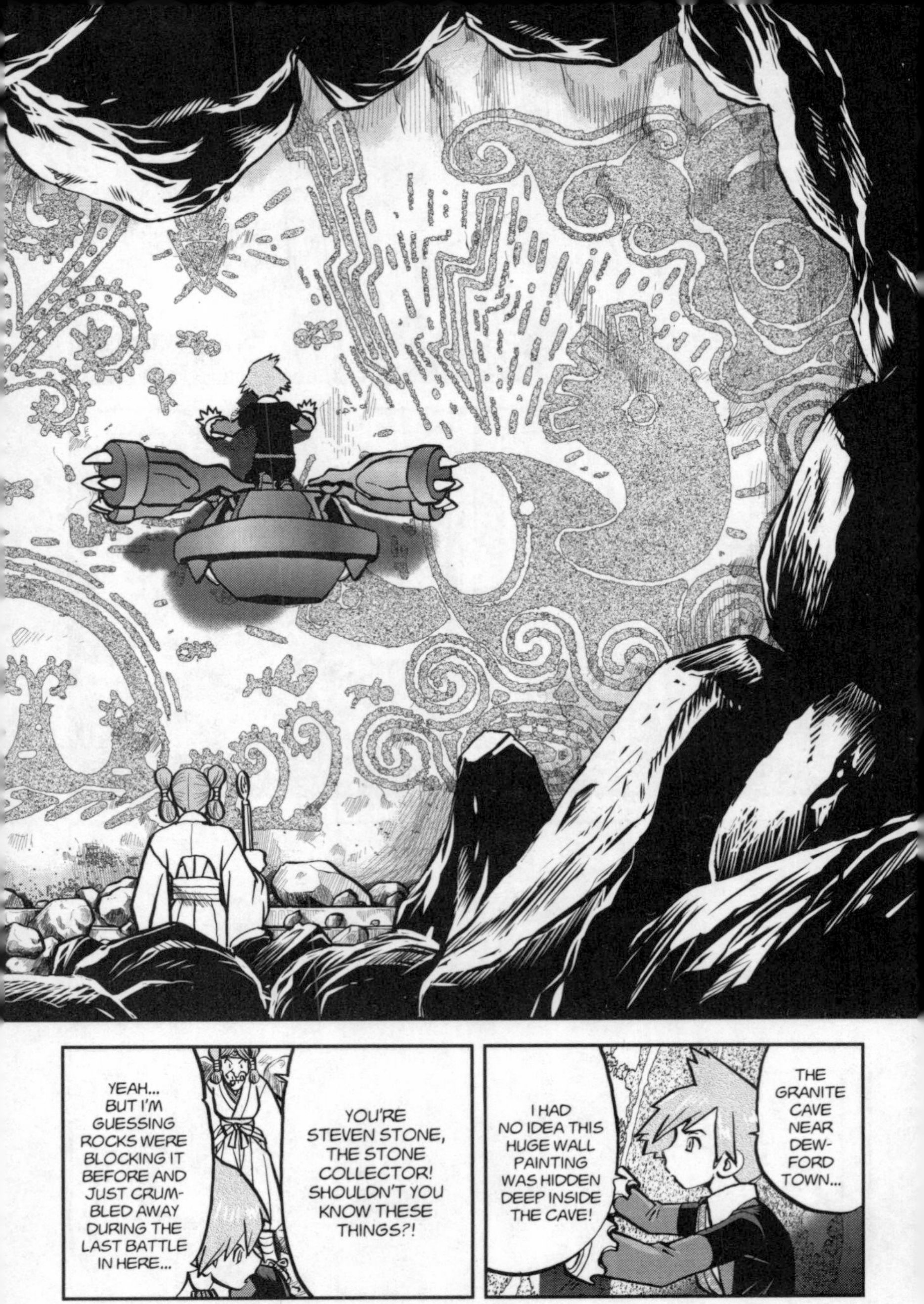
THE GRANITE CAVE NEAR DEW-FORD TOWN...
I HAD NO IDEA THIS HUGE WALL PAINTING WAS HIDDEN DEEP INSIDE THE CAVE!
YOU'RE STEVEN STONE, THE STONE COLLECTOR! SHOULDN'T YOU KNOW THESE THINGS?!
YEAH... BUT I'M GUESSING ROCKS WERE BLOCKING IT BEFORE AND JUST CRUM-BLED AWAY DURING THE LAST BATTLE IN HERE...

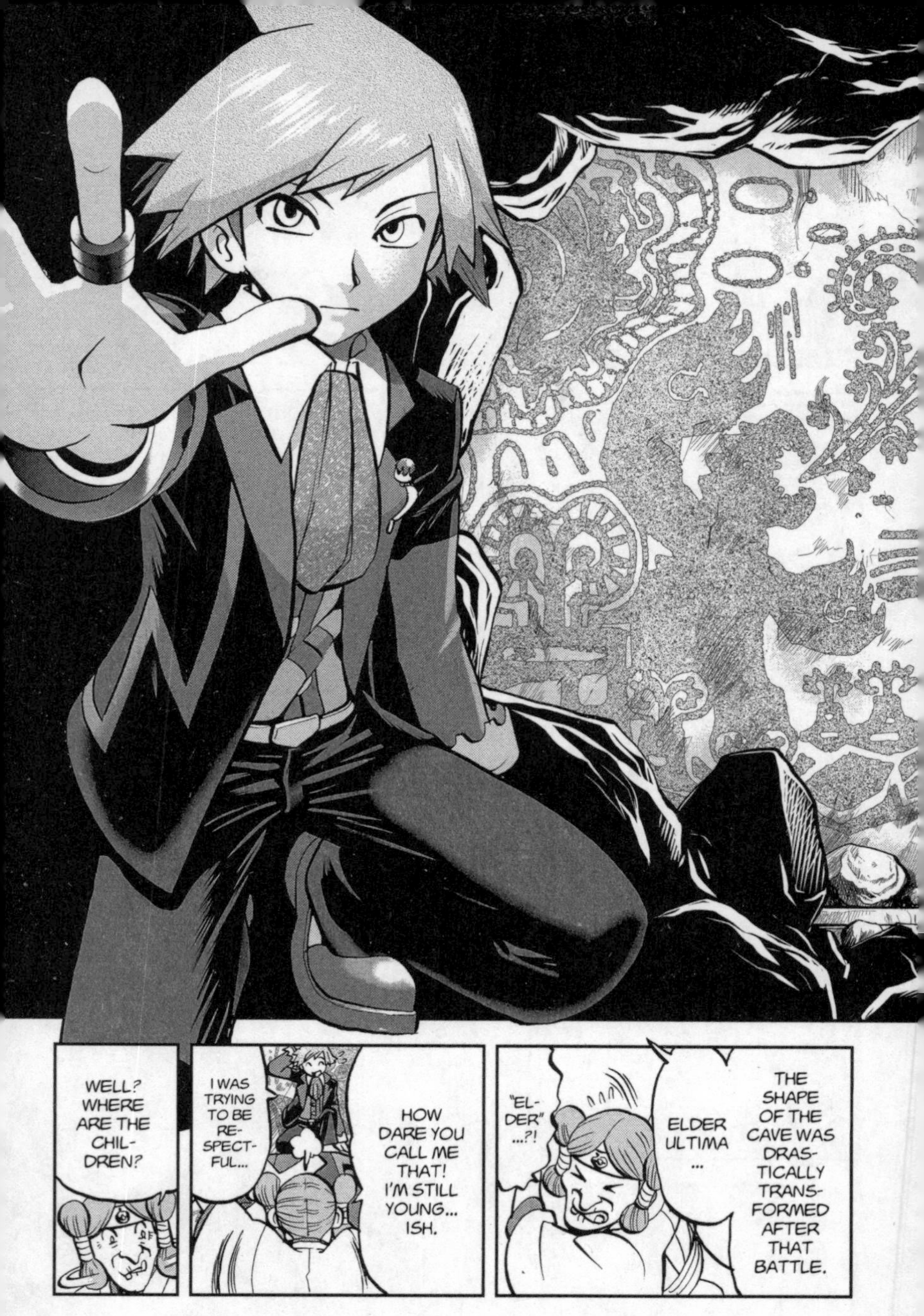
THE SHAPE OF THE CAVE WAS DRASTICALLY TRANSFORMED AFTER THAT BATTLE.
ELDER ULTIMA...
"EL-DER"...?!
HOW DARE YOU CALL ME THAT! I'M STILL YOUNG... ISH.
I WAS TRYING TO BE RESPECTFUL...
WELL? WHERE ARE THE CHILDREN?

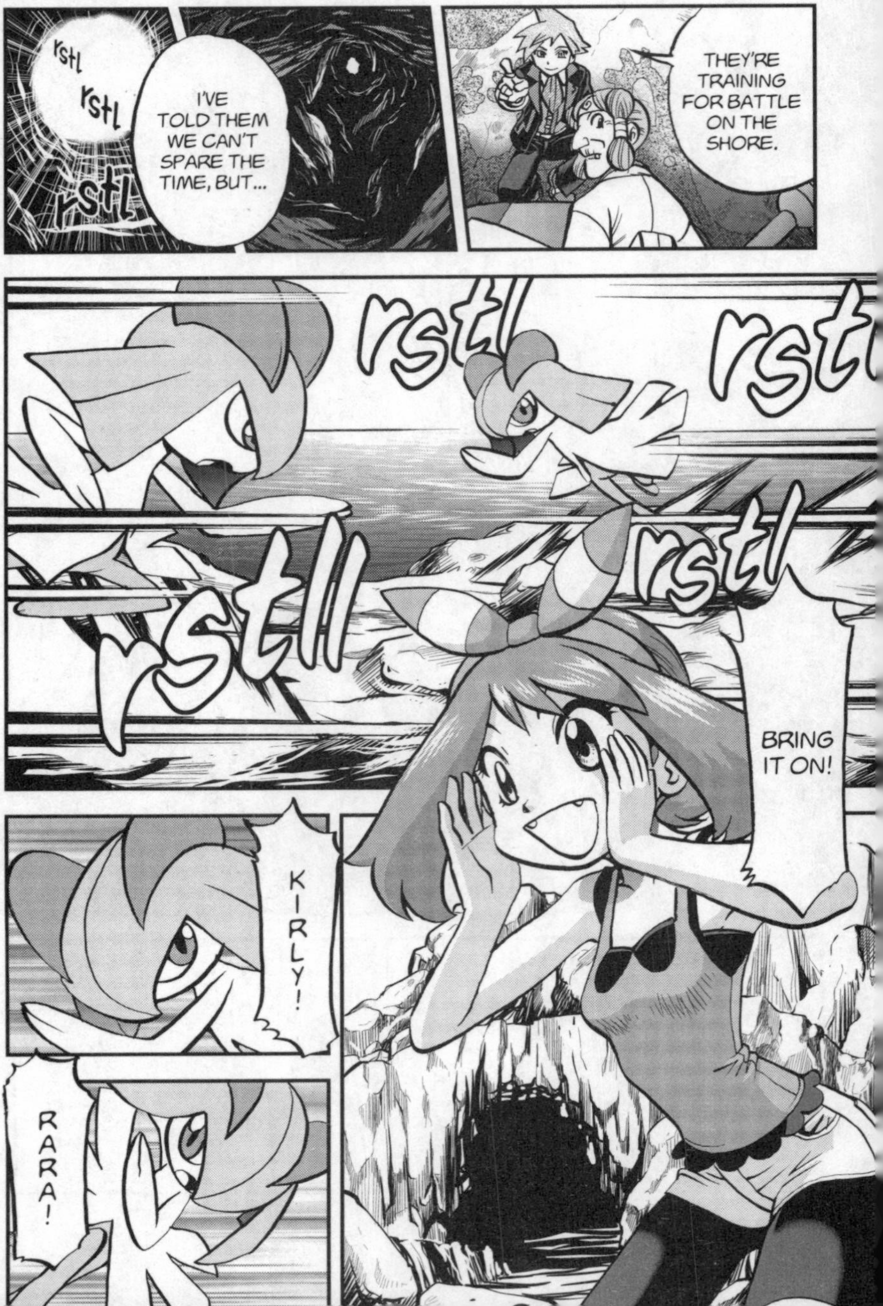
THEY'RE TRAINING FOR BATTLE ON THE SHORE.
rstl
rstl
rstl
I'VE TOLD THEM WE CAN'T SPARE THE TIME, BUT...
rstl
rstl
rstl
rstll
BRING IT ON!
KIRLY!
RARA!

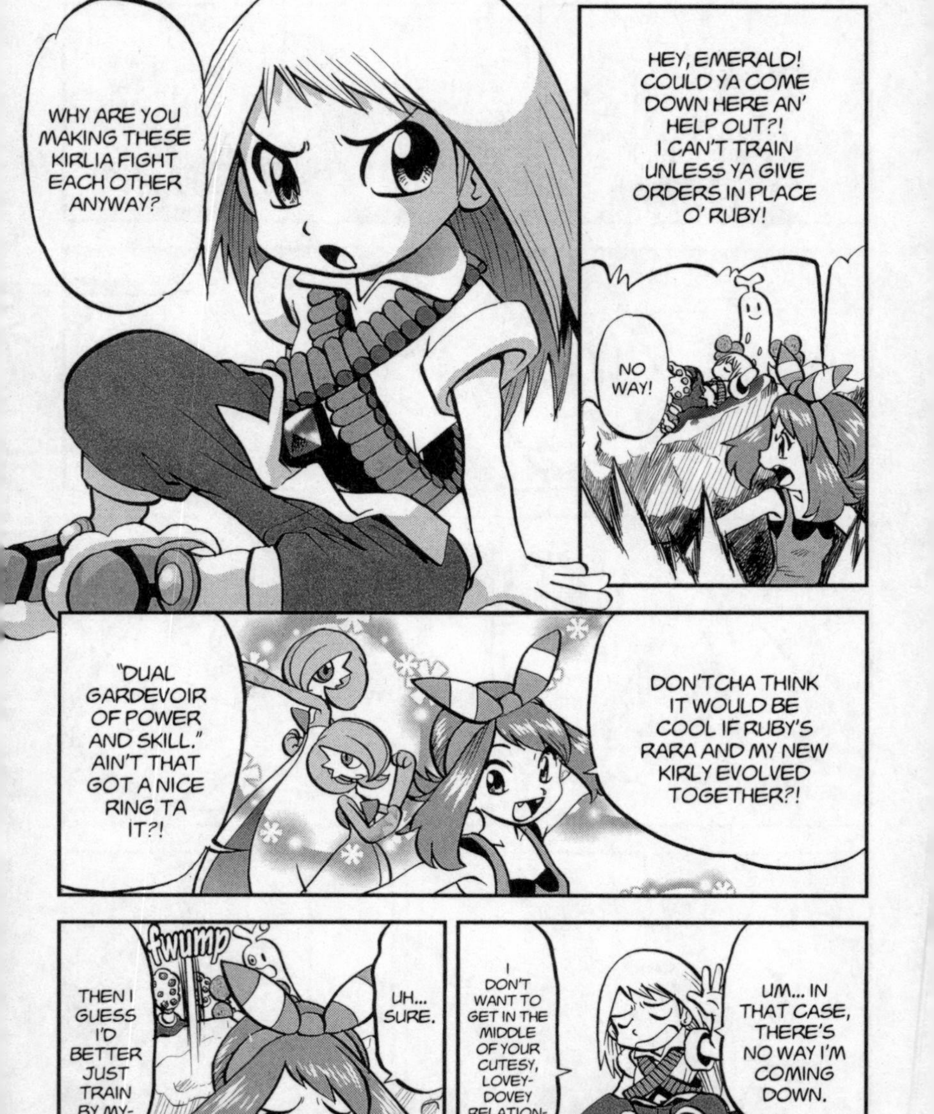
HEY, EMERALD! COULD YA COME DOWN HERE AN' HELP OUT?! I CAN'T TRAIN UNLESS YA GIVE ORDERS IN PLACE O' RUBY!
NO WAY!
WHY ARE YOU MAKING THESE KIRLIA FIGHT EACH OTHER ANYWAY?
DON'TCHA THINK IT WOULD BE COOL IF RUBY'S RARA AND MY NEW KIRLY EVOLVED TOGETHER?!
"DUAL GARDEVOIR OF POWER AND SKILL." AIN'T THAT GOT A NICE RING TA IT?!
UM... IN THAT CASE, THERE'S NO WAY I'M COMING DOWN.
I DON'T WANT TO GET IN THE MIDDLE OF YOUR CUTESY, LOVEY-DOVEY RELATIONSHIP.
UH... SURE.
fwump
THEN I GUESS I'D BETTER JUST TRAIN BY MYSELF!

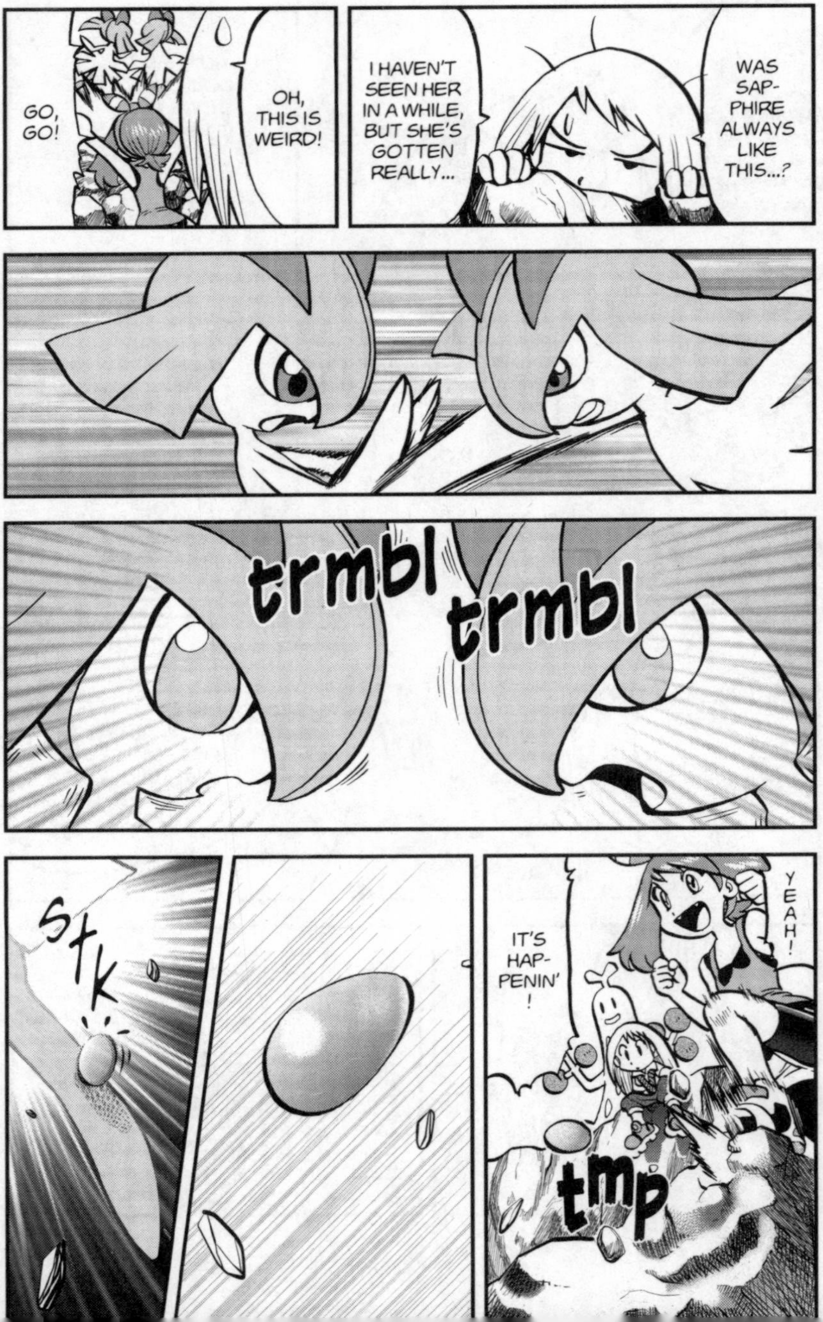
WAS SAP-PHIRE ALWAYS LIKE THIS...?
I HAVEN'T SEEN HER IN A WHILE, BUT SHE'S GOTTEN REALLY...
OH, THIS IS WEIRD!
GO, GO!
trmbl
trmbl
YEAH!
IT'S HAP-PENIN'!
tmp
stk

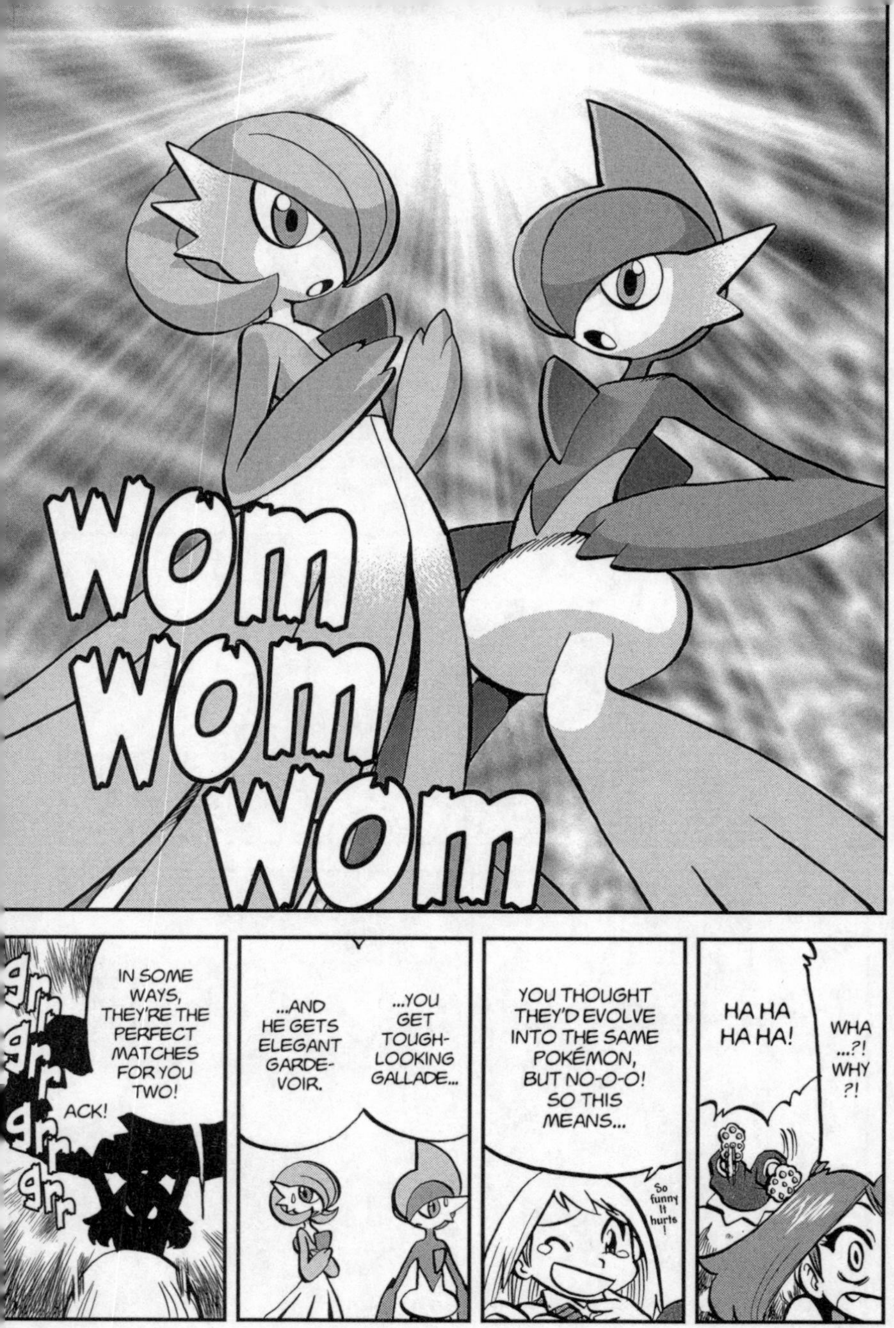
WOM
WOM
WOM
WHA ...?! WHY ?!
HA HA HA HA!
YOU THOUGHT THEY'D EVOLVE INTO THE SAME POKÉMON, BUT NO-O-O! SO THIS MEANS...
So funny it hurts!
...YOU GET TOUGH-LOOKING GALLADE...
...AND HE GETS ELEGANT GARDE-VOIR.
IN SOME WAYS, THEY'RE THE PERFECT MATCHES FOR YOU TWO!
ACK!
grr grr grr grr

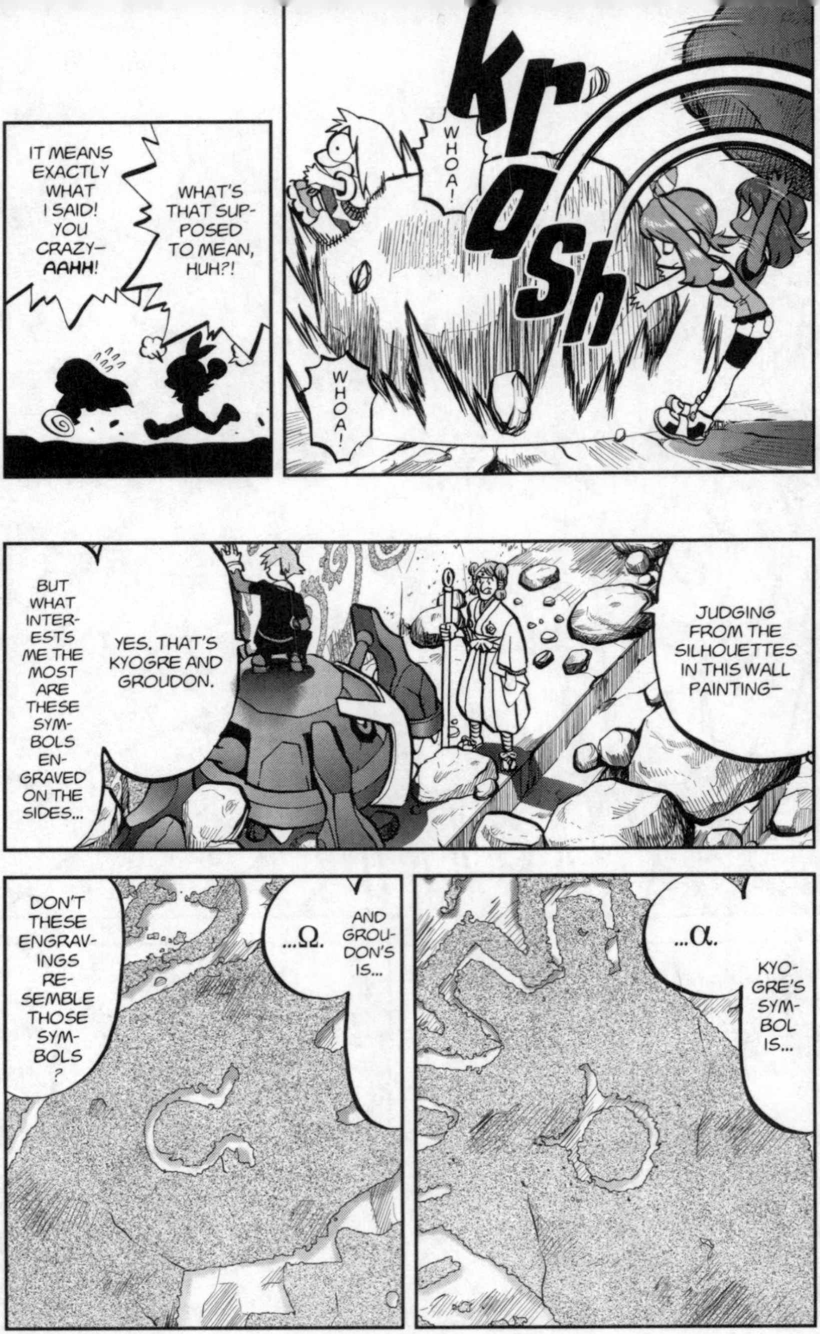
krash
WHOA!
WHOA!
WHAT'S THAT SUPPOSED TO MEAN, HUH?!
IT MEANS EXACTLY WHAT I SAID! YOU CRAZY—AAHH!
JUDGING FROM THE SILHOUETTES IN THIS WALL PAINTING—
YES. THAT'S KYOGRE AND GROUDON.
BUT WHAT INTERESTS ME THE MOST ARE THESE SYMBOLS ENGRAVED ON THE SIDES...
KYOGRE'S SYMBOL IS...
...α.
AND GROUDON'S IS...
...Ω.
DON'T THESE ENGRAVINGS RESEMBLE THOSE SYMBOLS?

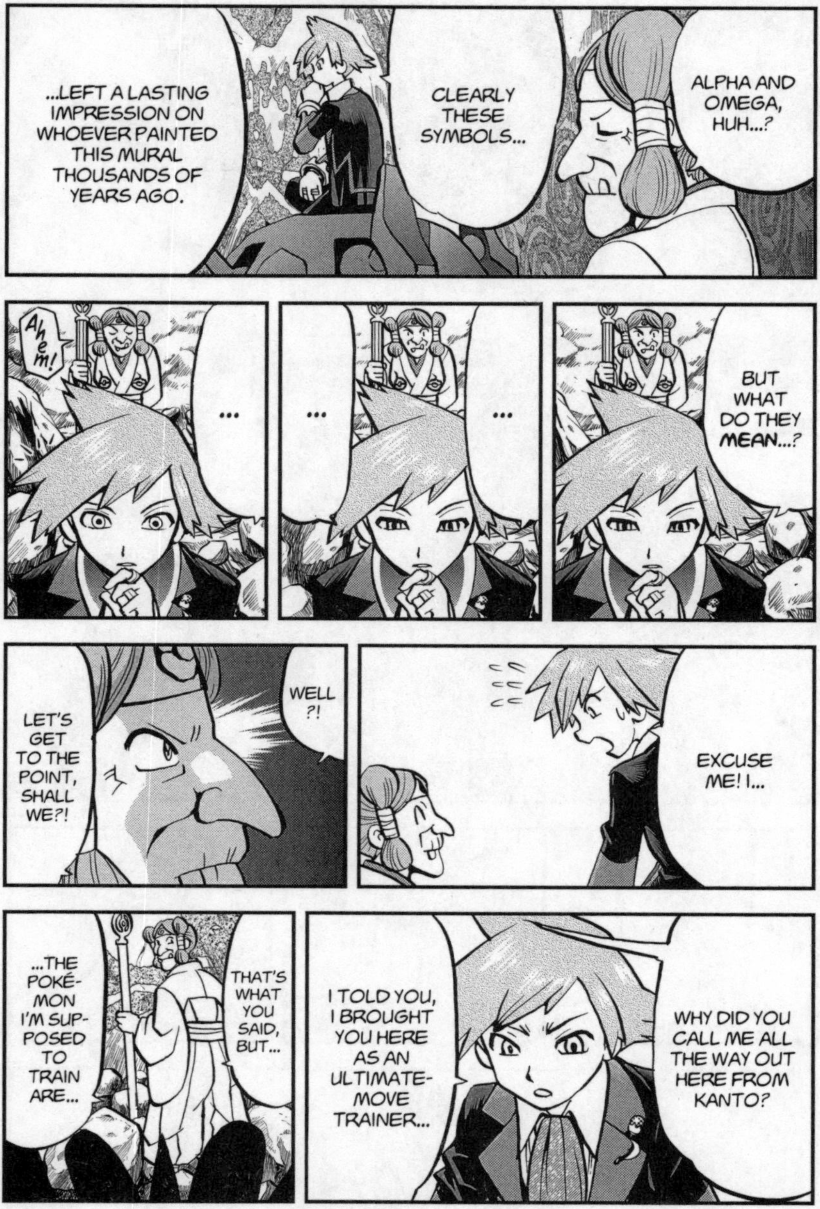
ALPHA AND OMEGA, HUH...?
CLEARLY THESE SYMBOLS...
...LEFT A LASTING IMPRESSION ON WHOEVER PAINTED THIS MURAL THOUSANDS OF YEARS AGO.
BUT WHAT DO THEY MEAN...?
...
...
...
Ahem!
EXCUSE ME! I...
WELL?!
LET'S GET TO THE POINT, SHALL WE?!
WHY DID YOU CALL ME ALL THE WAY OUT HERE FROM KANTO?
I TOLD YOU, I BROUGHT YOU HERE AS AN ULTIMATE-MOVE TRAINER...
THAT'S WHAT YOU SAID, BUT...
...THE POKÉMON I'M SUPPOSED TO TRAIN ARE...

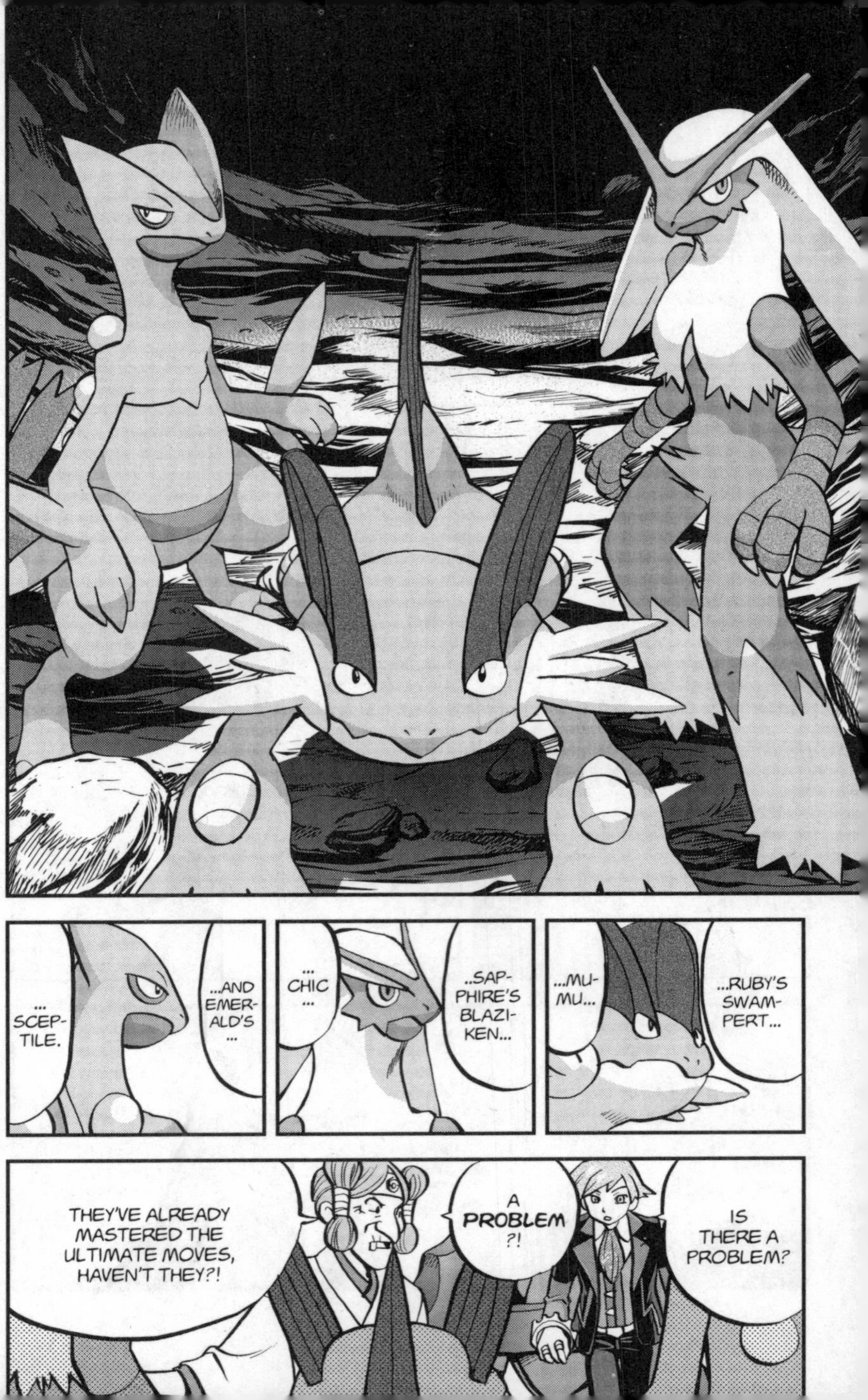
...RUBY'S SWAMPERT...
...MUMU...
..SAPPHIRE'S BLAZIKEN...
... CHIC ...
...AND EMERALD'S ...
... SCEPTILE.
IS THERE A PROBLEM?
A **PROBLEM** ?!
THEY'VE ALREADY MASTERED THE ULTIMATE MOVES, HAVEN'T THEY?!

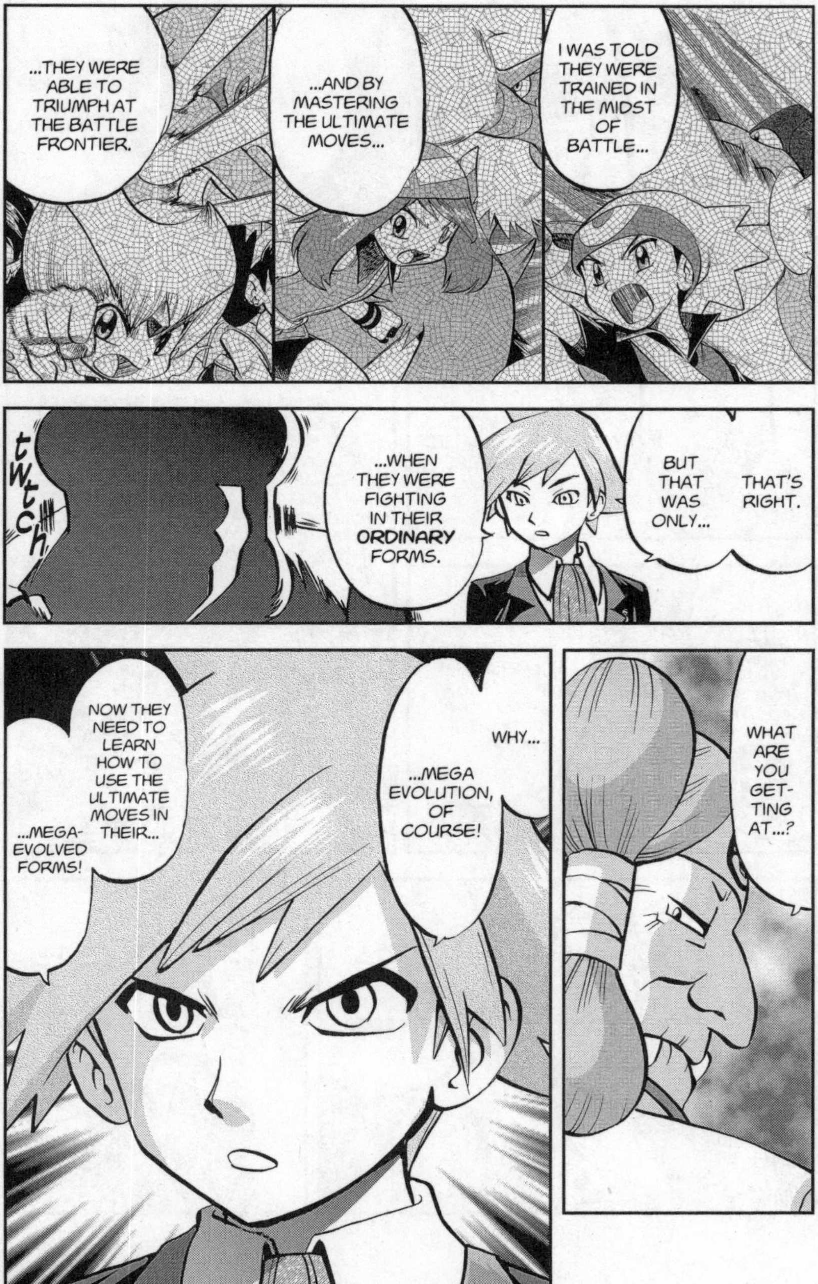

I WAS TOLD THEY WERE TRAINED IN THE MIDST OF BATTLE...
...AND BY MASTERING THE ULTIMATE MOVES...
...THEY WERE ABLE TO TRIUMPH AT THE BATTLE FRONTIER.
THAT'S RIGHT.
BUT THAT WAS ONLY...
...WHEN THEY WERE FIGHTING IN THEIR ORDINARY FORMS.
twtch
WHAT ARE YOU GET-TING AT...?
WHY...
...MEGA EVOLUTION, OF COURSE!
NOW THEY NEED TO LEARN HOW TO USE THE ULTIMATE MOVES IN THEIR...
...MEGA-EVOLVED FORMS!

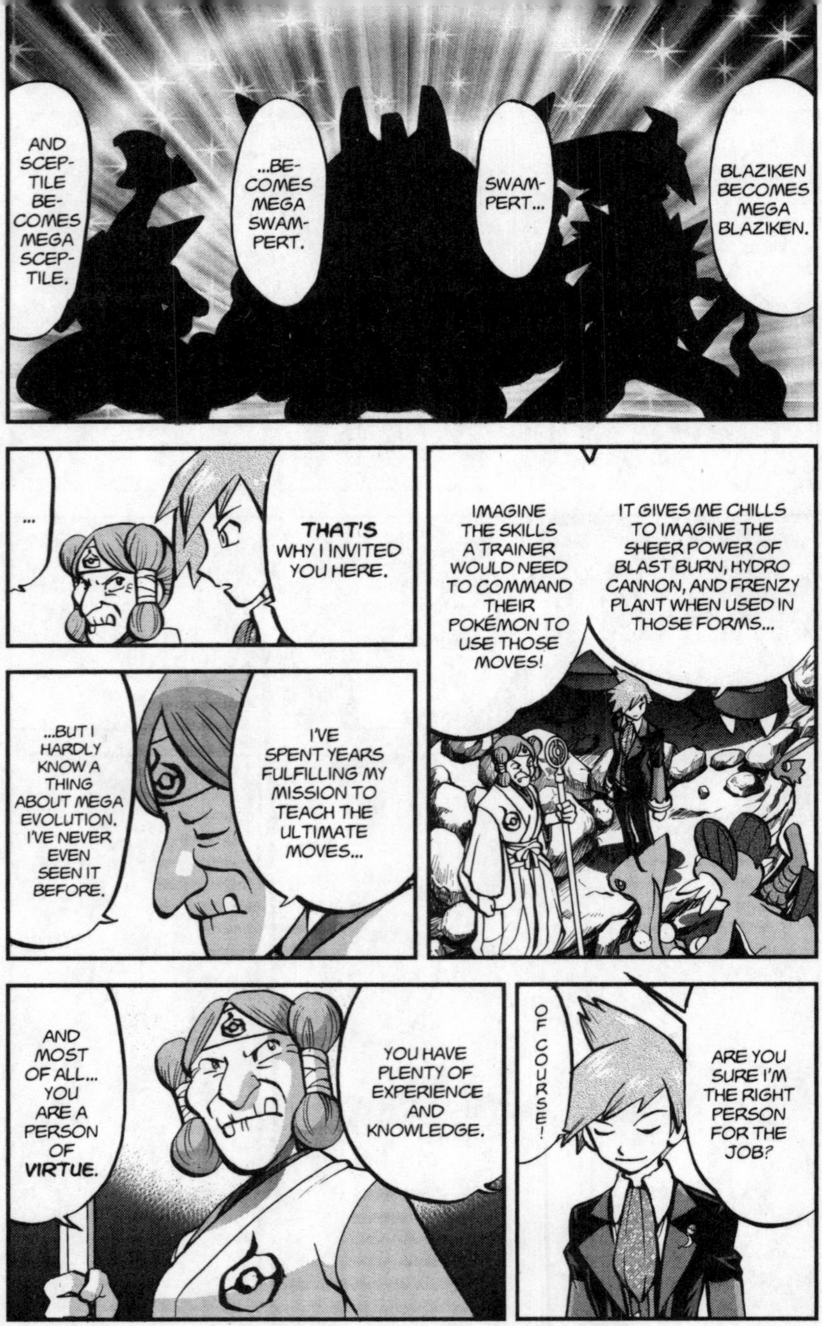
BLAZIKEN BECOMES MEGA BLAZIKEN.
SWAMPERT...
...BECOMES MEGA SWAMPERT.
AND SCEPTILE BECOMES MEGA SCEPTILE.
IT GIVES ME CHILLS TO IMAGINE THE SHEER POWER OF BLAST BURN, HYDRO CANNON, AND FRENZY PLANT WHEN USED IN THOSE FORMS...
IMAGINE THE SKILLS A TRAINER WOULD NEED TO COMMAND THEIR POKÉMON TO USE THOSE MOVES!
THAT'S WHY I INVITED YOU HERE.
...
I'VE SPENT YEARS FULFILLING MY MISSION TO TEACH THE ULTIMATE MOVES...
...BUT I HARDLY KNOW A THING ABOUT MEGA EVOLUTION. I'VE NEVER EVEN SEEN IT BEFORE.
ARE YOU SURE I'M THE RIGHT PERSON FOR THE JOB?
OF COURSE!
YOU HAVE PLENTY OF EXPERIENCE AND KNOWLEDGE.
AND MOST OF ALL... YOU ARE A PERSON OF **VIRTUE**.

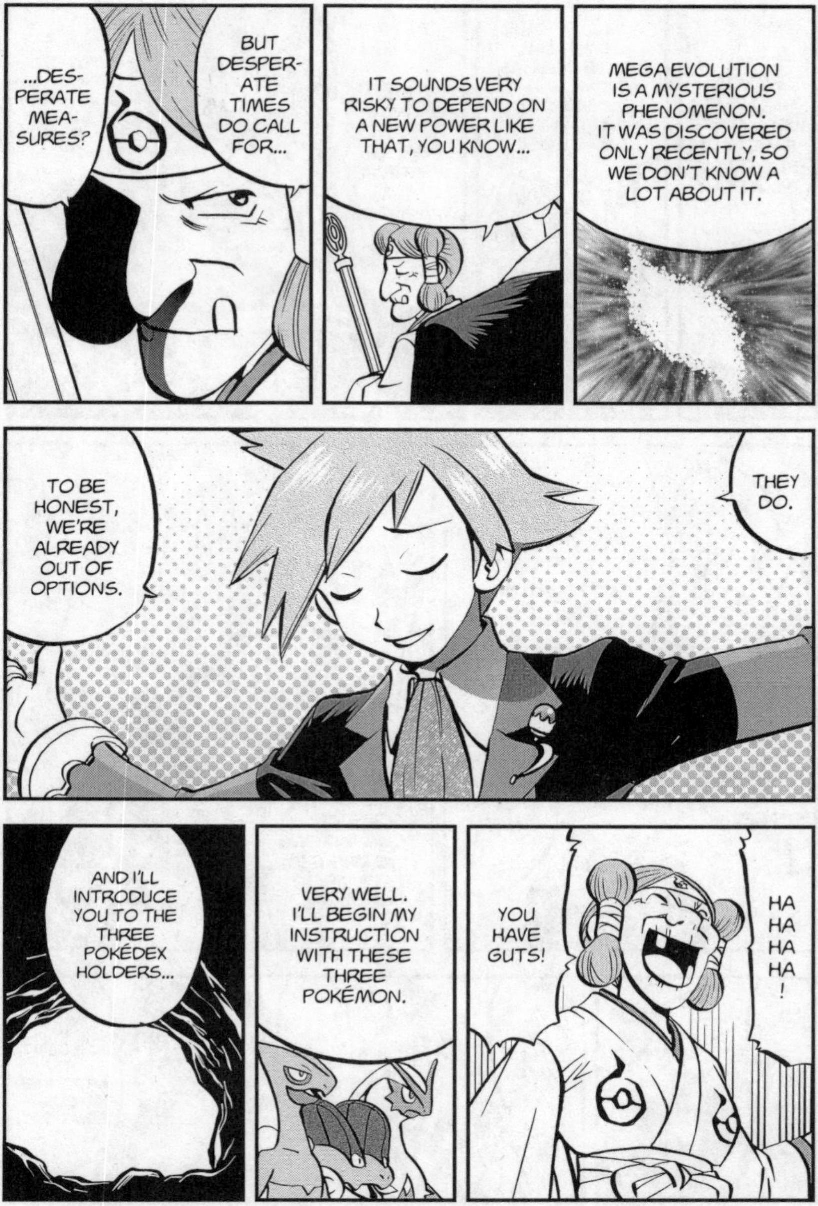

MEGA EVOLUTION IS A MYSTERIOUS PHENOMENON. IT WAS DISCOVERED ONLY RECENTLY, SO WE DON'T KNOW A LOT ABOUT IT.
IT SOUNDS VERY RISKY TO DEPEND ON A NEW POWER LIKE THAT, YOU KNOW...
BUT DESPER-ATE TIMES DO CALL FOR...
...DES-PERATE MEA-SURES?
THEY DO.
TO BE HONEST, WE'RE ALREADY OUT OF OPTIONS.
HA HA HA HA!
YOU HAVE GUTS!
VERY WELL. I'LL BEGIN MY INSTRUCTION WITH THESE THREE POKÉMON.
AND I'LL INTRODUCE YOU TO THE THREE POKÉDEX HOLDERS...

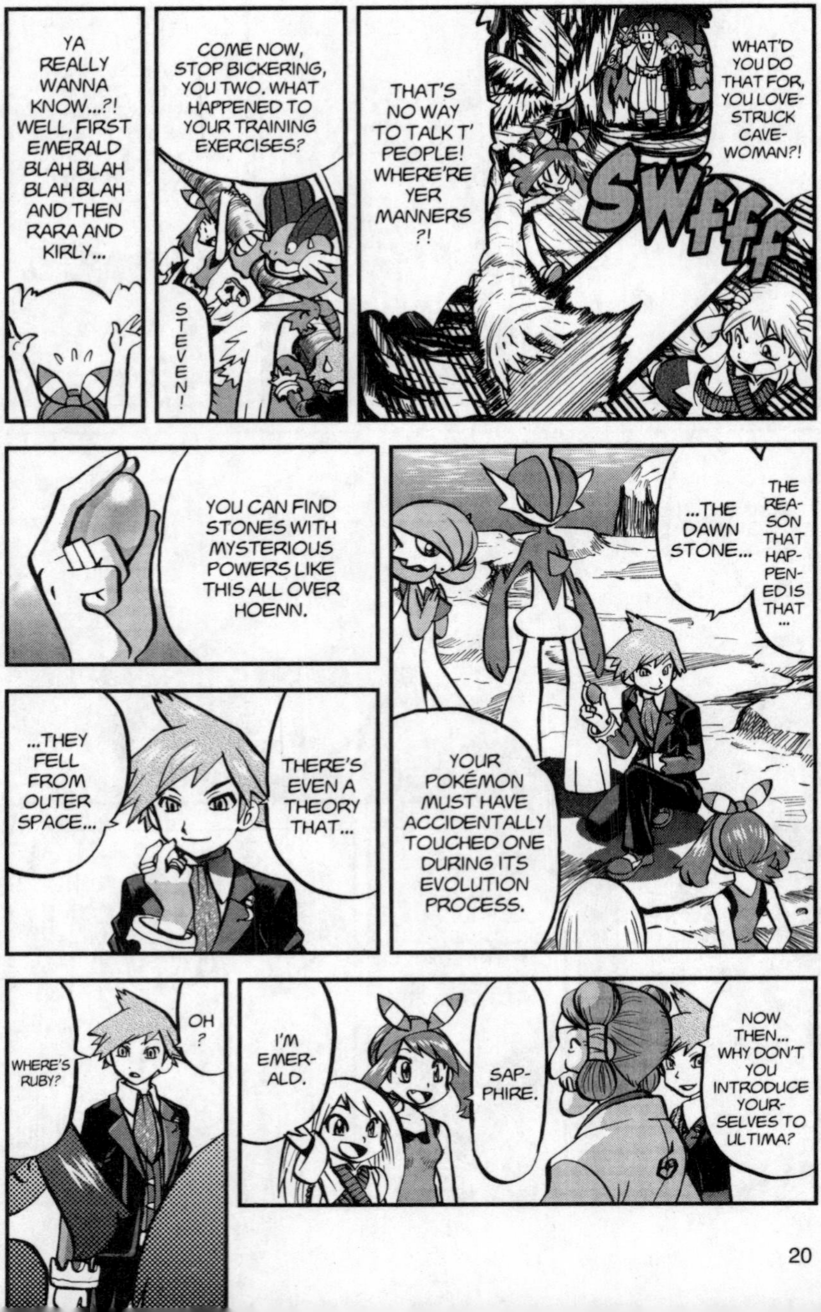
WHAT'D YOU DO THAT FOR, YOU LOVE-STRUCK CAVE-WOMAN?!
THAT'S NO WAY TO TALK T' PEOPLE! WHERE'RE YER MANNERS?!
SWFFF
COME NOW, STOP BICKERING, YOU TWO. WHAT HAPPENED TO YOUR TRAINING EXERCISES?
STEVEN!
YA REALLY WANNA KNOW...?! WELL, FIRST EMERALD BLAH BLAH BLAH BLAH AND THEN RARA AND KIRLY...
THE REA-SON THAT HAP-PEN-ED IS THAT...
...THE DAWN STONE...
YOUR POKÉMON MUST HAVE ACCIDENTALLY TOUCHED ONE DURING ITS EVOLUTION PROCESS.
YOU CAN FIND STONES WITH MYSTERIOUS POWERS LIKE THIS ALL OVER HOENN.
THERE'S EVEN A THEORY THAT...
...THEY FELL FROM OUTER SPACE...
NOW THEN... WHY DON'T YOU INTRODUCE YOUR-SELVES TO ULTIMA?
SAP-PHIRE.
I'M EMER-ALD.
OH?
WHERE'S RUBY?

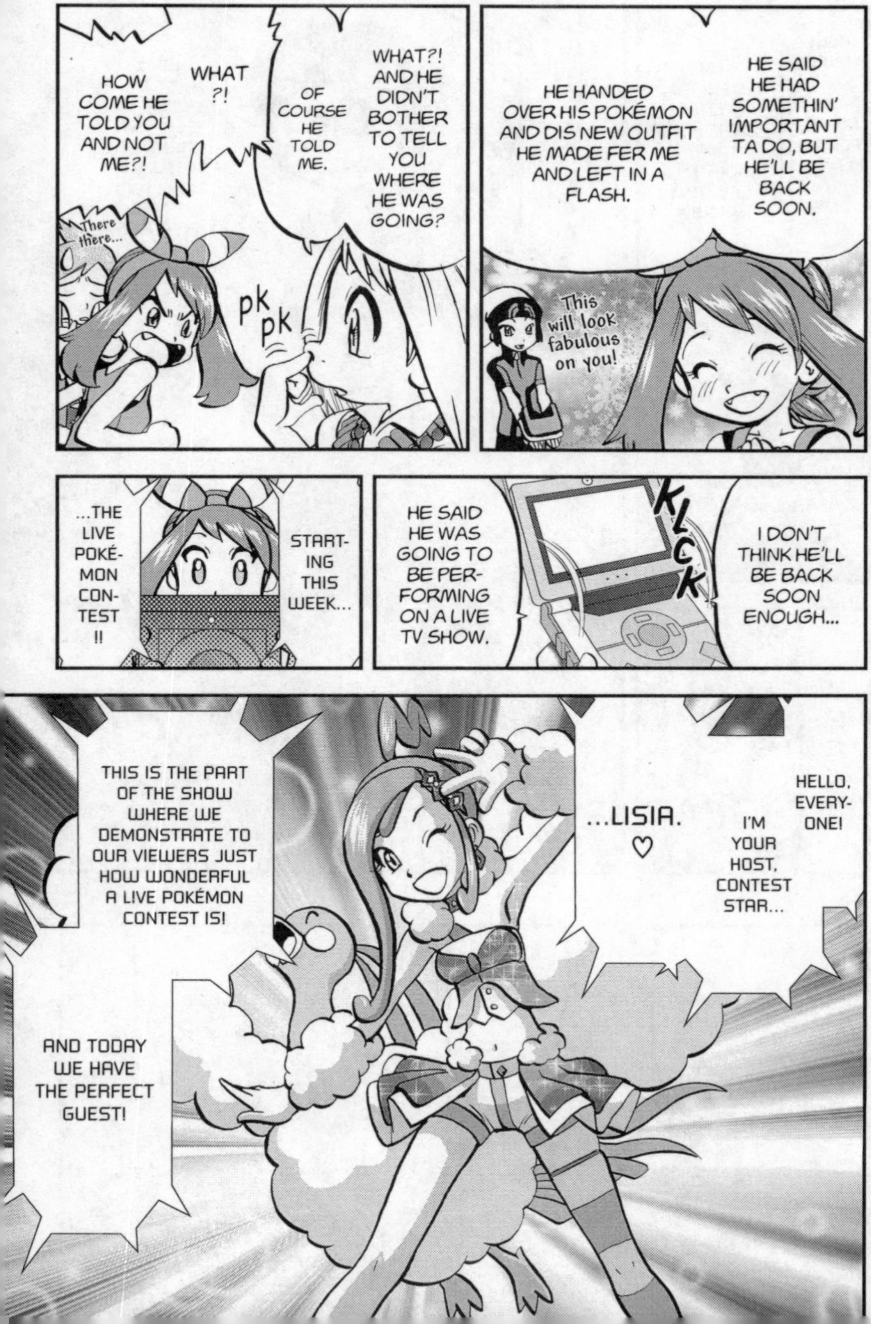

HE SAID HE HAD SOMETHIN' IMPORTANT TA DO, BUT HE'LL BE BACK SOON.
HE HANDED OVER HIS POKÉMON AND DIS NEW OUTFIT HE MADE FER ME AND LEFT IN A FLASH.
This will look fabulous on you!
WHAT?! AND HE DIDN'T BOTHER TO TELL YOU WHERE HE WAS GOING?
OF COURSE HE TOLD ME.
WHAT ?!
HOW COME HE TOLD YOU AND NOT ME?!
pk pk
There there...
I DON'T THINK HE'LL BE BACK SOON ENOUGH...
KLICK
HE SAID HE WAS GOING TO BE PER-FORMING ON A LIVE TV SHOW.
START-ING THIS WEEK...
...THE LIVE POKÉ-MON CON-TEST !!
HELLO, EVERY-ONE!
I'M YOUR HOST, CONTEST STAR...
...LISIA. ♡
THIS IS THE PART OF THE SHOW WHERE WE DEMONSTRATE TO OUR VIEWERS JUST HOW WONDERFUL A LIVE POKÉMON CONTEST IS!
AND TODAY WE HAVE THE PERFECT GUEST!

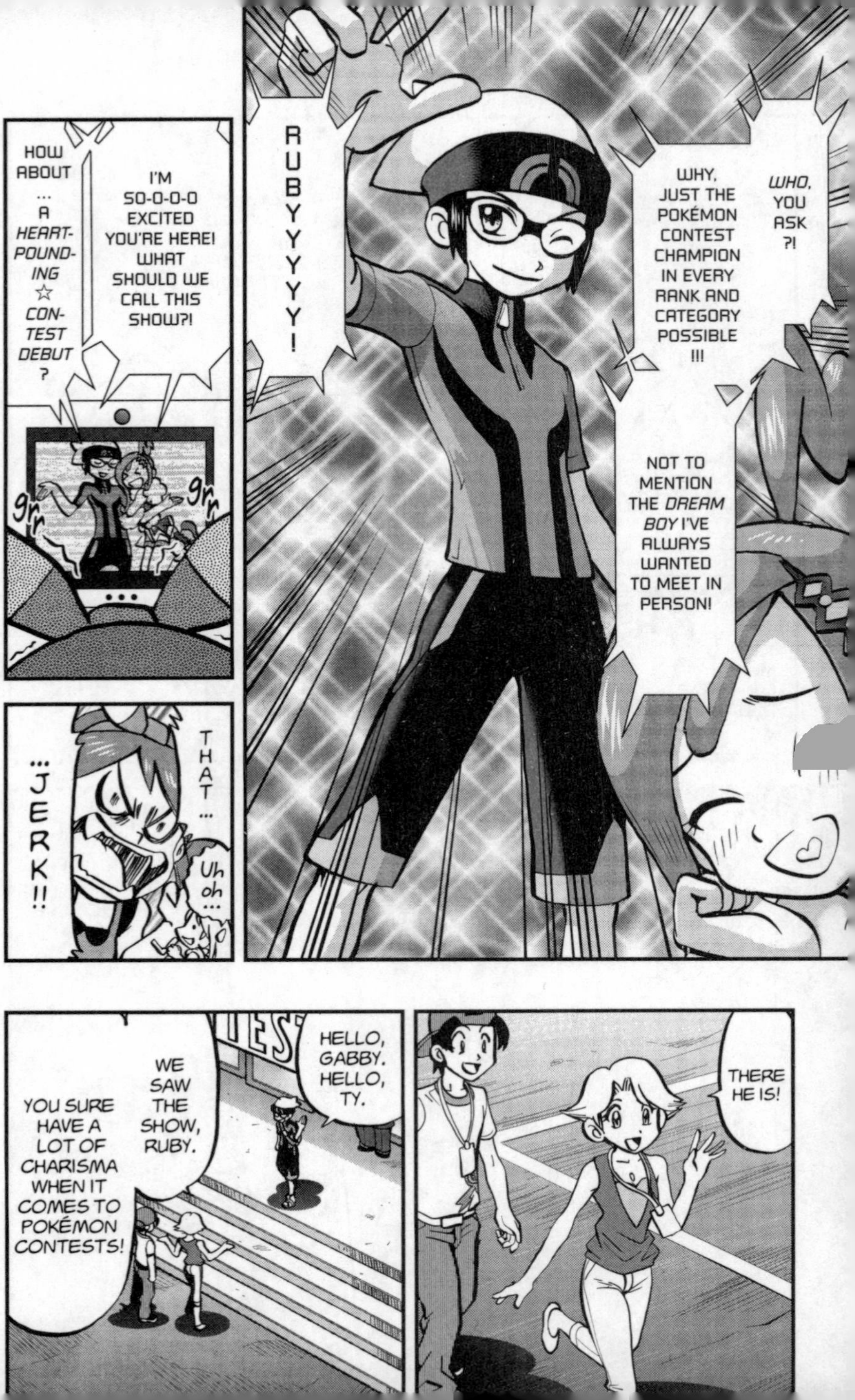
WHO, YOU ASK?!
WHY, JUST THE POKÉMON CONTEST CHAMPION IN EVERY RANK AND CATEGORY POSSIBLE!!!
NOT TO MENTION THE DREAM BOY I'VE ALWAYS WANTED TO MEET IN PERSON!
RUBYYYYY!
I'M SO-O-O-O EXCITED YOU'RE HERE! WHAT SHOULD WE CALL THIS SHOW?!
HOW ABOUT... A HEART-POUNDING ☆ CON-TEST DEBUT?
grr
grr
THAT...
...JERK!!
Uh oh...
THERE HE IS!
HELLO, GABBY. HELLO, TY.
WE SAW THE SHOW, RUBY.
YOU SURE HAVE A LOT OF CHARISMA WHEN IT COMES TO POKÉMON CONTESTS!

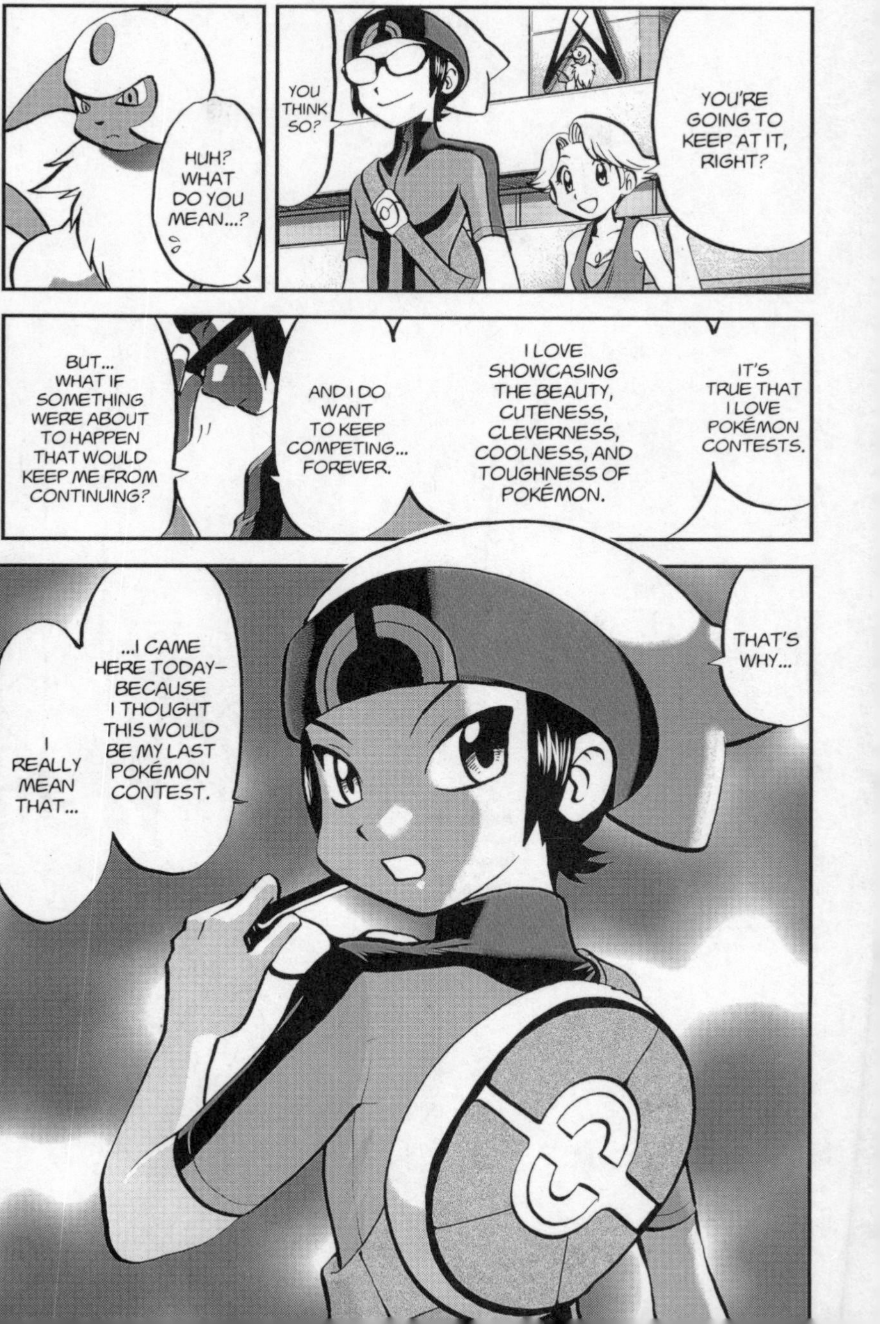
YOU'RE GOING TO KEEP AT IT, RIGHT?
YOU THINK SO?
HUH? WHAT DO YOU MEAN...?
IT'S TRUE THAT I LOVE POKéMON CONTESTS.
I LOVE SHOWCASING THE BEAUTY, CUTENESS, CLEVERNESS, COOLNESS, AND TOUGHNESS OF POKéMON.
AND I DO WANT TO KEEP COMPETING... FOREVER.
BUT... WHAT IF SOMETHING WERE ABOUT TO HAPPEN THAT WOULD KEEP ME FROM CONTINUING?
THAT'S WHY...
...I CAME HERE TODAY—BECAUSE I THOUGHT THIS WOULD BE MY LAST POKéMON CONTEST.
I REALLY MEAN THAT...

RUBY

ADVENTURE #2
Latias Flies

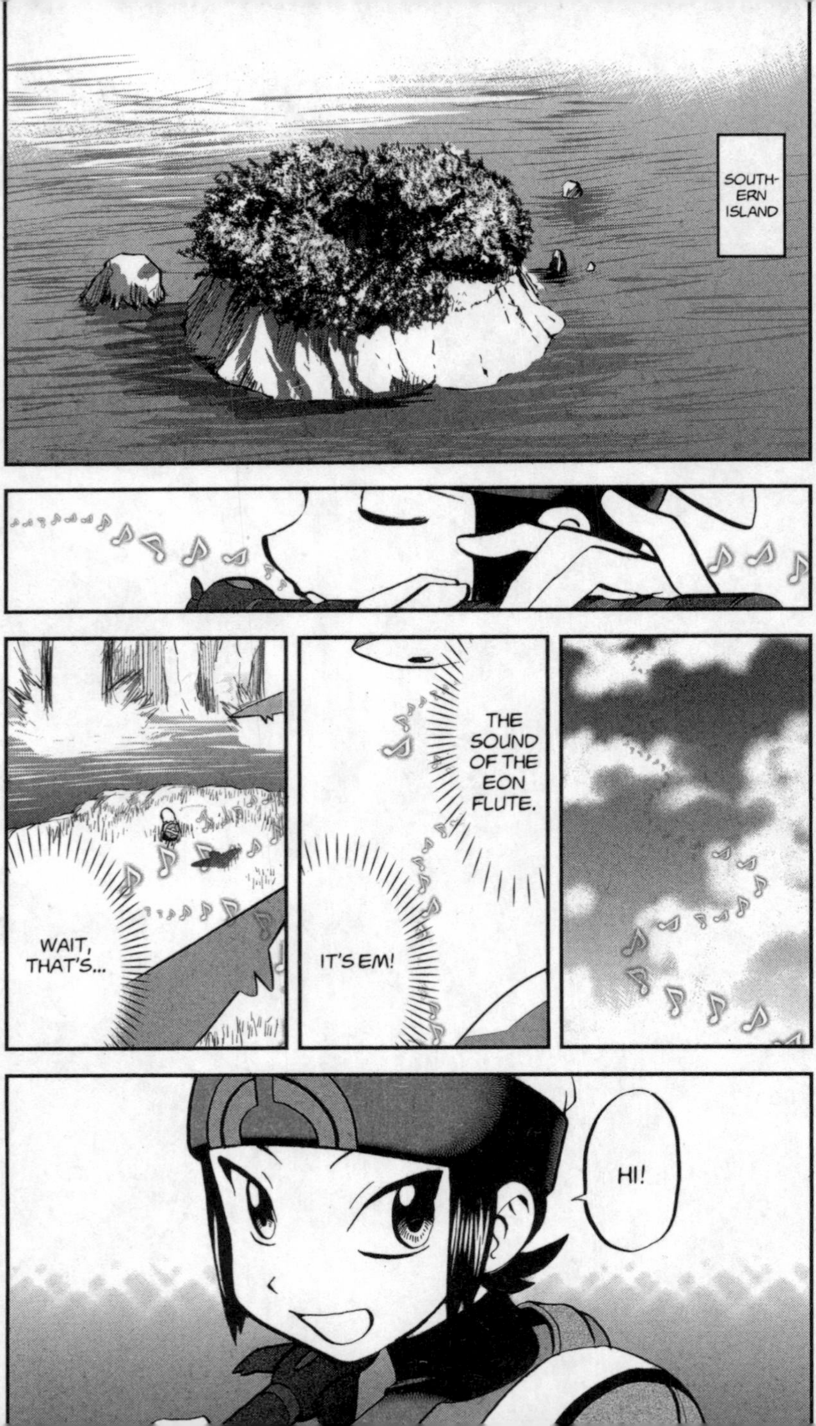
SOUTH-
ERN
ISLAND
THE SOUND OF THE EON FLUTE.
IT'S EM!
WAIT, THAT'S...
HI!

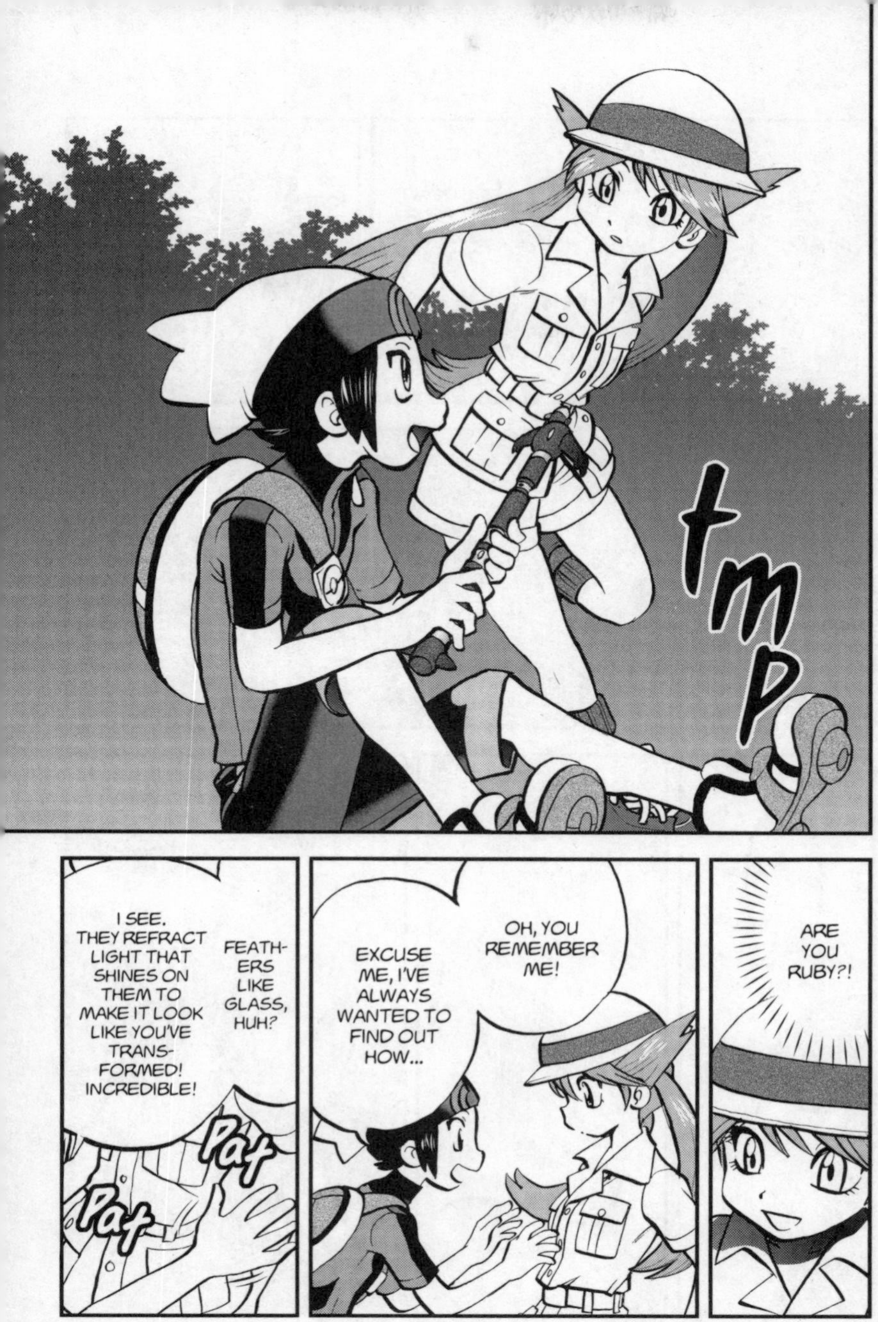
tmp
ARE YOU RUBY?!
OH, YOU REMEMBER ME!
EXCUSE ME, I'VE ALWAYS WANTED TO FIND OUT HOW...
FEATH-ERS LIKE GLASS, HUH?
I SEE. THEY REFRACT LIGHT THAT SHINES ON THEM TO MAKE IT LOOK LIKE YOU'VE TRANS-FORMED! INCREDIBLE!
Pat
Pat

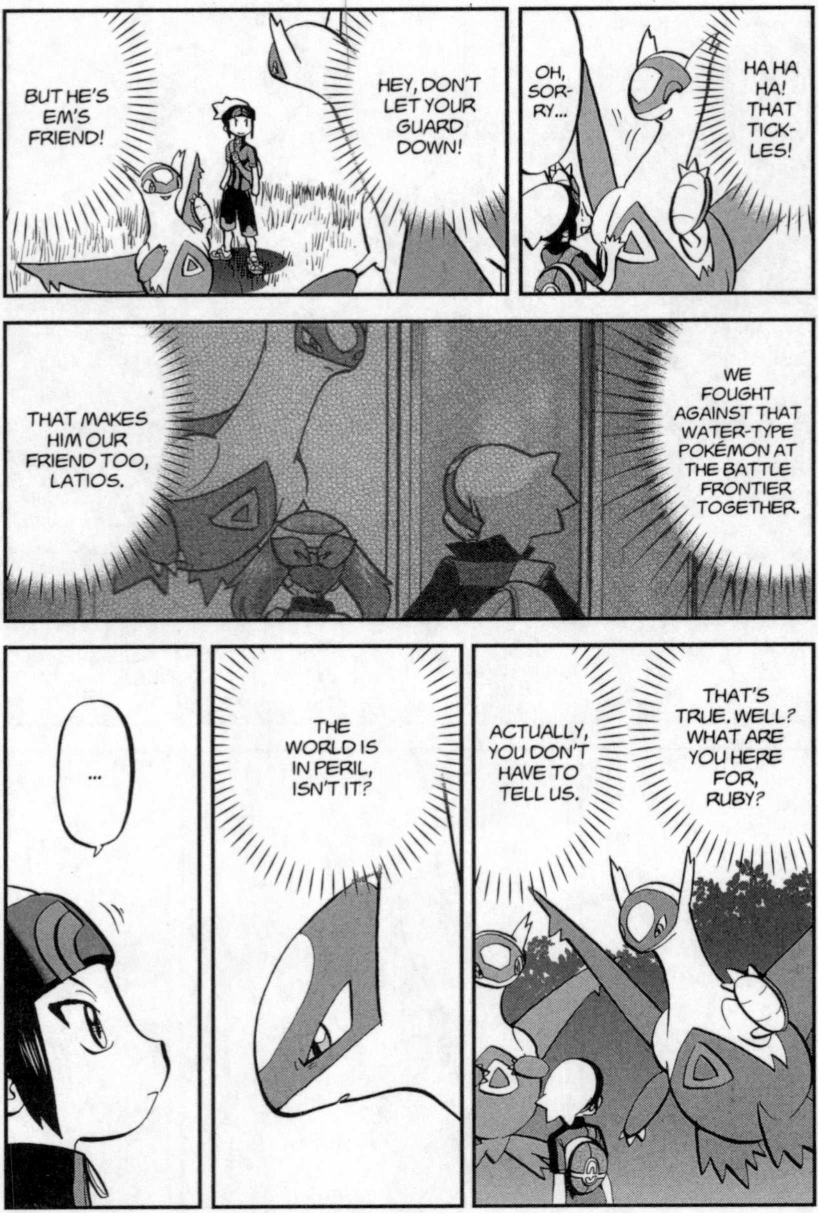
HA HA HA! THAT TICKLES!
OH, SORRY...
HEY, DON'T LET YOUR GUARD DOWN!
BUT HE'S EM'S FRIEND!
WE FOUGHT AGAINST THAT WATER-TYPE POKÉMON AT THE BATTLE FRONTIER TOGETHER.
THAT MAKES HIM OUR FRIEND TOO, LATIOS.
THAT'S TRUE. WELL? WHAT ARE YOU HERE FOR, RUBY?
ACTUALLY, YOU DON'T HAVE TO TELL US.
THE WORLD IS IN PERIL, ISN'T IT?
...

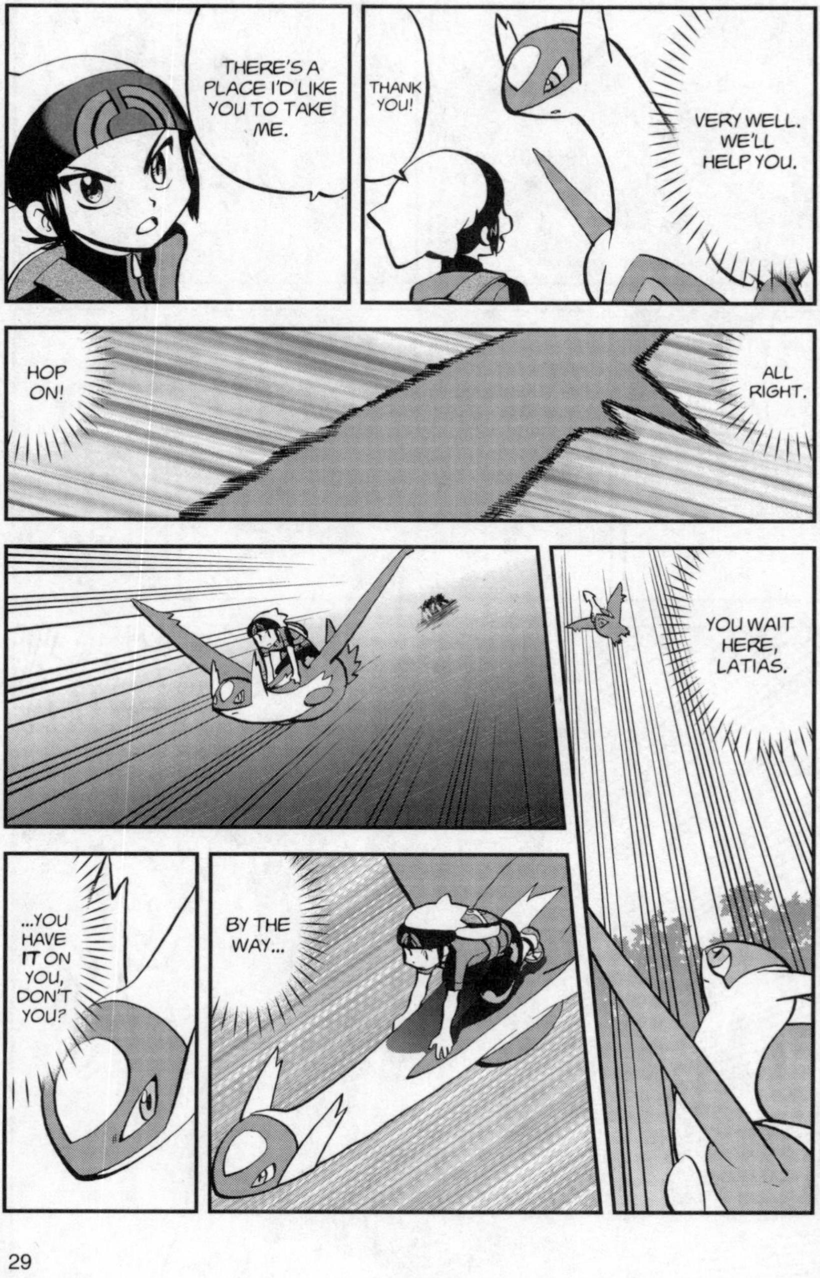
VERY WELL. WE'LL HELP YOU.
THANK YOU!
THERE'S A PLACE I'D LIKE YOU TO TAKE ME.
ALL RIGHT.
HOP ON!
YOU WAIT HERE, LATIAS.
BY THE WAY...
...YOU HAVE IT ON YOU, DON'T YOU?

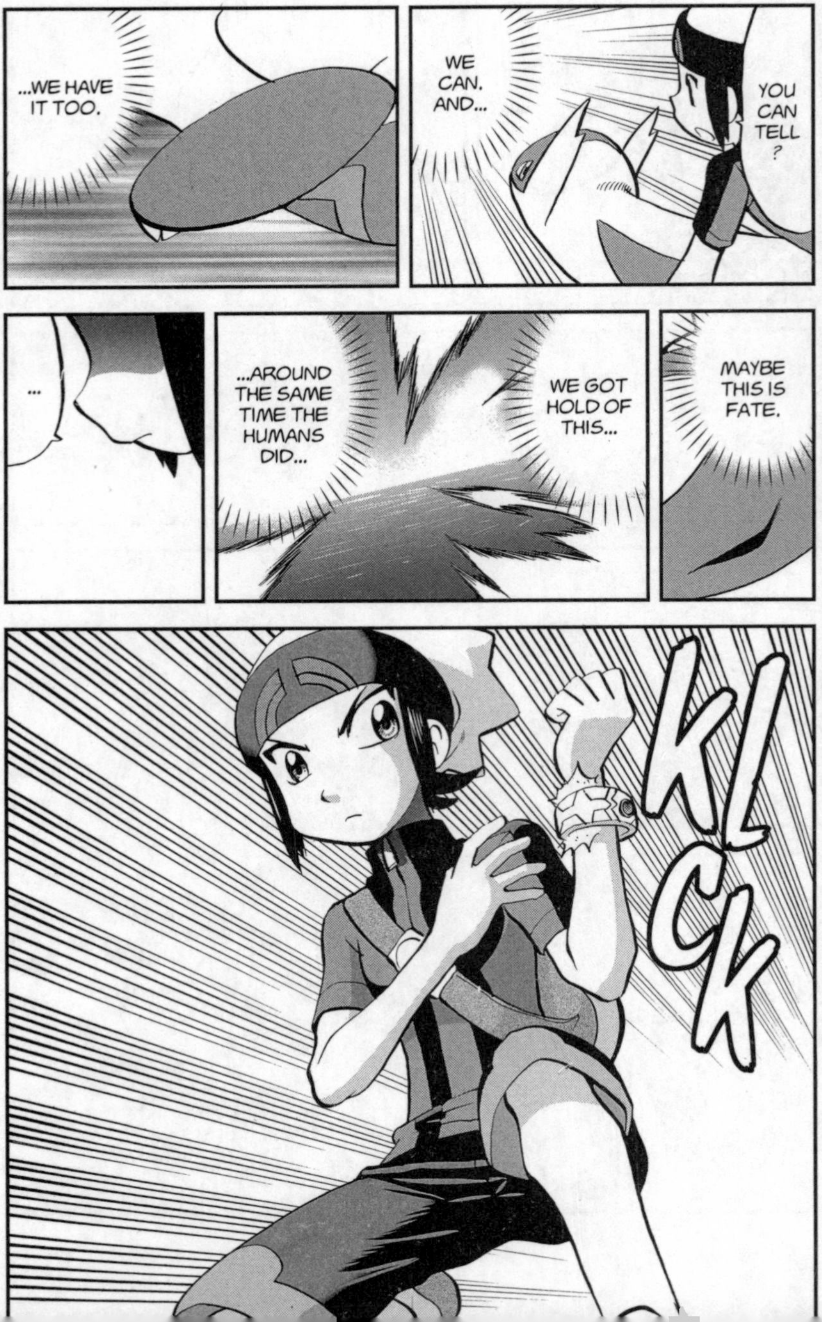
YOU CAN TELL?
WE CAN. AND...
...WE HAVE IT TOO.
MAYBE THIS IS FATE.
WE GOT HOLD OF THIS...
...AROUND THE SAME TIME THE HUMANS DID...
...
KLICK

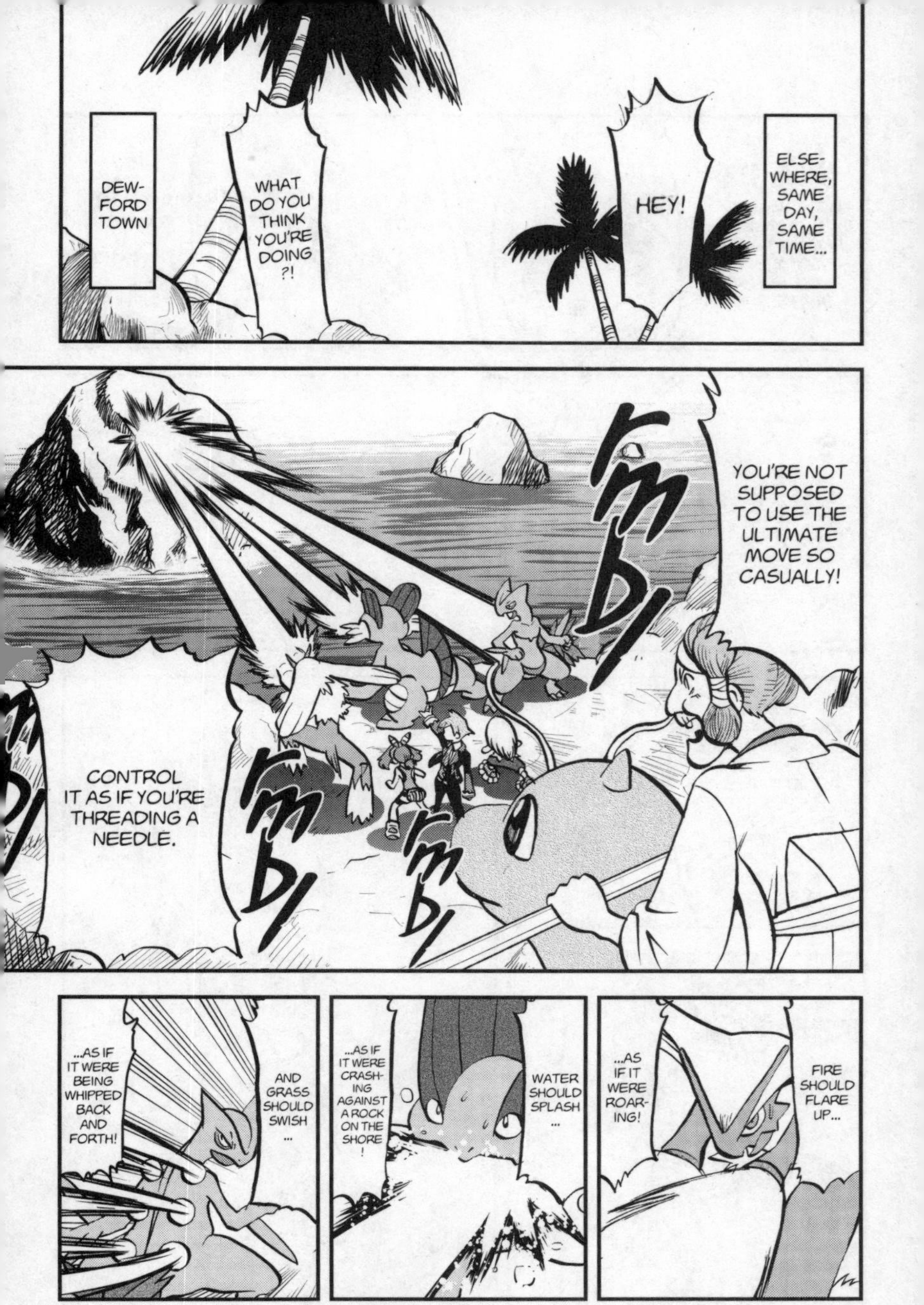
ELSE-WHERE, SAME DAY, SAME TIME...
HEY!
WHAT DO YOU THINK YOU'RE DOING?!
DEW-FORD TOWN
YOU'RE NOT SUPPOSED TO USE THE ULTIMATE MOVE SO CASUALLY!
CONTROL IT AS IF YOU'RE THREADING A NEEDLE.
FIRE SHOULD FLARE UP...
...AS IF IT WERE ROAR-ING!
WATER SHOULD SPLASH...
...AS IF IT WERE CRASH-ING AGAINST A ROCK ON THE SHORE!
AND GRASS SHOULD SWISH...
...AS IF IT WERE BEING WHIPPED BACK AND FORTH!

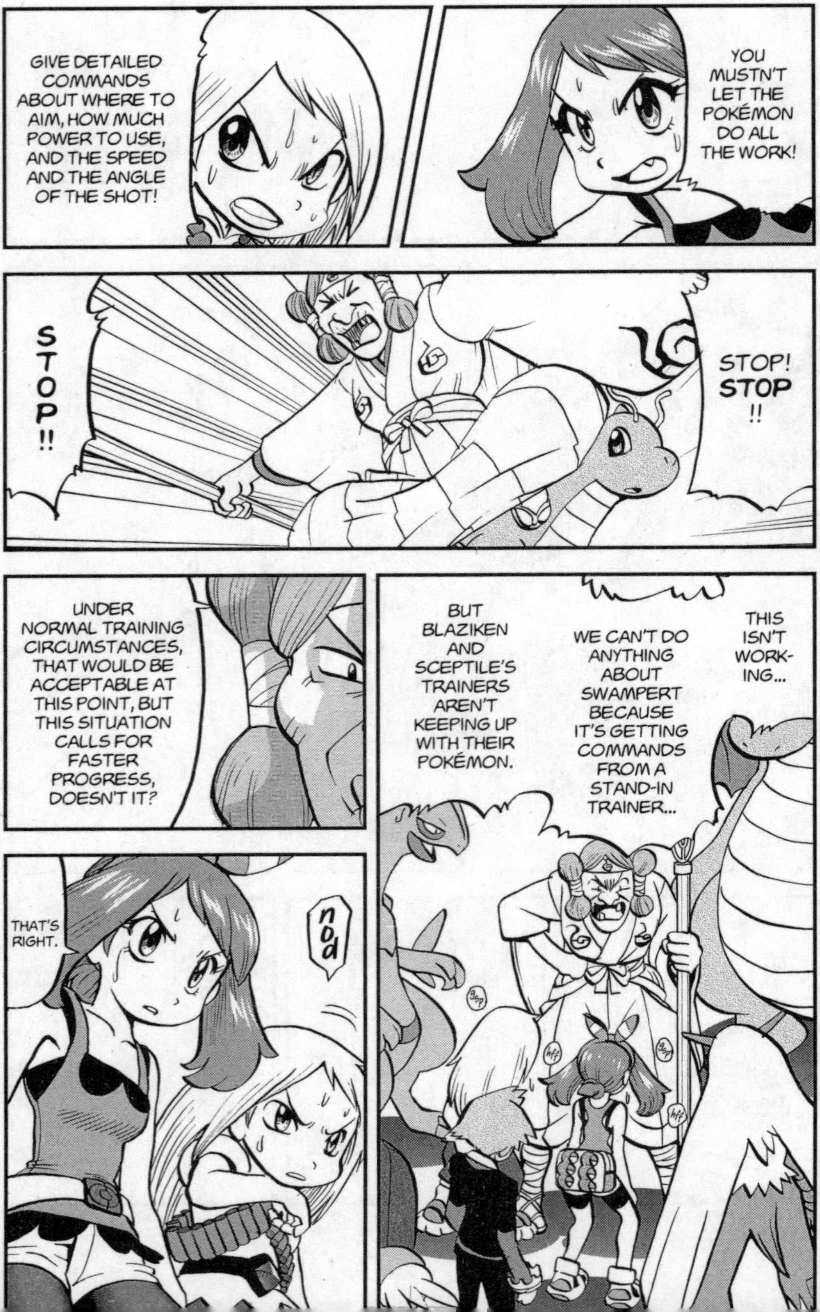
YOU MUSTN'T LET THE POKÉMON DO ALL THE WORK!
GIVE DETAILED COMMANDS ABOUT WHERE TO AIM, HOW MUCH POWER TO USE, AND THE SPEED AND THE ANGLE OF THE SHOT!
STOP! STOP!!
STOP!!
THIS ISN'T WORK-ING...
WE CAN'T DO ANYTHING ABOUT SWAMPERT BECAUSE IT'S GETTING COMMANDS FROM A STAND-IN TRAINER...
BUT BLAZIKEN AND SCEPTILE'S TRAINERS AREN'T KEEPING UP WITH THEIR POKÉMON.
UNDER NORMAL TRAINING CIRCUMSTANCES, THAT WOULD BE ACCEPTABLE AT THIS POINT, BUT THIS SITUATION CALLS FOR FASTER PROGRESS, DOESN'T IT?
nod
THAT'S RIGHT.

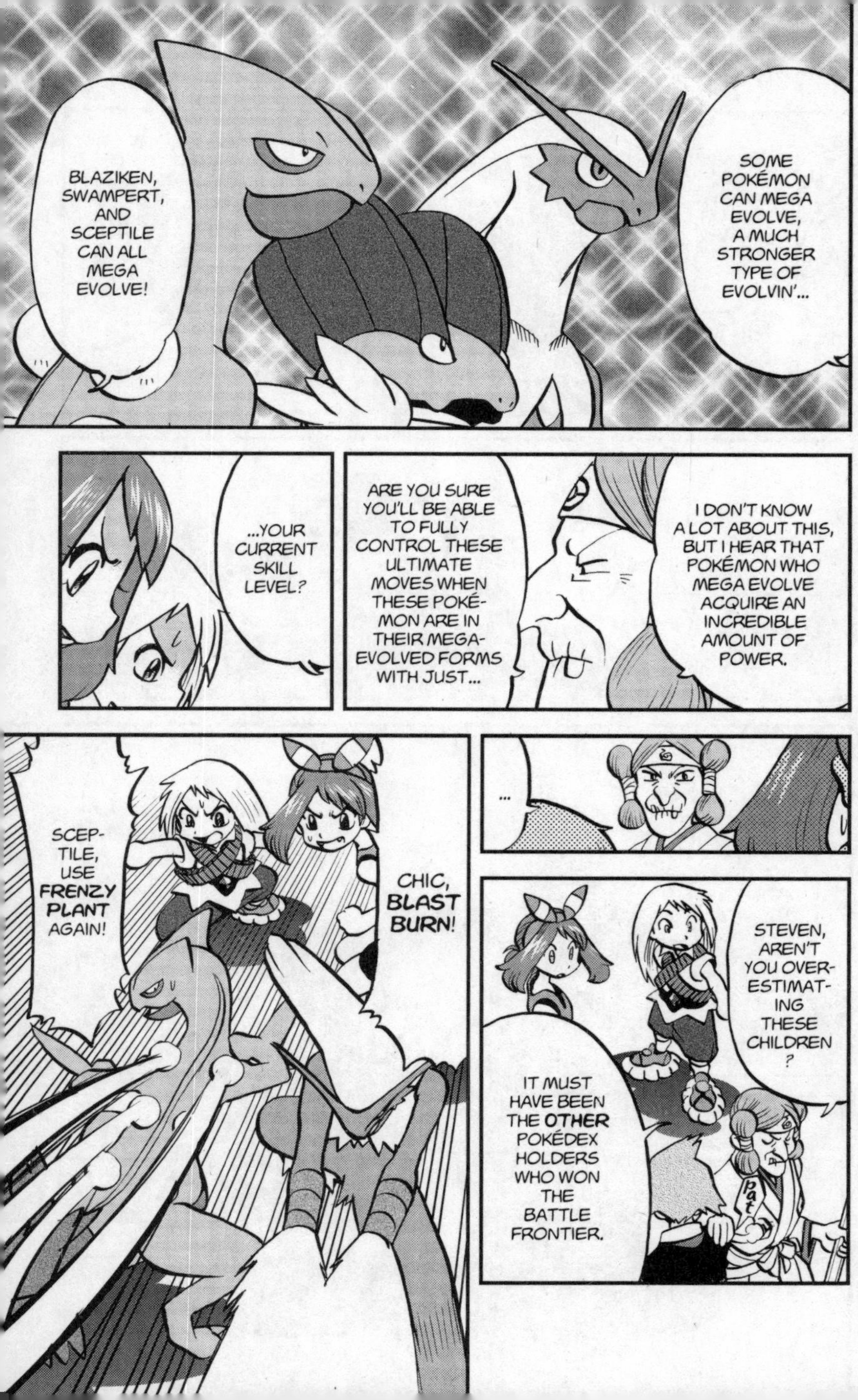
SOME POKÉMON CAN MEGA EVOLVE, A MUCH STRONGER TYPE OF EVOLVIN'...
BLAZIKEN, SWAMPERT, AND SCEPTILE CAN ALL MEGA EVOLVE!
I DON'T KNOW A LOT ABOUT THIS, BUT I HEAR THAT POKÉMON WHO MEGA EVOLVE ACQUIRE AN INCREDIBLE AMOUNT OF POWER.
ARE YOU SURE YOU'LL BE ABLE TO FULLY CONTROL THESE ULTIMATE MOVES WHEN THESE POKÉMON ARE IN THEIR MEGA-EVOLVED FORMS WITH JUST...
...YOUR CURRENT SKILL LEVEL?
...
STEVEN, AREN'T YOU OVERESTIMATING THESE CHILDREN?
IT MUST HAVE BEEN THE OTHER POKÉDEX HOLDERS WHO WON THE BATTLE FRONTIER.
pat
CHIC, BLAST BURN!
SCEPTILE, USE FRENZY PLANT AGAIN!

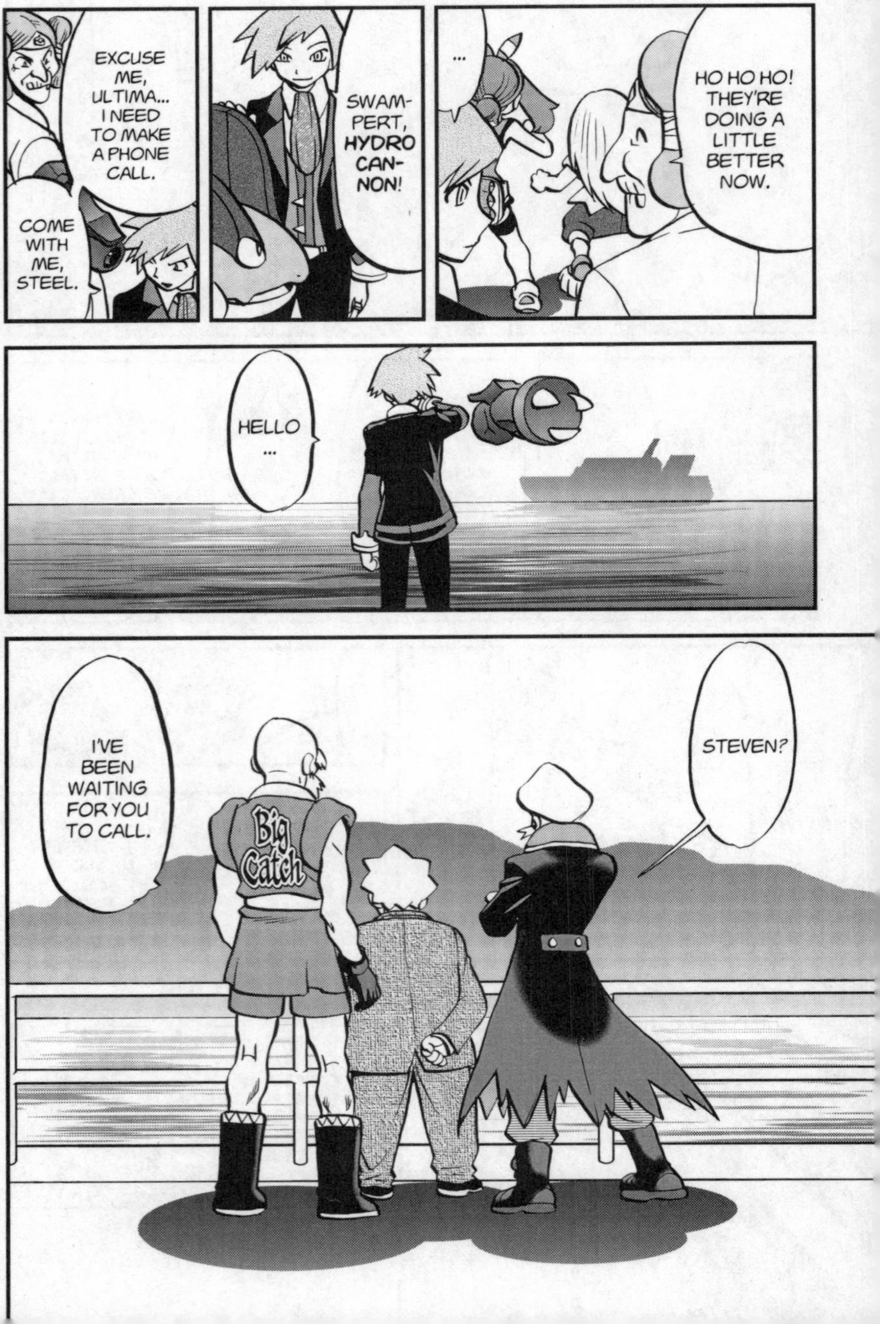
HO HO HO! THEY'RE DOING A LITTLE BETTER NOW.
...
SWAMPERT, HYDRO CANNON!
EXCUSE ME, ULTIMA... I NEED TO MAKE A PHONE CALL.
COME WITH ME, STEEL.
HELLO ...
STEVEN?
I'VE BEEN WAITING FOR YOU TO CALL.
Big Catch

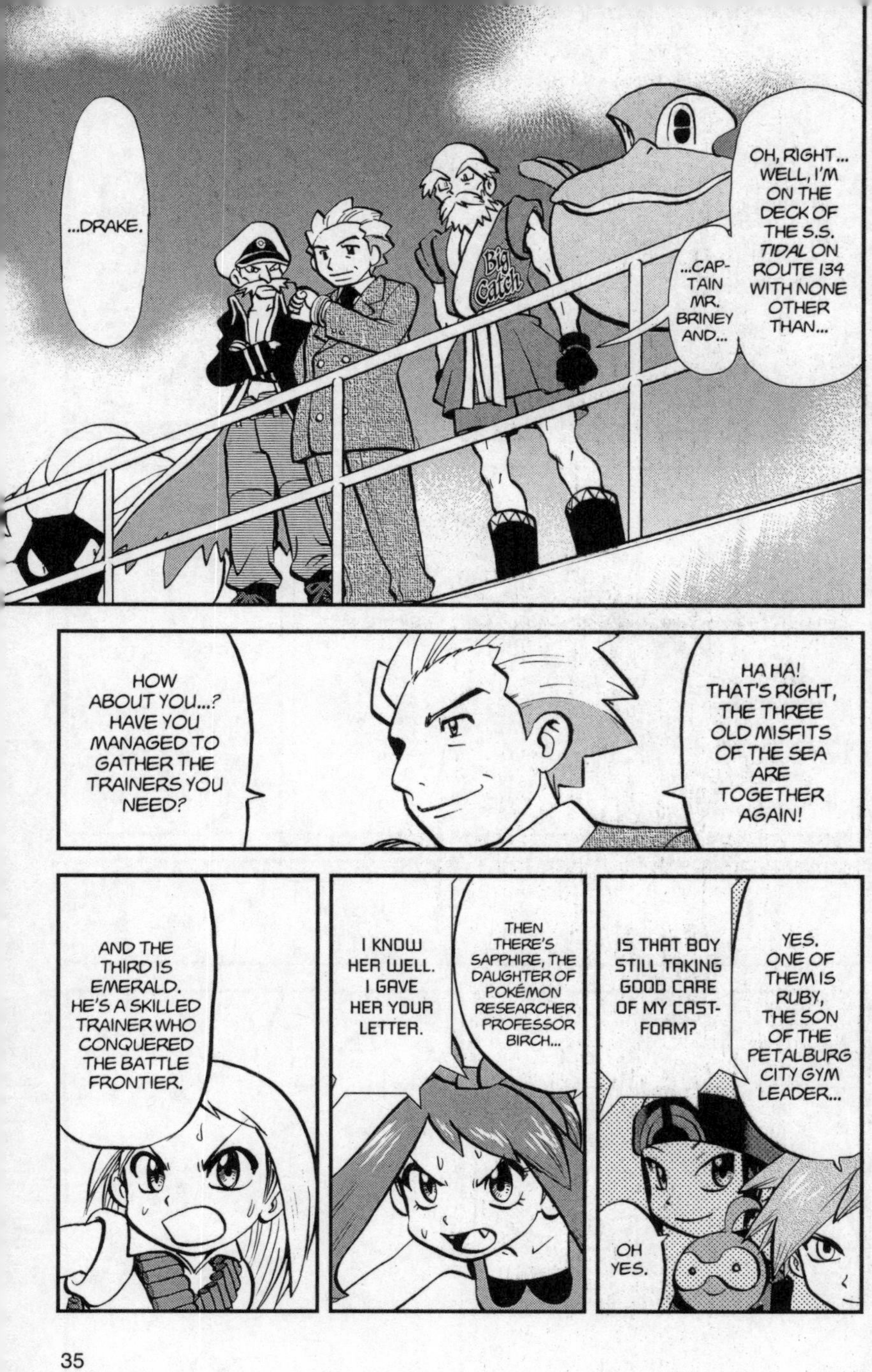
OH, RIGHT... WELL, I'M ON THE DECK OF THE S.S. *TIDAL* ON ROUTE 134 WITH NONE OTHER THAN...
...CAPTAIN MR. BRINEY AND...
...DRAKE.
HA HA! THAT'S RIGHT, THE THREE OLD MISFITS OF THE SEA ARE TOGETHER AGAIN!
HOW ABOUT YOU...? HAVE YOU MANAGED TO GATHER THE TRAINERS YOU NEED?
YES. ONE OF THEM IS RUBY, THE SON OF THE PETALBURG CITY GYM LEADER...
IS THAT BOY STILL TAKING GOOD CARE OF MY CASTFORM?
OH YES.
THEN THERE'S SAPPHIRE, THE DAUGHTER OF POKÉMON RESEARCHER PROFESSOR BIRCH...
I KNOW HER WELL. I GAVE HER YOUR LETTER.
AND THE THIRD IS EMERALD. HE'S A SKILLED TRAINER WHO CONQUERED THE BATTLE FRONTIER.

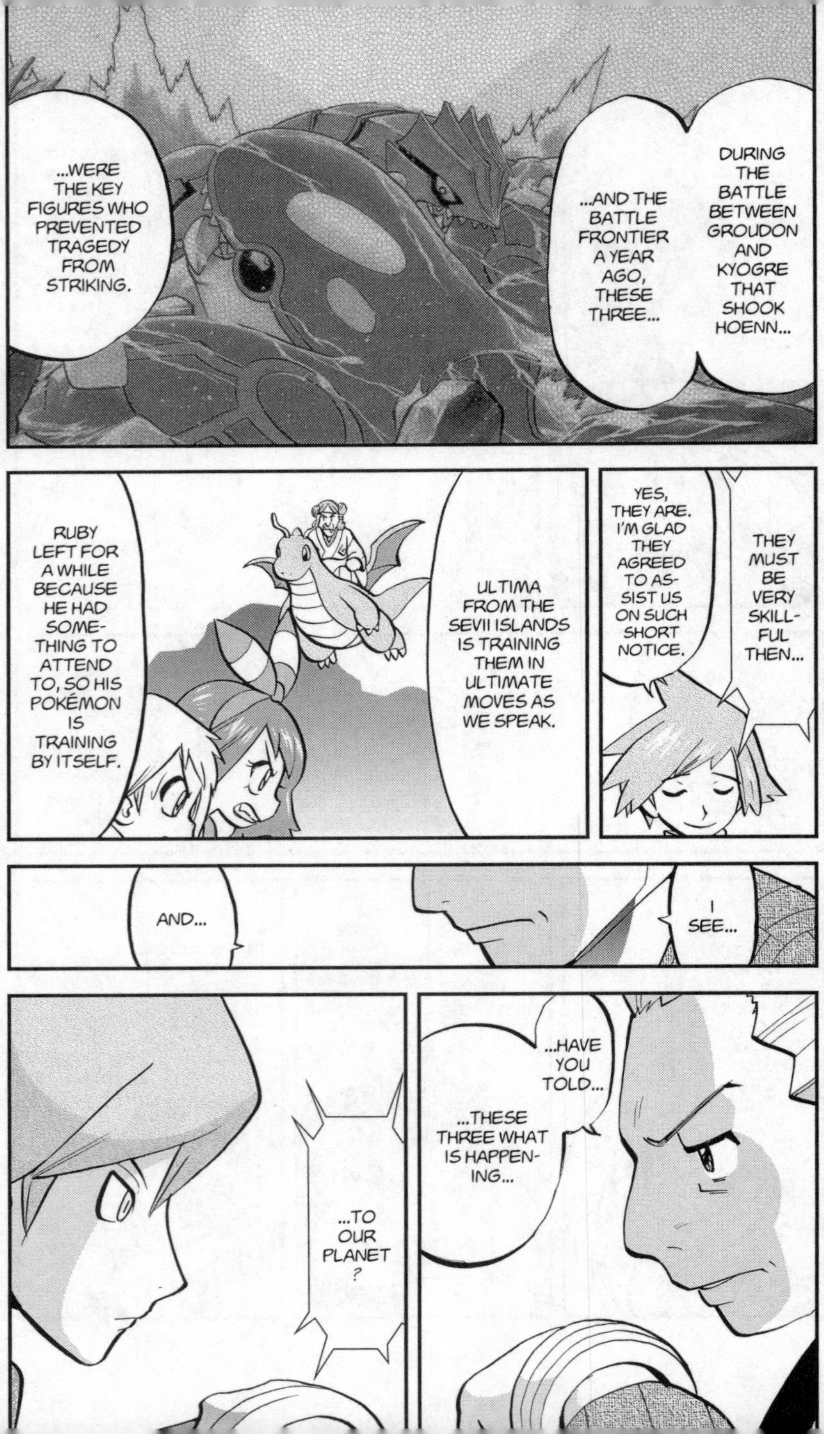
DURING THE BATTLE BETWEEN GROUDON AND KYOGRE THAT SHOOK HOENN...
...AND THE BATTLE FRONTIER A YEAR AGO, THESE THREE...
...WERE THE KEY FIGURES WHO PREVENTED TRAGEDY FROM STRIKING.
THEY MUST BE VERY SKILLFUL THEN...
YES, THEY ARE. I'M GLAD THEY AGREED TO ASSIST US ON SUCH SHORT NOTICE.
ULTIMA FROM THE SEVII ISLANDS IS TRAINING THEM IN ULTIMATE MOVES AS WE SPEAK.
RUBY LEFT FOR A WHILE BECAUSE HE HAD SOMETHING TO ATTEND TO, SO HIS POKÉMON IS TRAINING BY ITSELF.
I SEE...
AND...
...HAVE YOU TOLD...
...THESE THREE WHAT IS HAPPENING...
...TO OUR PLANET?

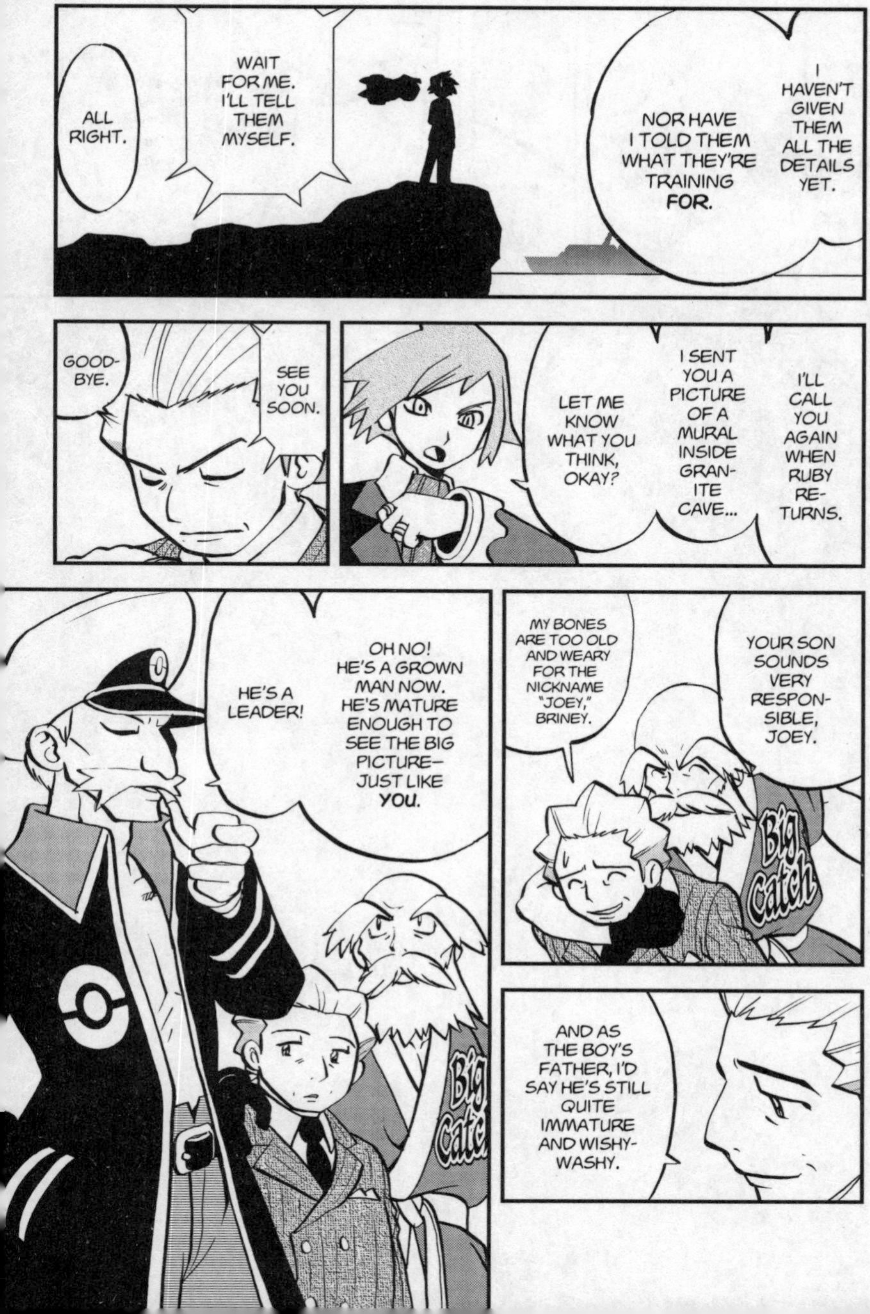
I HAVEN'T GIVEN THEM ALL THE DETAILS YET.
NOR HAVE I TOLD THEM WHAT THEY'RE TRAINING **FOR**.
WAIT FOR ME. I'LL TELL THEM MYSELF.
ALL RIGHT.
I'LL CALL YOU AGAIN WHEN RUBY RE-TURNS.
I SENT YOU A PICTURE OF A MURAL INSIDE GRAN-ITE CAVE...
LET ME KNOW WHAT YOU THINK, OKAY?
SEE YOU SOON.
GOOD-BYE.
YOUR SON SOUNDS VERY RESPON-SIBLE, JOEY.
MY BONES ARE TOO OLD AND WEARY FOR THE NICKNAME "JOEY," BRINEY.
AND AS THE BOY'S FATHER, I'D SAY HE'S STILL QUITE IMMATURE AND WISHY-WASHY.
OH NO! HE'S A GROWN MAN NOW. HE'S MATURE ENOUGH TO SEE THE BIG PICTURE—JUST LIKE **YOU**.
HE'S A LEADER!
Big Catch

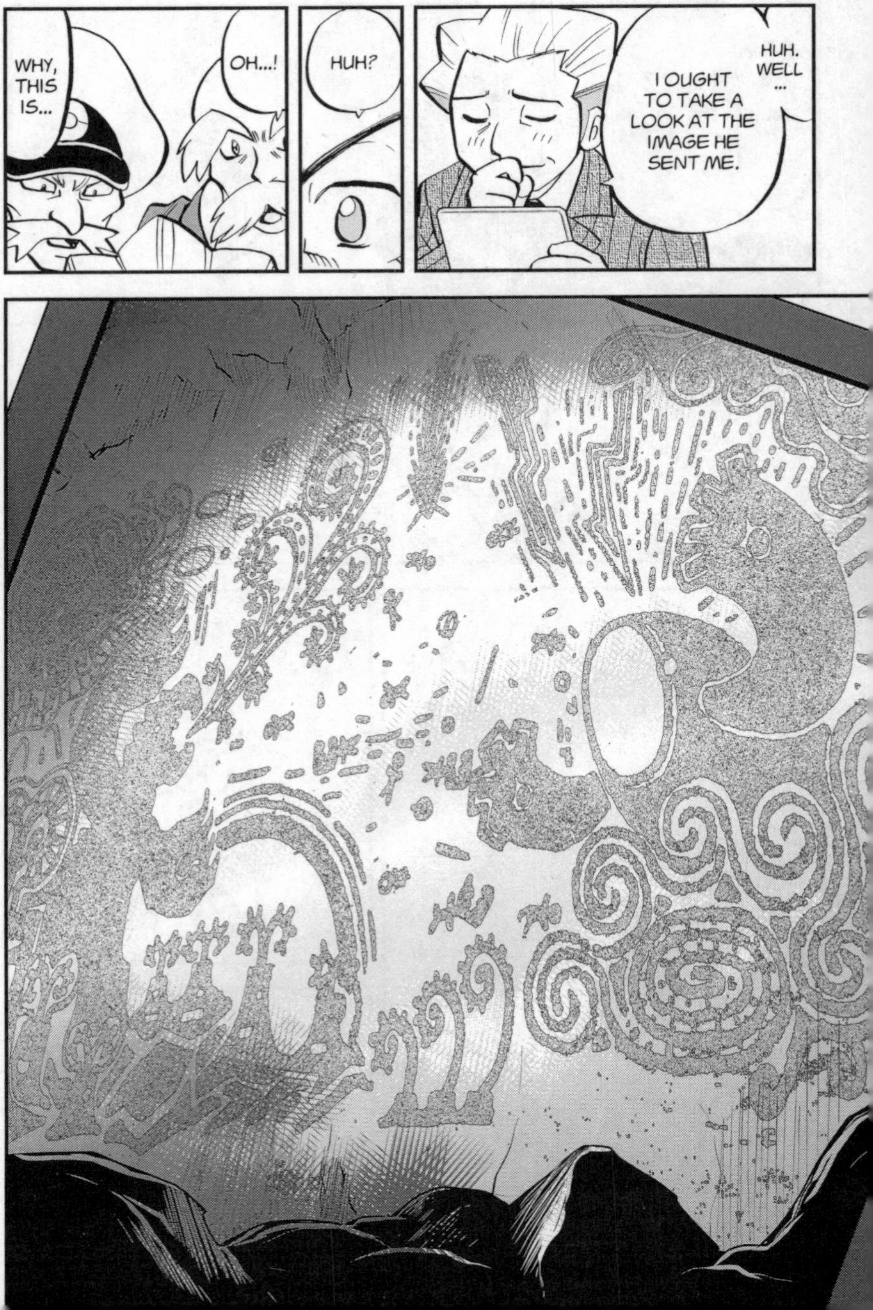
HUH. WELL ...
I OUGHT TO TAKE A LOOK AT THE IMAGE HE SENT ME.
HUH?
OH...!
WHY, THIS IS...

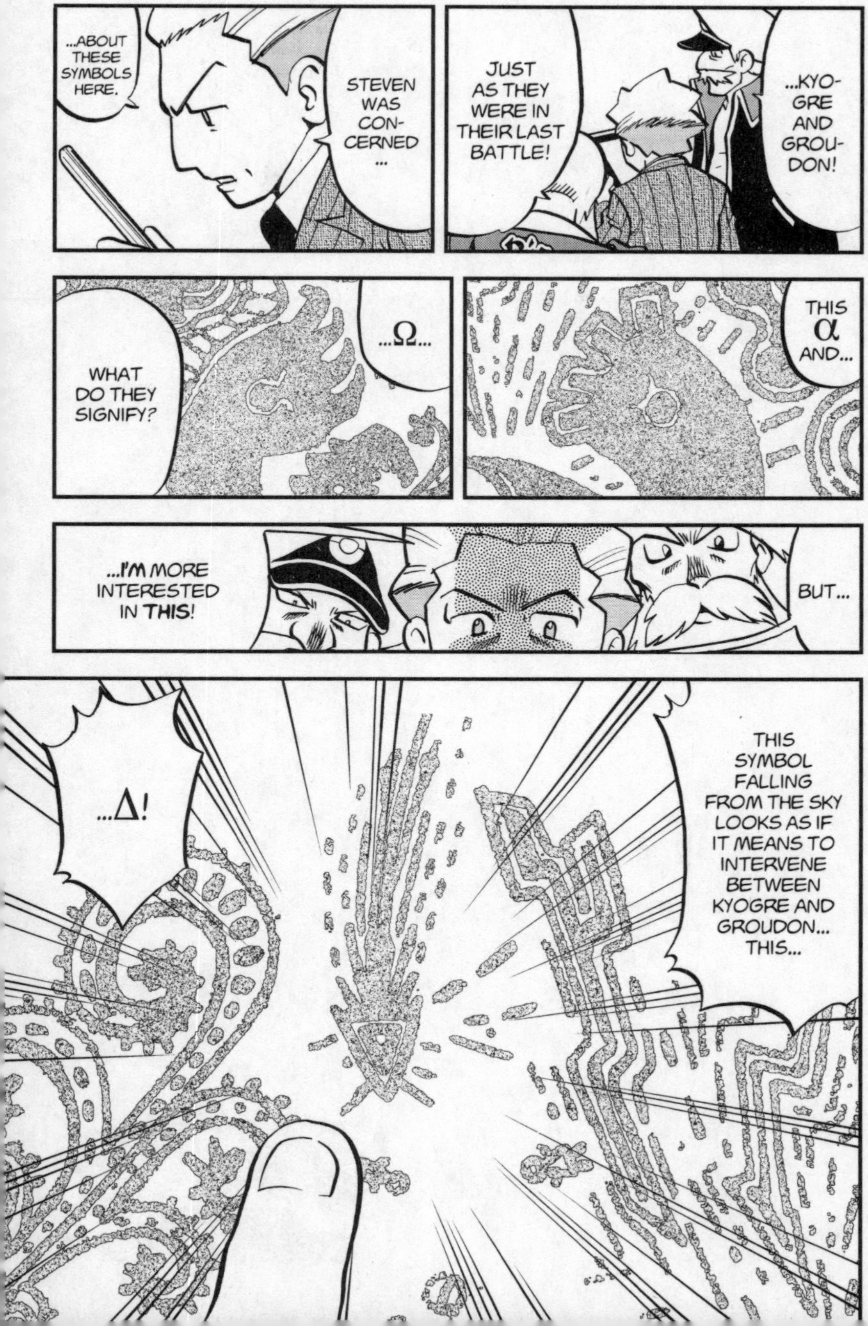
...KYOGRE AND GROUDON!
JUST AS THEY WERE IN THEIR LAST BATTLE!
STEVEN WAS CONCERNED...
...ABOUT THESE SYMBOLS HERE.
THIS α AND...
...Ω...
WHAT DO THEY SIGNIFY?
BUT...
...I'M MORE INTERESTED IN **THIS**!
THIS SYMBOL FALLING FROM THE SKY LOOKS AS IF IT MEANS TO INTERVENE BETWEEN KYOGRE AND GROUDON... THIS...
...Δ!

POKéMON™

ADVENTURES

Ω OMEGA RUBY α ALPHA SAPPHIRE

ADVENTURE #3
Claydol Unleashes

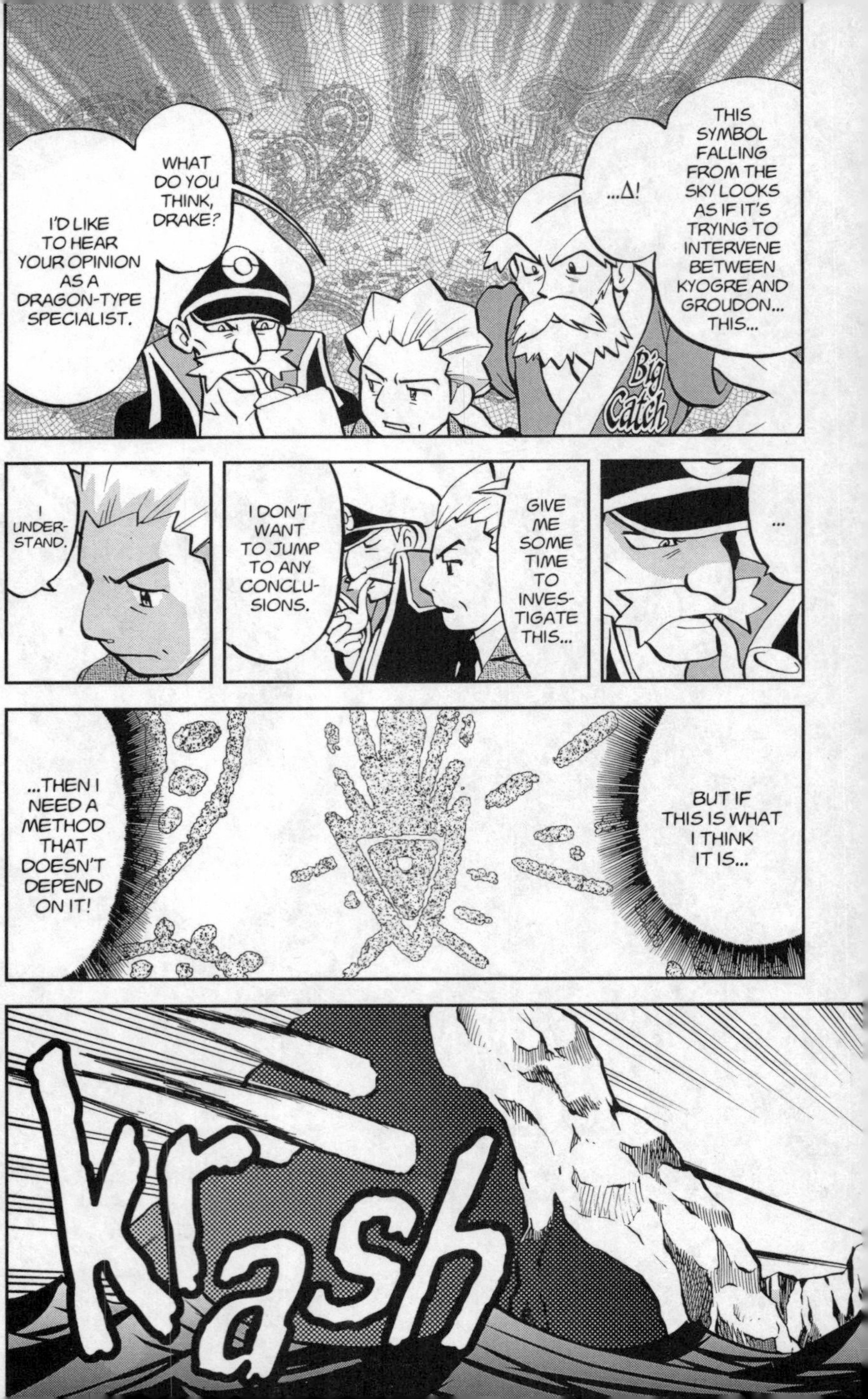
THIS SYMBOL FALLING FROM THE SKY LOOKS AS IF IT'S TRYING TO INTERVENE BETWEEN KYOGRE AND GROUDON... THIS...
...Δ!
WHAT DO YOU THINK, DRAKE?
I'D LIKE TO HEAR YOUR OPINION AS A DRAGON-TYPE SPECIALIST.
Big Catch
...
GIVE ME SOME TIME TO INVESTIGATE THIS...
I DON'T WANT TO JUMP TO ANY CONCLUSIONS.
I UNDERSTAND.
BUT IF THIS IS WHAT I THINK IT IS...
...THEN I NEED A METHOD THAT DOESN'T DEPEND ON IT!
Krash

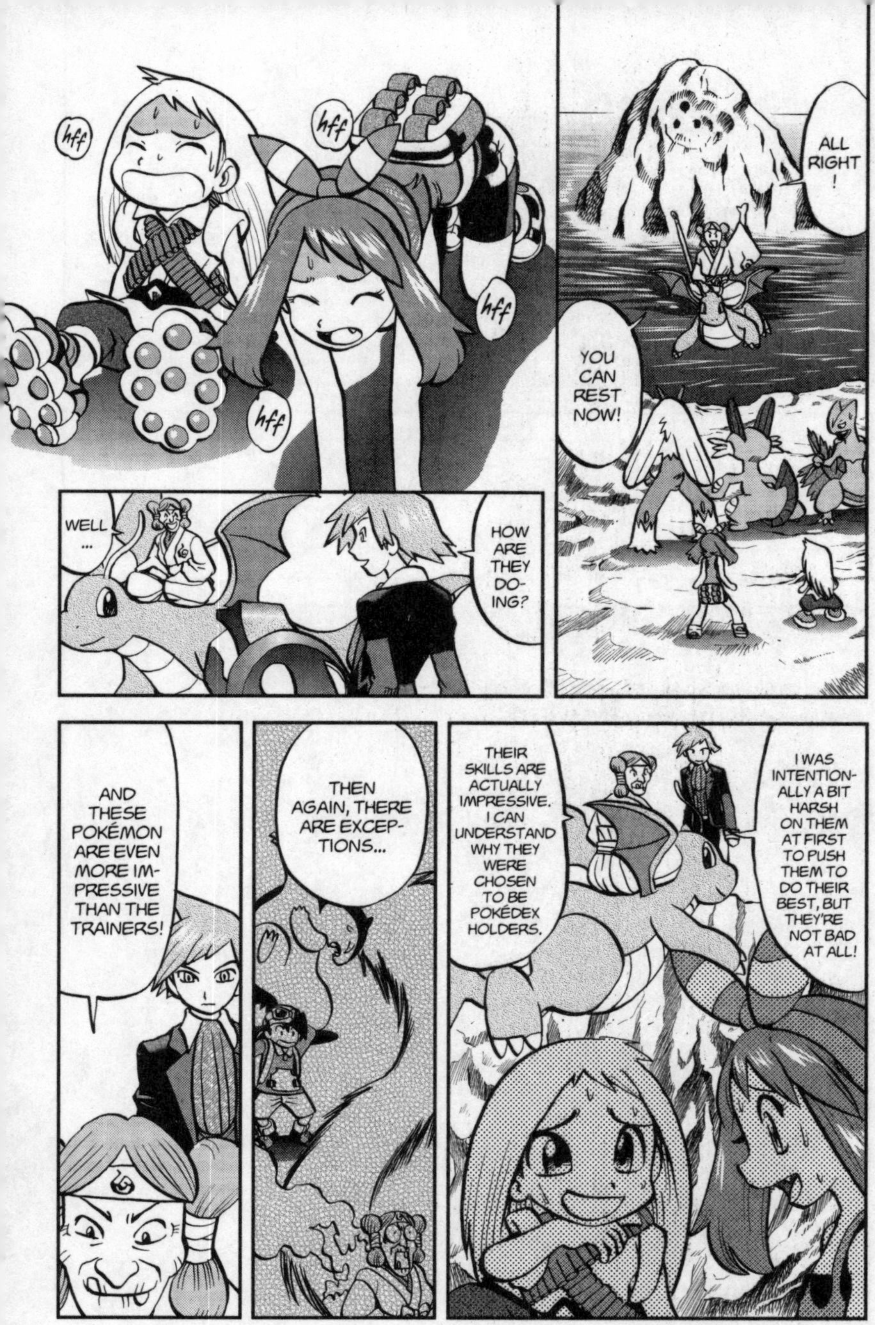
ALL RIGHT!
YOU CAN REST NOW!
hff
hff
hff
hff
HOW ARE THEY DOING?
WELL...
I WAS INTENTIONALLY A BIT HARSH ON THEM AT FIRST TO PUSH THEM TO DO THEIR BEST, BUT THEY'RE NOT BAD AT ALL!
THEIR SKILLS ARE ACTUALLY IMPRESSIVE. I CAN UNDERSTAND WHY THEY WERE CHOSEN TO BE POKÉDEX HOLDERS.
THEN AGAIN, THERE ARE EXCEPTIONS...
AND THESE POKÉMON ARE EVEN MORE IMPRESSIVE THAN THE TRAINERS!

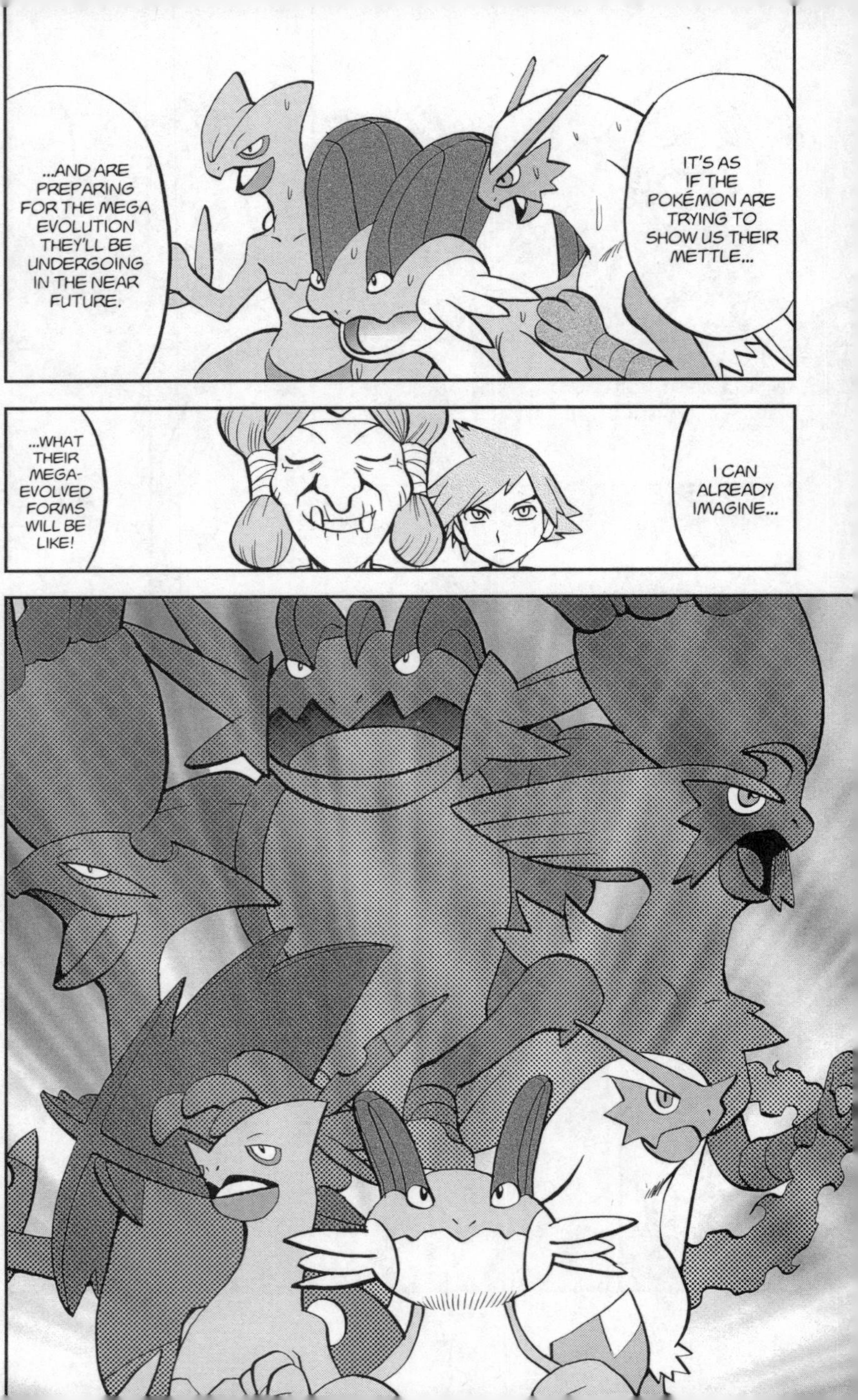
IT'S AS IF THE POKÉMON ARE TRYING TO SHOW US THEIR METTLE...
...AND ARE PREPARING FOR THE MEGA EVOLUTION THEY'LL BE UNDERGOING IN THE NEAR FUTURE.
I CAN ALREADY IMAGINE...
...WHAT THEIR MEGA-EVOLVED FORMS WILL BE LIKE!

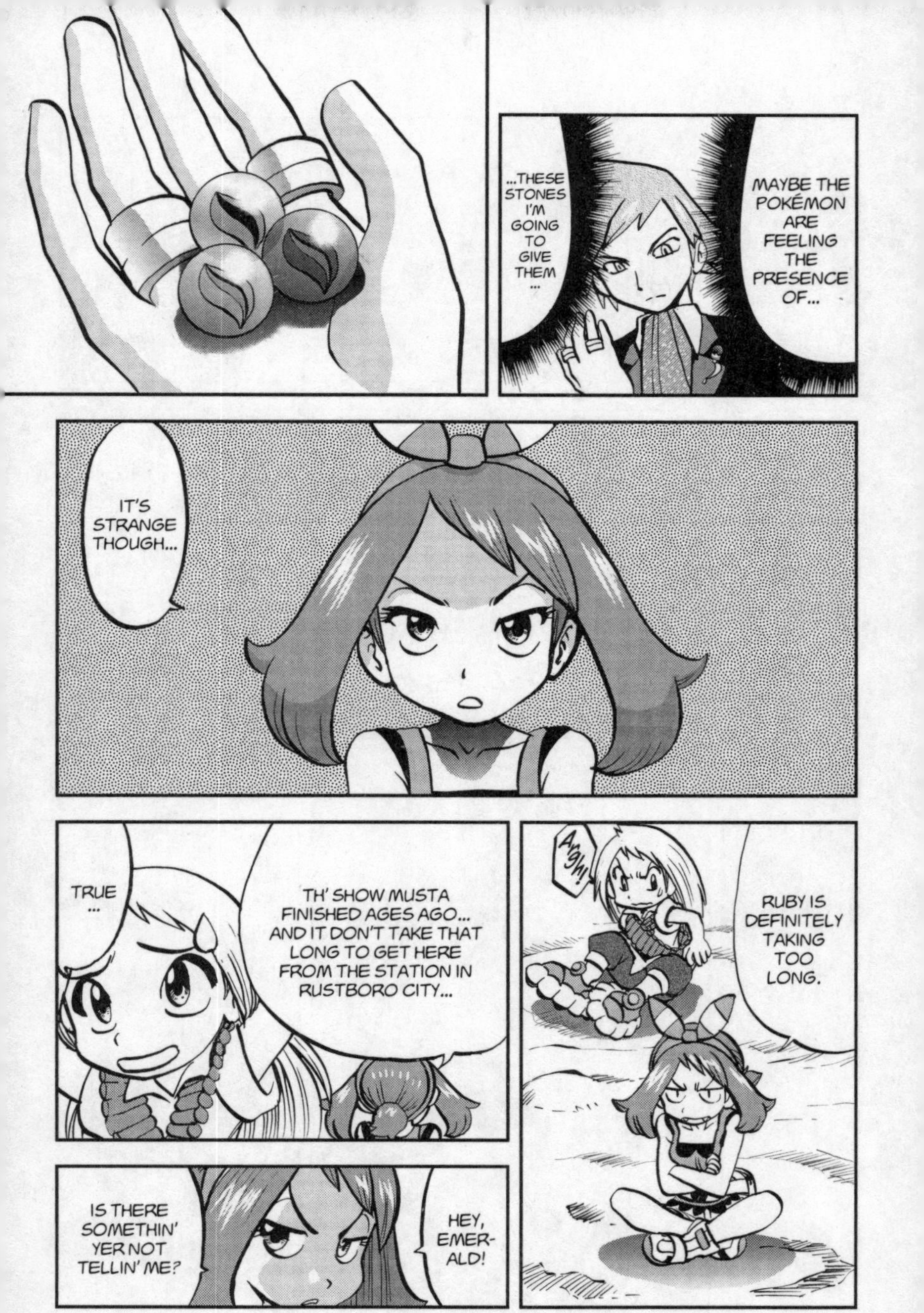

MAYBE THE POKÉMON ARE FEELING THE PRESENCE OF...
...THESE STONES I'M GOING TO GIVE THEM...
IT'S STRANGE THOUGH...
RUBY IS DEFINITELY TAKING TOO LONG.
Argh!
TH' SHOW MUSTA FINISHED AGES AGO... AND IT DON'T TAKE THAT LONG TO GET HERE FROM THE STATION IN RUSTBORO CITY...
TRUE...
HEY, EMER-ALD!
IS THERE SOMETHIN' YER NOT TELLIN' ME?

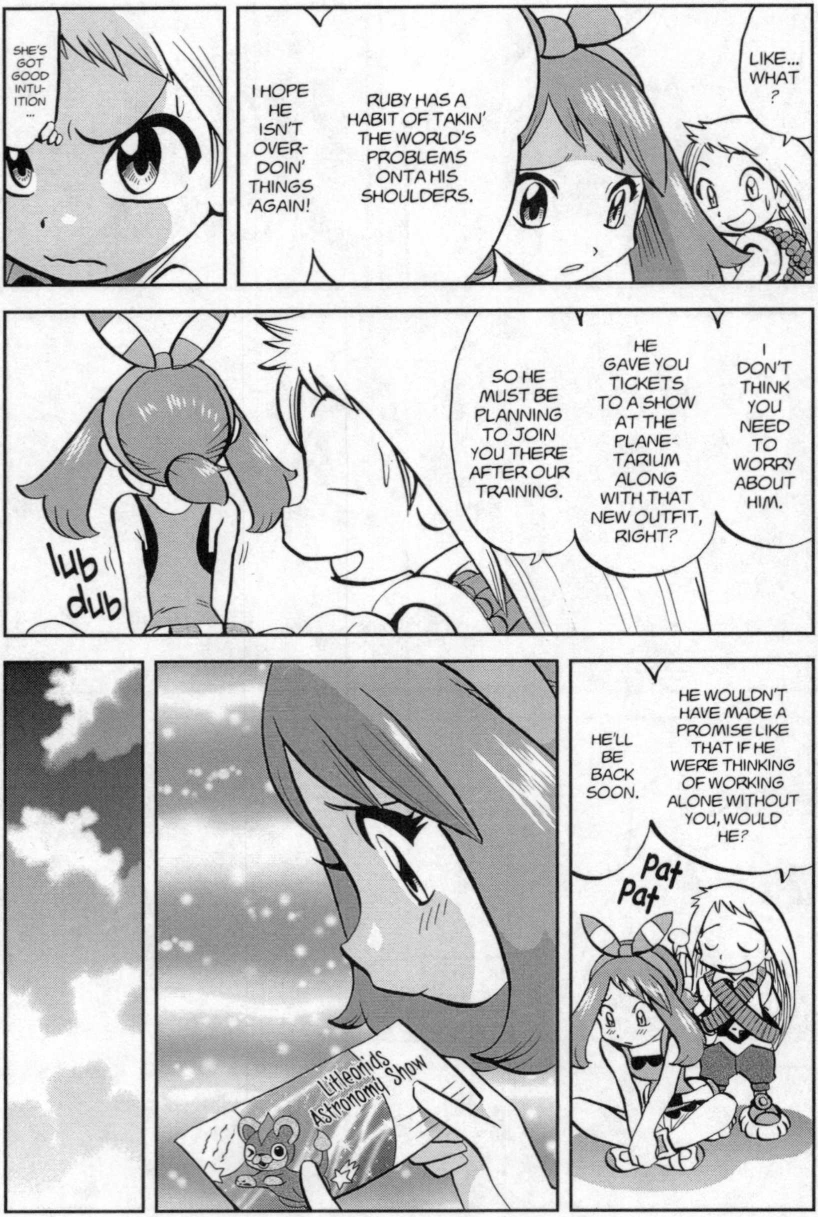
LIKE... WHAT?
RUBY HAS A HABIT OF TAKIN' THE WORLD'S PROBLEMS ONTA HIS SHOULDERS.
I HOPE HE ISN'T OVER-DOIN' THINGS AGAIN!
SHE'S GOT GOOD INTU-ITION ...
I DON'T THINK YOU NEED TO WORRY ABOUT HIM.
HE GAVE YOU TICKETS TO A SHOW AT THE PLANE-TARIUM ALONG WITH THAT NEW OUTFIT, RIGHT?
SO HE MUST BE PLANNING TO JOIN YOU THERE AFTER OUR TRAINING.
lub dub
HE WOULDN'T HAVE MADE A PROMISE LIKE THAT IF HE WERE THINKING OF WORKING ALONE WITHOUT YOU, WOULD HE?
HE'LL BE BACK SOON.
Pat Pat
Litleonids Astronomy Show

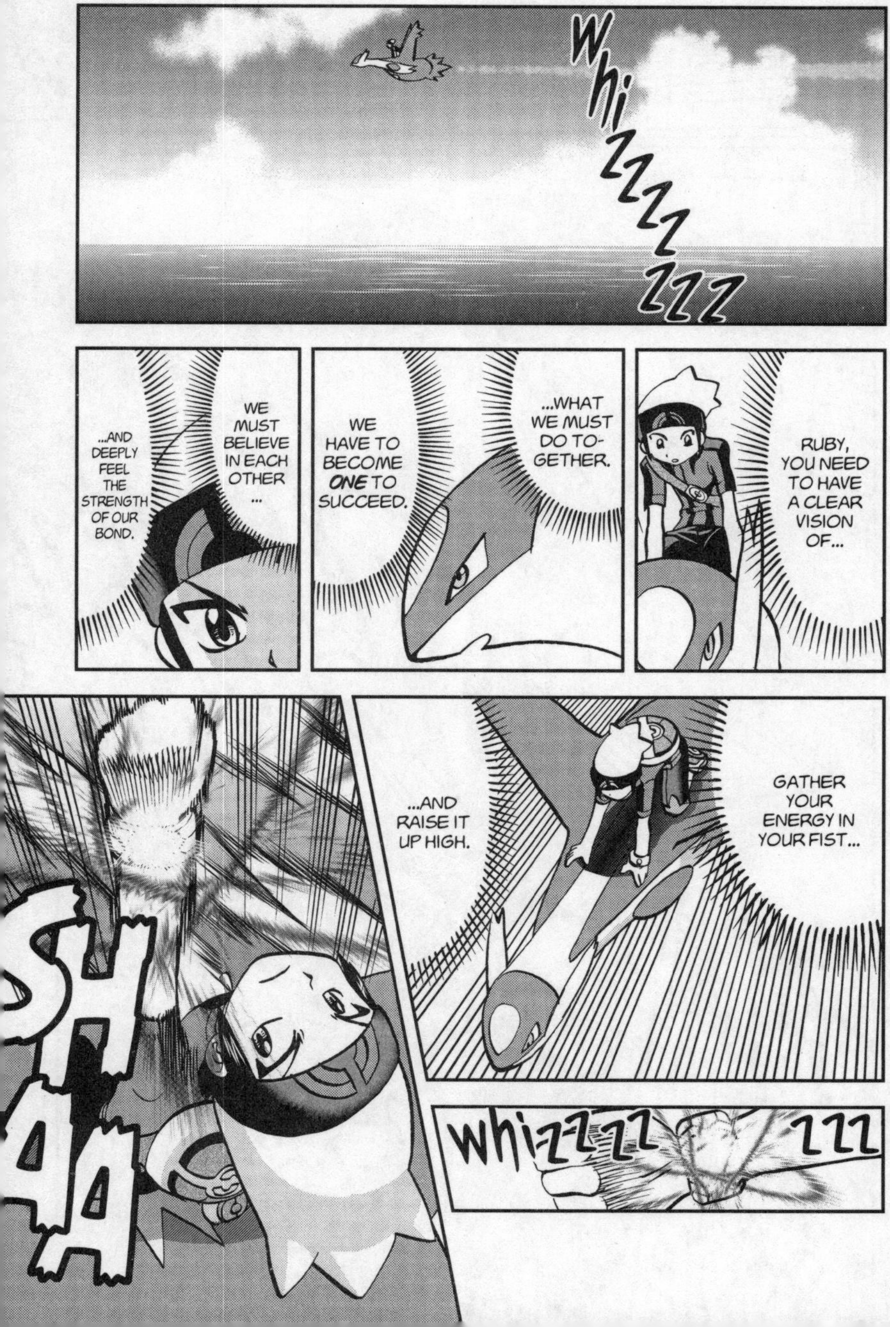
Whizzzzzzz
RUBY, YOU NEED TO HAVE A CLEAR VISION OF...
...WHAT WE MUST DO TO-GETHER.
WE HAVE TO BECOME *ONE* TO SUCCEED.
WE MUST BELIEVE IN EACH OTHER ...
...AND DEEPLY FEEL THE STRENGTH OF OUR BOND.
GATHER YOUR ENERGY IN YOUR FIST...
...AND RAISE IT UP HIGH.
whizzzzz zzz
SHAA

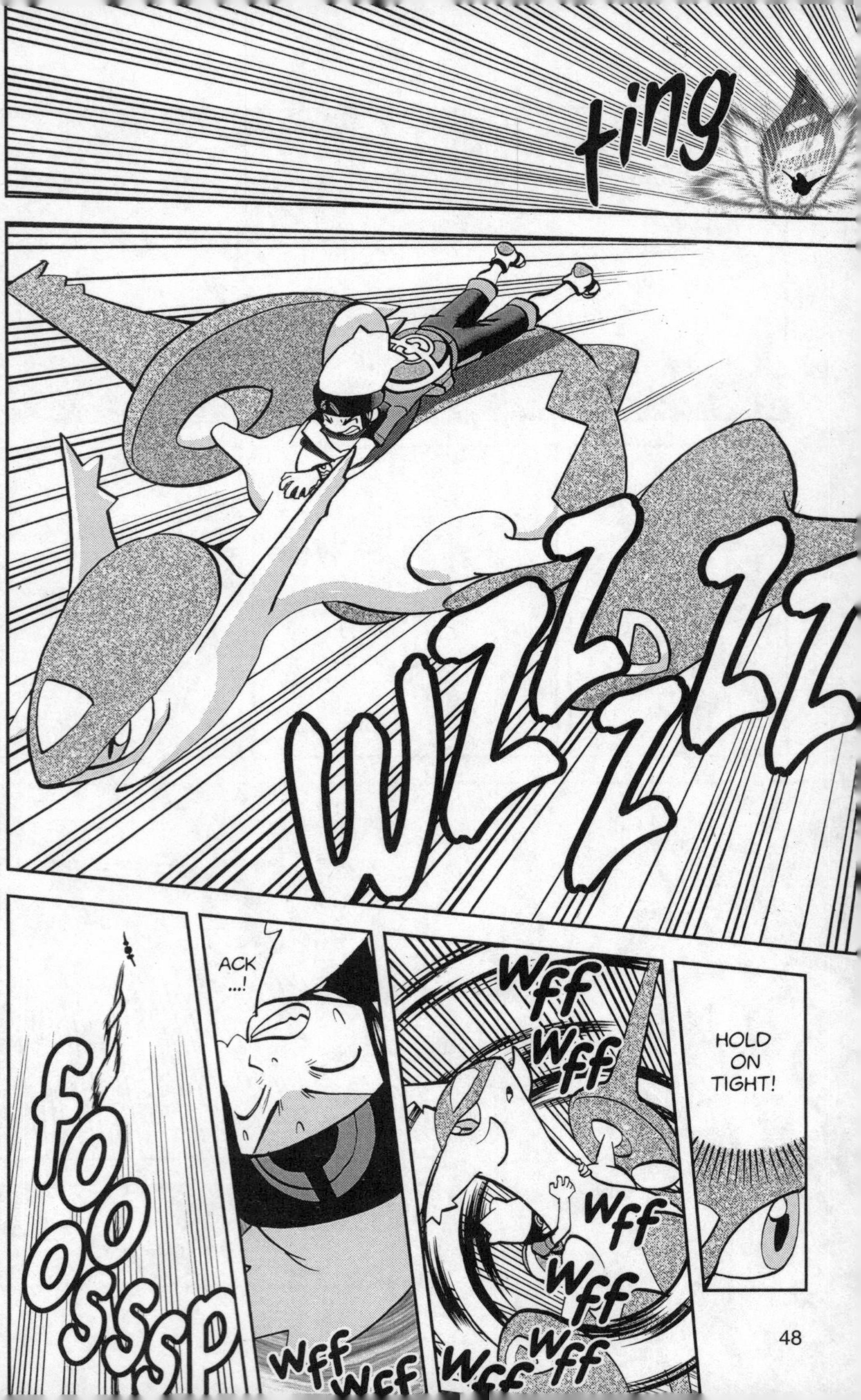
ting
WZZZZZZ
HOLD ON TIGHT!
wff wff wff wff wff
ACK ...!
wff wff
fooossssp

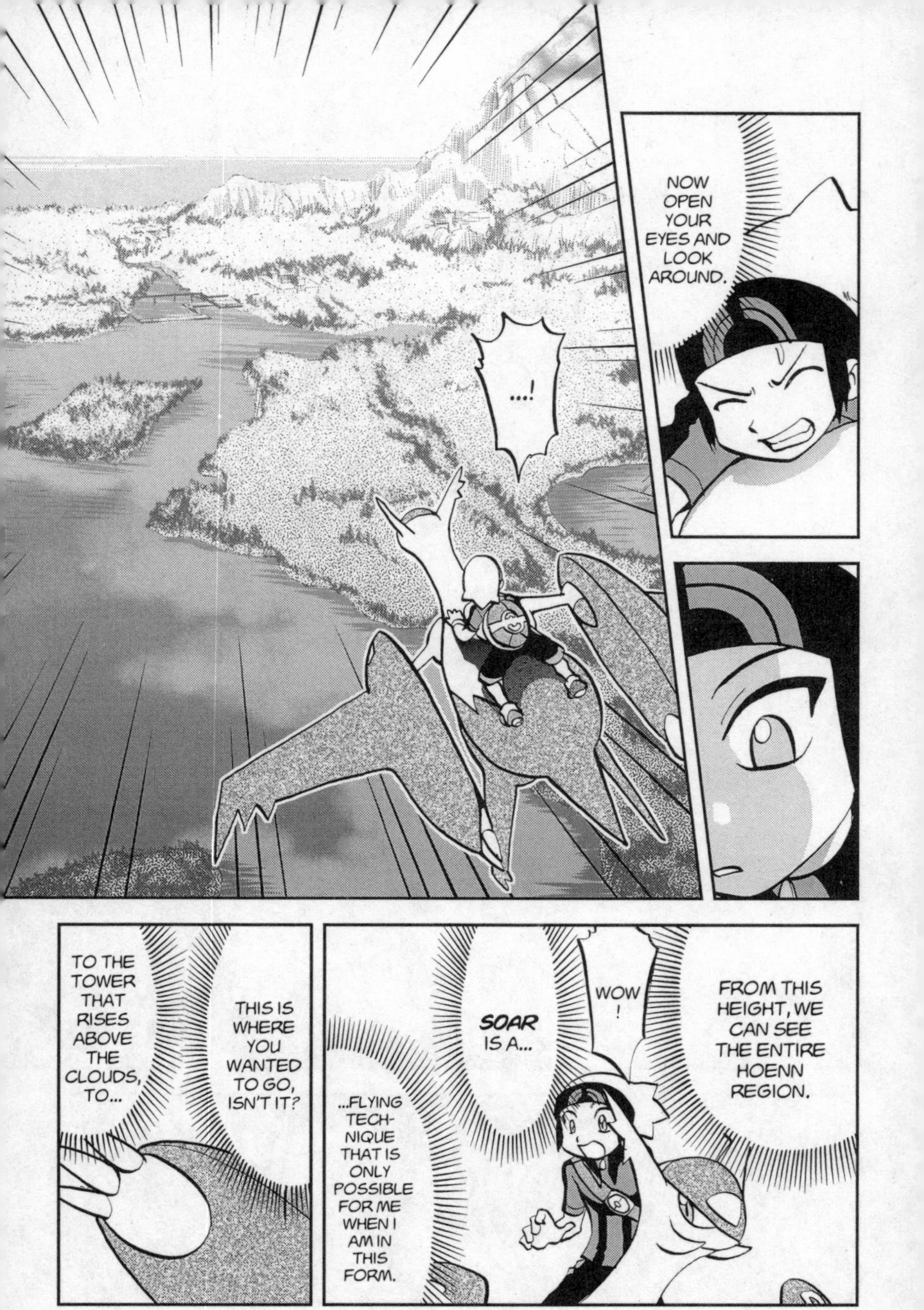
NOW OPEN YOUR EYES AND LOOK AROUND.
...!
FROM THIS HEIGHT, WE CAN SEE THE ENTIRE HOENN REGION.
WOW!
SOAR IS A...
...FLYING TECHNIQUE THAT IS ONLY POSSIBLE FOR ME WHEN I AM IN THIS FORM.
THIS IS WHERE YOU WANTED TO GO, ISN'T IT?
TO THE TOWER THAT RISES ABOVE THE CLOUDS, TO...

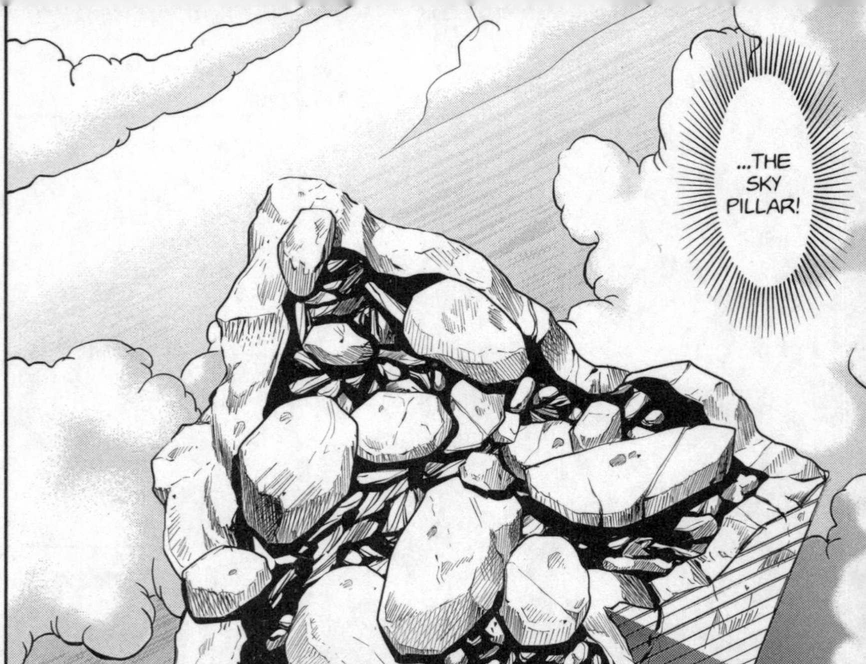
...THE SKY PILLAR!

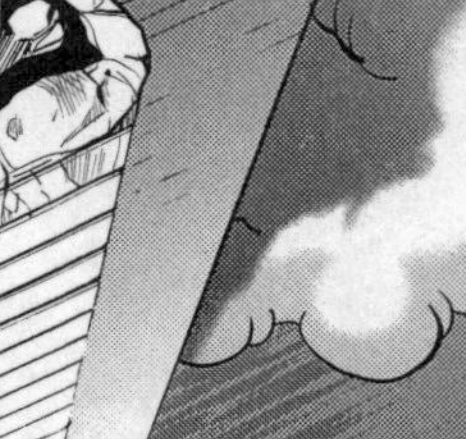
ZWOOOP

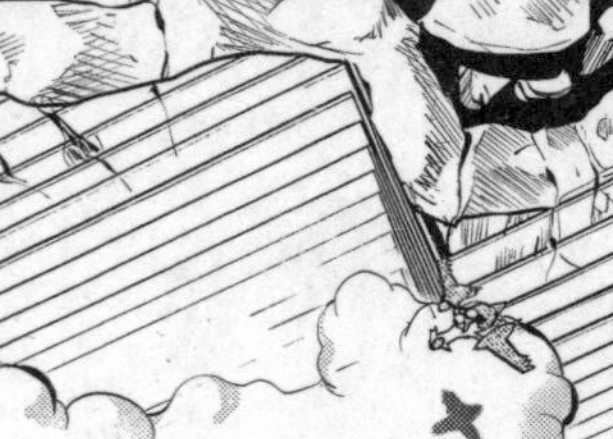
fmmmp

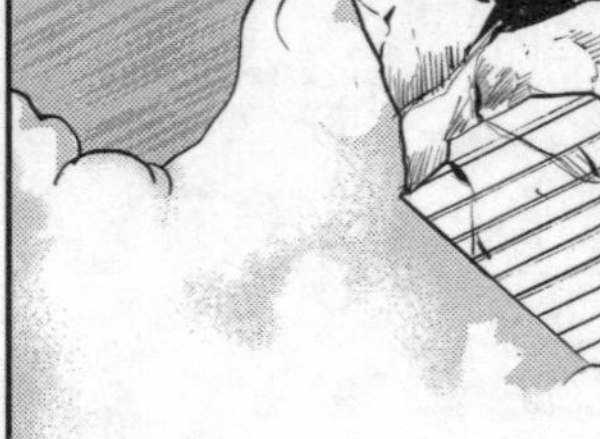

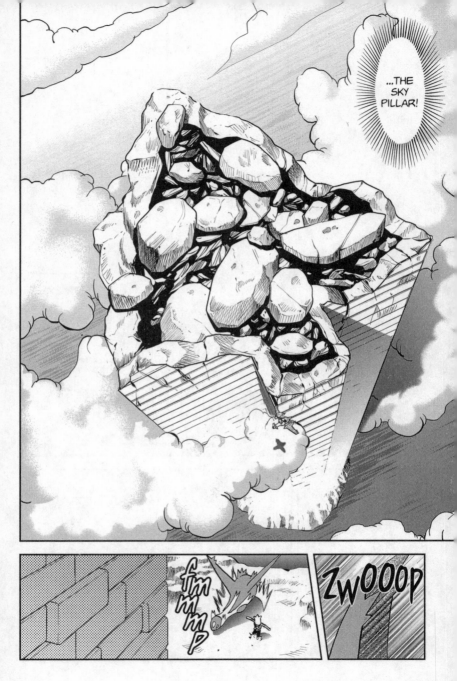

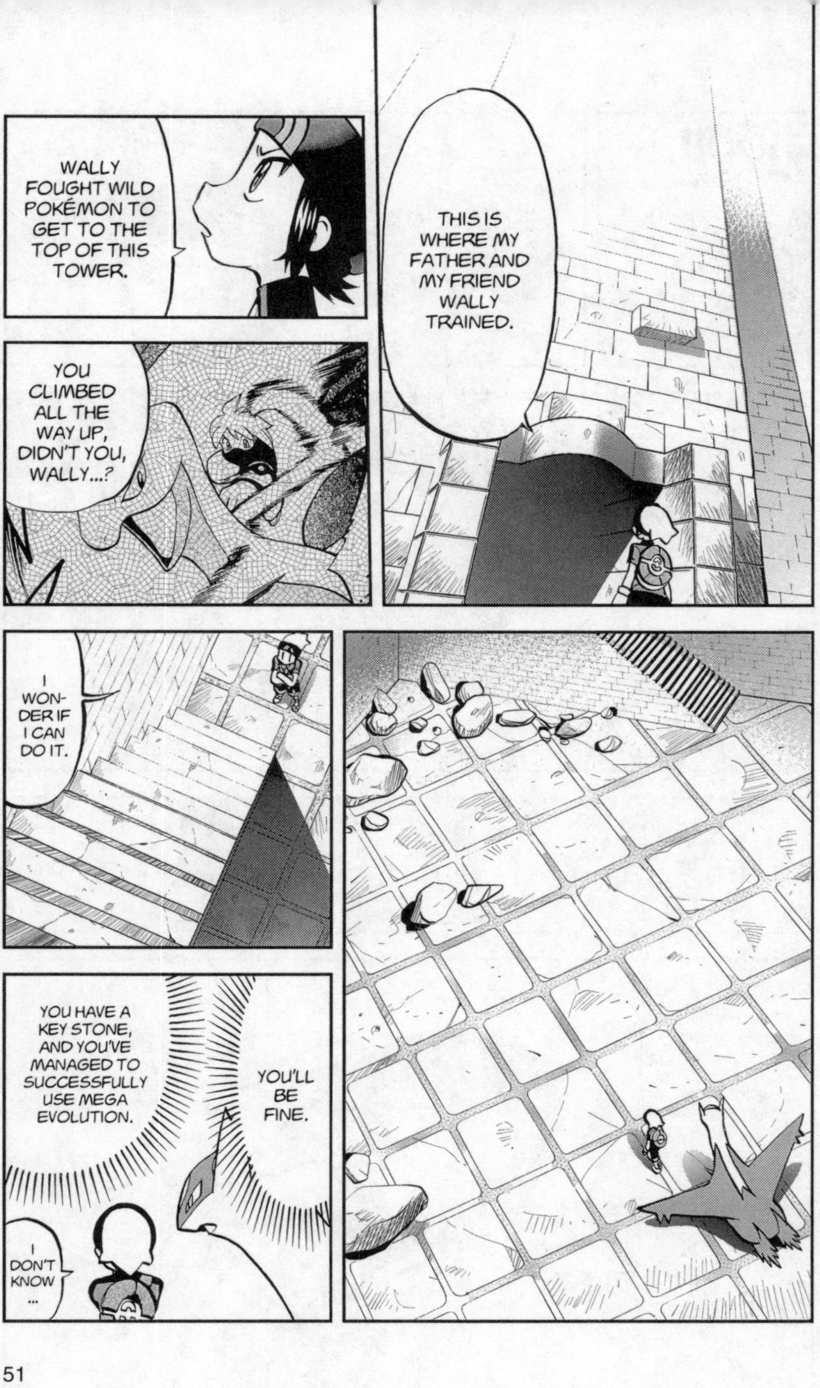
THIS IS WHERE MY FATHER AND MY FRIEND WALLY TRAINED.
WALLY FOUGHT WILD POKÉMON TO GET TO THE TOP OF THIS TOWER.
YOU CLIMBED ALL THE WAY UP, DIDN'T YOU, WALLY...?
I WON-DER IF I CAN DO IT.
YOU'LL BE FINE.
YOU HAVE A KEY STONE, AND YOU'VE MANAGED TO SUCCESSFULLY USE MEGA EVOLUTION.
I DON'T KNOW...

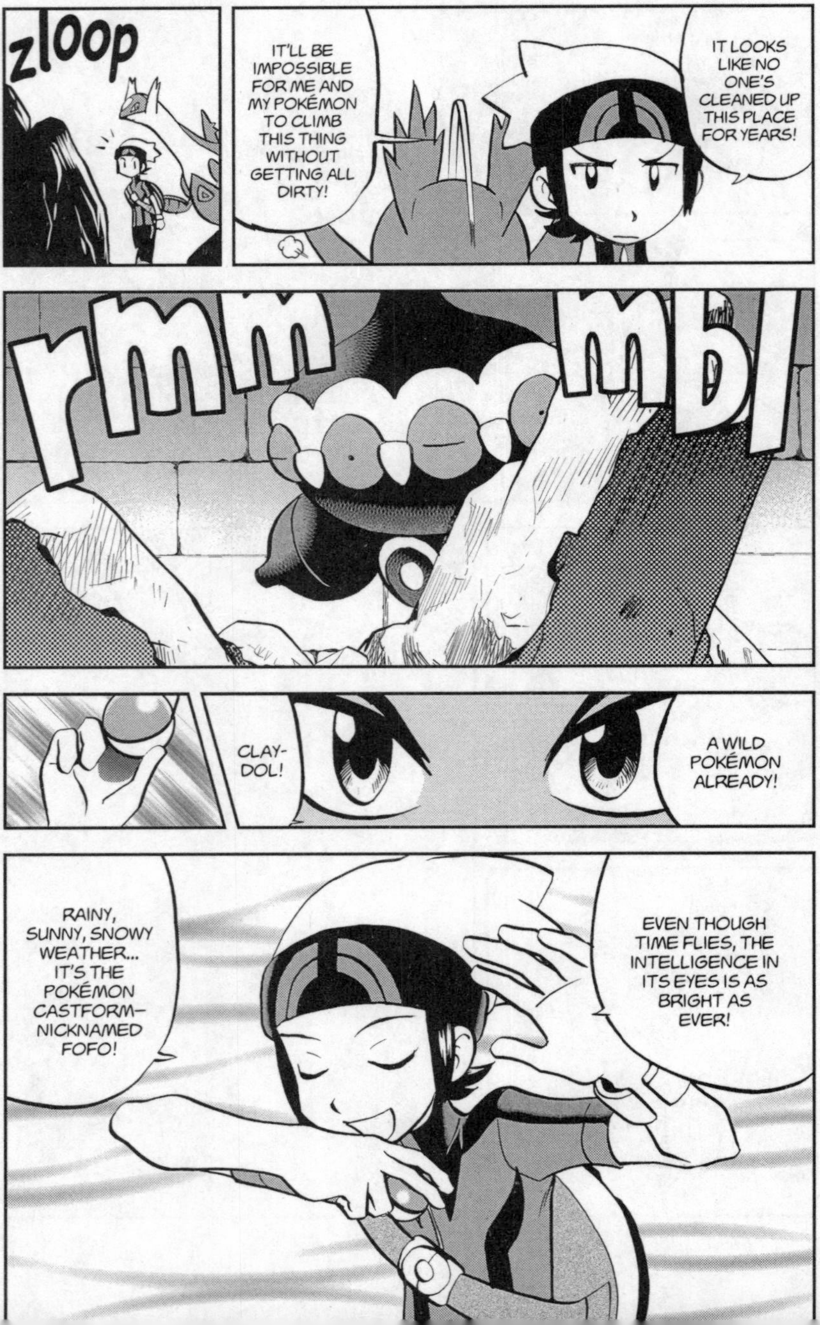
IT LOOKS LIKE NO ONE'S CLEANED UP THIS PLACE FOR YEARS!
IT'LL BE IMPOSSIBLE FOR ME AND MY POKÉMON TO CLIMB THIS THING WITHOUT GETTING ALL DIRTY!
zloop
rmm mbl
A WILD POKÉMON ALREADY!
CLAY-DOL!
EVEN THOUGH TIME FLIES, THE INTELLIGENCE IN ITS EYES IS AS BRIGHT AS EVER!
RAINY, SUNNY, SNOWY WEATHER... IT'S THE POKÉMON CASTFORM—NICKNAMED FOFO!

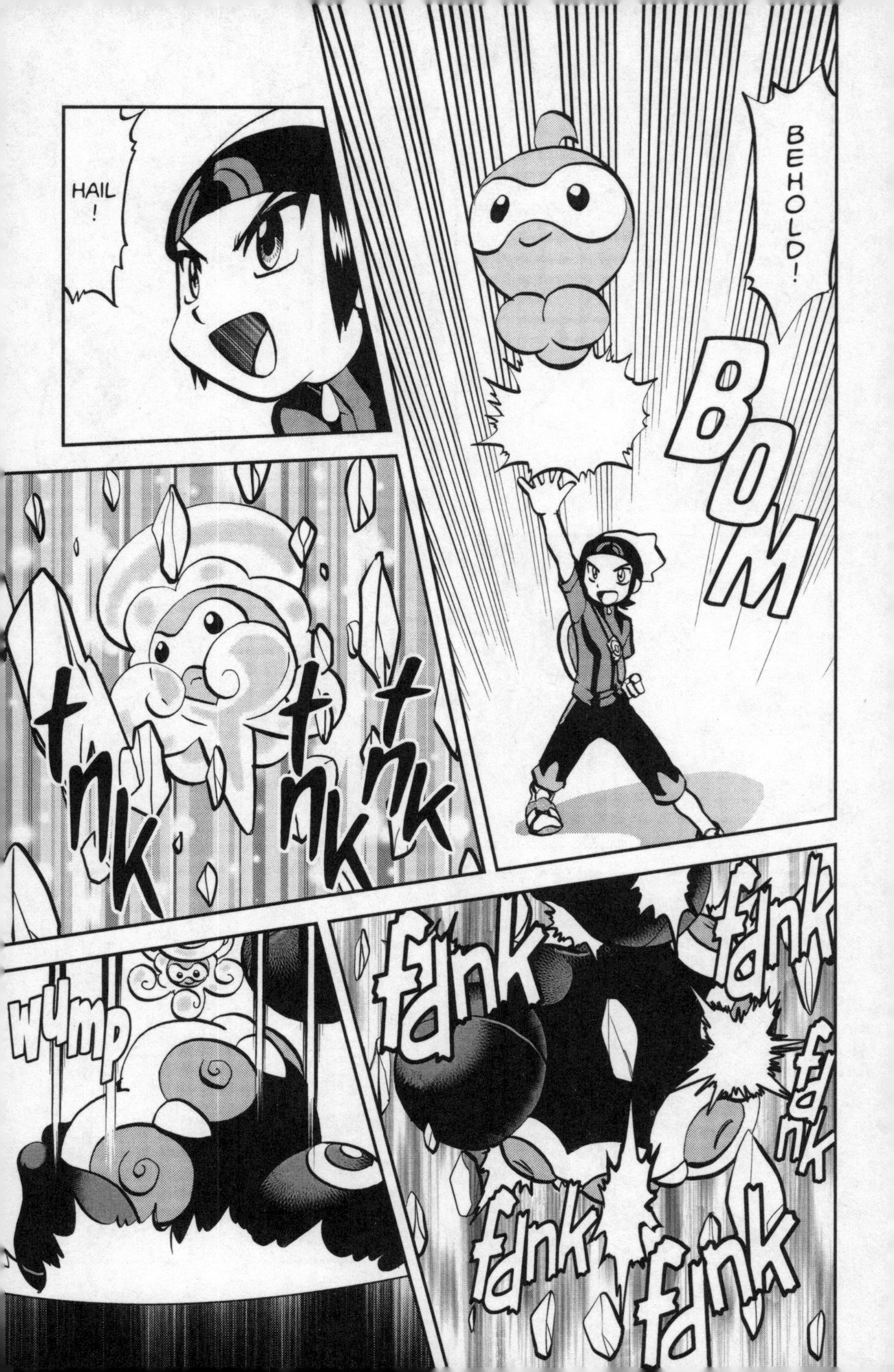
BEHOLD!
BOOM
HAIL!
tnk
tnk
tnk
fdnk
fdnk
fdnk
fdnk
fdnk
wump

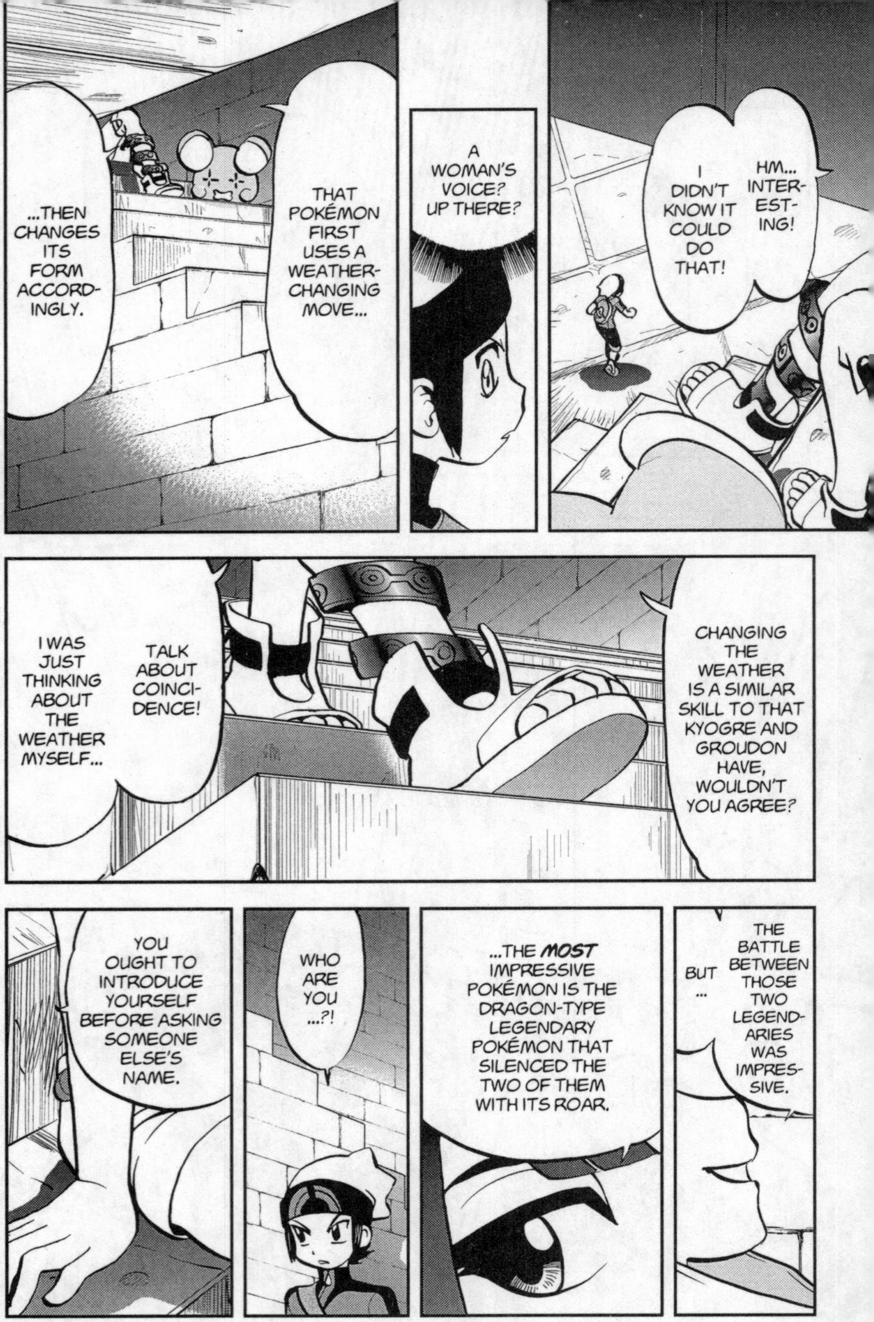
HM... INTERESTING!
I DIDN'T KNOW IT COULD DO THAT!
A WOMAN'S VOICE? UP THERE?
THAT POKÉMON FIRST USES A WEATHER-CHANGING MOVE...
...THEN CHANGES ITS FORM ACCORDINGLY.
CHANGING THE WEATHER IS A SIMILAR SKILL TO THAT KYOGRE AND GROUDON HAVE, WOULDN'T YOU AGREE?
TALK ABOUT COINCIDENCE!
I WAS JUST THINKING ABOUT THE WEATHER MYSELF...
THE BATTLE BETWEEN THOSE TWO LEGENDARIES WAS IMPRESSIVE.
BUT...
...THE *MOST* IMPRESSIVE POKÉMON IS THE DRAGON-TYPE LEGENDARY POKÉMON THAT SILENCED THE TWO OF THEM WITH ITS ROAR.
WHO ARE YOU...?!
YOU OUGHT TO INTRODUCE YOURSELF BEFORE ASKING SOMEONE ELSE'S NAME.

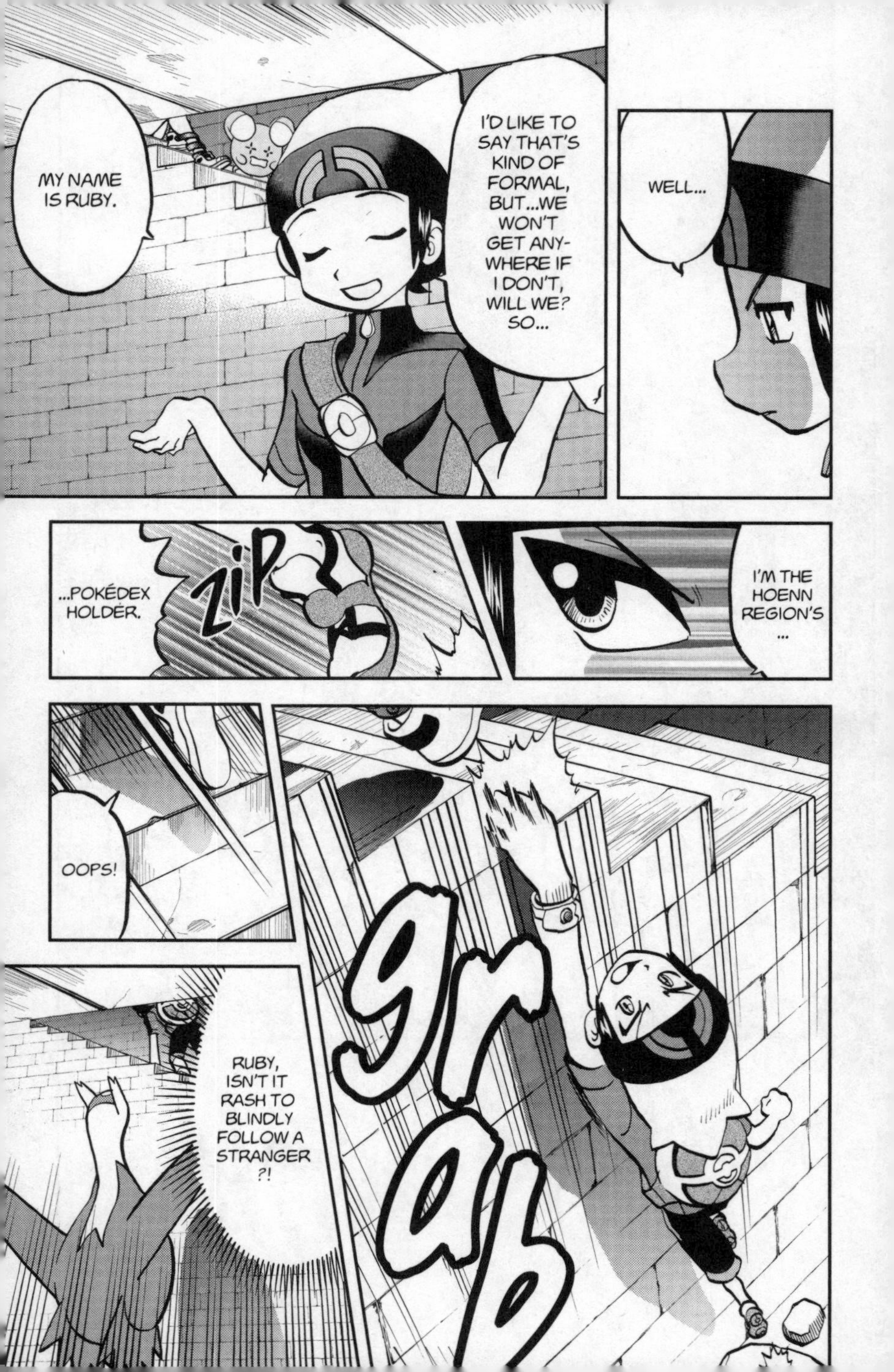
WELL...
I'D LIKE TO SAY THAT'S KIND OF FORMAL, BUT...WE WON'T GET ANYWHERE IF I DON'T, WILL WE? SO...
MY NAME IS RUBY.
I'M THE HOENN REGION'S ...
ZIP
...POKÉDEX HOLDER.
grab
OOPS!
RUBY, ISN'T IT RASH TO BLINDLY FOLLOW A STRANGER ?!

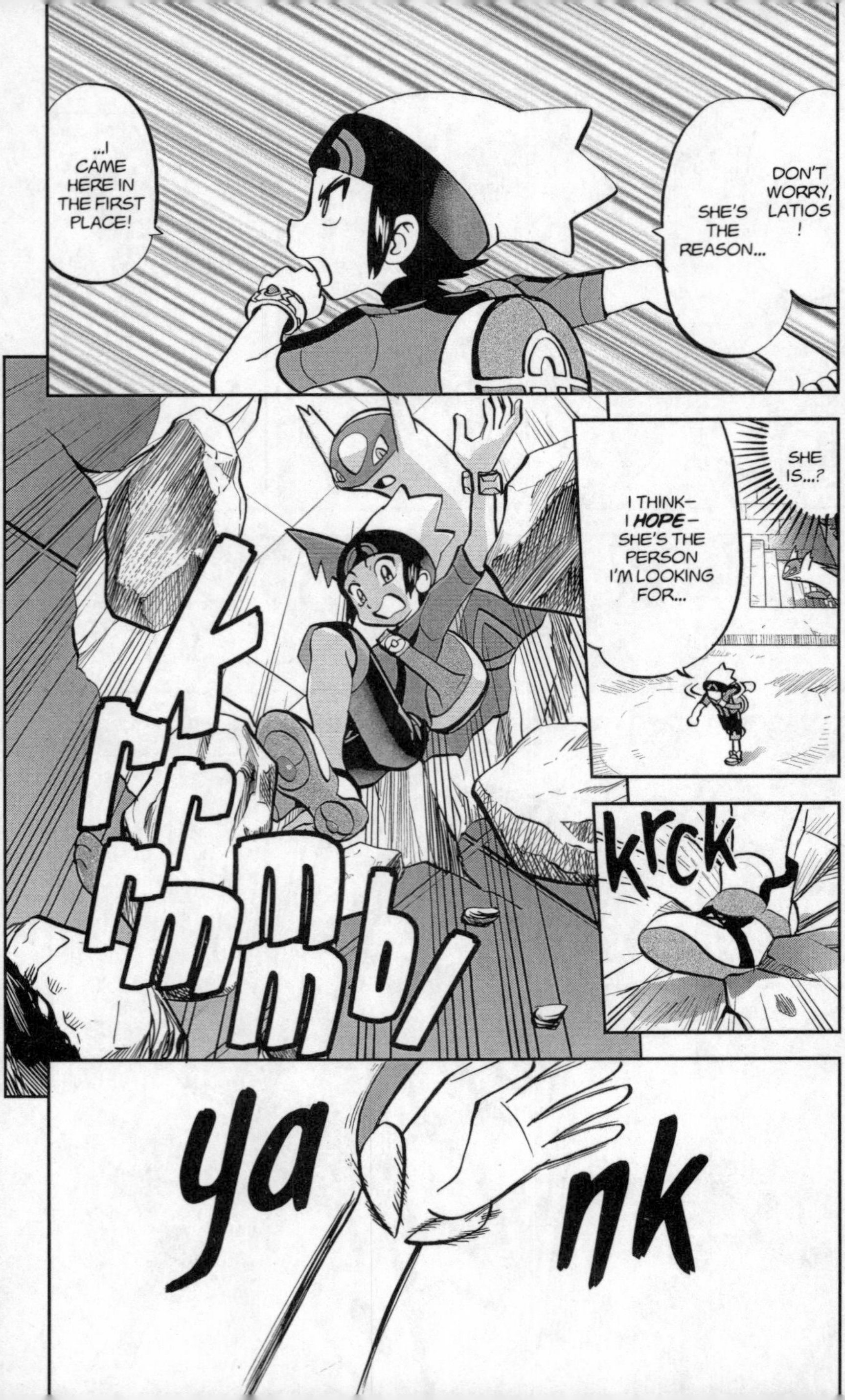
DON'T WORRY, LATIOS!
SHE'S THE REASON...
...I CAME HERE IN THE FIRST PLACE!
SHE IS...?
I THINK—I ***HOPE***—SHE'S THE PERSON I'M LOOKING FOR...
krck
krrrmmmbl
yank

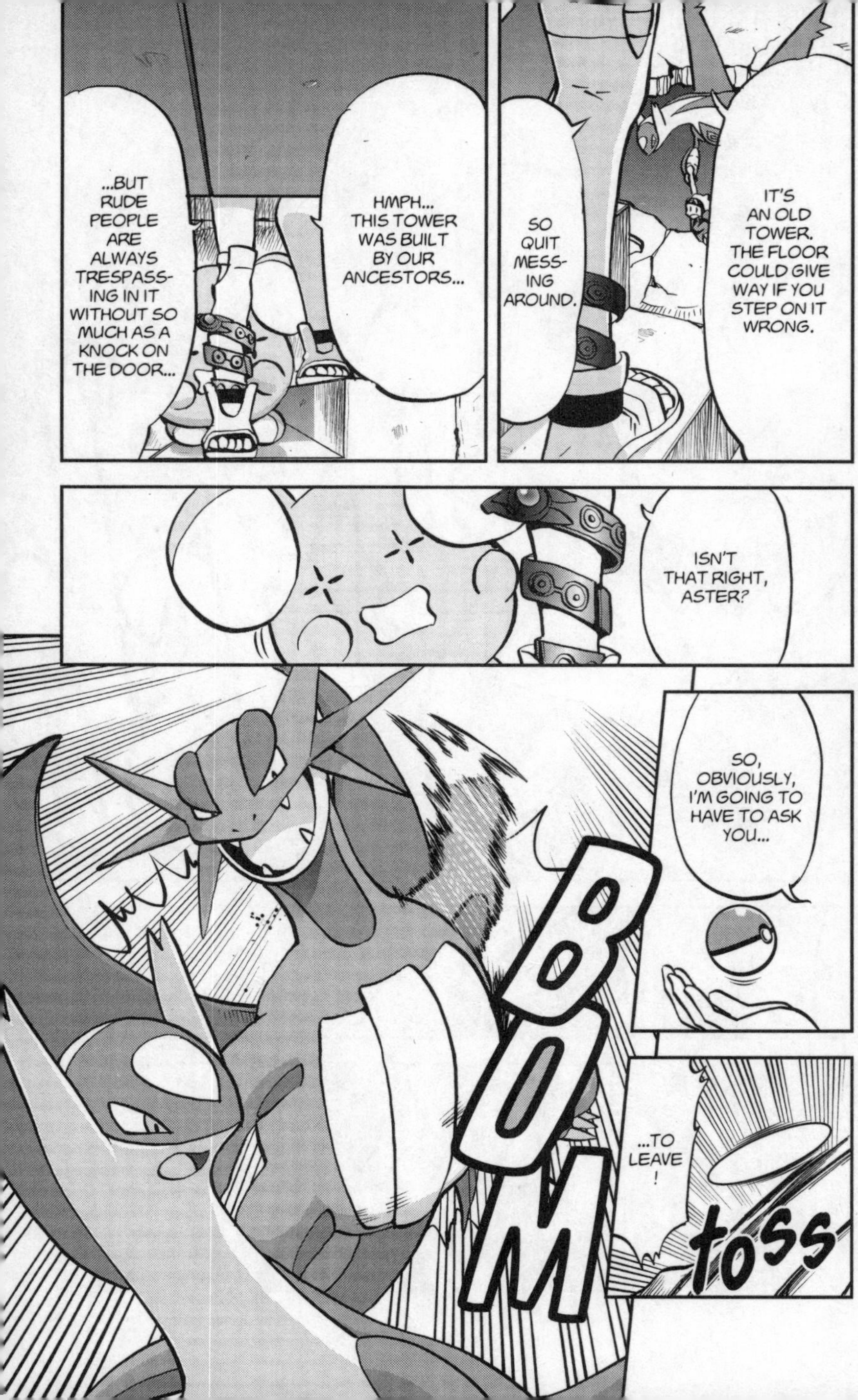
IT'S AN OLD TOWER. THE FLOOR COULD GIVE WAY IF YOU STEP ON IT WRONG.
SO QUIT MESS-ING AROUND.
HMPH... THIS TOWER WAS BUILT BY OUR ANCESTORS...
...BUT RUDE PEOPLE ARE ALWAYS TRESPASS-ING IN IT WITHOUT SO MUCH AS A KNOCK ON THE DOOR...
ISN'T THAT RIGHT, ASTER?
SO, OBVIOUSLY, I'M GOING TO HAVE TO ASK YOU...
...TO LEAVE!
toss
BOOM

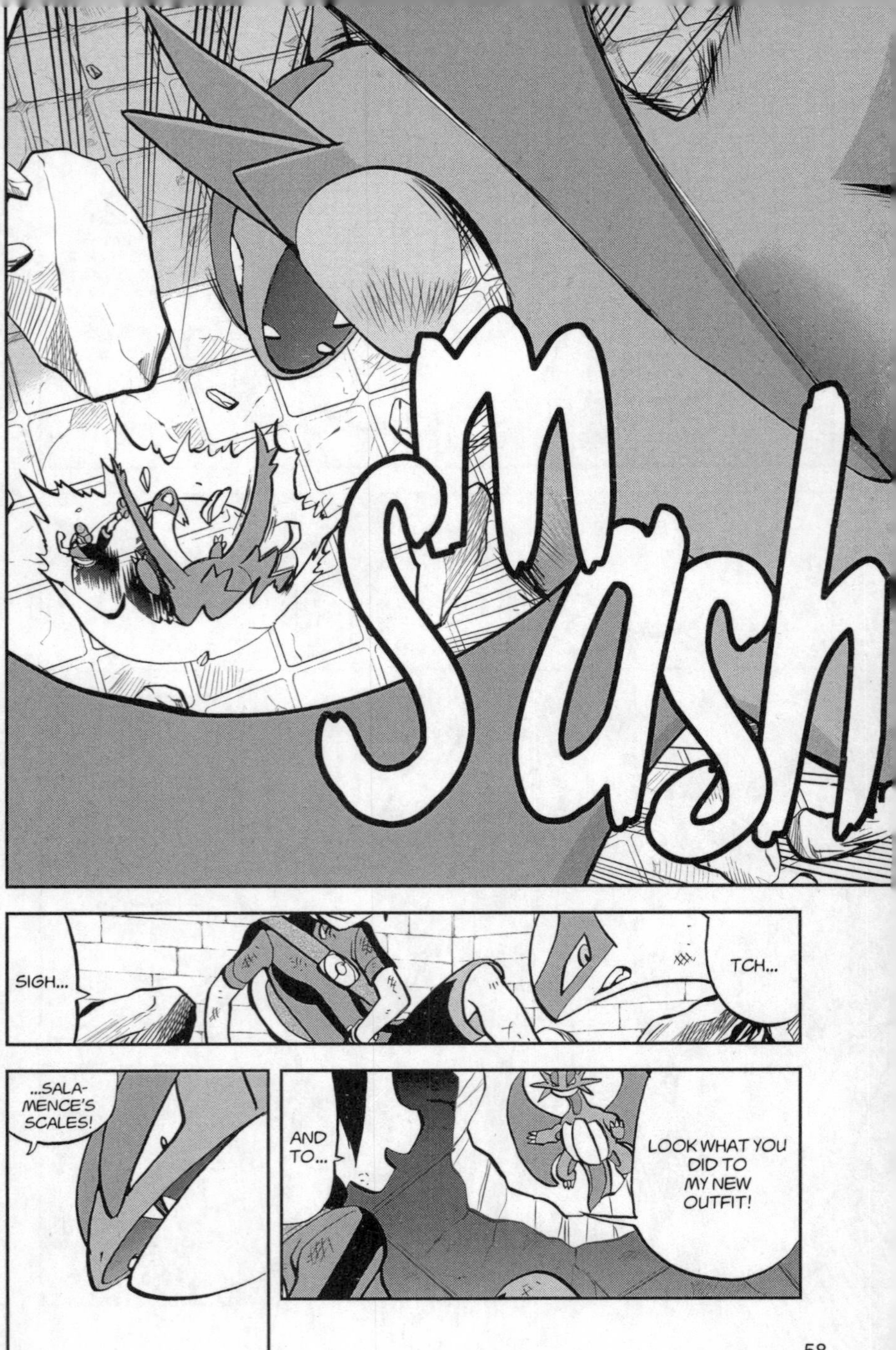
SMASH
TCH...
SIGH...
LOOK WHAT YOU DID TO MY NEW OUTFIT!
AND TO...
...SALA-MENCE'S SCALES!

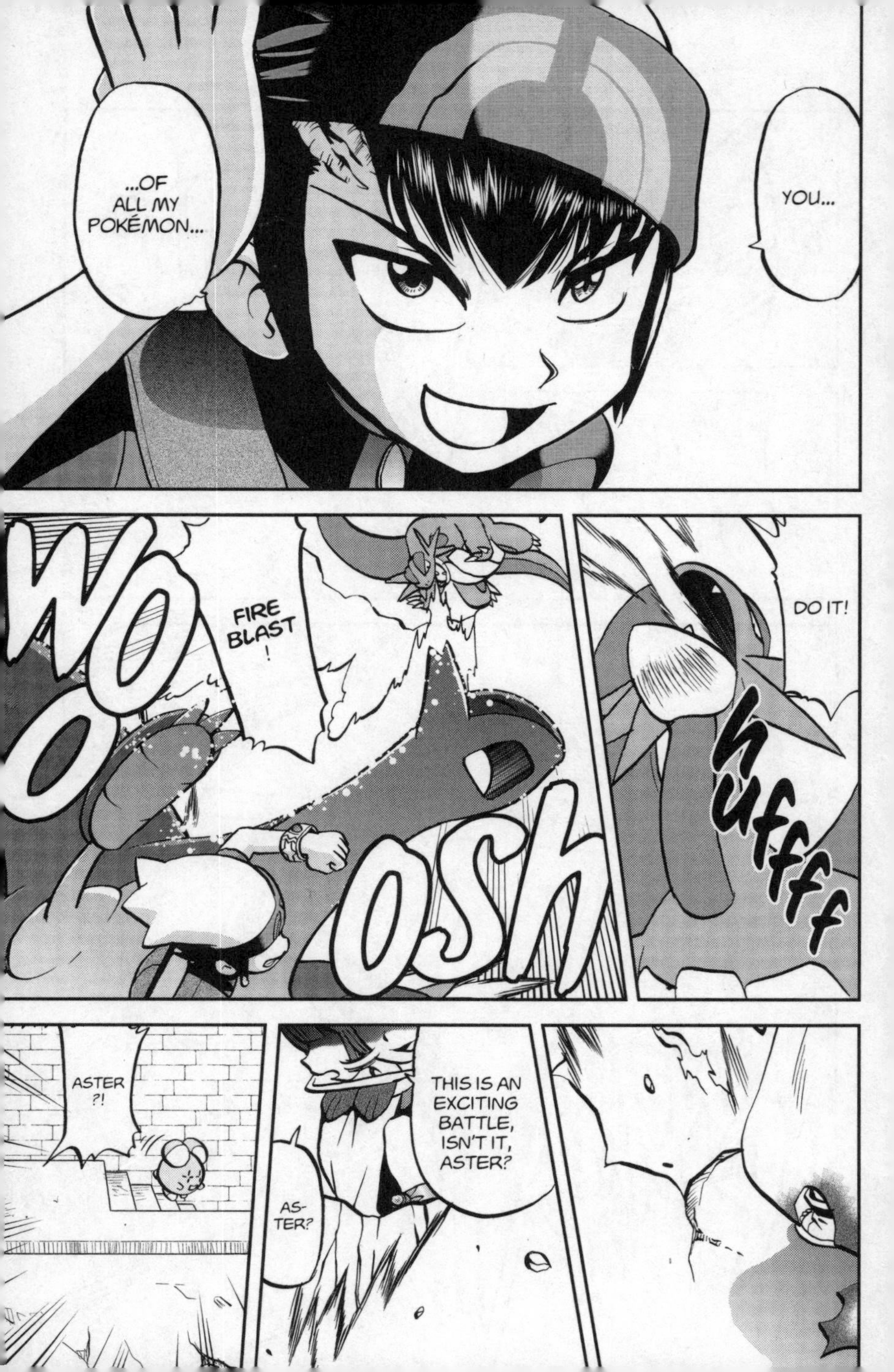
YOU...
...OF ALL MY POKÉMON...
DO IT!
huffff
FIRE BLAST!
WOOOSH
THIS IS AN EXCITING BATTLE, ISN'T IT, ASTER?
AS-TER?
ASTER?!

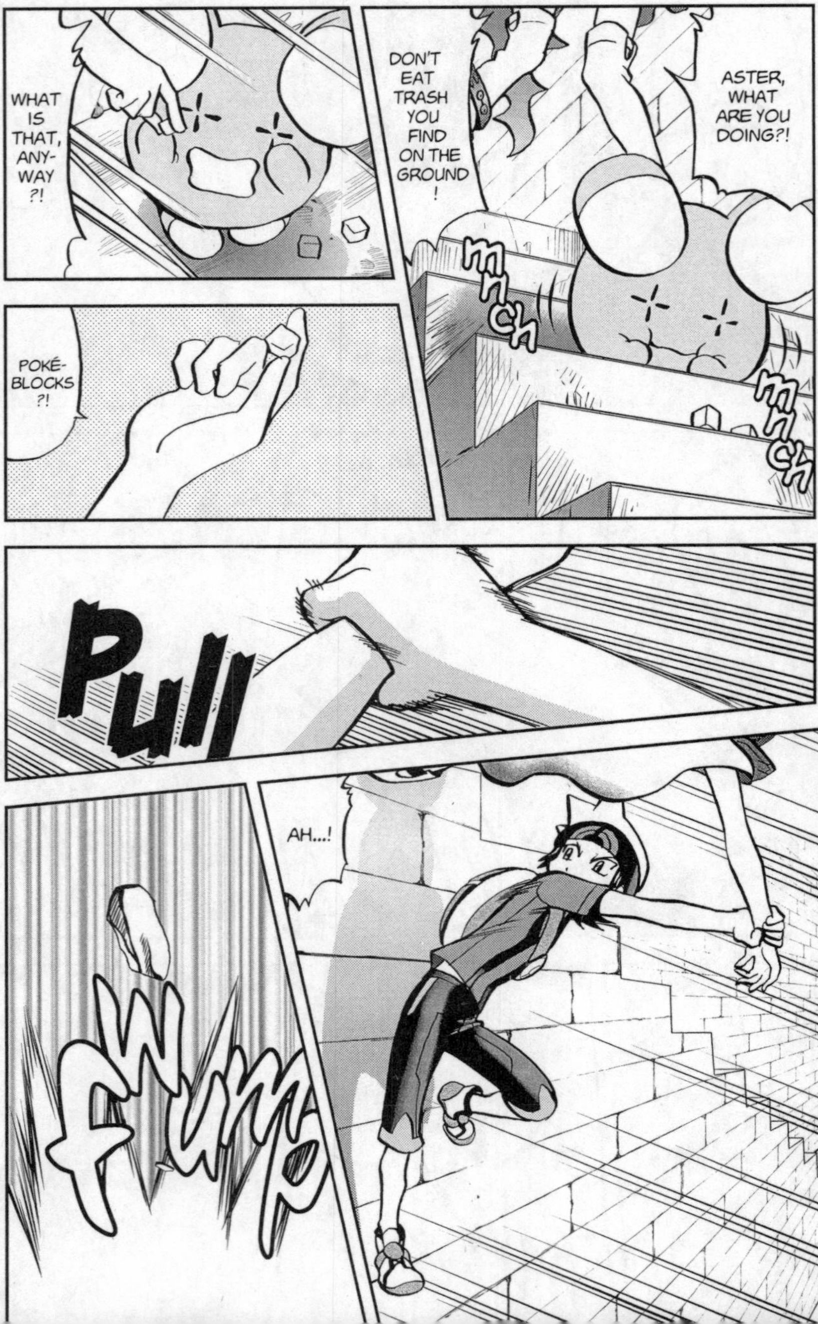
ASTER, WHAT ARE YOU DOING?!
DON'T EAT TRASH YOU FIND ON THE GROUND!
mnch
mnch
WHAT IS THAT, ANYWAY?!
POKÉBLOCKS?!
Pull
AH...!
fwump

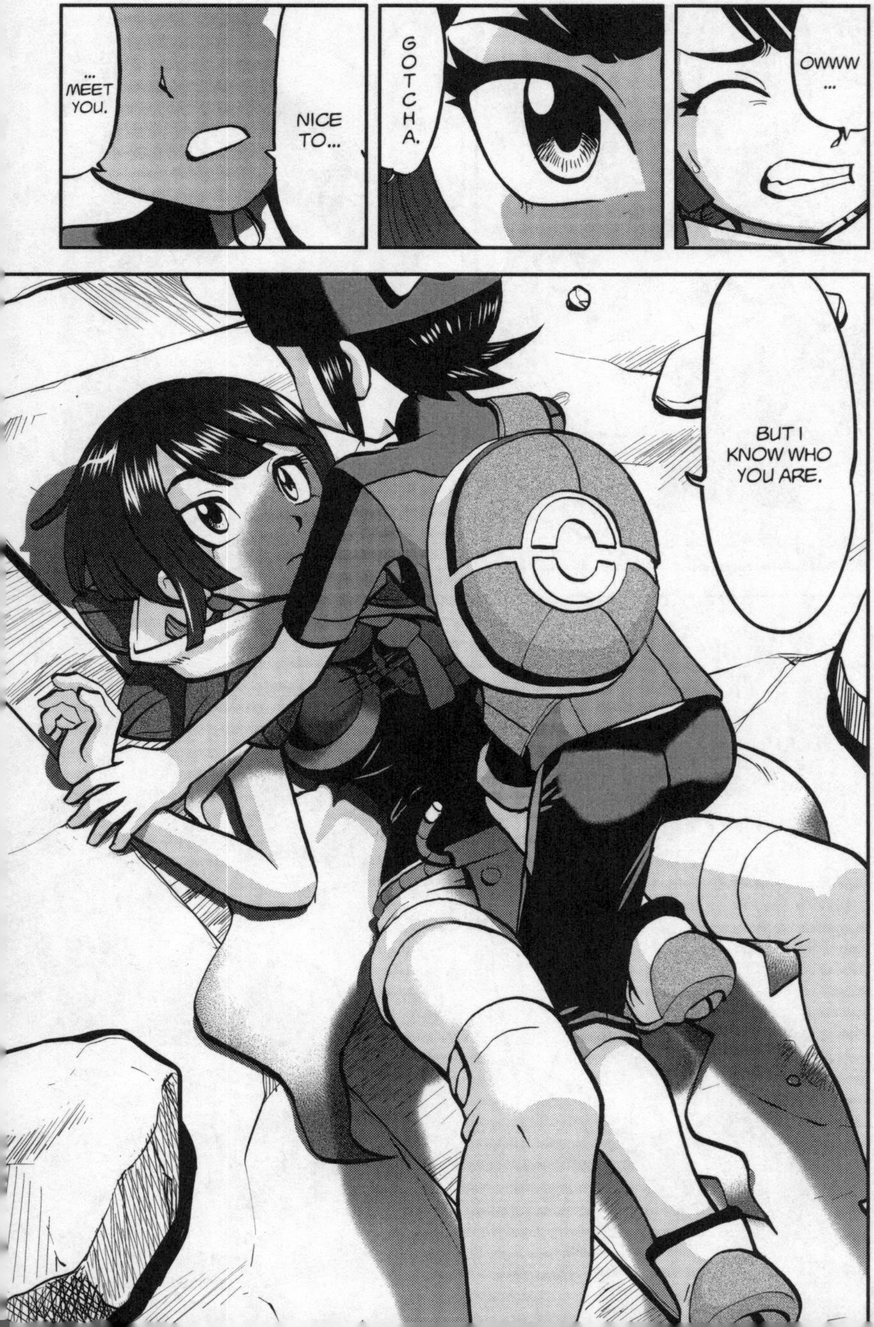
OWWW ...
GOTCHA.
NICE TO...
... MEET YOU.
BUT I KNOW WHO YOU ARE.

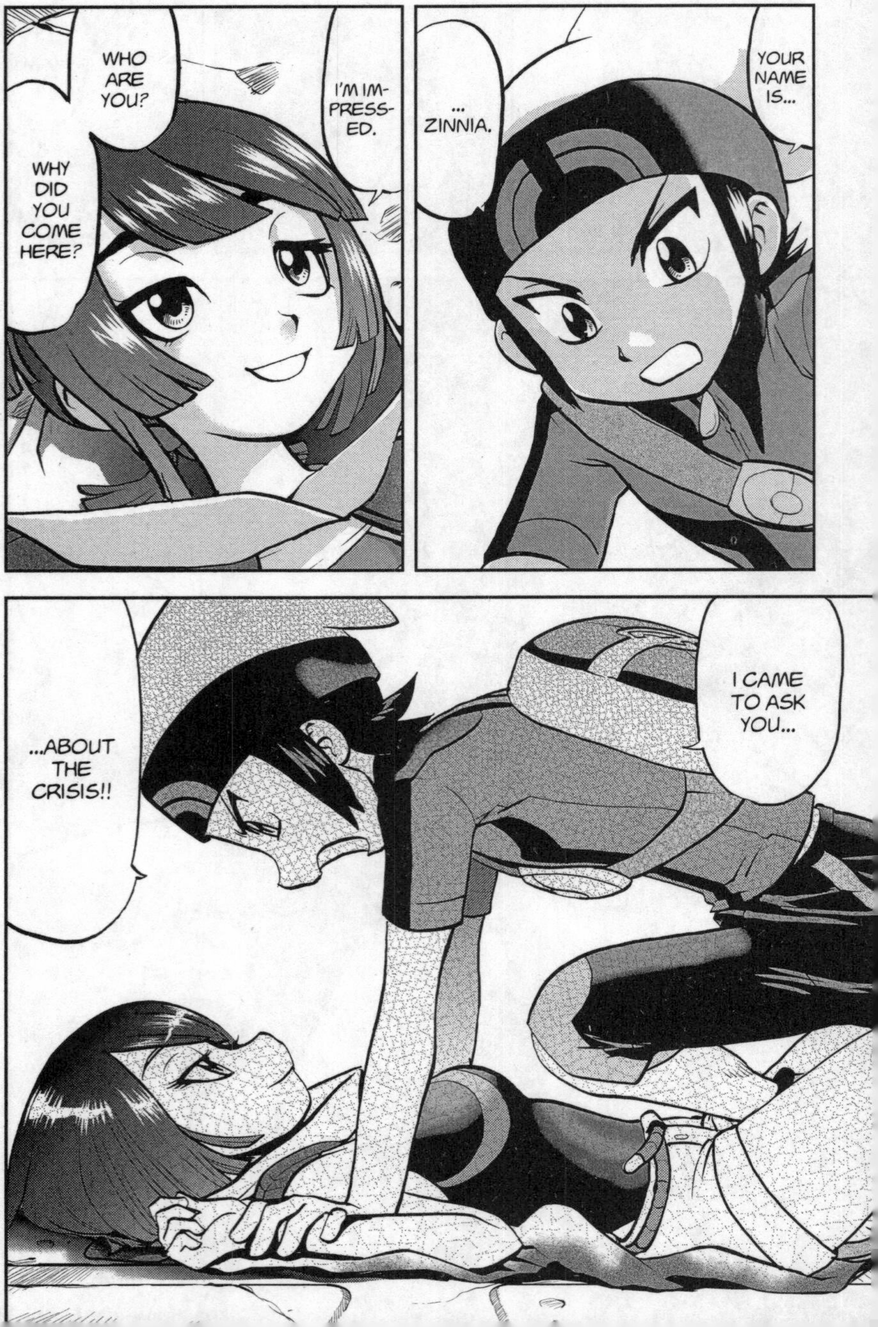
YOUR NAME IS...
... ZINNIA.
I'M IM-PRESS-ED.
WHO ARE YOU?
WHY DID YOU COME HERE?
I CAME TO ASK YOU...
...ABOUT THE CRISIS!!

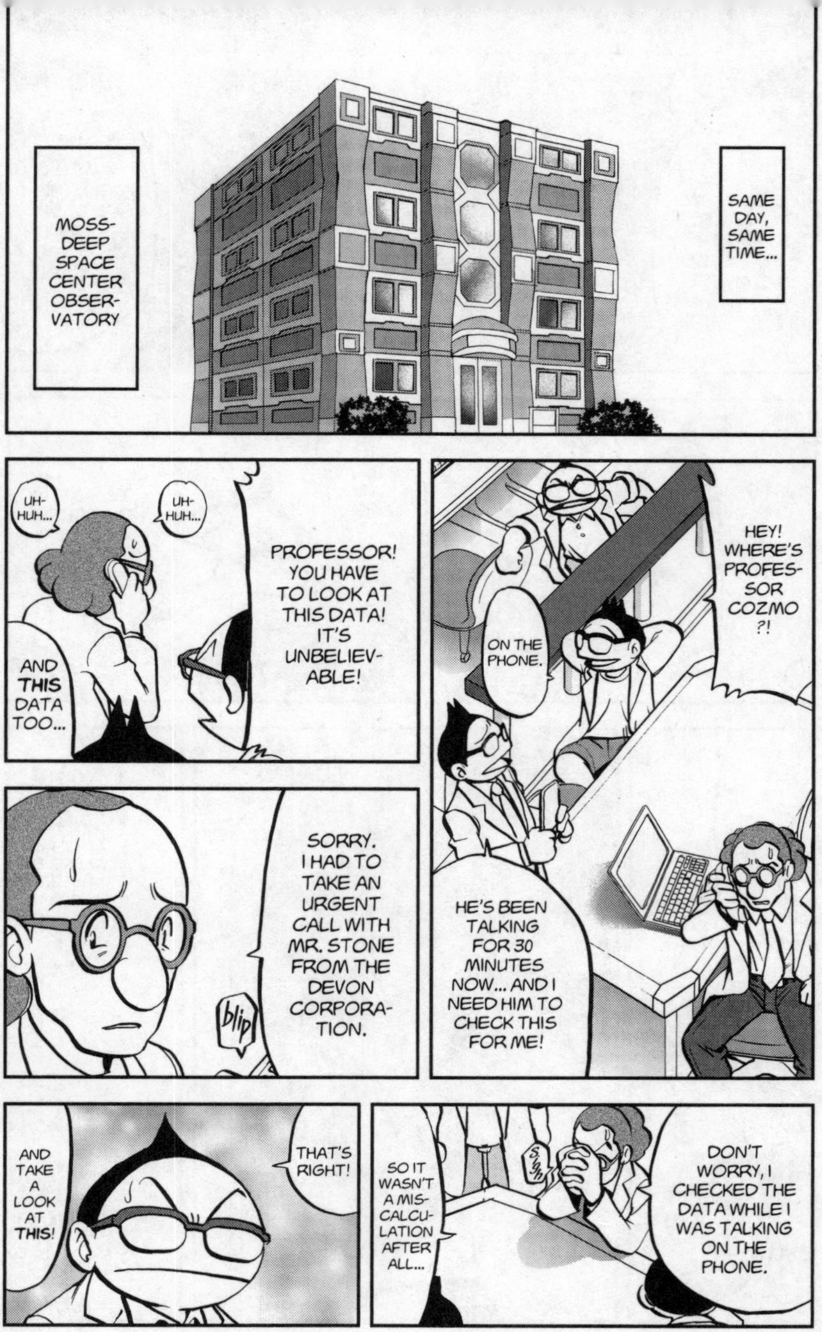
SAME DAY, SAME TIME...
MOSS-DEEP SPACE CENTER OBSERVATORY
HEY! WHERE'S PROFES-SOR COZMO ?!
ON THE PHONE.
HE'S BEEN TALKING FOR 30 MINUTES NOW... AND I NEED HIM TO CHECK THIS FOR ME!
PROFESSOR! YOU HAVE TO LOOK AT THIS DATA! IT'S UNBELIEV-ABLE!
UH-HUH...
UH-HUH...
AND **THIS** DATA TOO...
SORRY. I HAD TO TAKE AN URGENT CALL WITH MR. STONE FROM THE DEVON CORPORA-TION.
blip
DON'T WORRY, I CHECKED THE DATA WHILE I WAS TALKING ON THE PHONE.
SO IT WASN'T A MIS-CALCU-LATION AFTER ALL...
THAT'S RIGHT!
AND TAKE A LOOK AT **THIS**!

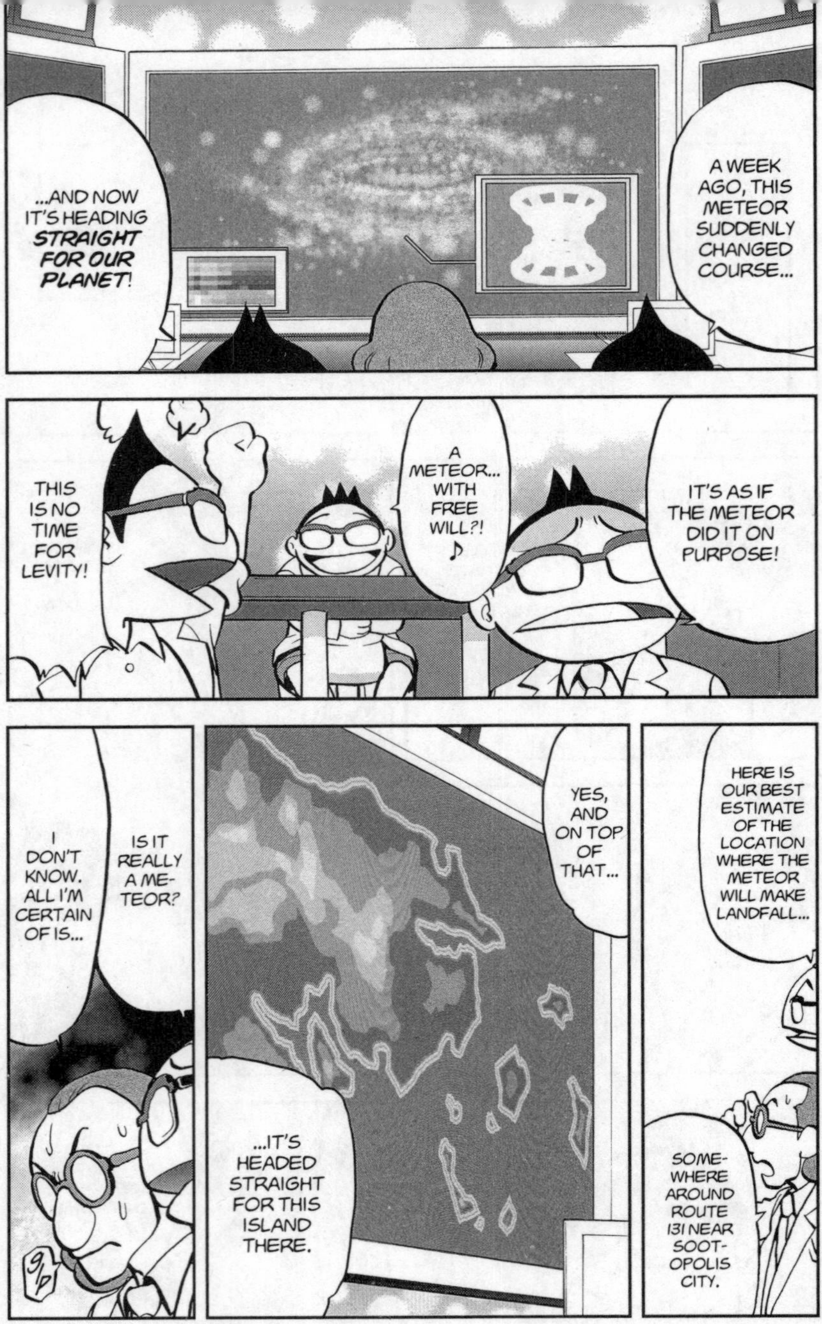
A WEEK AGO, THIS METEOR SUDDENLY CHANGED COURSE...
...AND NOW IT'S HEADING **STRAIGHT FOR OUR PLANET**!
IT'S AS IF THE METEOR DID IT ON PURPOSE!
A METEOR... WITH FREE WILL?! ♪
THIS IS NO TIME FOR LEVITY!
HERE IS OUR BEST ESTIMATE OF THE LOCATION WHERE THE METEOR WILL MAKE LANDFALL...
SOMEWHERE AROUND ROUTE 131 NEAR SOOTOPOLIS CITY.
YES, AND ON TOP OF THAT...
...IT'S HEADED STRAIGHT FOR THIS ISLAND THERE.
IS IT REALLY A METEOR?
I DON'T KNOW. ALL I'M CERTAIN OF IS...

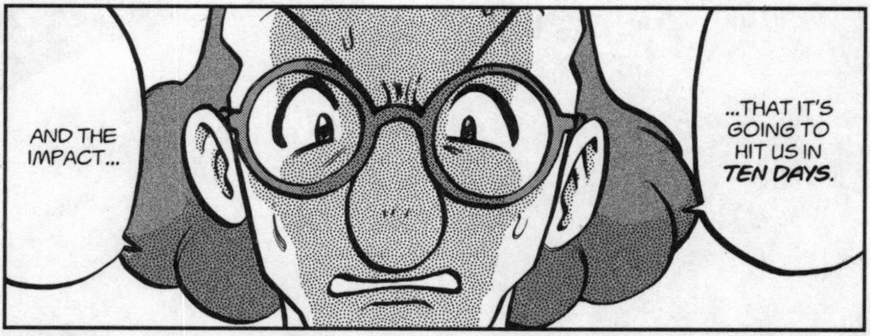
...THAT IT'S GOING TO HIT US IN *TEN DAYS*.
AND THE IMPACT...

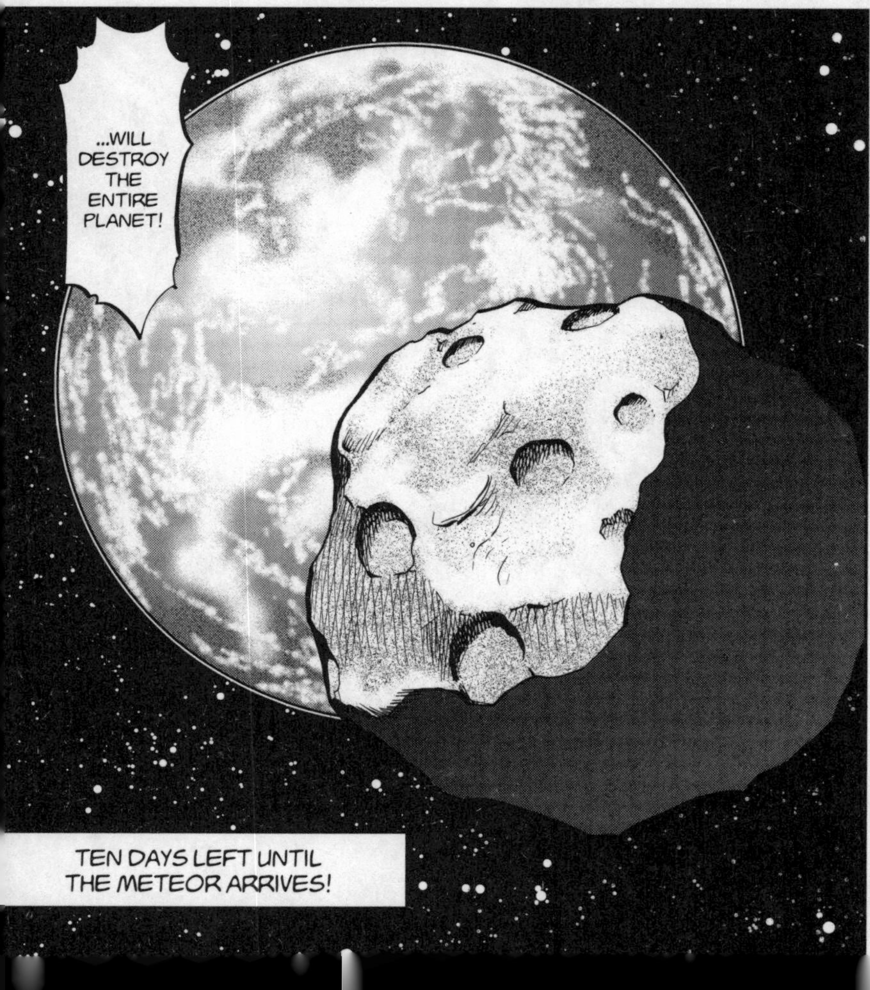
...WILL DESTROY THE ENTIRE PLANET!
TEN DAYS LEFT UNTIL THE METEOR ARRIVES!

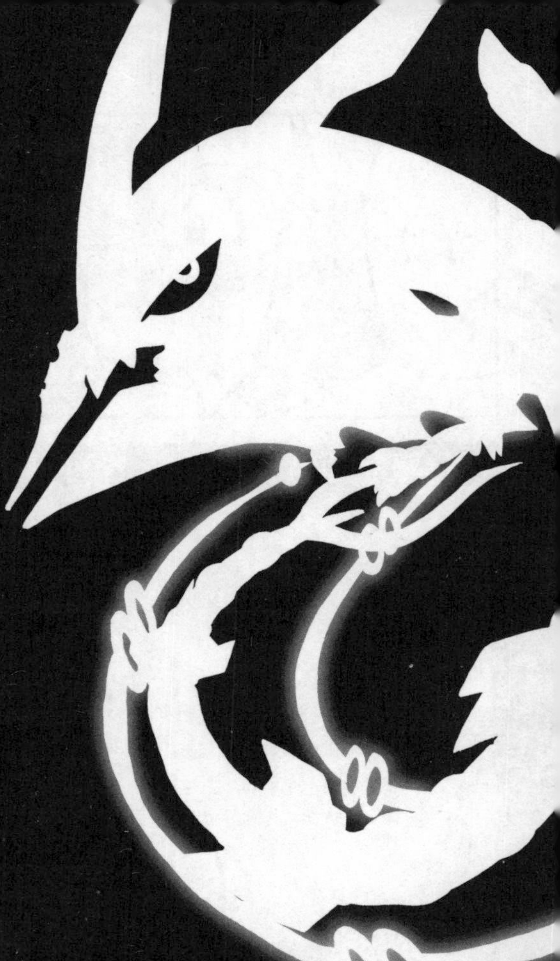

ADVENTURE #4

Salamence Evolves

POKÉMON ADVENTURES Ω RUBY α SAPPHIRE

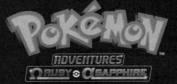

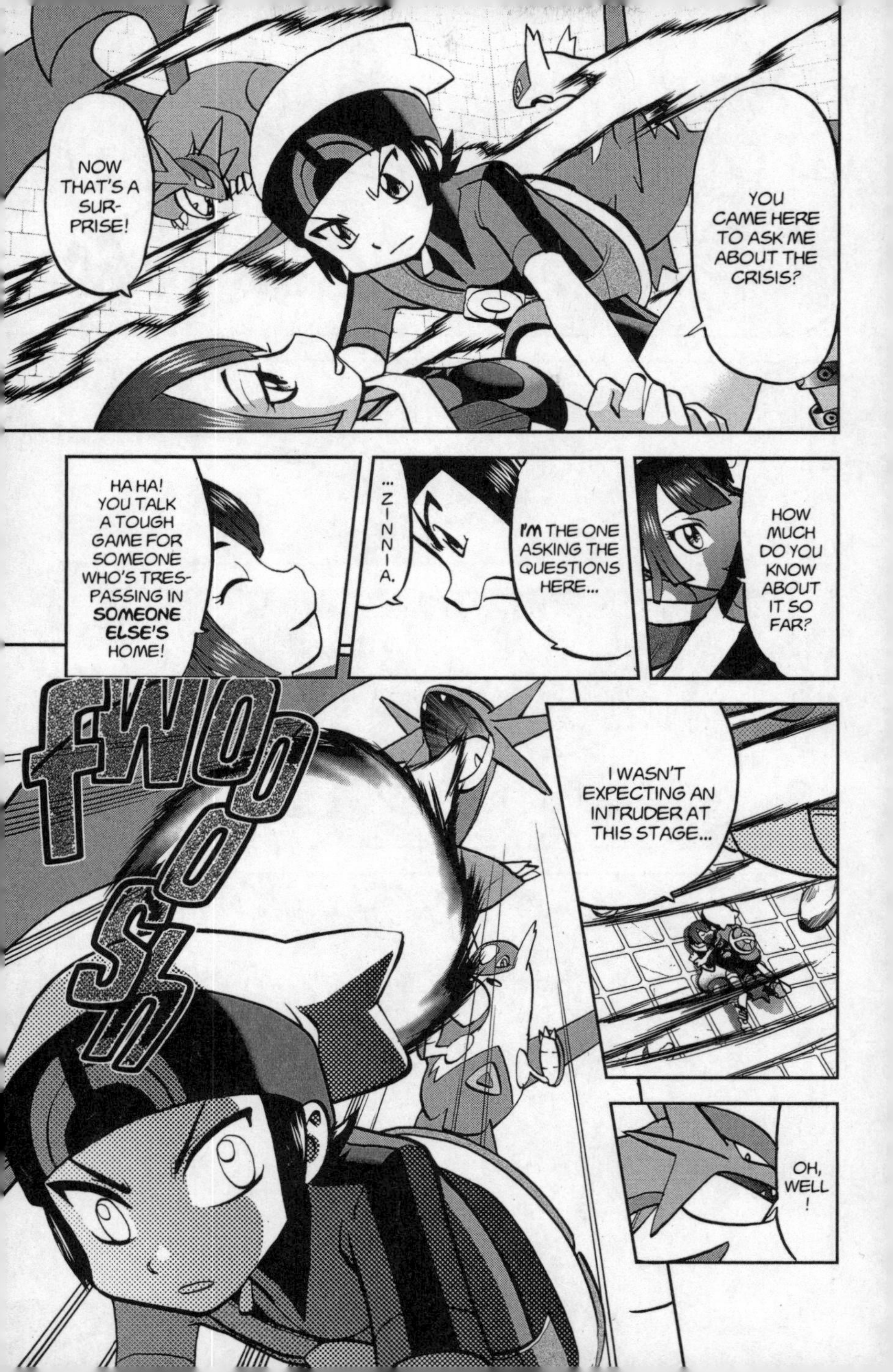
YOU CAME HERE TO ASK ME ABOUT THE CRISIS?
NOW THAT'S A SUR-PRISE!
HOW MUCH DO YOU KNOW ABOUT IT SO FAR?
I'M THE ONE ASKING THE QUESTIONS HERE...
...ZINNIA.
HA HA! YOU TALK A TOUGH GAME FOR SOMEONE WHO'S TRES-PASSING IN SOMEONE ELSE'S HOME!
I WASN'T EXPECTING AN INTRUDER AT THIS STAGE...
OH, WELL!
FWOOOSH

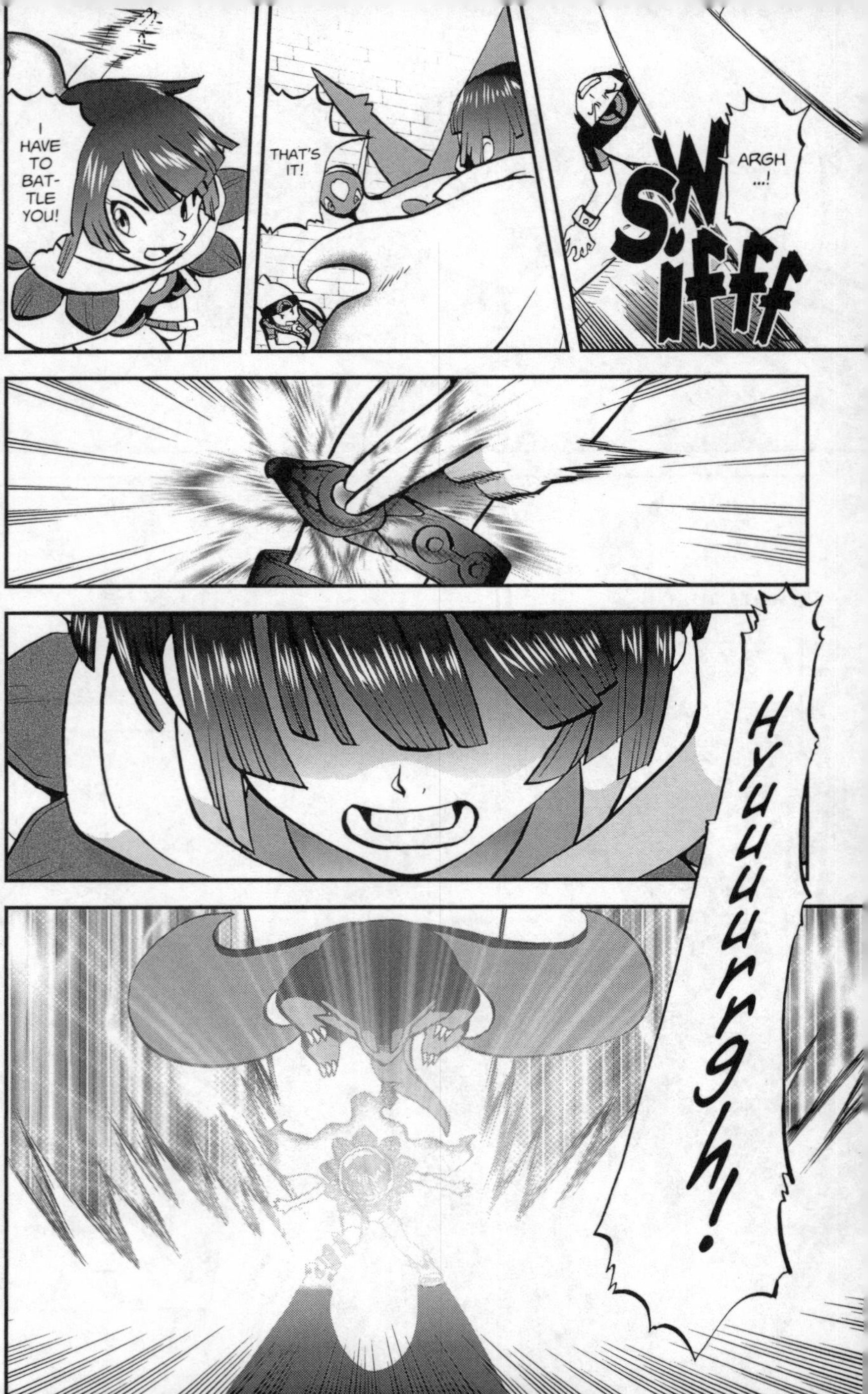
ARGH ...!
SWIFFF
THAT'S IT!
I HAVE TO BAT-TLE YOU!
HYUUURRGH!

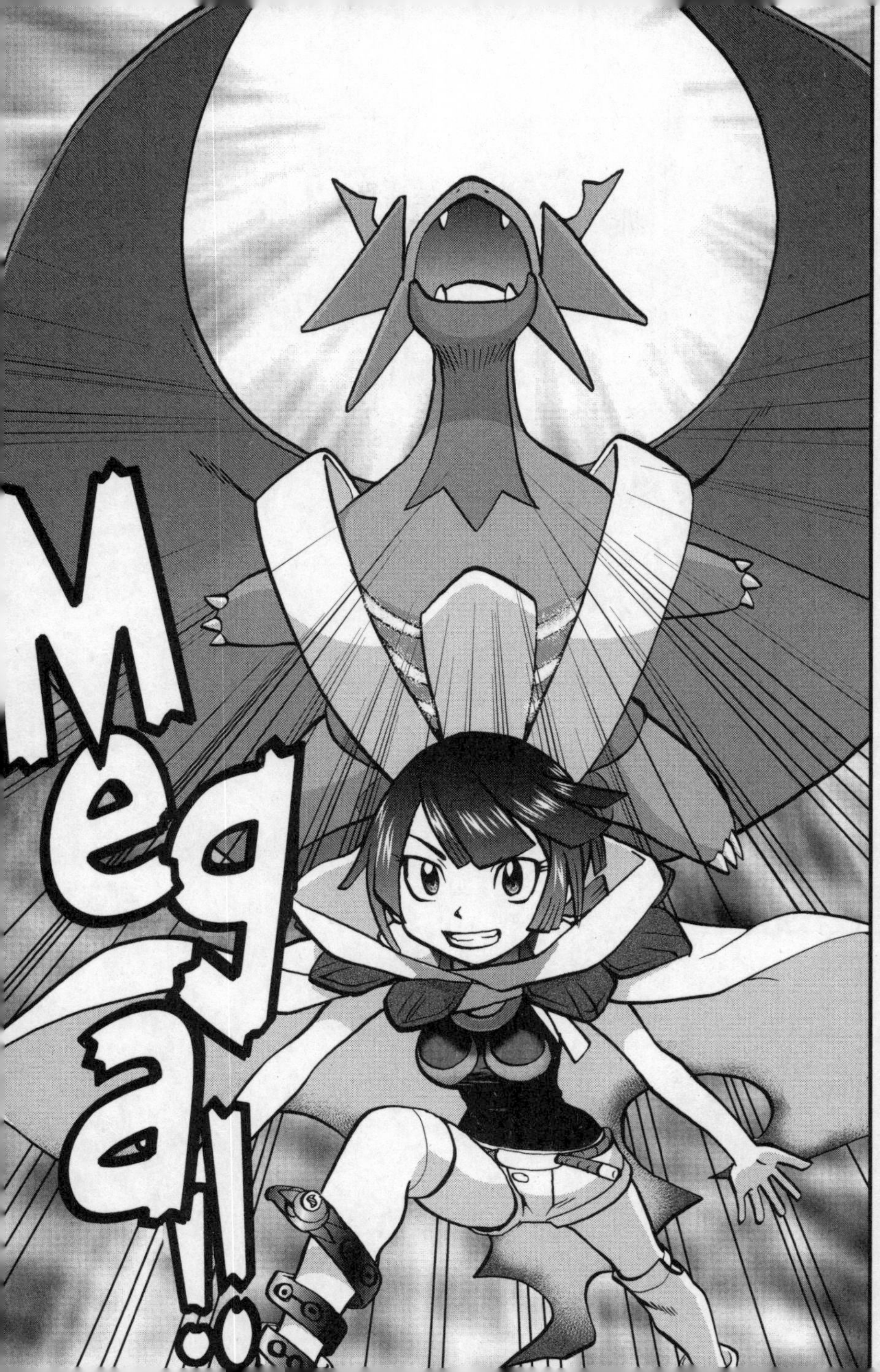
Mega!!

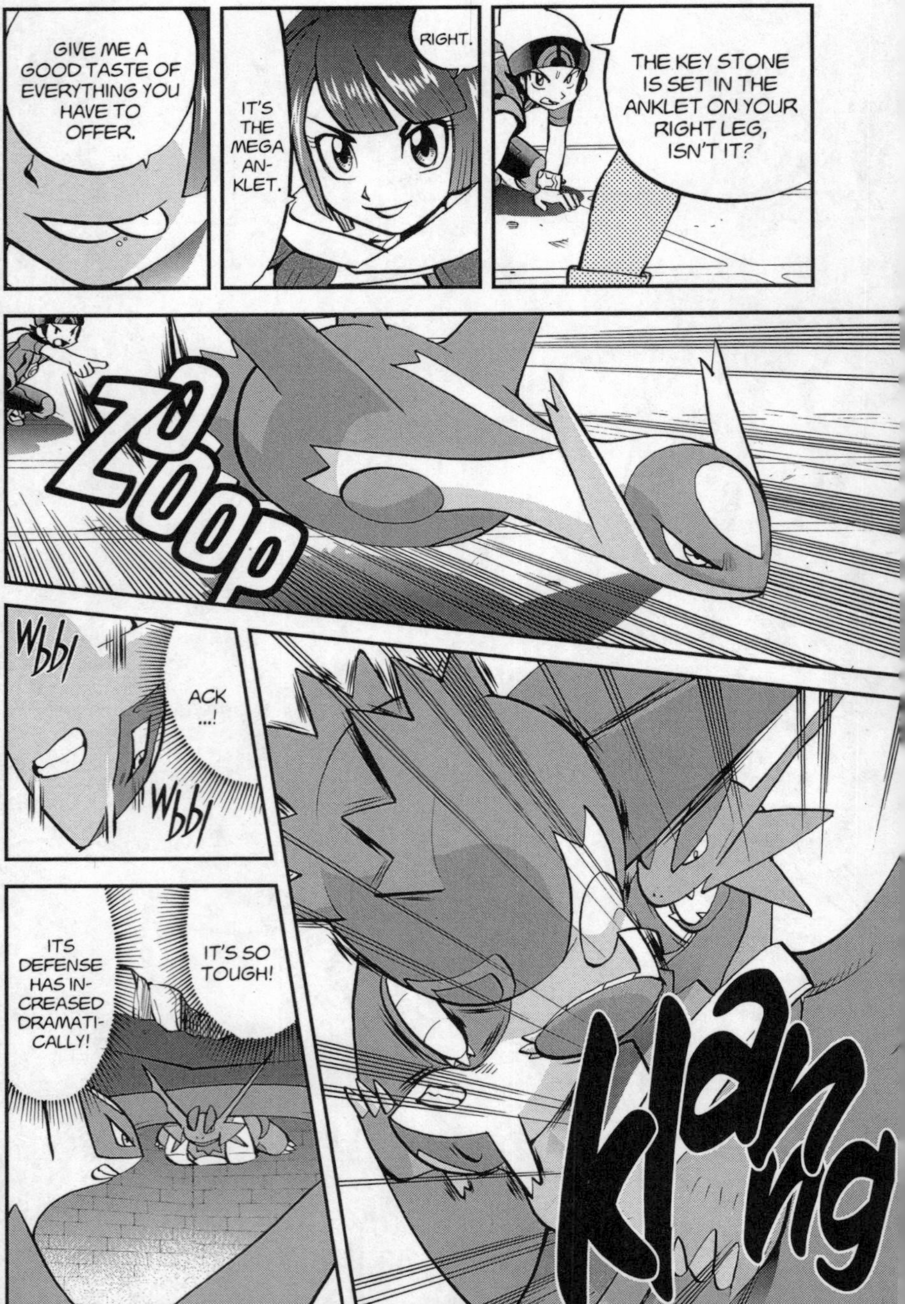
THE KEY STONE IS SET IN THE ANKLET ON YOUR RIGHT LEG, ISN'T IT?
RIGHT.
IT'S THE MEGA AN-KLET.
GIVE ME A GOOD TASTE OF EVERYTHING YOU HAVE TO OFFER.
ZOOOP
KLANG
WBBL
ACK ...!
WBBL
IT'S SO TOUGH!
ITS DEFENSE HAS IN-CREASED DRAMATI-CALLY!

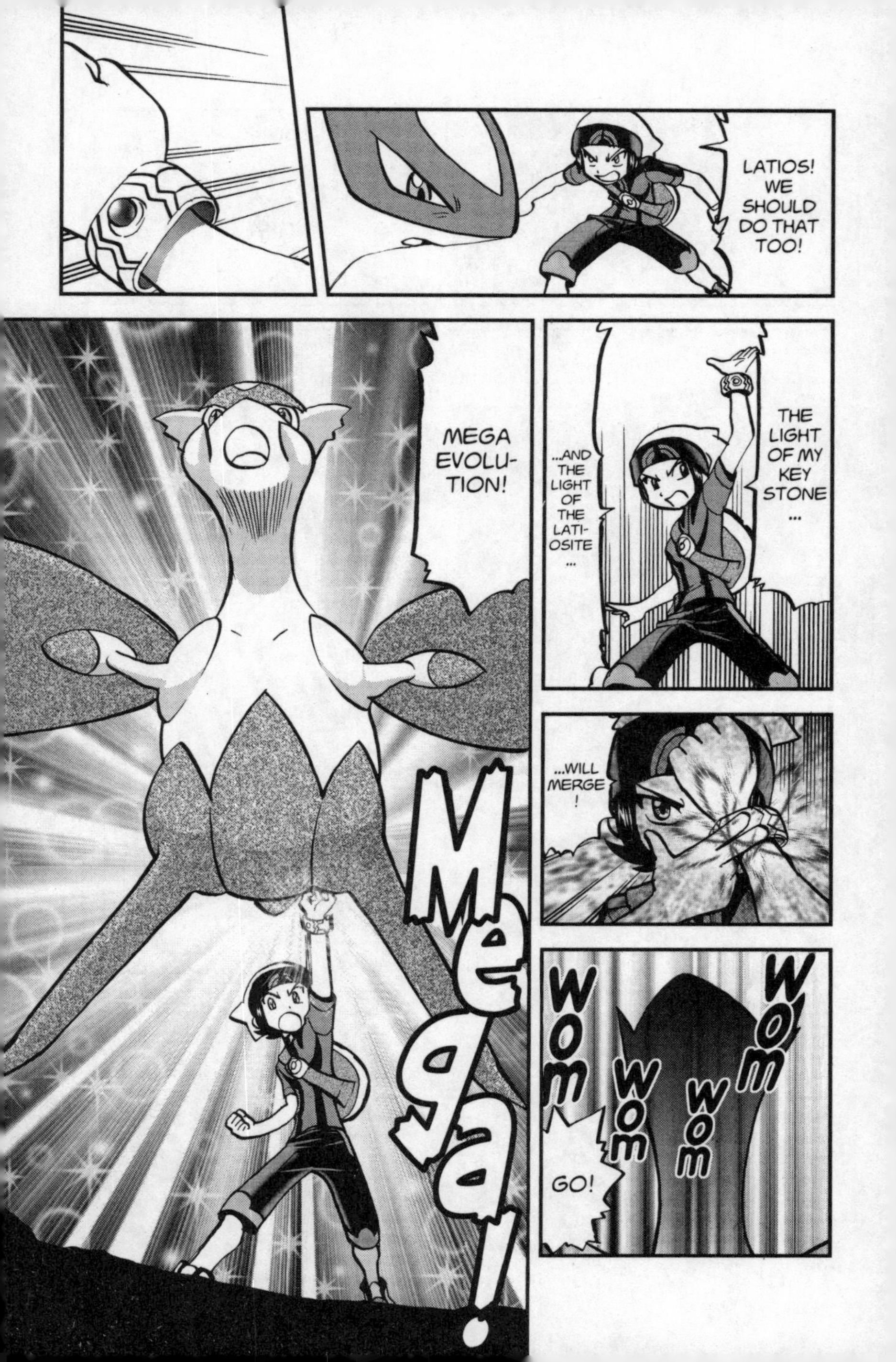
LATIOS! WE SHOULD DO THAT TOO!
THE LIGHT OF MY KEY STONE ...
...AND THE LIGHT OF THE LATI-OSITE ...
...WILL MERGE!
WOM WOM WOM WOM WOM WOM
GO!
MEGA EVOLU-TION!
Mega!

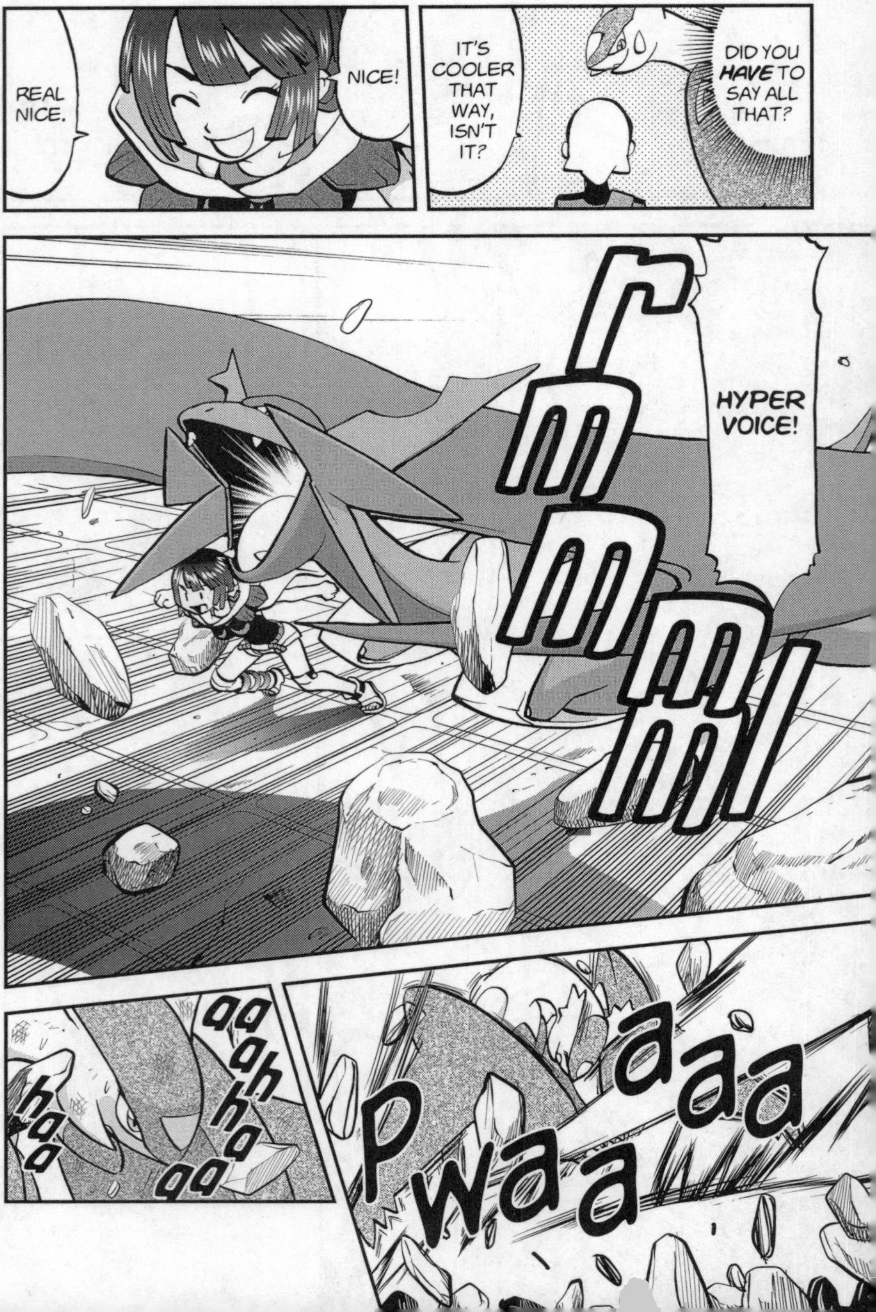
DID YOU HAVE TO SAY ALL THAT?
IT'S COOLER THAT WAY, ISN'T IT?
NICE!
REAL NICE.
HYPER VOICE!
rmmmm
Pwaaaaa
aaahhaaaa
haa

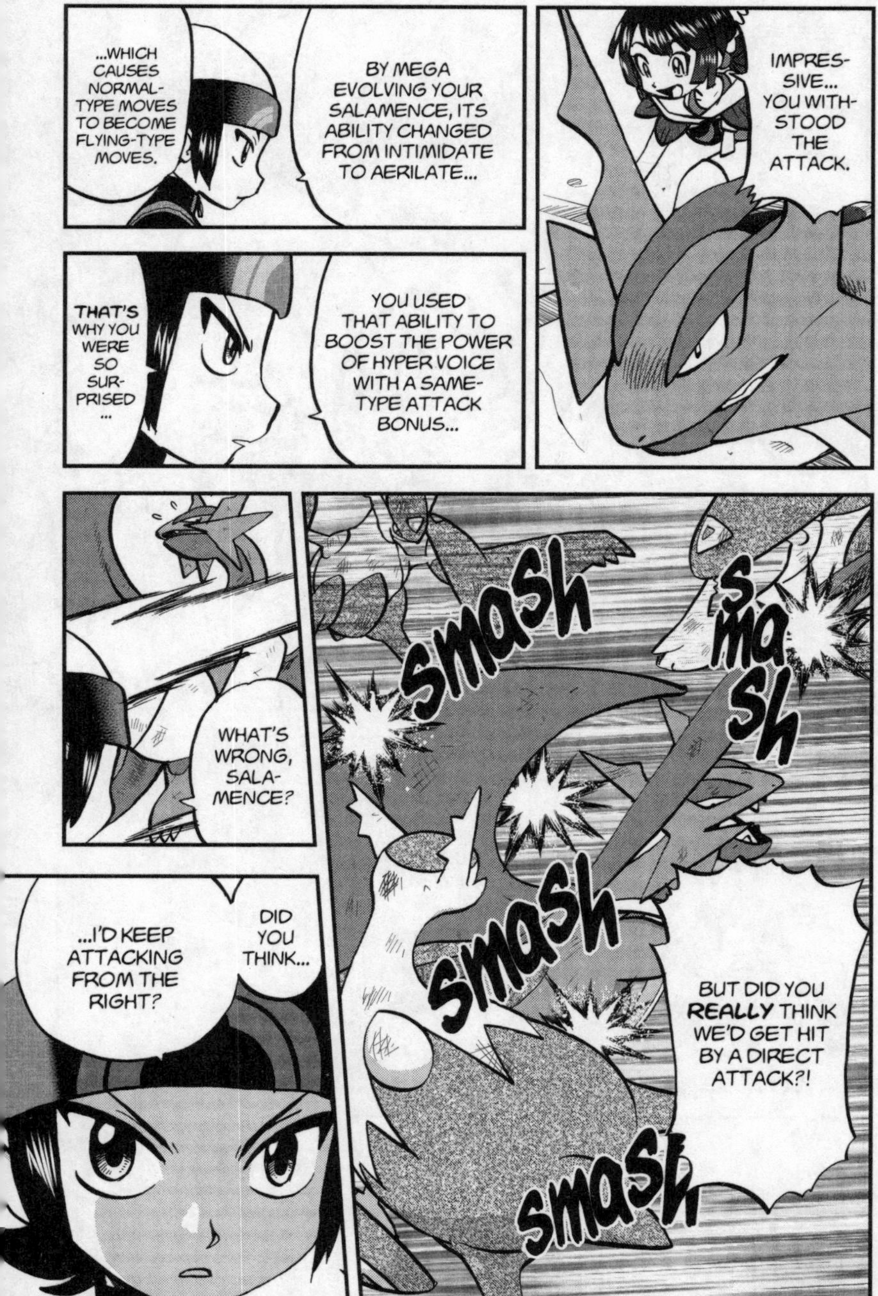

IMPRESSIVE... YOU WITHSTOOD THE ATTACK.
BY MEGA EVOLVING YOUR SALAMENCE, ITS ABILITY CHANGED FROM INTIMIDATE TO AERILATE...
...WHICH CAUSES NORMAL-TYPE MOVES TO BECOME FLYING-TYPE MOVES.
YOU USED THAT ABILITY TO BOOST THE POWER OF HYPER VOICE WITH A SAME-TYPE ATTACK BONUS...
THAT'S WHY YOU WERE SO SURPRISED...
SMASH
SMASH
SMASH
SMASH
BUT DID YOU **REALLY** THINK WE'D GET HIT BY A DIRECT ATTACK?!
WHAT'S WRONG, SALAMENCE?
DID YOU THINK...
...I'D KEEP ATTACKING FROM THE RIGHT?

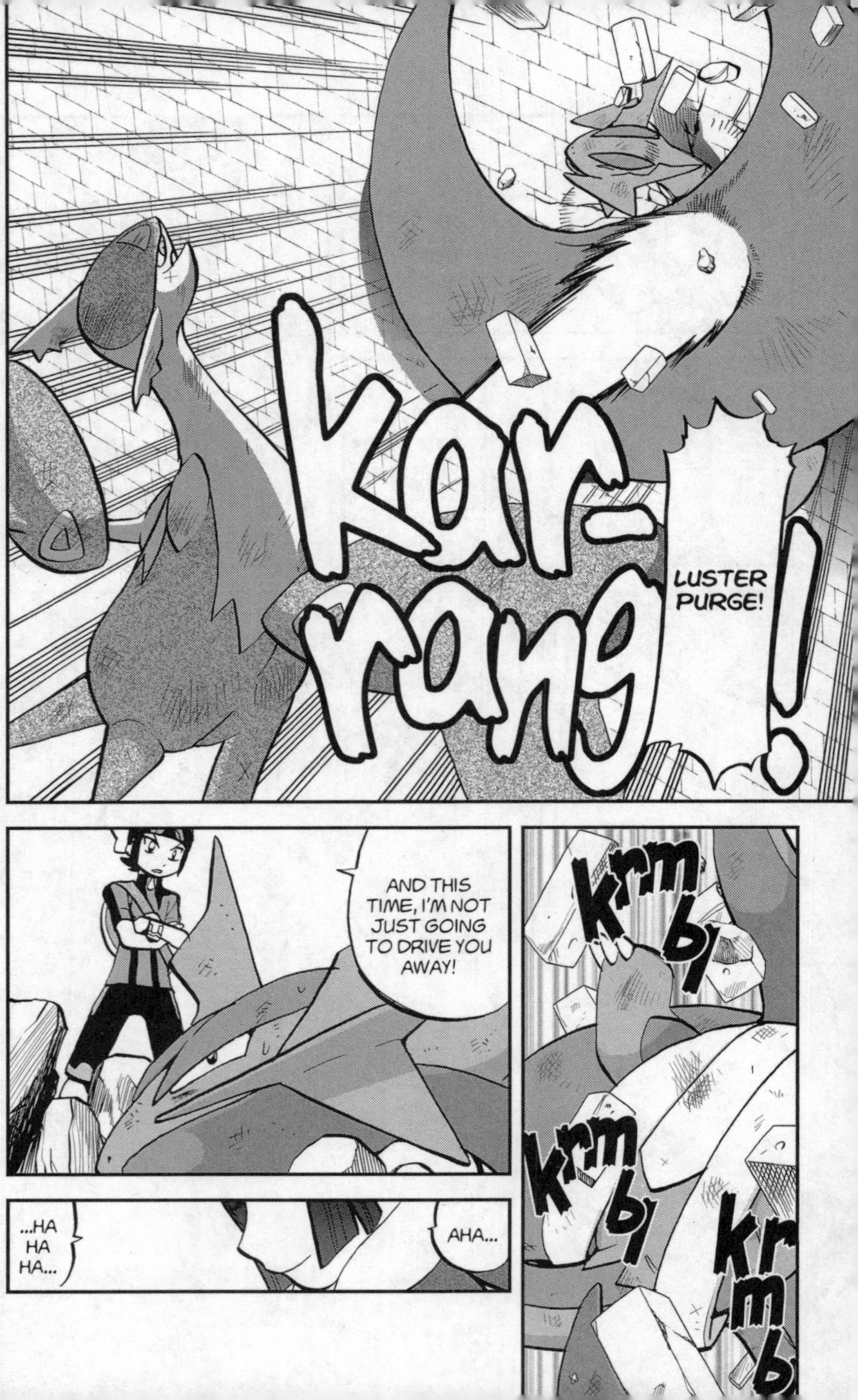
kar-rang!
LUSTER PURGE!
krmbl
krmbl
krmb
AND THIS TIME, I'M NOT JUST GOING TO DRIVE YOU AWAY!
AHA...
...HA HA HA...

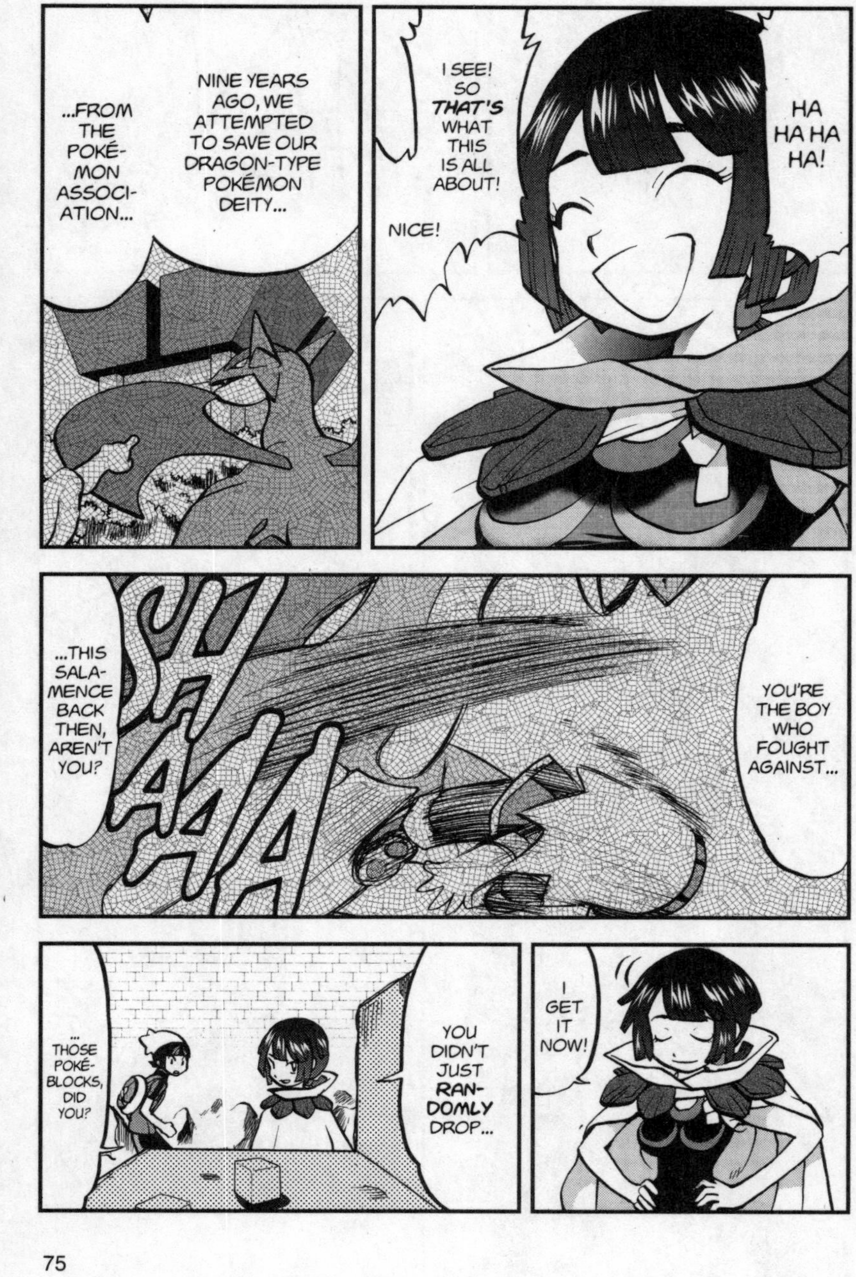
HA HA HA HA!
I SEE! SO *THAT'S* WHAT THIS IS ALL ABOUT!
NICE!
NINE YEARS AGO, WE ATTEMPTED TO SAVE OUR DRAGON-TYPE POKÉMON DEITY...
...FROM THE POKÉMON ASSOCIATION...
YOU'RE THE BOY WHO FOUGHT AGAINST...
...THIS SALAMENCE BACK THEN, AREN'T YOU?
I GET IT NOW!
YOU DIDN'T JUST **RANDOMLY** DROP...
...THOSE POKÉBLOCKS, DID YOU?

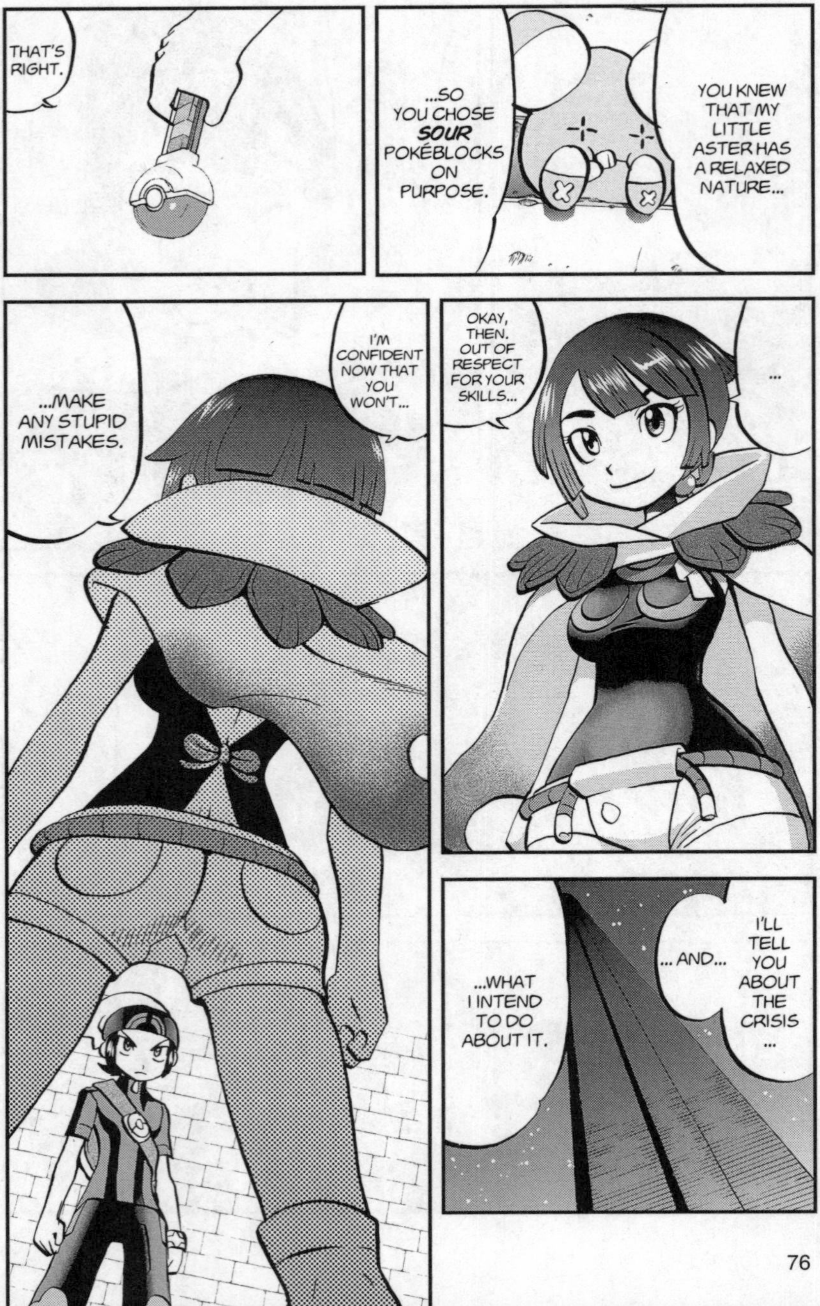
YOU KNEW THAT MY LITTLE ASTER HAS A RELAXED NATURE...
...SO YOU CHOSE SOUR POKÉBLOCKS ON PURPOSE.
THAT'S RIGHT.
...
OKAY, THEN. OUT OF RESPECT FOR YOUR SKILLS...
I'LL TELL YOU ABOUT THE CRISIS ...
... AND...
...WHAT I INTEND TO DO ABOUT IT.
I'M CONFIDENT NOW THAT YOU WON'T...
...MAKE ANY STUPID MISTAKES.

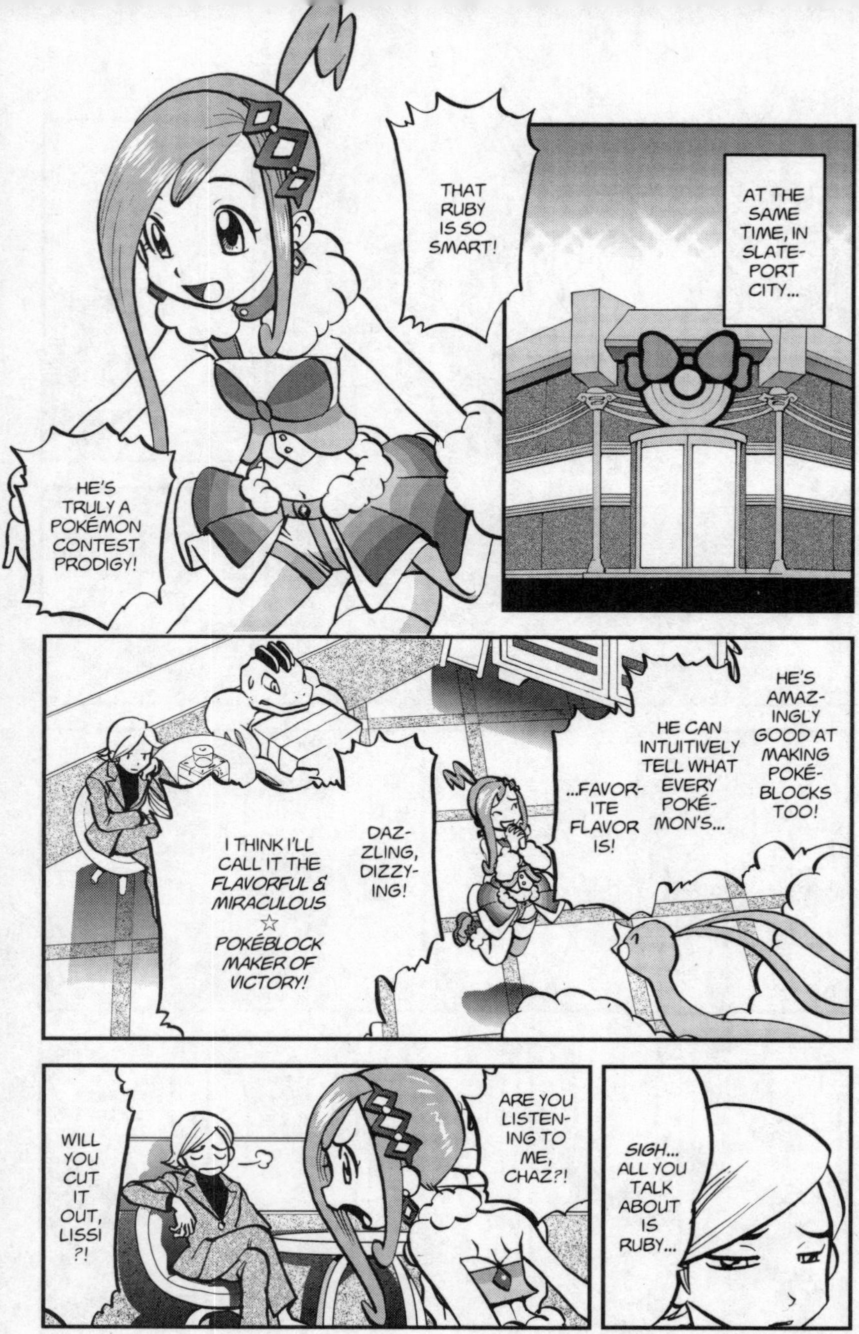
AT THE SAME TIME, IN SLATEPORT CITY...
THAT RUBY IS SO SMART!
HE'S TRULY A POKÉMON CONTEST PRODIGY!
HE'S AMAZINGLY GOOD AT MAKING POKÉBLOCKS TOO!
HE CAN INTUITIVELY TELL WHAT EVERY POKÉMON'S...
...FAVORITE FLAVOR IS!
DAZZLING, DIZZYING!
I THINK I'LL CALL IT THE *FLAVORFUL & MIRACULOUS ☆ POKÉBLOCK MAKER OF VICTORY!*
SIGH... ALL YOU TALK ABOUT IS RUBY...
ARE YOU LISTENING TO ME, CHAZ?!
WILL YOU CUT IT OUT, LISSI?!

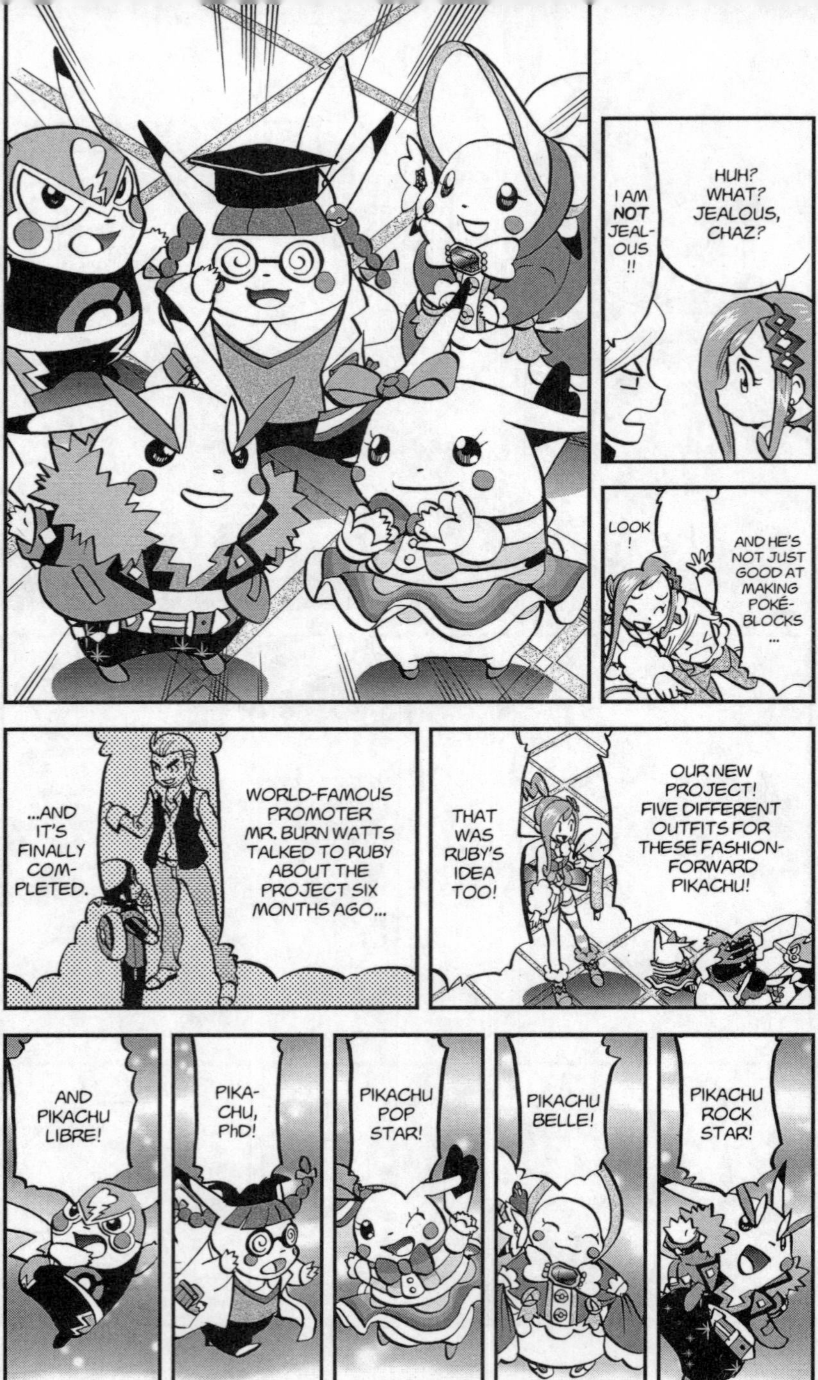
HUH? WHAT? JEALOUS, CHAZ?
I AM **NOT** JEALOUS!!
AND HE'S NOT JUST GOOD AT MAKING POKÉBLOCKS...
LOOK!
OUR NEW PROJECT! FIVE DIFFERENT OUTFITS FOR THESE FASHION-FORWARD PIKACHU!
THAT WAS RUBY'S IDEA TOO!
WORLD-FAMOUS PROMOTER MR. BURN WATTS TALKED TO RUBY ABOUT THE PROJECT SIX MONTHS AGO...
...AND IT'S FINALLY COMPLETED.
PIKACHU ROCK STAR!
PIKACHU BELLE!
PIKACHU POP STAR!
PIKACHU, PhD!
AND PIKACHU LIBRE!

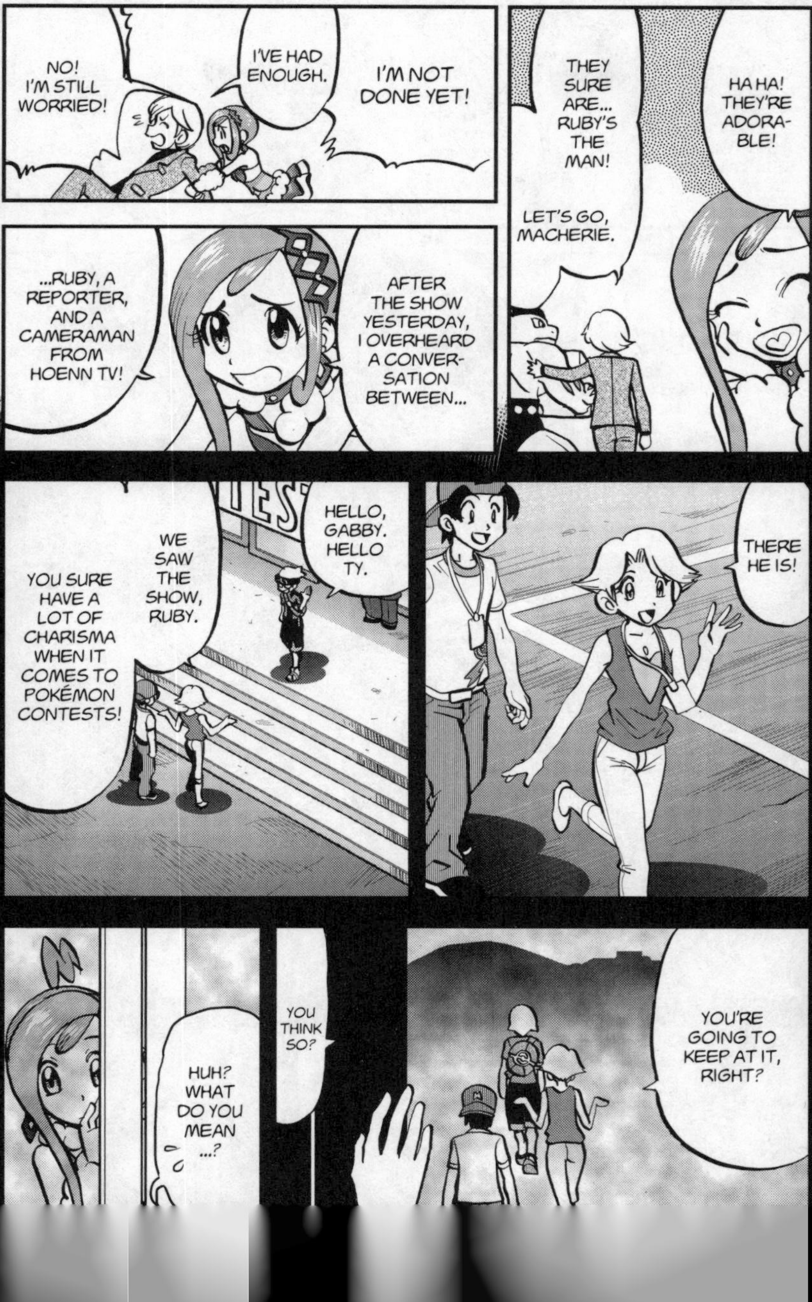
HA HA! THEY'RE ADORA-BLE!
THEY SURE ARE... RUBY'S THE MAN!
LET'S GO, MACHERIE.
I'M NOT DONE YET!
I'VE HAD ENOUGH.
NO! I'M STILL WORRIED!
AFTER THE SHOW YESTERDAY, I OVERHEARD A CONVER-SATION BETWEEN...
...RUBY, A REPORTER, AND A CAMERAMAN FROM HOENN TV!
THERE HE IS!
HELLO, GABBY. HELLO TY.
WE SAW THE SHOW, RUBY.
YOU SURE HAVE A LOT OF CHARISMA WHEN IT COMES TO POKÉMON CONTESTS!
YOU'RE GOING TO KEEP AT IT, RIGHT?
YOU THINK SO?
HUH? WHAT DO YOU MEAN ...?

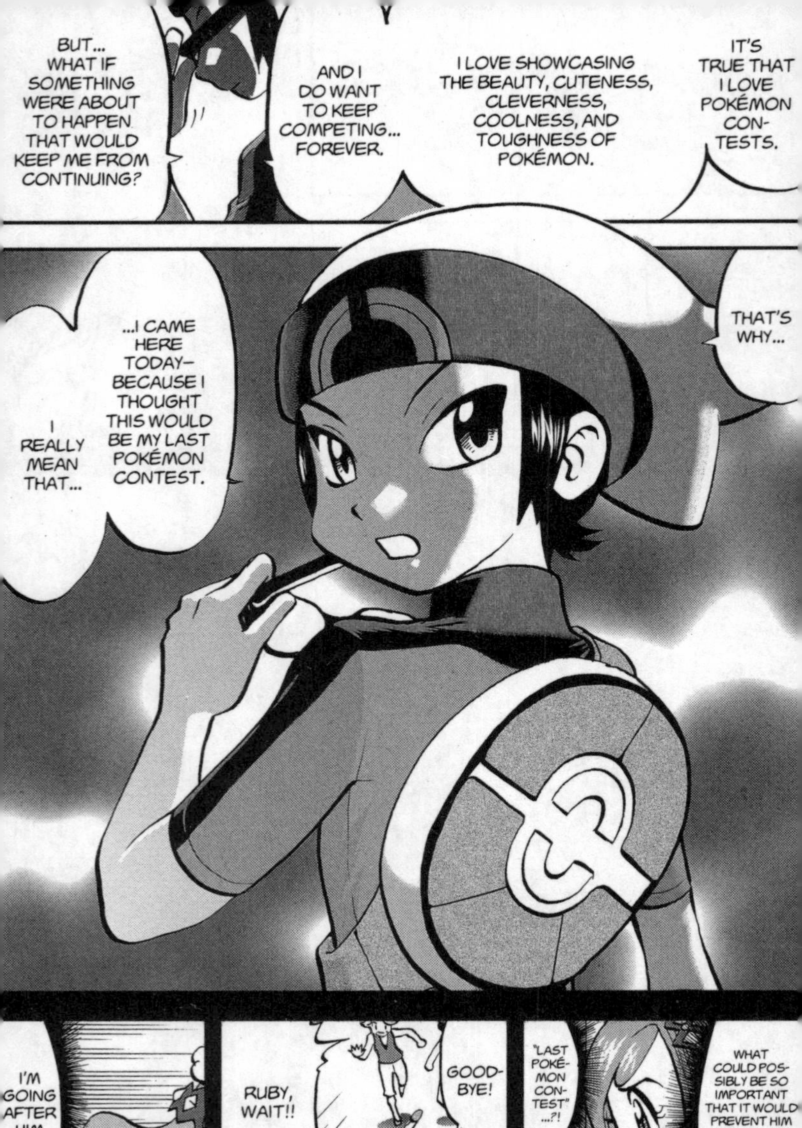
IT'S TRUE THAT I LOVE POKÉMON CONTESTS.
I LOVE SHOWCASING THE BEAUTY, CUTENESS, CLEVERNESS, COOLNESS, AND TOUGHNESS OF POKÉMON.
AND I DO WANT TO KEEP COMPETING... FOREVER.
BUT... WHAT IF SOMETHING WERE ABOUT TO HAPPEN THAT WOULD KEEP ME FROM CONTINUING?
THAT'S WHY...
...I CAME HERE TODAY—BECAUSE I THOUGHT THIS WOULD BE MY LAST POKÉMON CONTEST.
I REALLY MEAN THAT...
WHAT COULD POSSIBLY BE SO IMPORTANT THAT IT WOULD PREVENT HIM FROM TAKING PART IN MORE CONTESTS IN THE FUTURE ...?!
"LAST POKÉMON CONTEST" ...?!
GOOD-BYE!
RUBY, WAIT!!
I'M GOING AFTER HIM TOO!

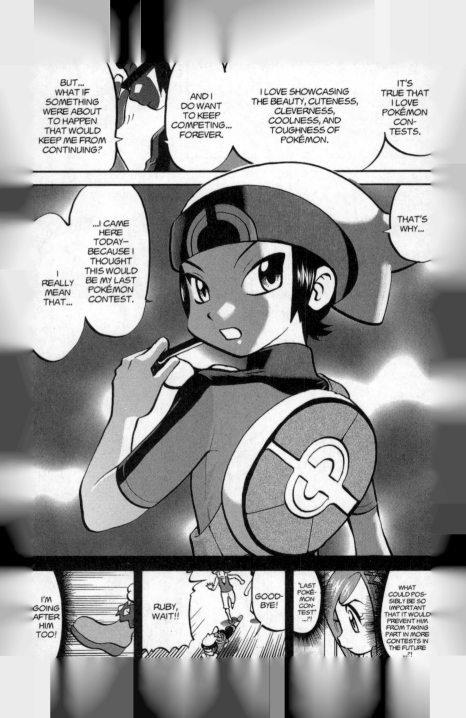

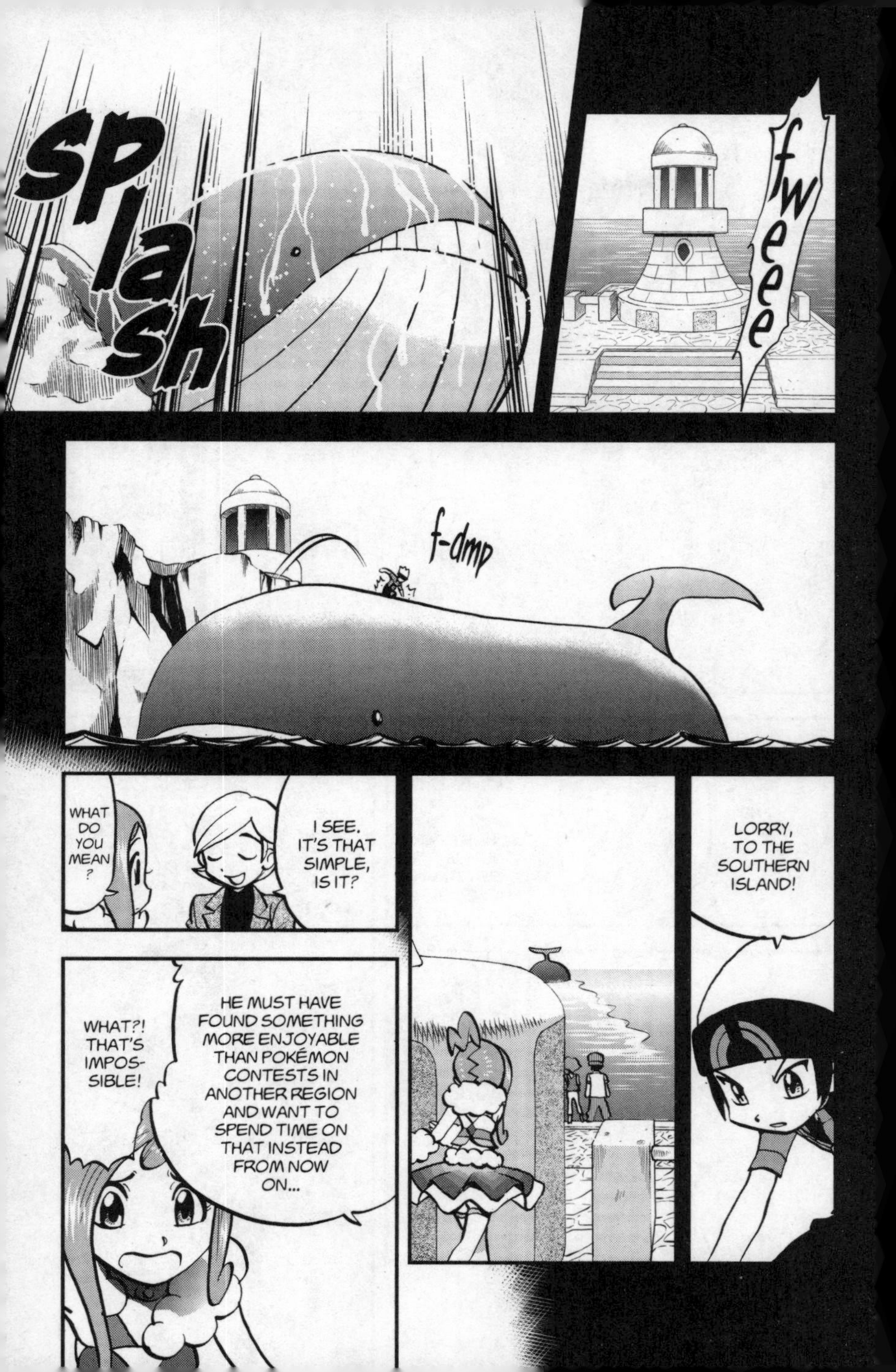
fweee
splash
f-dmp
LORRY, TO THE SOUTHERN ISLAND!
I SEE. IT'S THAT SIMPLE, IS IT?
WHAT DO YOU MEAN?
HE MUST HAVE FOUND SOMETHING MORE ENJOYABLE THAN POKÉMON CONTESTS IN ANOTHER REGION AND WANT TO SPEND TIME ON THAT INSTEAD FROM NOW ON...
WHAT?! THAT'S IMPOS-SIBLE!

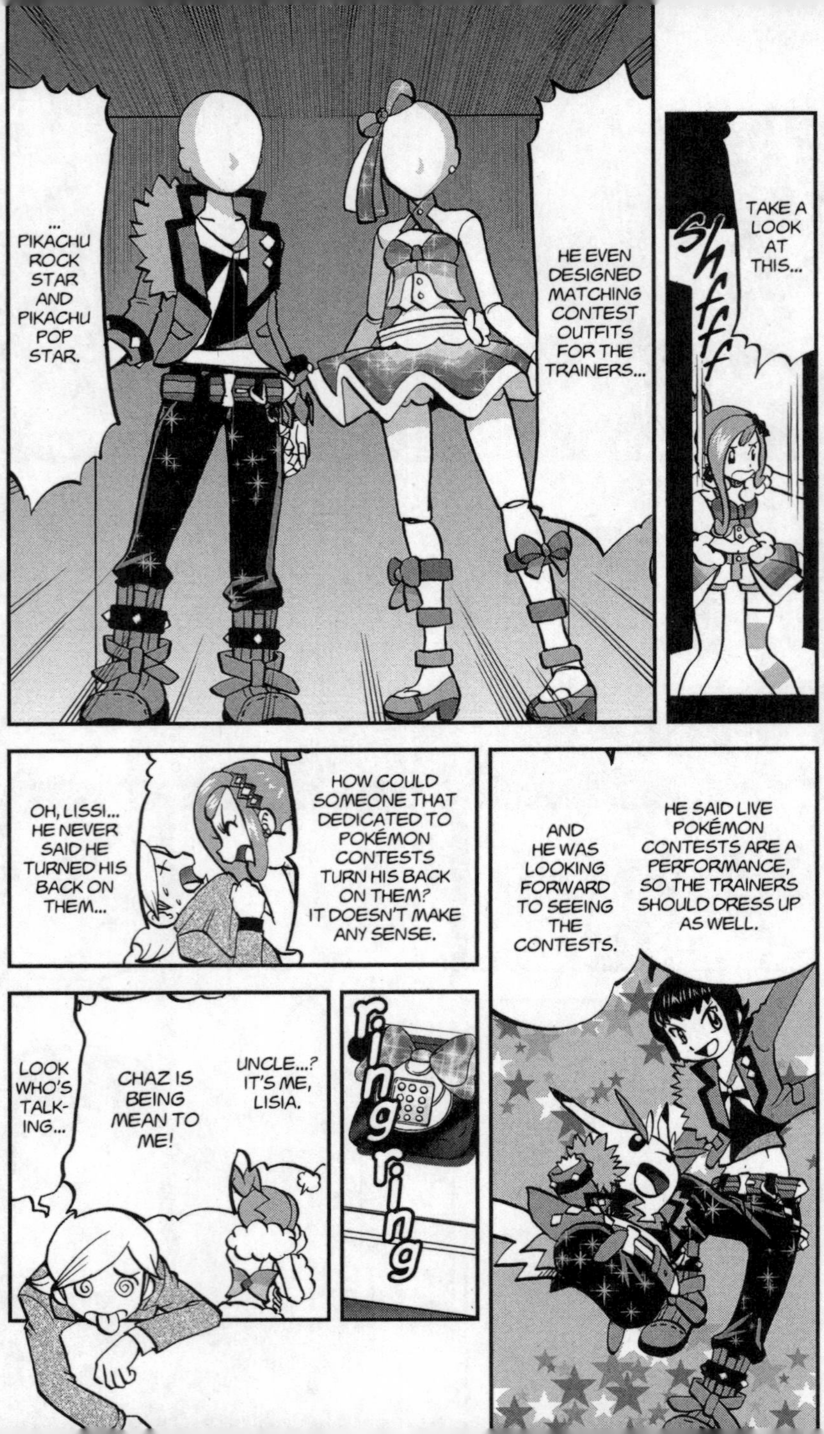
TAKE A LOOK AT THIS...
SHFFF
HE EVEN DESIGNED MATCHING CONTEST OUTFITS FOR THE TRAINERS...
... PIKACHU ROCK STAR AND PIKACHU POP STAR.
HE SAID LIVE POKÉMON CONTESTS ARE A PERFORMANCE, SO THE TRAINERS SHOULD DRESS UP AS WELL.
AND HE WAS LOOKING FORWARD TO SEEING THE CONTESTS.
HOW COULD SOMEONE THAT DEDICATED TO POKÉMON CONTESTS TURN HIS BACK ON THEM? IT DOESN'T MAKE ANY SENSE.
OH, LISSI... HE NEVER SAID HE TURNED HIS BACK ON THEM...
RING RING
UNCLE...? IT'S ME, LISIA.
CHAZ IS BEING MEAN TO ME!
LOOK WHO'S TALK-ING...

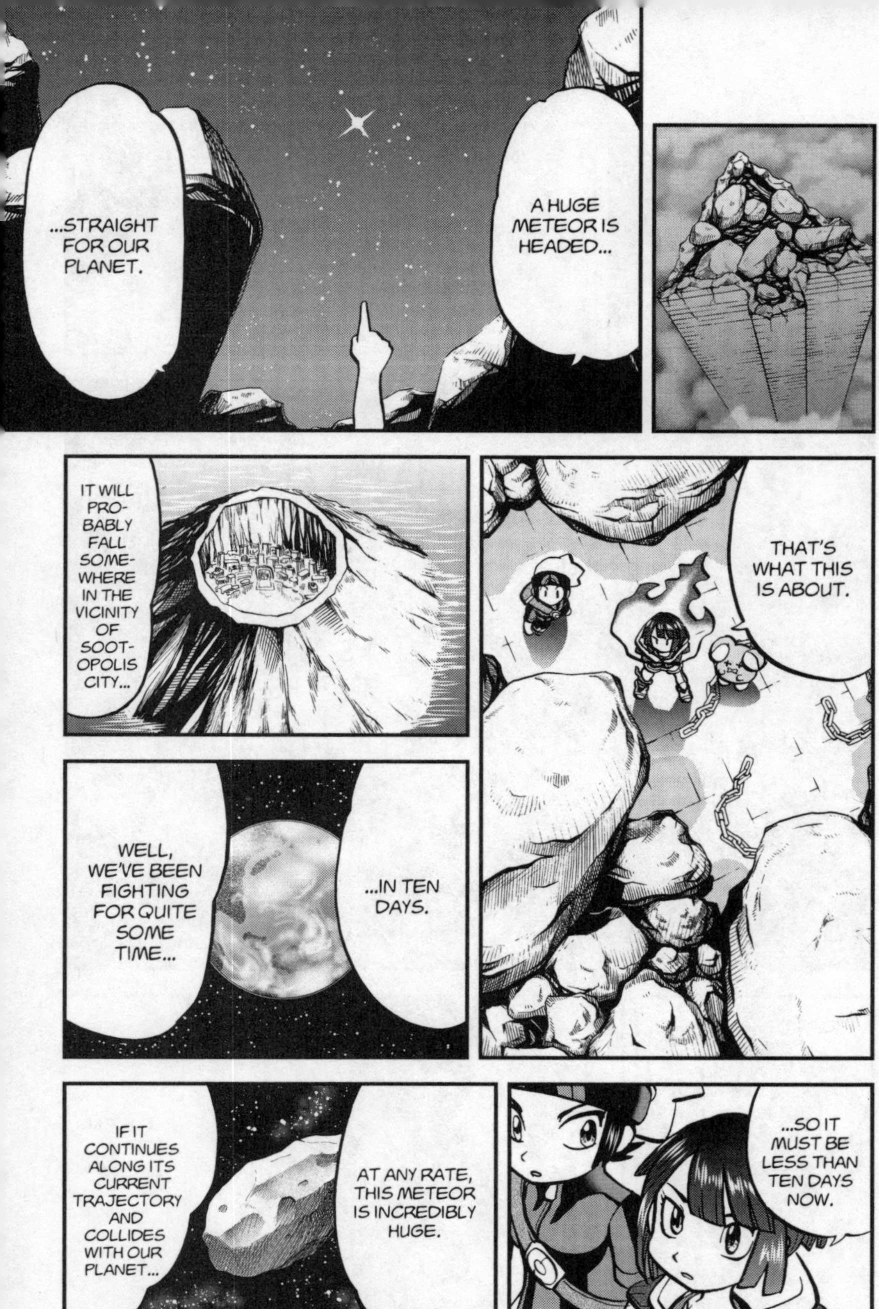
A HUGE METEOR IS HEADED...
...STRAIGHT FOR OUR PLANET.
THAT'S WHAT THIS IS ABOUT.
IT WILL PRO-BABLY FALL SOME-WHERE IN THE VICINITY OF SOOT-OPOLIS CITY...
...IN TEN DAYS.
WELL, WE'VE BEEN FIGHTING FOR QUITE SOME TIME...
...SO IT MUST BE LESS THAN TEN DAYS NOW.
AT ANY RATE, THIS METEOR IS INCREDIBLY HUGE.
IF IT CONTINUES ALONG ITS CURRENT TRAJECTORY AND COLLIDES WITH OUR PLANET...

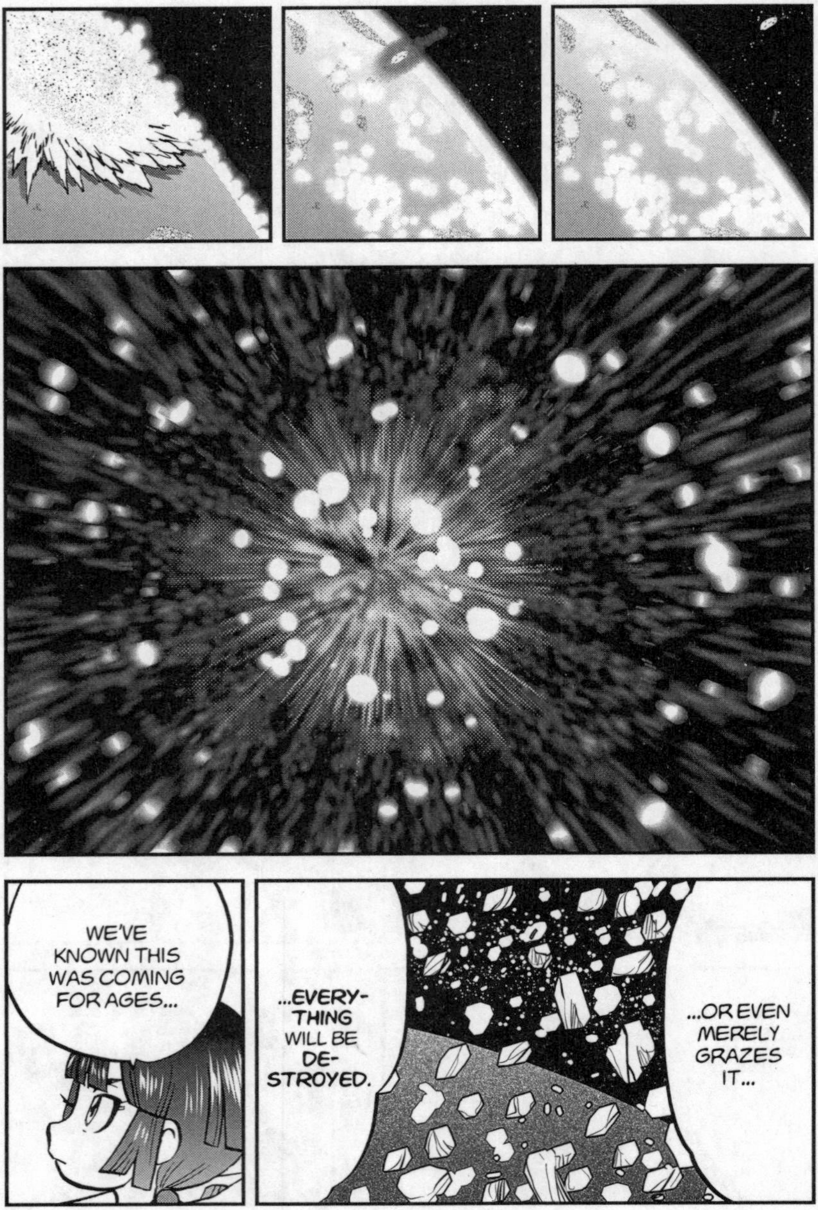
...OR EVEN MERELY GRAZES IT...
...EVERY-THING WILL BE DE-STROYED.
WE'VE KNOWN THIS WAS COMING FOR AGES...

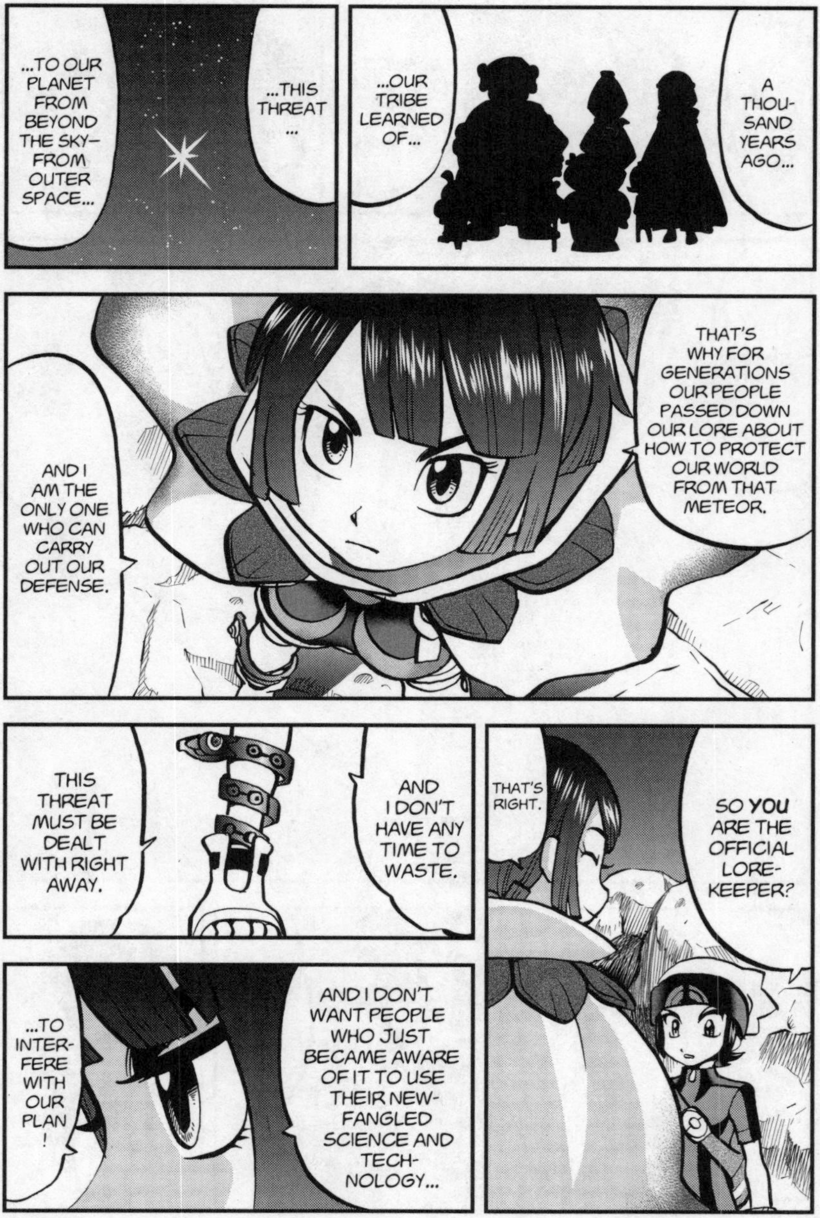
A THOUSAND YEARS AGO...
...OUR TRIBE LEARNED OF...
...THIS THREAT ...
...TO OUR PLANET FROM BEYOND THE SKY—FROM OUTER SPACE...
THAT'S WHY FOR GENERATIONS OUR PEOPLE PASSED DOWN OUR LORE ABOUT HOW TO PROTECT OUR WORLD FROM THAT METEOR.
AND I AM THE ONLY ONE WHO CAN CARRY OUT OUR DEFENSE.
SO **YOU** ARE THE OFFICIAL LORE-KEEPER?
THAT'S RIGHT.
AND I DON'T HAVE ANY TIME TO WASTE.
THIS THREAT MUST BE DEALT WITH RIGHT AWAY.
AND I DON'T WANT PEOPLE WHO JUST BECAME AWARE OF IT TO USE THEIR NEW-FANGLED SCIENCE AND TECHNOLOGY...
...TO INTERFERE WITH OUR PLAN!

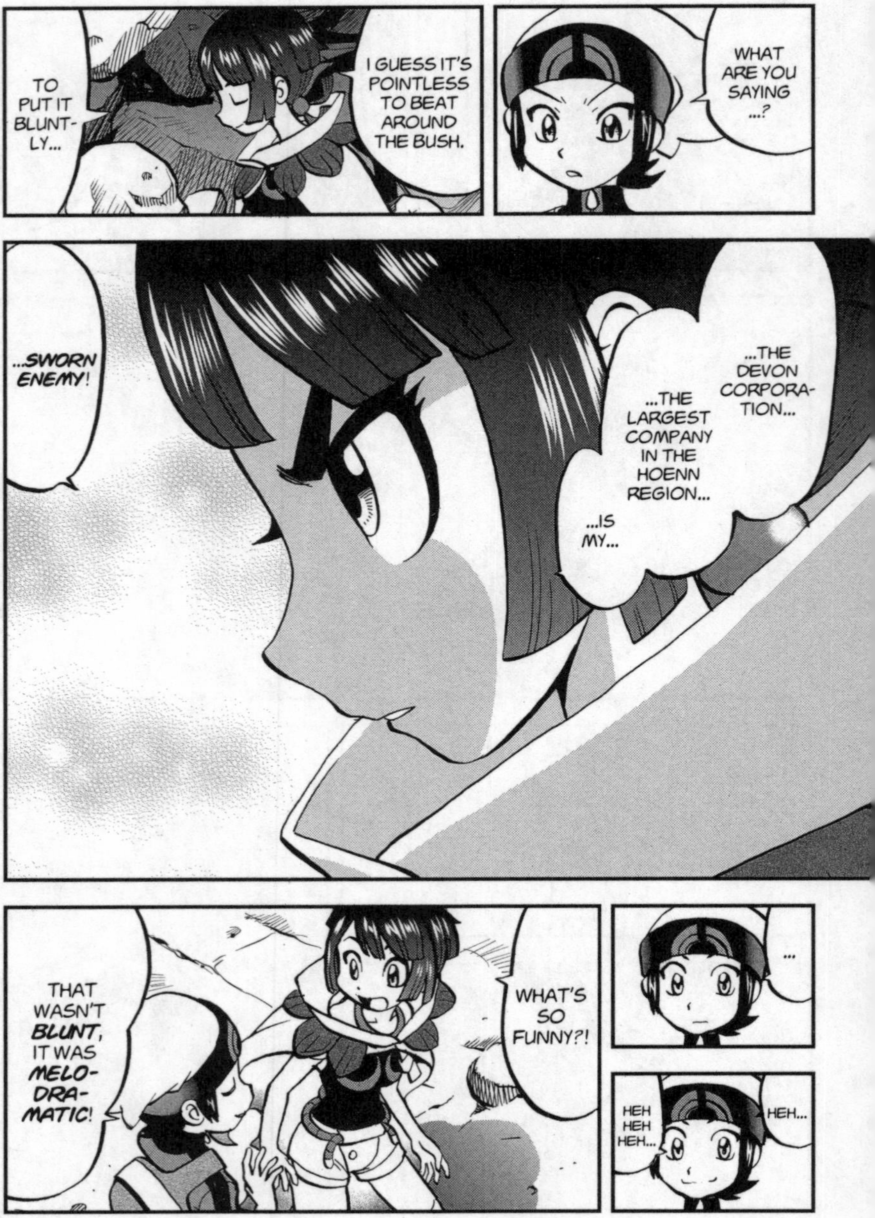

WHAT ARE YOU SAYING ...?
I GUESS IT'S POINTLESS TO BEAT AROUND THE BUSH.
TO PUT IT BLUNT-LY...
...THE DEVON CORPORA-TION...
...THE LARGEST COMPANY IN THE HOENN REGION...
...IS MY...
...**SWORN ENEMY**!
...
HEH...
HEH HEH HEH...
WHAT'S SO FUNNY?!
THAT WASN'T **BLUNT**, IT WAS **MELO-DRA-MATIC**!

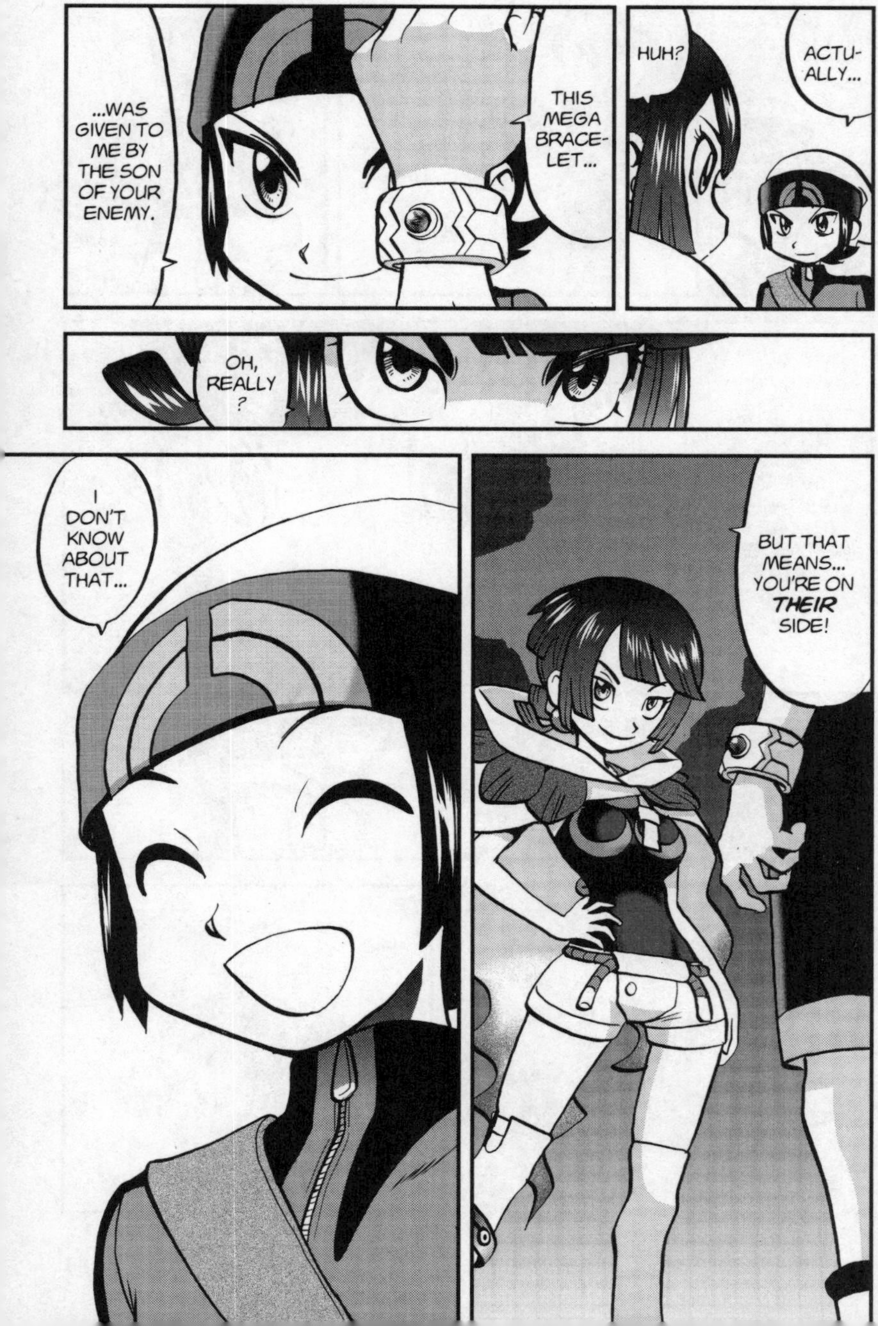
ACTUALLY...
HUH?
THIS MEGA BRACELET...
...WAS GIVEN TO ME BY THE SON OF YOUR ENEMY.
OH, REALLY?
BUT THAT MEANS... YOU'RE ON **THEIR** SIDE!
I DON'T KNOW ABOUT THAT...

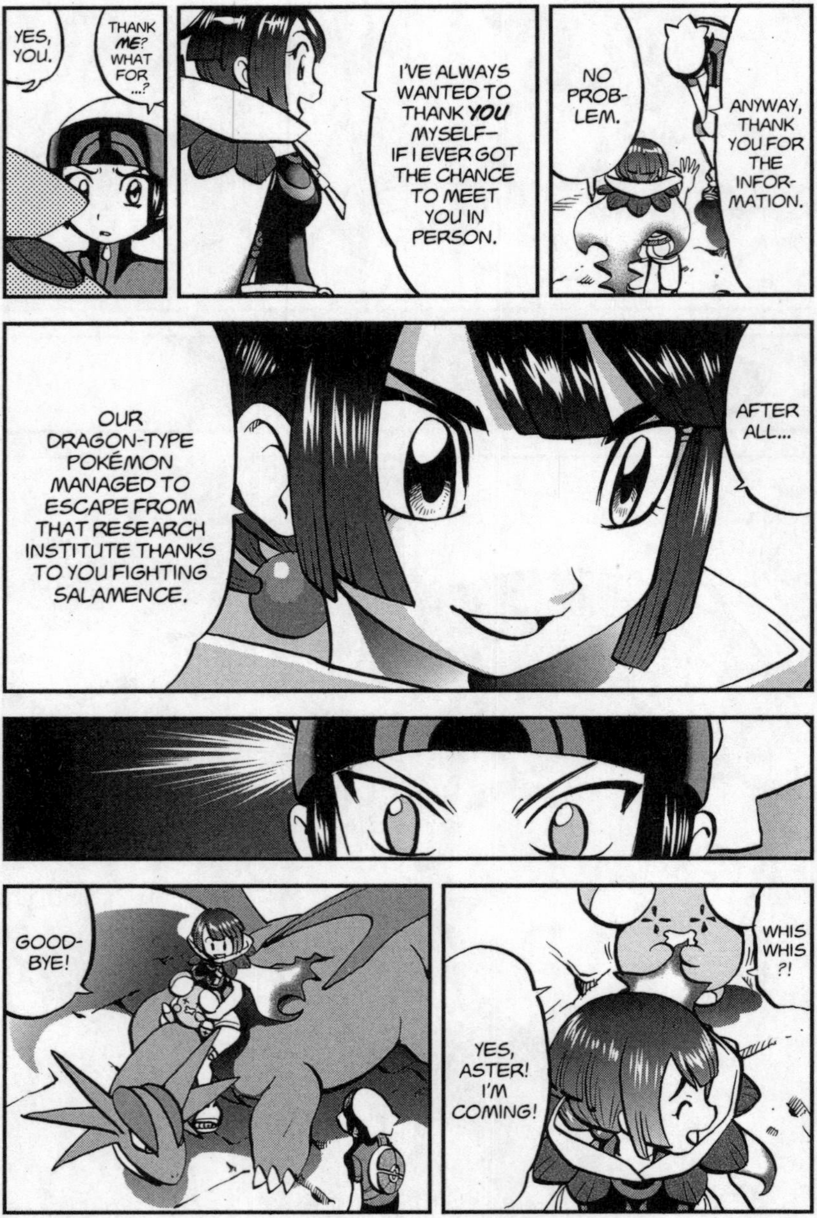
ANYWAY, THANK YOU FOR THE INFORMATION.
NO PROBLEM.
I'VE ALWAYS WANTED TO THANK *YOU* MYSELF— IF I EVER GOT THE CHANCE TO MEET YOU IN PERSON.
THANK *ME*? WHAT FOR ...?
YES, YOU.
AFTER ALL...
OUR DRAGON-TYPE POKÉMON MANAGED TO ESCAPE FROM THAT RESEARCH INSTITUTE THANKS TO YOU FIGHTING SALAMENCE.
WHIS WHIS ?!
YES, ASTER! I'M COMING!
GOOD-BYE!

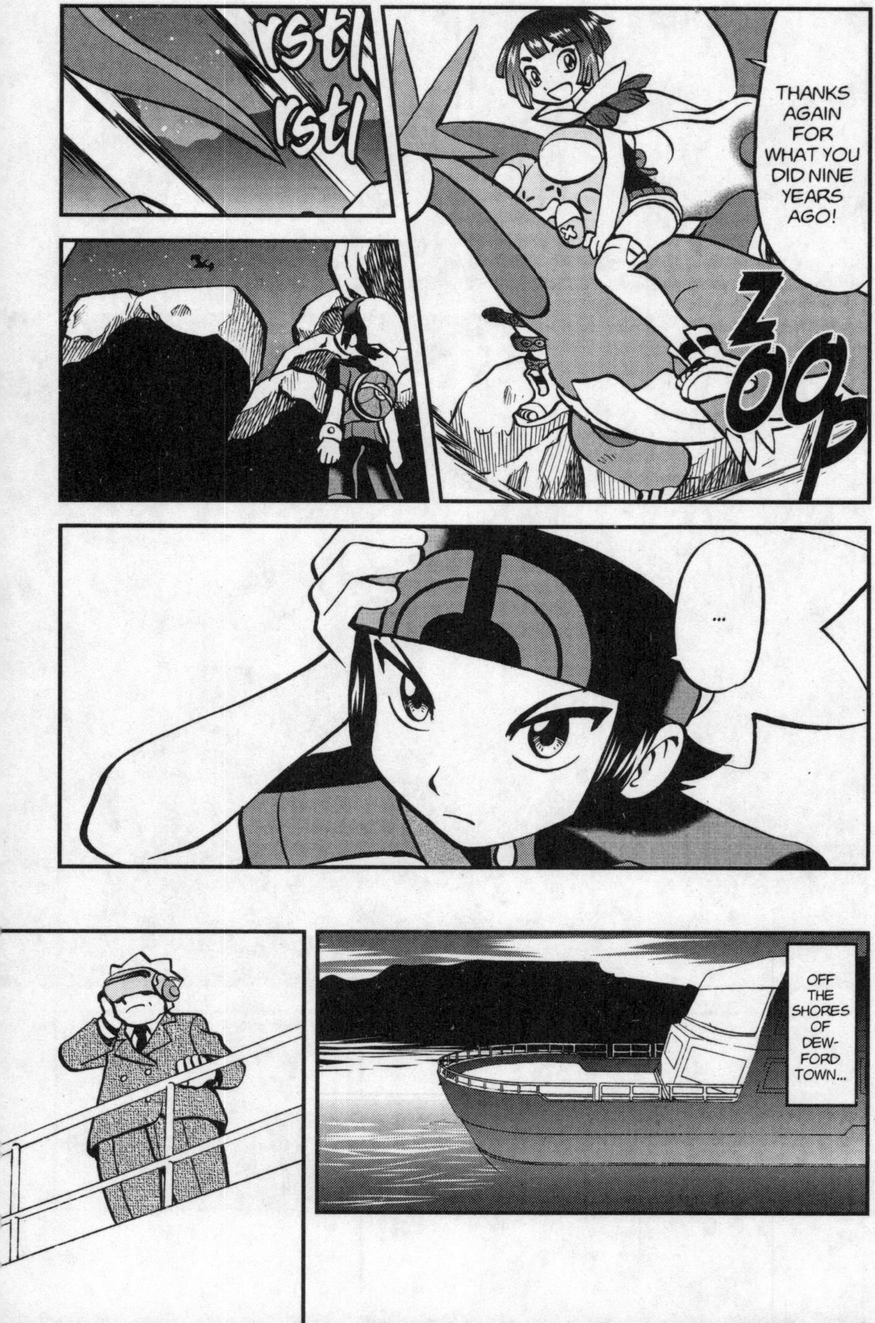
THANKS AGAIN FOR WHAT YOU DID NINE YEARS AGO!
ZOOOP
rstl rstl
...
OFF THE SHORES OF DEW-FORD TOWN...

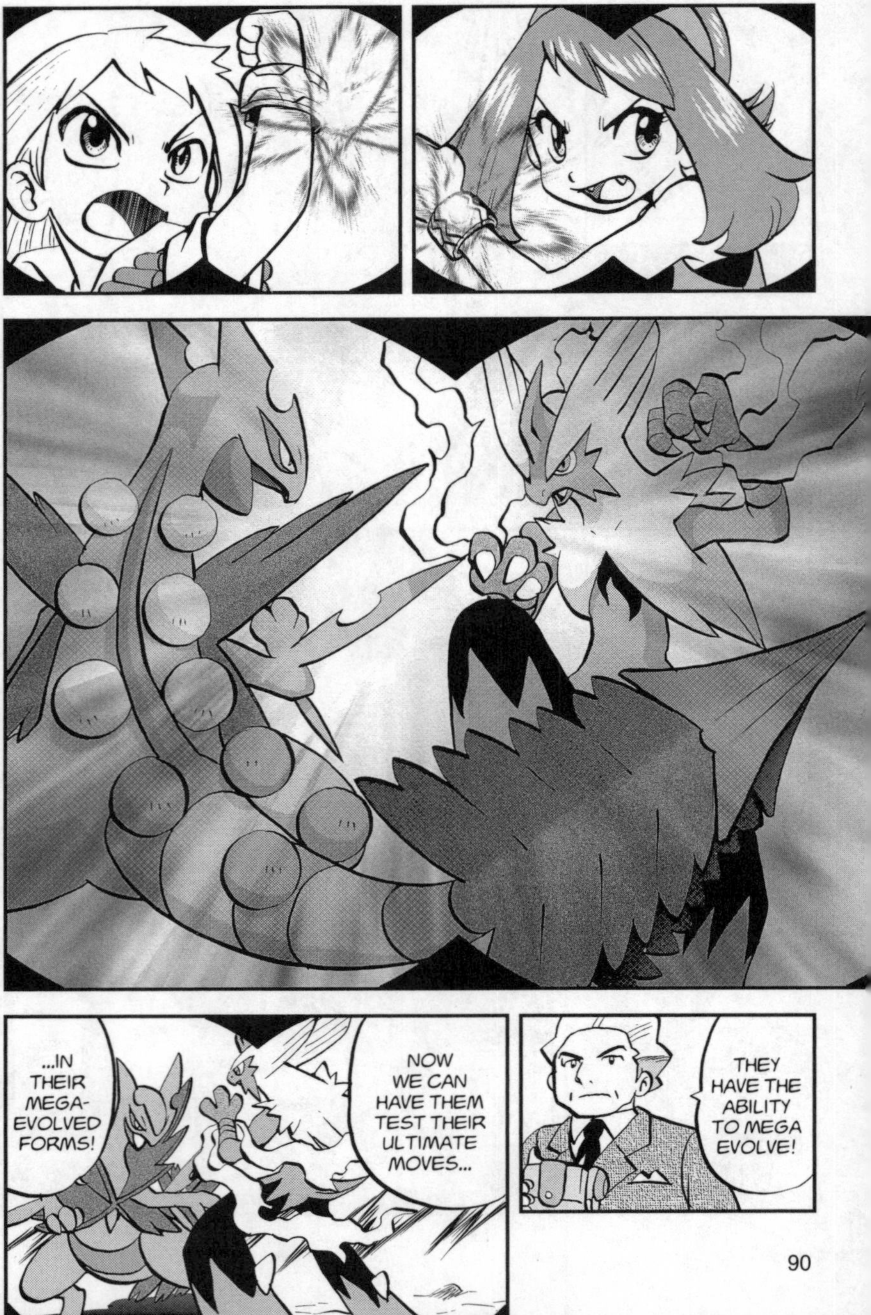
THEY HAVE THE ABILITY TO MEGA EVOLVE!
NOW WE CAN HAVE THEM TEST THEIR ULTIMATE MOVES...
...IN THEIR MEGA-EVOLVED FORMS!

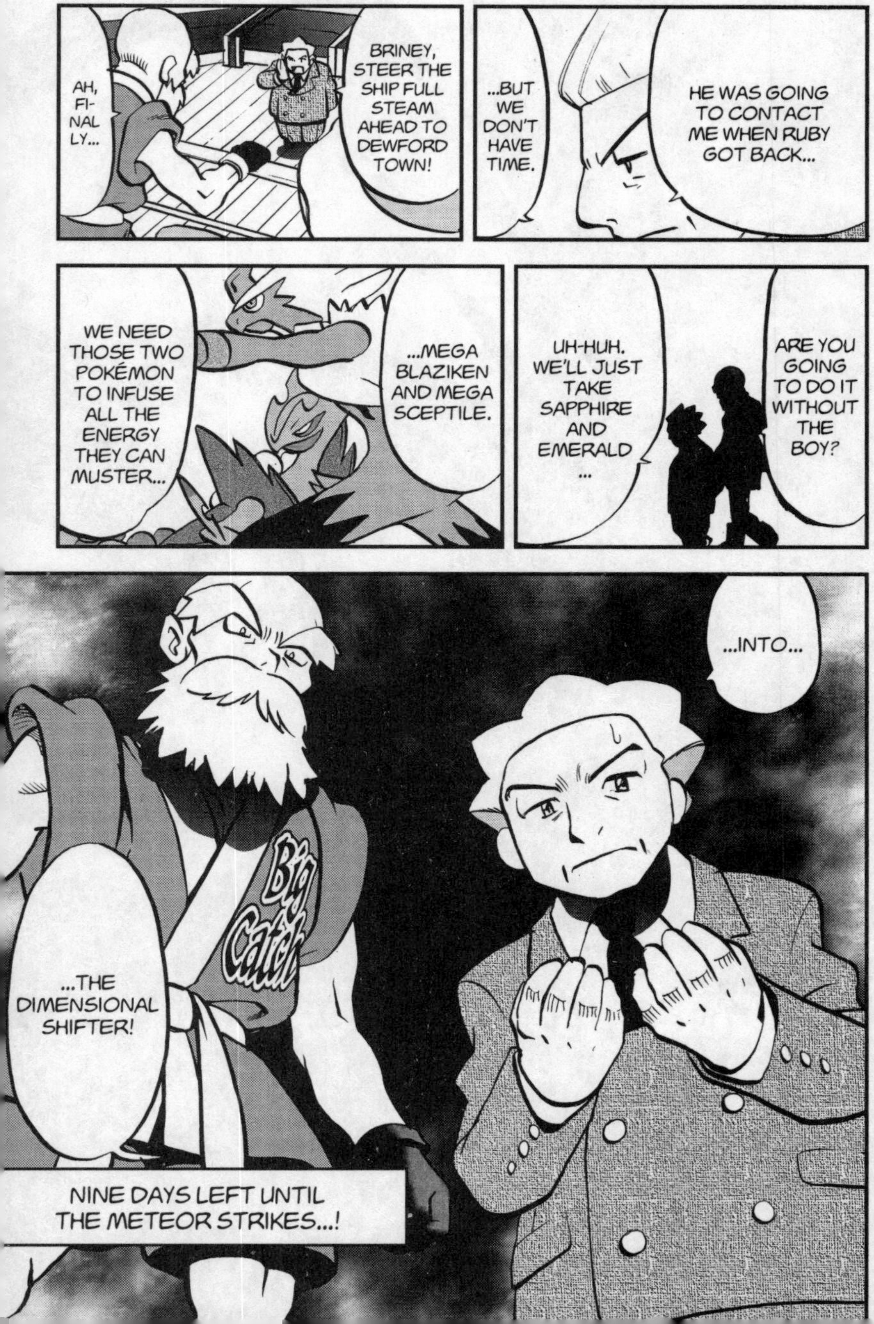
HE WAS GOING TO CONTACT ME WHEN RUBY GOT BACK...
...BUT WE DON'T HAVE TIME.
BRINEY, STEER THE SHIP FULL STEAM AHEAD TO DEWFORD TOWN!
AH, FI-NAL LY...
ARE YOU GOING TO DO IT WITHOUT THE BOY?
UH-HUH. WE'LL JUST TAKE SAPPHIRE AND EMERALD ...
...MEGA BLAZIKEN AND MEGA SCEPTILE.
WE NEED THOSE TWO POKÉMON TO INFUSE ALL THE ENERGY THEY CAN MUSTER...
...INTO...
...THE DIMENSIONAL SHIFTER!
NINE DAYS LEFT UNTIL THE METEOR STRIKES...!

ADVENTURE #5
Gorebyss Changes Color

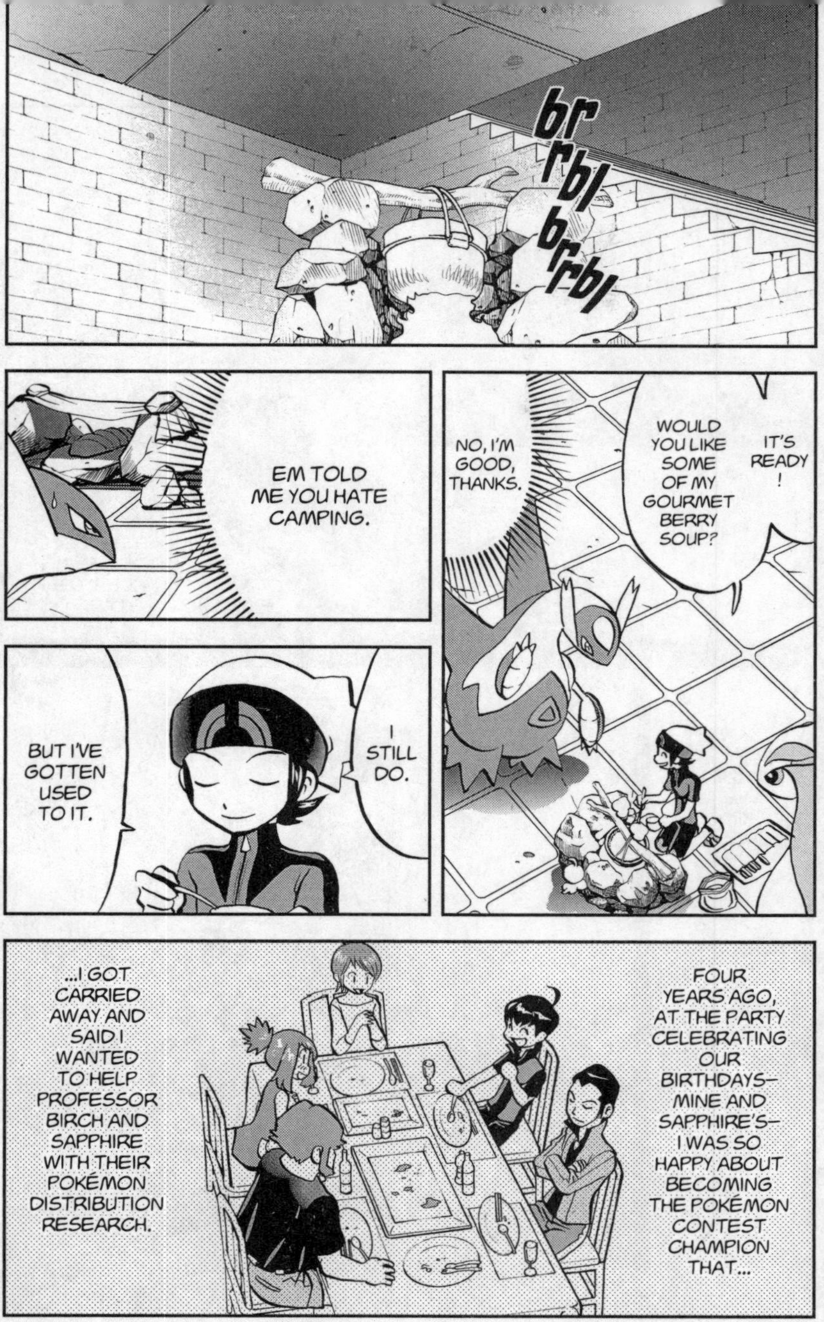
brrbl brrbl
IT'S READY!
WOULD YOU LIKE SOME OF MY GOURMET BERRY SOUP?
NO, I'M GOOD, THANKS.
EM TOLD ME YOU HATE CAMPING.
I STILL DO.
BUT I'VE GOTTEN USED TO IT.
FOUR YEARS AGO, AT THE PARTY CELEBRATING OUR BIRTHDAYS—MINE AND SAPPHIRE'S—I WAS SO HAPPY ABOUT BECOMING THE POKÉMON CONTEST CHAMPION THAT...
...I GOT CARRIED AWAY AND SAID I WANTED TO HELP PROFESSOR BIRCH AND SAPPHIRE WITH THEIR POKÉMON DISTRIBUTION RESEARCH.

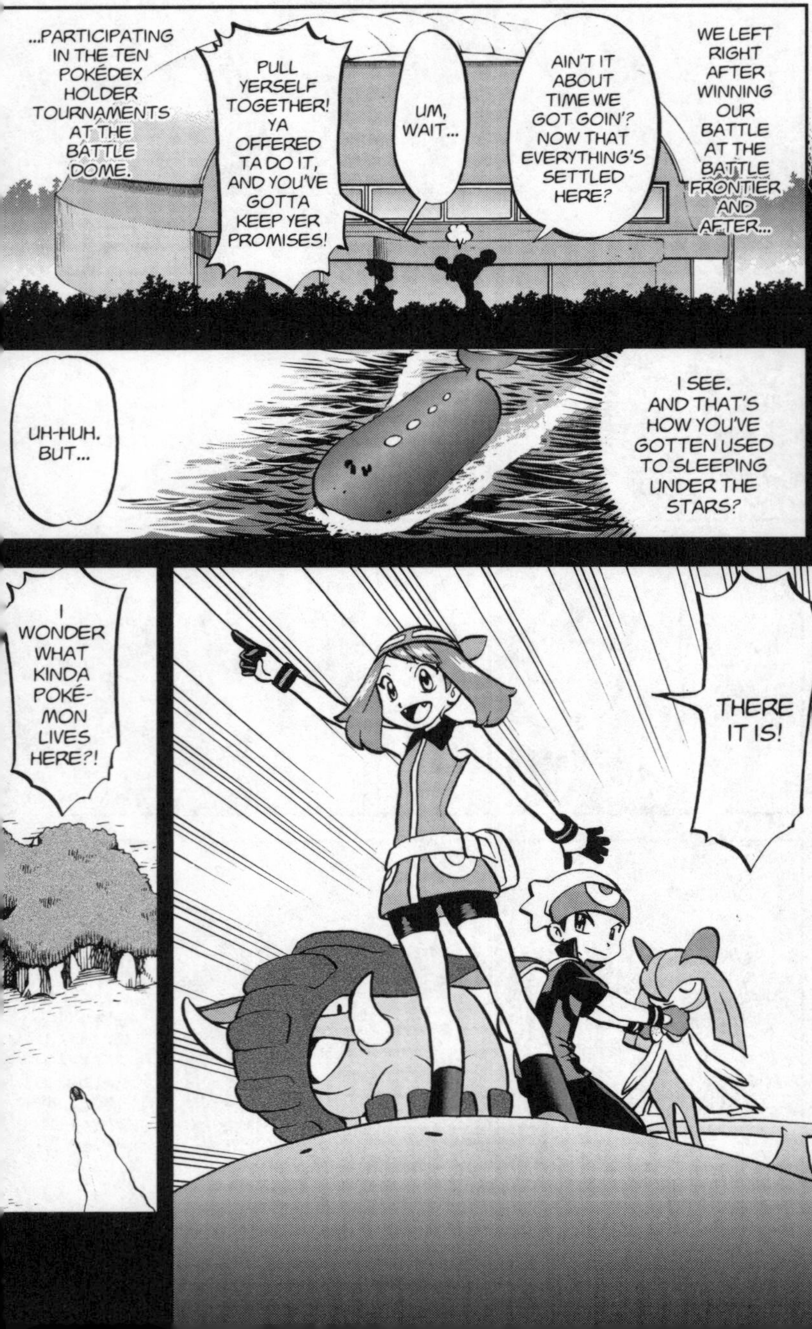
WE LEFT RIGHT AFTER WINNING OUR BATTLE AT THE BATTLE FRONTIER AND AFTER...
AIN'T IT ABOUT TIME WE GOT GOIN'? NOW THAT EVERYTHING'S SETTLED HERE?
UM, WAIT...
PULL YERSELF TOGETHER! YA OFFERED TA DO IT, AND YOU'VE GOTTA KEEP YER PROMISES!
...PARTICIPATING IN THE TEN POKÉDEX HOLDER TOURNAMENTS AT THE BATTLE DOME.
I SEE. AND THAT'S HOW YOU'VE GOTTEN USED TO SLEEPING UNDER THE STARS?
UH-HUH. BUT...
THERE IT IS!
I WONDER WHAT KINDA POKÉ-MON LIVES HERE?!

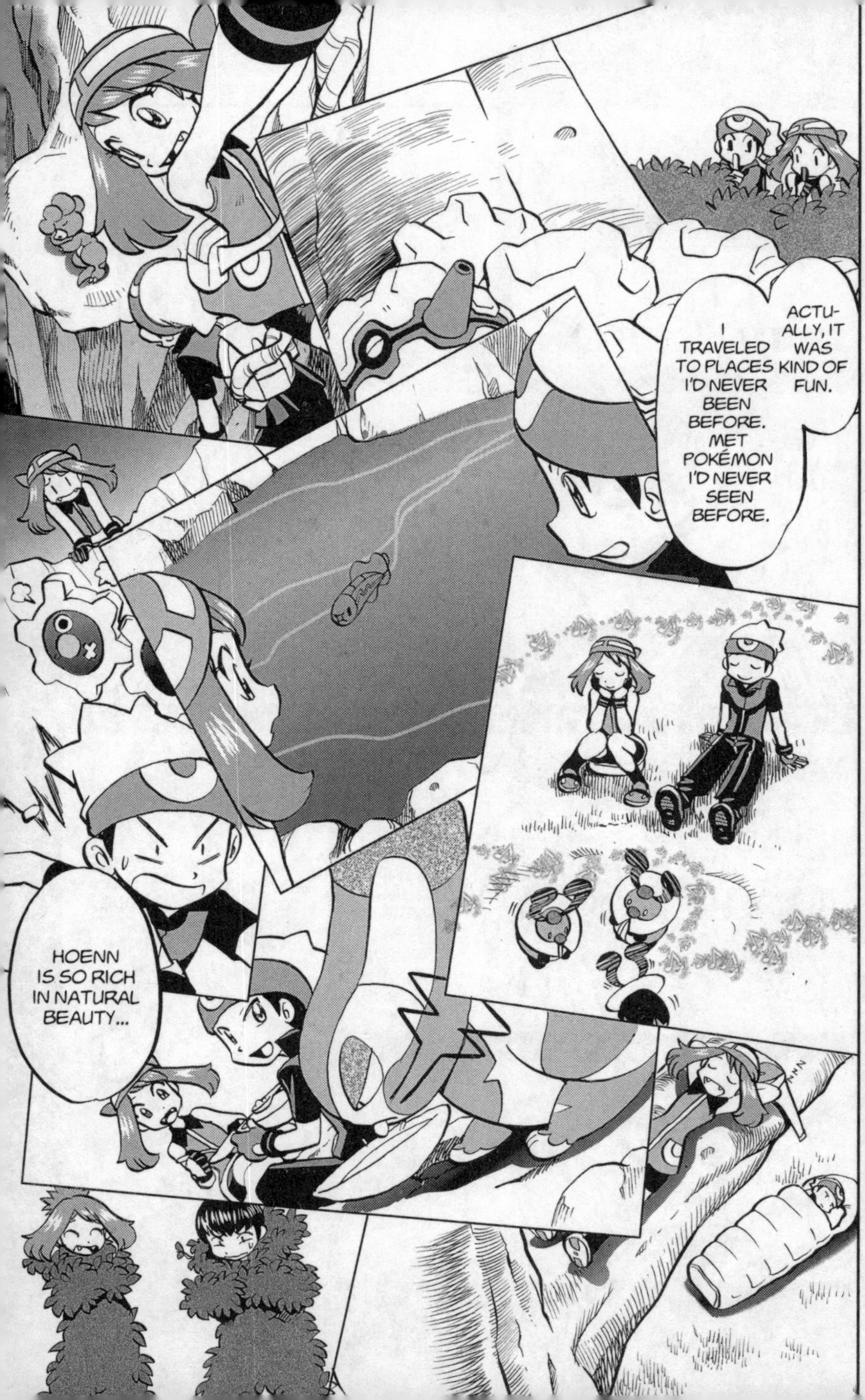
ACTUALLY, IT WAS KIND OF FUN.
I TRAVELED TO PLACES I'D NEVER BEEN BEFORE. MET POKÉMON I'D NEVER SEEN BEFORE.
HOENN IS SO RICH IN NATURAL BEAUTY...

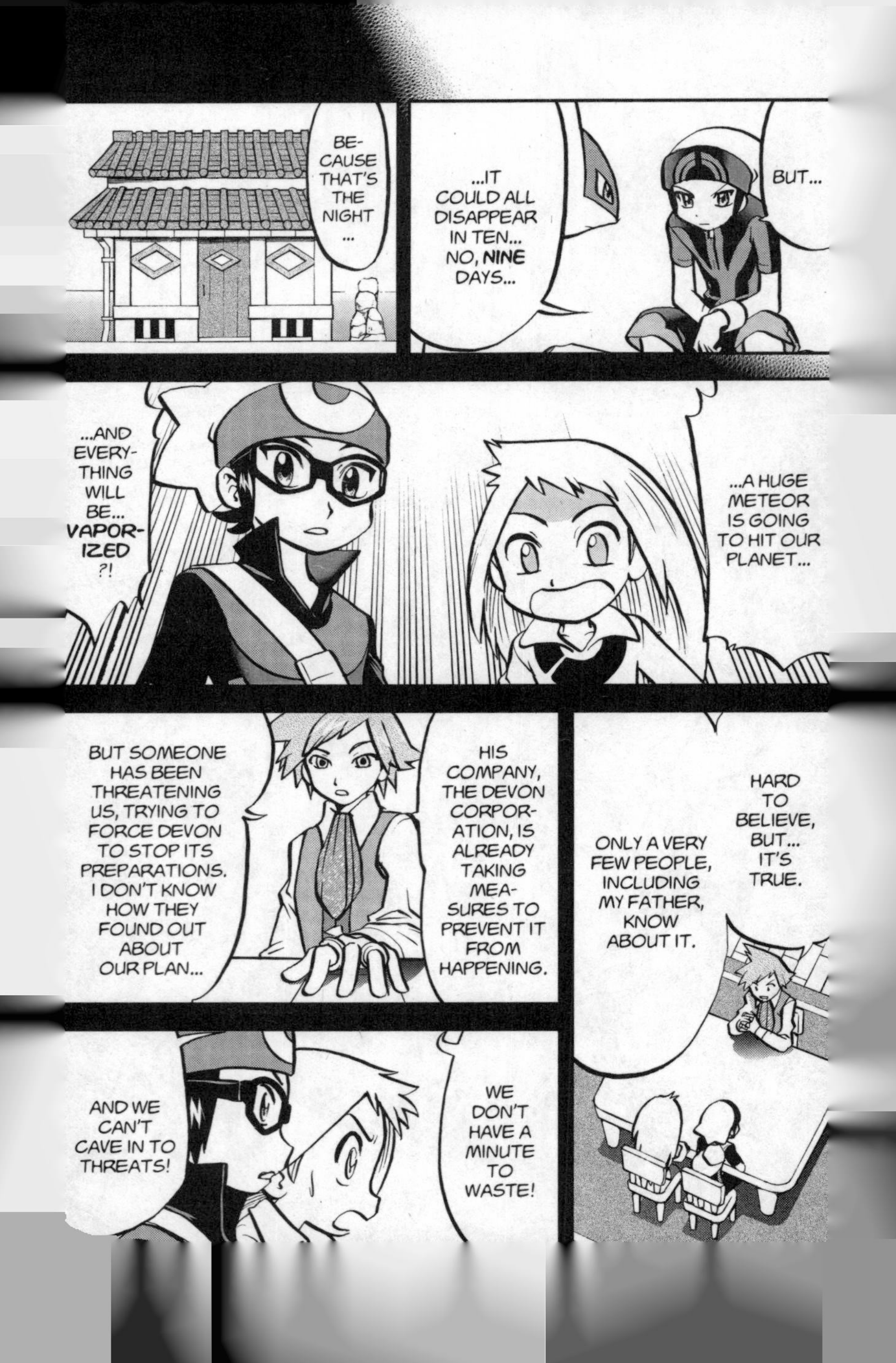
BUT...
...IT COULD ALL DISAPPEAR IN TEN... NO, NINE DAYS...
BE-CAUSE THAT'S THE NIGHT ...
...A HUGE METEOR IS GOING TO HIT OUR PLANET...
...AND EVERYTHING WILL BE... VAPORIZED?!
HARD TO BELIEVE, BUT... IT'S TRUE.
ONLY A VERY FEW PEOPLE, INCLUDING MY FATHER, KNOW ABOUT IT.
HIS COMPANY, THE DEVON CORPORATION, IS ALREADY TAKING MEA-SURES TO PREVENT IT FROM HAPPENING.
BUT SOMEONE HAS BEEN THREATENING US, TRYING TO FORCE DEVON TO STOP ITS PREPARATIONS. I DON'T KNOW HOW THEY FOUND OUT ABOUT OUR PLAN...
WE DON'T HAVE A MINUTE TO WASTE!
AND WE CAN'T CAVE IN TO THREATS!

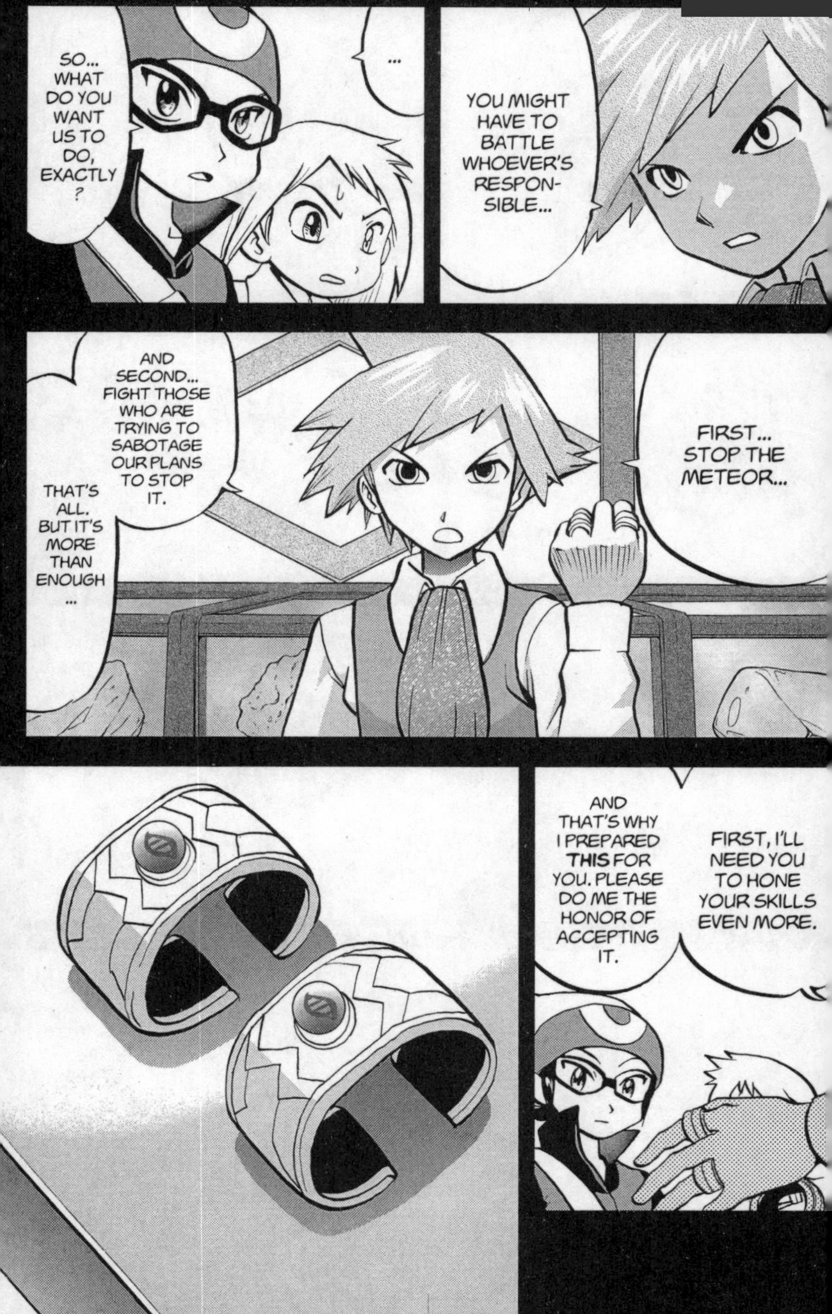
YOU MIGHT HAVE TO BATTLE WHOEVER'S RESPONSIBLE...
...
SO... WHAT DO YOU WANT US TO DO, EXACTLY?
FIRST... STOP THE METEOR...
AND SECOND... FIGHT THOSE WHO ARE TRYING TO SABOTAGE OUR PLANS TO STOP IT.
THAT'S ALL. BUT IT'S MORE THAN ENOUGH...
FIRST, I'LL NEED YOU TO HONE YOUR SKILLS EVEN MORE.
AND THAT'S WHY I PREPARED **THIS** FOR YOU. PLEASE DO ME THE HONOR OF ACCEPTING IT.

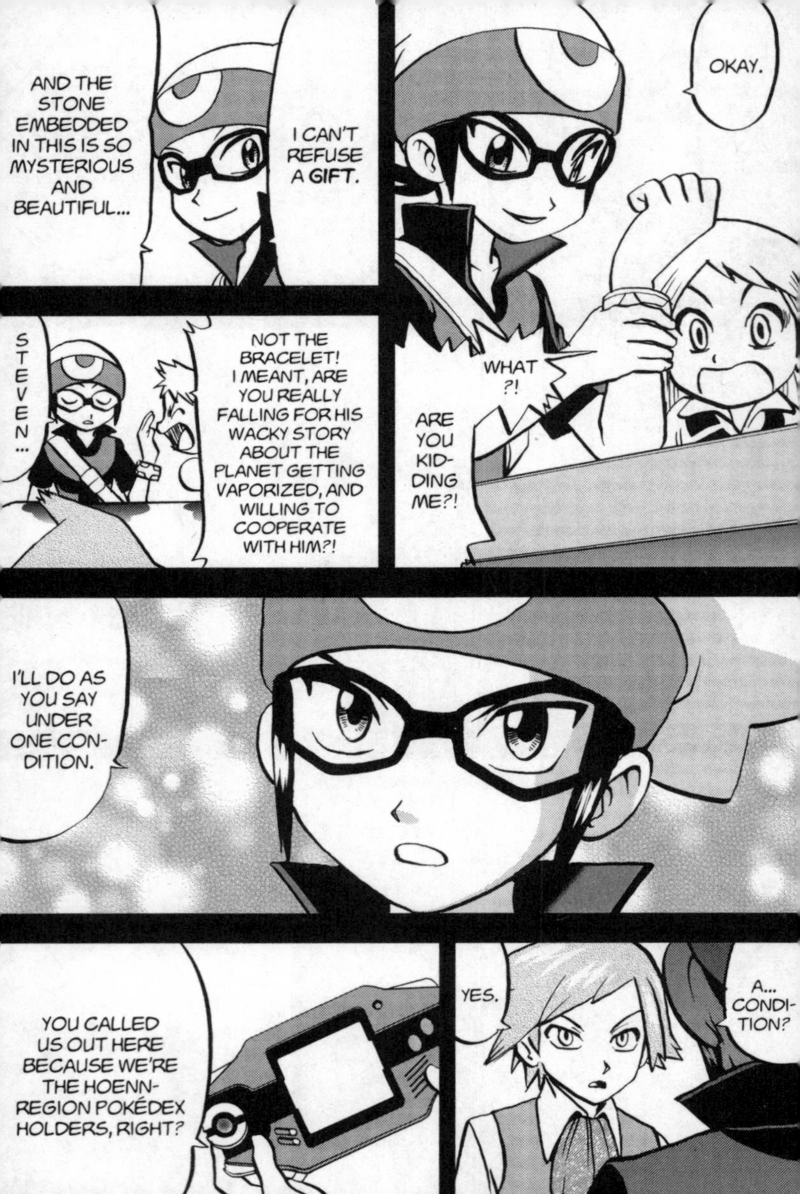
OKAY.
WHAT?!
ARE YOU KIDDING ME?!
I CAN'T REFUSE A GIFT.
AND THE STONE EMBEDDED IN THIS IS SO MYSTERIOUS AND BEAUTIFUL...
NOT THE BRACELET! I MEANT, ARE YOU REALLY FALLING FOR HIS WACKY STORY ABOUT THE PLANET GETTING VAPORIZED, AND WILLING TO COOPERATE WITH HIM?!
STEVEN...
I'LL DO AS YOU SAY UNDER ONE CONDITION.
A... CONDITION?
YES.
YOU CALLED US OUT HERE BECAUSE WE'RE THE HOENN-REGION POKÉDEX HOLDERS, RIGHT?

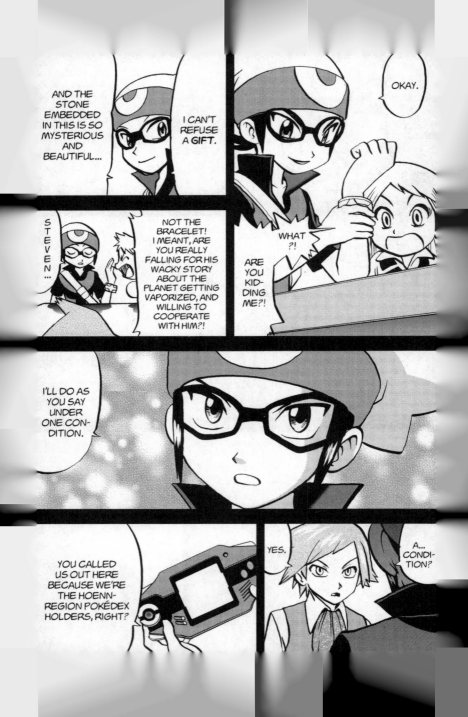

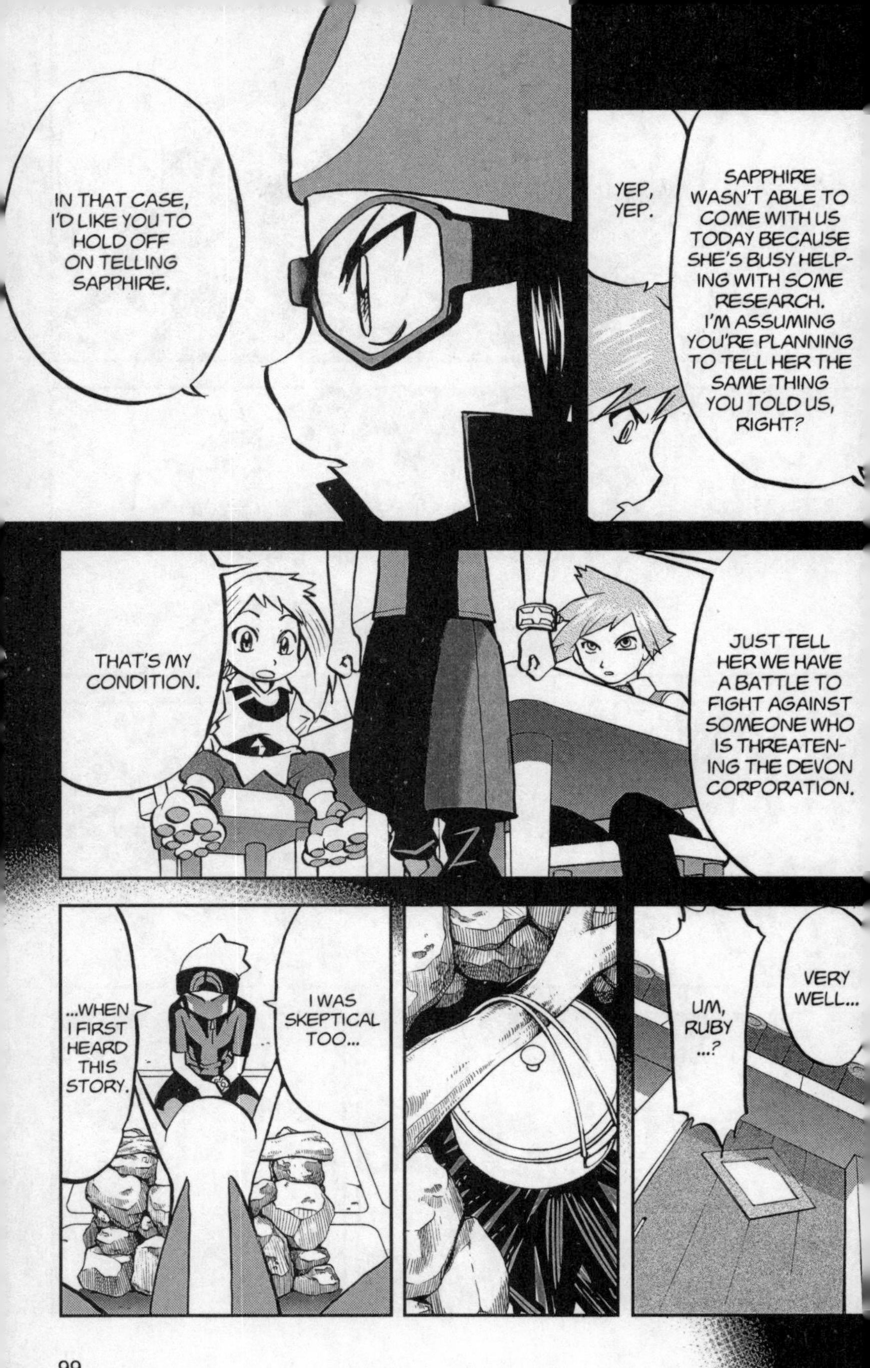
SAPPHIRE WASN'T ABLE TO COME WITH US TODAY BECAUSE SHE'S BUSY HELPING WITH SOME RESEARCH. I'M ASSUMING YOU'RE PLANNING TO TELL HER THE SAME THING YOU TOLD US, RIGHT?
YEP, YEP.
IN THAT CASE, I'D LIKE YOU TO HOLD OFF ON TELLING SAPPHIRE.
JUST TELL HER WE HAVE A BATTLE TO FIGHT AGAINST SOMEONE WHO IS THREATENING THE DEVON CORPORATION.
THAT'S MY CONDITION.
VERY WELL...
UM, RUBY ...?
I WAS SKEPTICAL TOO...
...WHEN I FIRST HEARD THIS STORY.

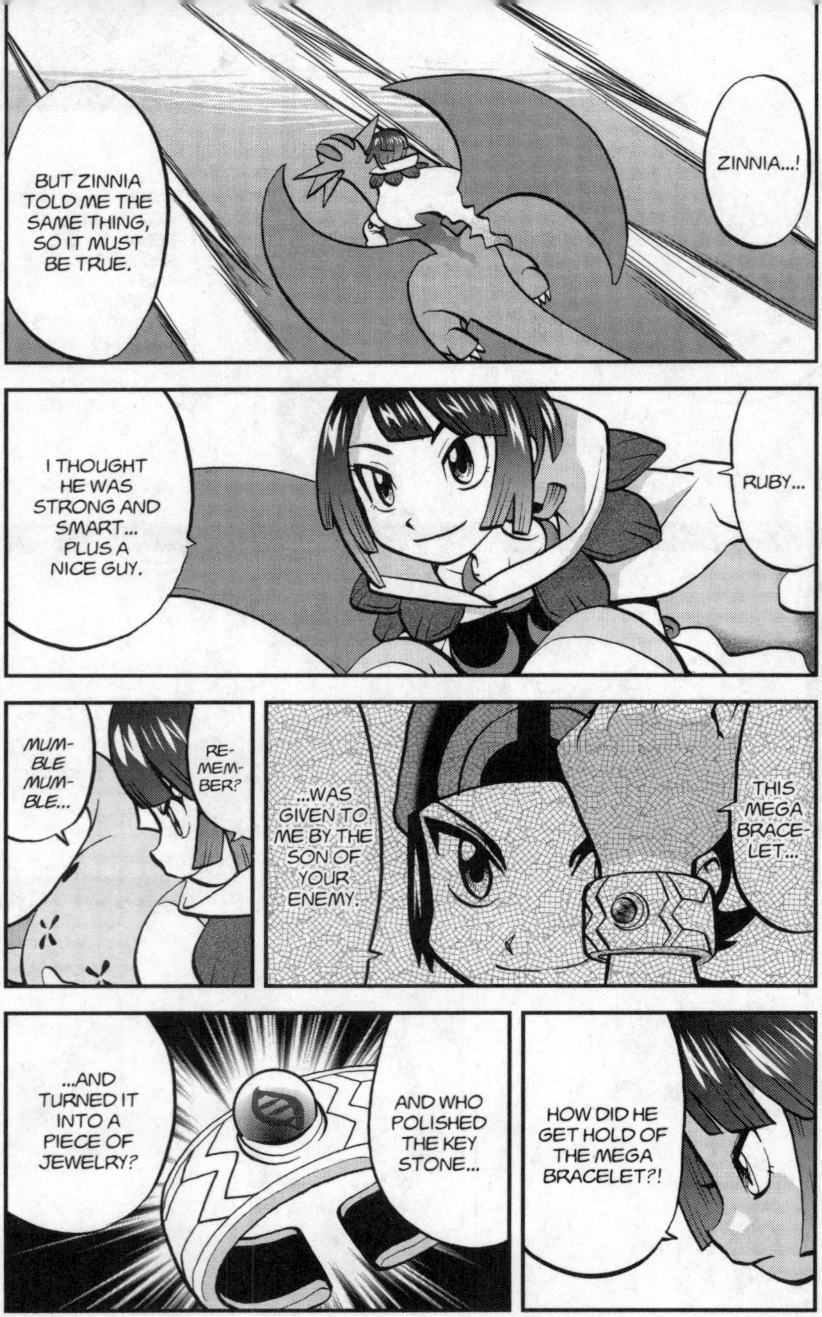
ZINNIA...!
BUT ZINNIA TOLD ME THE SAME THING, SO IT MUST BE TRUE.
RUBY...
I THOUGHT HE WAS STRONG AND SMART... PLUS A NICE GUY.
THIS MEGA BRACE-LET...
...WAS GIVEN TO ME BY THE SON OF YOUR ENEMY.
RE-MEM-BER?
MUM-BLE MUM-BLE...
HOW DID HE GET HOLD OF THE MEGA BRACELET?!
AND WHO POLISHED THE KEY STONE...
...AND TURNED IT INTO A PIECE OF JEWELRY?

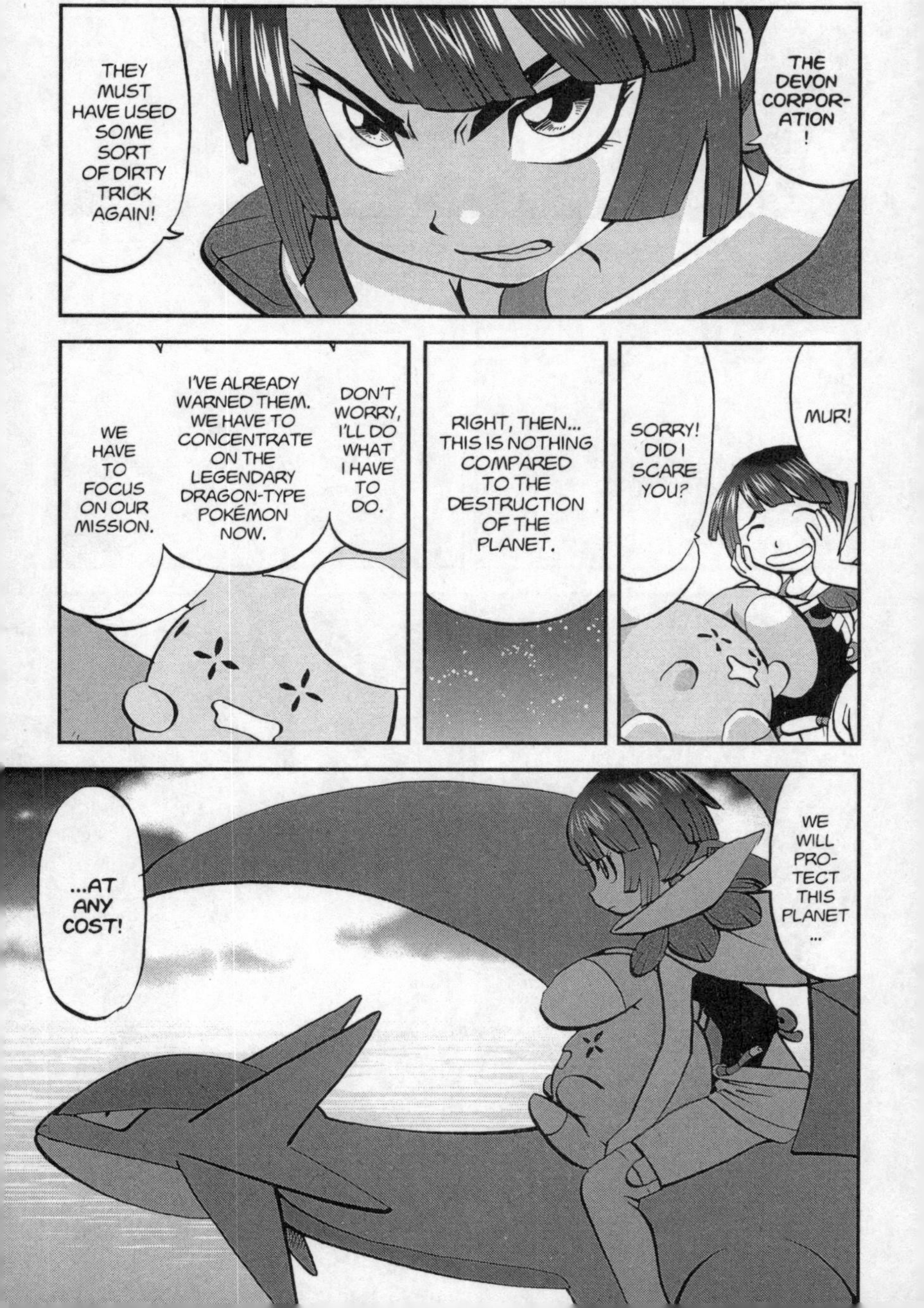
THE DEVON CORPORATION!
THEY MUST HAVE USED SOME SORT OF DIRTY TRICK AGAIN!
MUR!
SORRY! DID I SCARE YOU?
RIGHT, THEN... THIS IS NOTHING COMPARED TO THE DESTRUCTION OF THE PLANET.
DON'T WORRY, I'LL DO WHAT I HAVE TO DO.
I'VE ALREADY WARNED THEM. WE HAVE TO CONCENTRATE ON THE LEGENDARY DRAGON-TYPE POKÉMON NOW.
WE HAVE TO FOCUS ON OUR MISSION.
WE WILL PROTECT THIS PLANET...
...AT ANY COST!

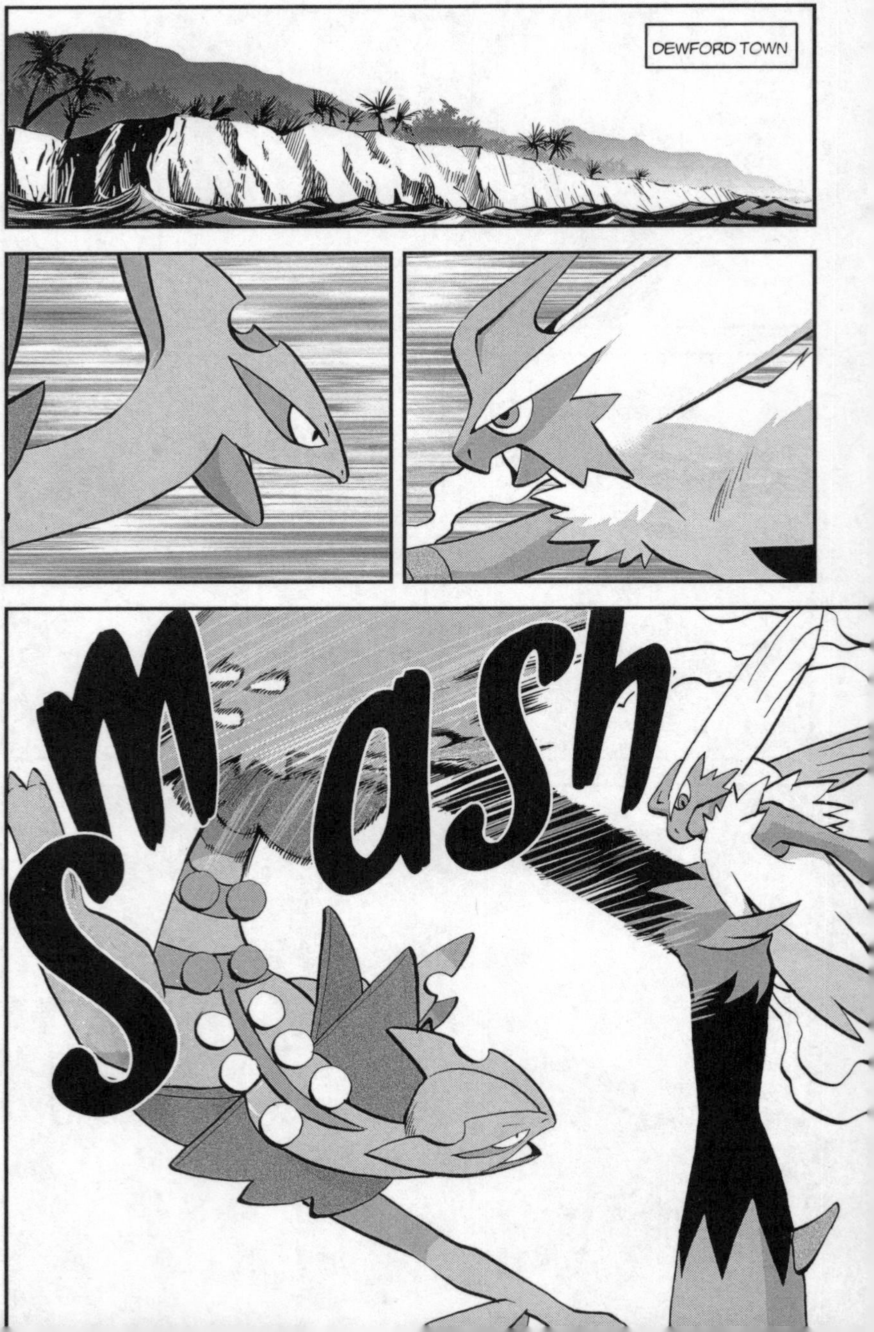
DEWFORD TOWN
SMASH

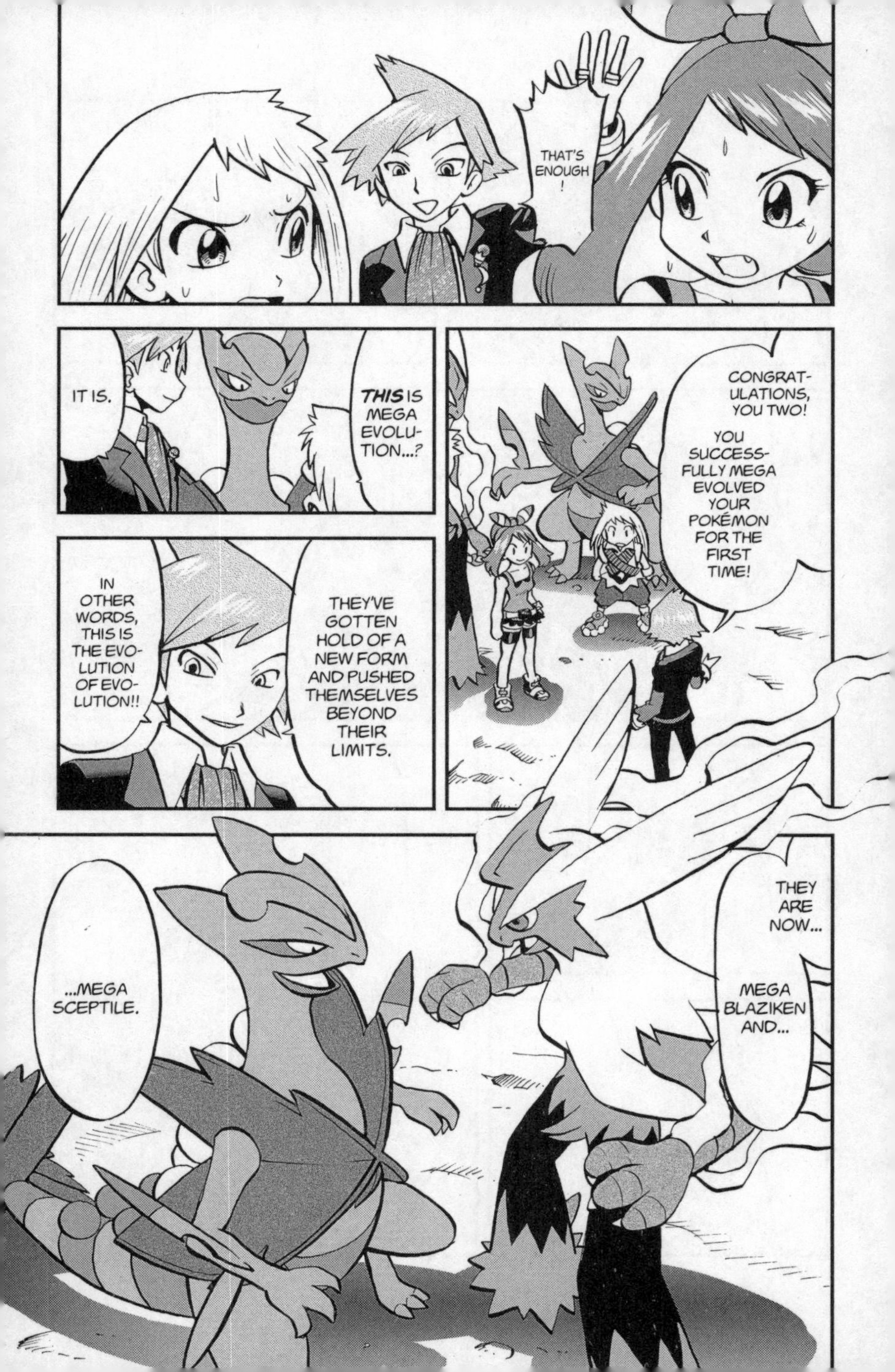
THAT'S ENOUGH!
CONGRATULATIONS, YOU TWO!
YOU SUCCESSFULLY MEGA EVOLVED YOUR POKÉMON FOR THE FIRST TIME!
THIS IS MEGA EVOLUTION...?
IT IS.
THEY'VE GOTTEN HOLD OF A NEW FORM AND PUSHED THEMSELVES BEYOND THEIR LIMITS.
IN OTHER WORDS, THIS IS THE EVOLUTION OF EVOLUTION!!
THEY ARE NOW...
MEGA BLAZIKEN AND...
...MEGA SCEPTILE.

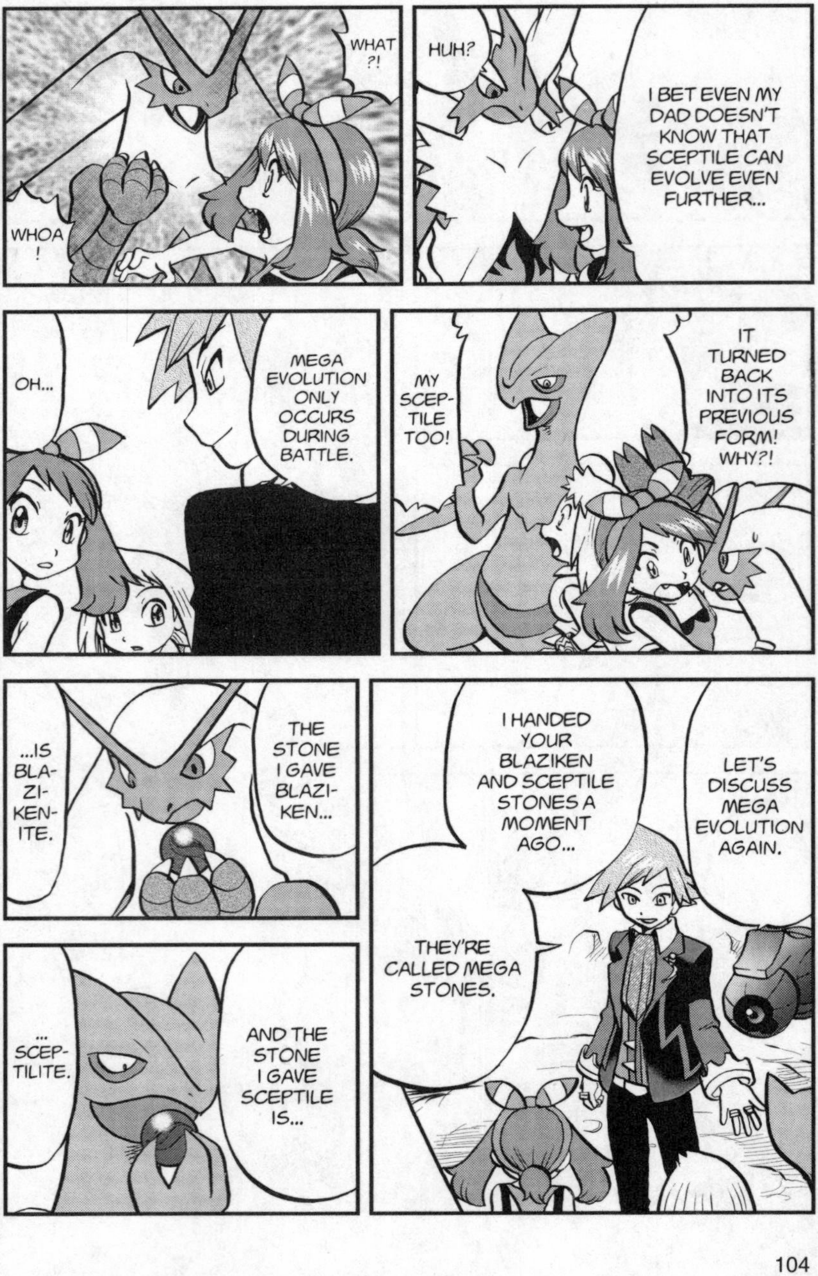
HUH?
I BET EVEN MY DAD DOESN'T KNOW THAT SCEPTILE CAN EVOLVE EVEN FURTHER...
WHAT ?!
WHOA !
IT TURNED BACK INTO ITS PREVIOUS FORM! WHY?!
MY SCEP-TILE TOO!
MEGA EVOLUTION ONLY OCCURS DURING BATTLE.
OH...
LET'S DISCUSS MEGA EVOLUTION AGAIN.
I HANDED YOUR BLAZIKEN AND SCEPTILE STONES A MOMENT AGO...
THEY'RE CALLED MEGA STONES.
THE STONE I GAVE BLAZI-KEN...
...IS BLA-ZI-KEN-ITE.
AND THE STONE I GAVE SCEPTILE IS...
... SCEP-TILITE.

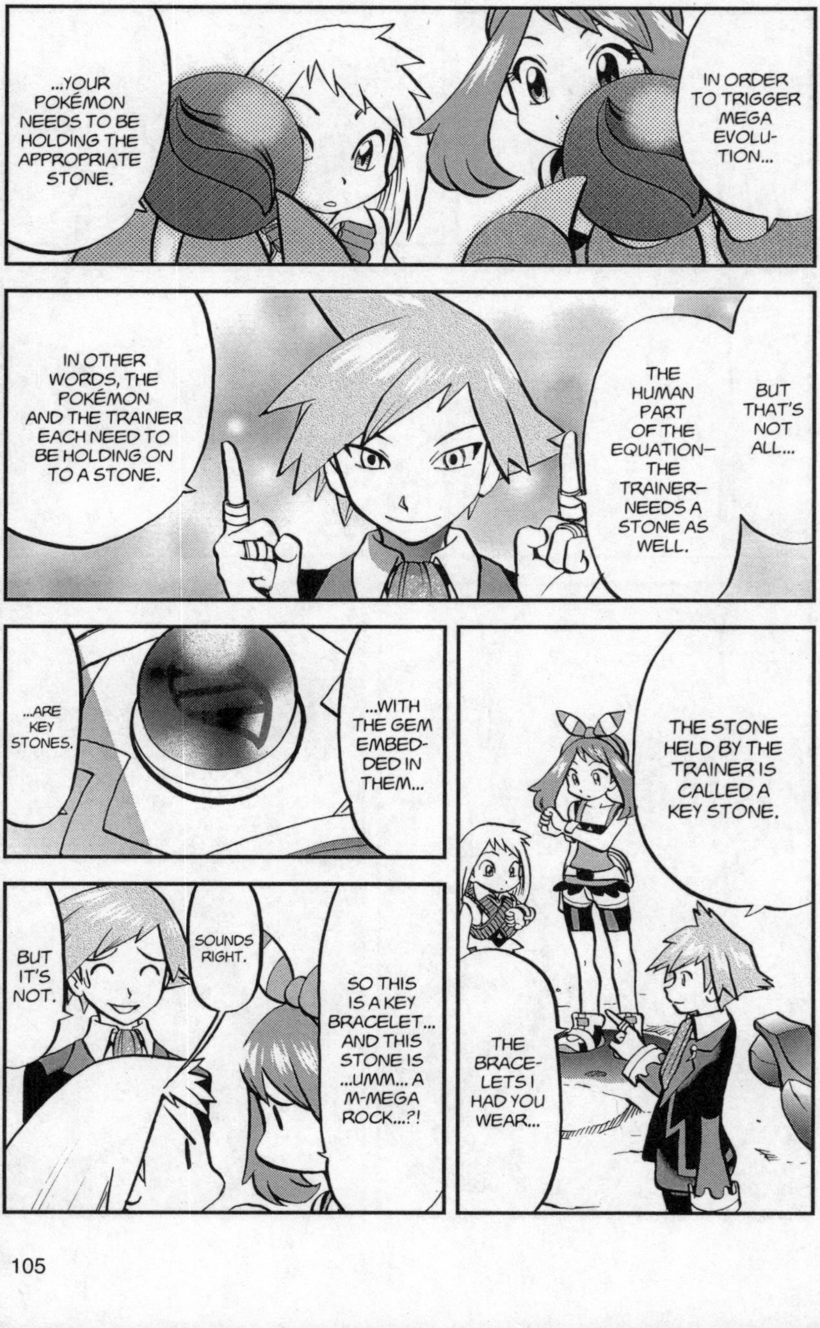

IN ORDER TO TRIGGER MEGA EVOLUTION...
...YOUR POKÉMON NEEDS TO BE HOLDING THE APPROPRIATE STONE.
BUT THAT'S NOT ALL...
THE HUMAN PART OF THE EQUATION—THE TRAINER—NEEDS A STONE AS WELL.
IN OTHER WORDS, THE POKÉMON AND THE TRAINER EACH NEED TO BE HOLDING ON TO A STONE.
THE STONE HELD BY THE TRAINER IS CALLED A KEY STONE.
THE BRACELETS I HAD YOU WEAR...
...WITH THE GEM EMBEDDED IN THEM...
...ARE KEY STONES.
SO THIS IS A KEY BRACELET... AND THIS STONE IS ...UMM... A M-MEGA ROCK...?!
SOUNDS RIGHT.
BUT IT'S NOT.

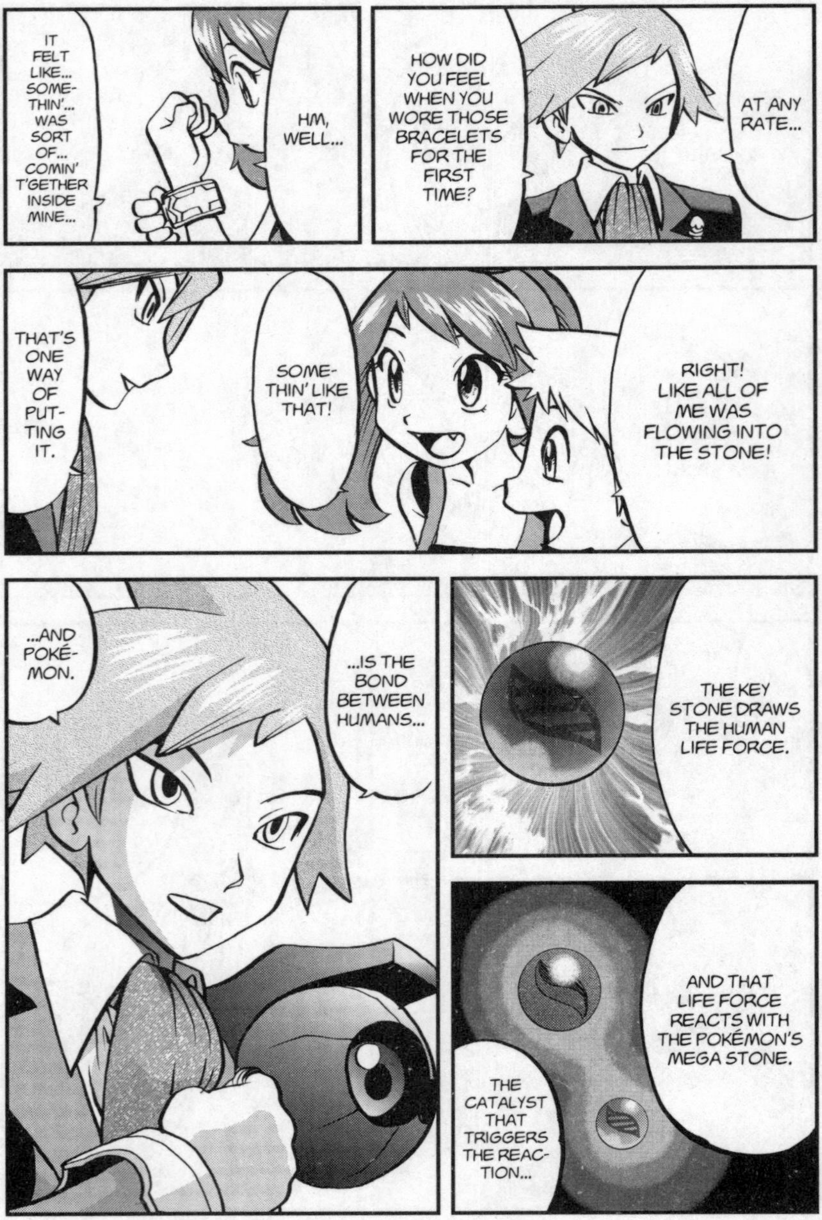
AT ANY RATE...
HOW DID YOU FEEL WHEN YOU WORE THOSE BRACELETS FOR THE FIRST TIME?
HM, WELL...
IT FELT LIKE... SOMETHIN'... WAS SORT OF... COMIN' T'GETHER INSIDE MINE...
RIGHT! LIKE ALL OF ME WAS FLOWING INTO THE STONE!
SOMETHIN' LIKE THAT!
THAT'S ONE WAY OF PUTTING IT.
THE KEY STONE DRAWS THE HUMAN LIFE FORCE.
AND THAT LIFE FORCE REACTS WITH THE POKÉMON'S MEGA STONE.
THE CATALYST THAT TRIGGERS THE REACTION...
...IS THE BOND BETWEEN HUMANS...
...AND POKÉMON.

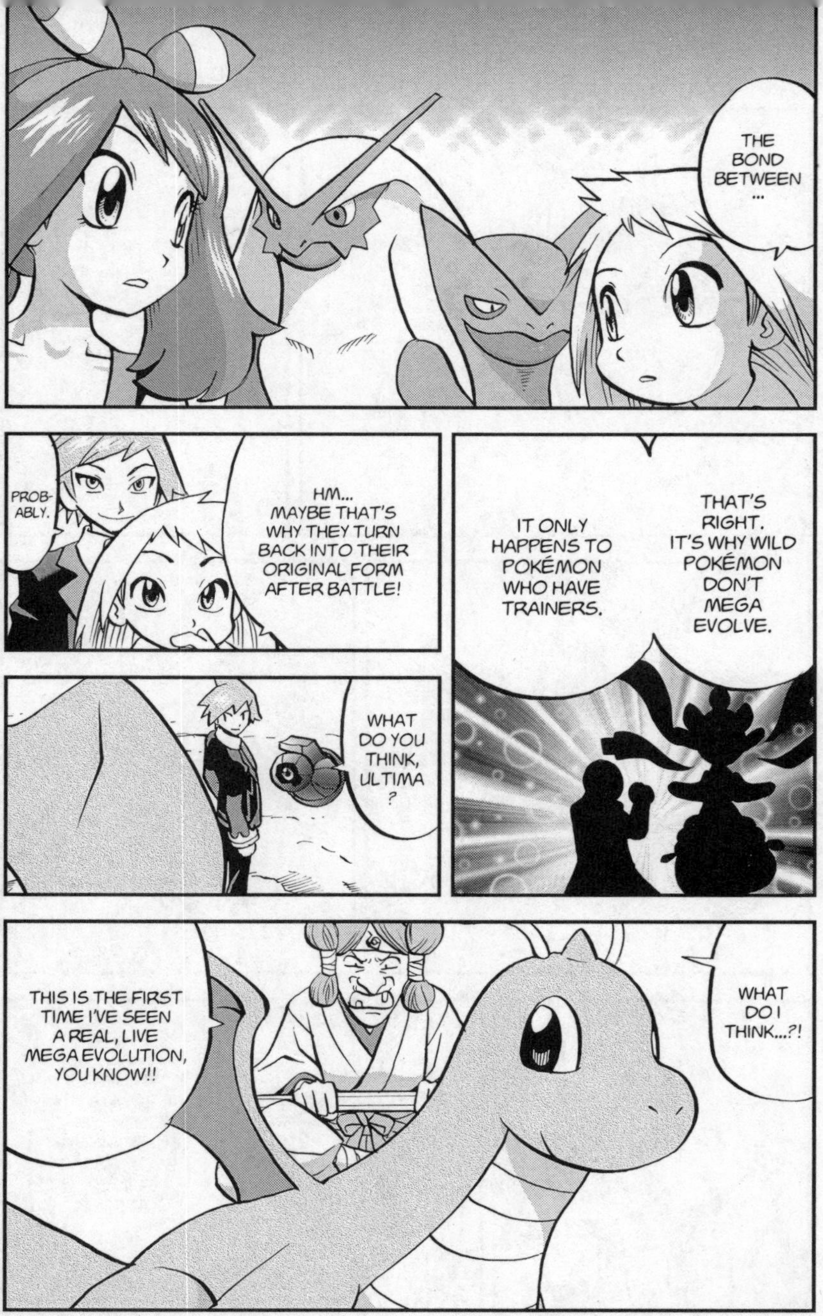
THE BOND BETWEEN ...
THAT'S RIGHT. IT'S WHY WILD POKÉMON DON'T MEGA EVOLVE.
IT ONLY HAPPENS TO POKÉMON WHO HAVE TRAINERS.
HM... MAYBE THAT'S WHY THEY TURN BACK INTO THEIR ORIGINAL FORM AFTER BATTLE!
PROB-ABLY.
WHAT DO YOU THINK, ULTIMA ?
WHAT DO I THINK...?!
THIS IS THE FIRST TIME I'VE SEEN A REAL, LIVE MEGA EVOLUTION, YOU KNOW!!

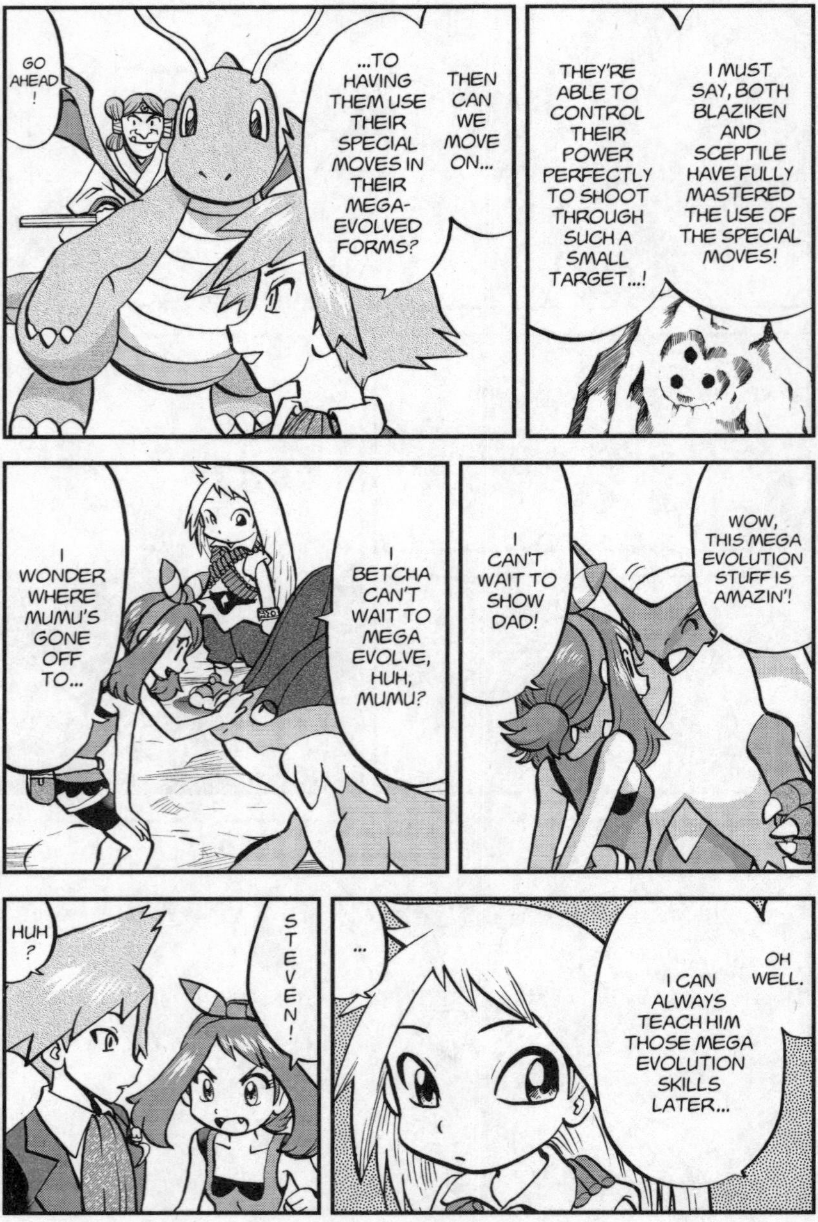
I MUST SAY, BOTH BLAZIKEN AND SCEPTILE HAVE FULLY MASTERED THE USE OF THE SPECIAL MOVES!
THEY'RE ABLE TO CONTROL THEIR POWER PERFECTLY TO SHOOT THROUGH SUCH A SMALL TARGET...!
THEN CAN WE MOVE ON...
...TO HAVING THEM USE THEIR SPECIAL MOVES IN THEIR MEGA-EVOLVED FORMS?
GO AHEAD!
WOW, THIS MEGA EVOLUTION STUFF IS AMAZIN'!
I CAN'T WAIT TO SHOW DAD!
I BETCHA CAN'T WAIT TO MEGA EVOLVE, HUH, MUMU?
I WONDER WHERE MUMU'S GONE OFF TO...
OH WELL.
I CAN ALWAYS TEACH HIM THOSE MEGA EVOLUTION SKILLS LATER...
...
STEVEN!
HUH?

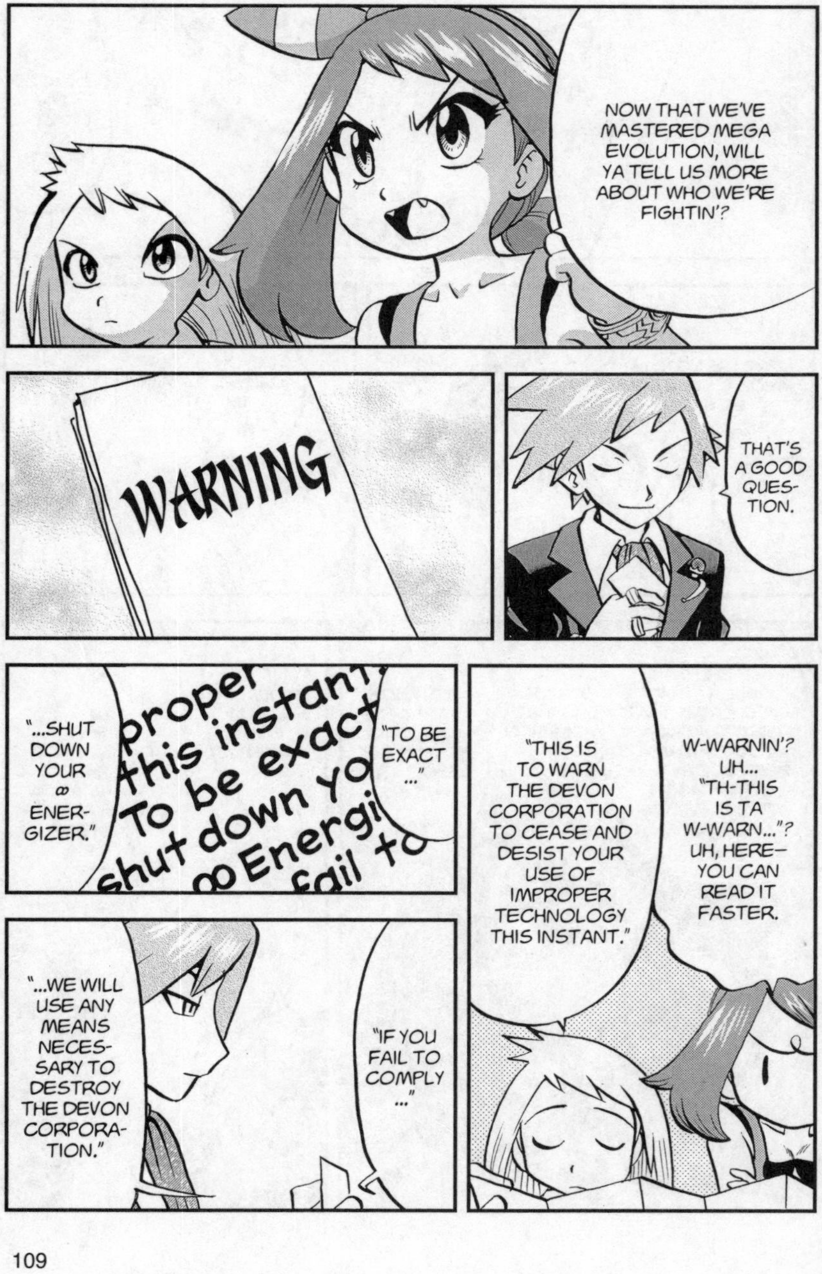
NOW THAT WE'VE MASTERED MEGA EVOLUTION, WILL YA TELL US MORE ABOUT WHO WE'RE FIGHTIN'?
THAT'S A GOOD QUES-TION.
WARNING
W-WARNIN'? UH... "TH-THIS IS TA W-WARN..."? UH, HERE— YOU CAN READ IT FASTER.
"THIS IS TO WARN THE DEVON CORPORATION TO CEASE AND DESIST YOUR USE OF IMPROPER TECHNOLOGY THIS INSTANT."
"TO BE EXACT..."
proper
this instant.
To be exact
shut down yo
∞Energi
fail to
"...SHUT DOWN YOUR ∞ ENER-GIZER."
"IF YOU FAIL TO COMPLY..."
"...WE WILL USE ANY MEANS NECES-SARY TO DESTROY THE DEVON CORPORA-TION."

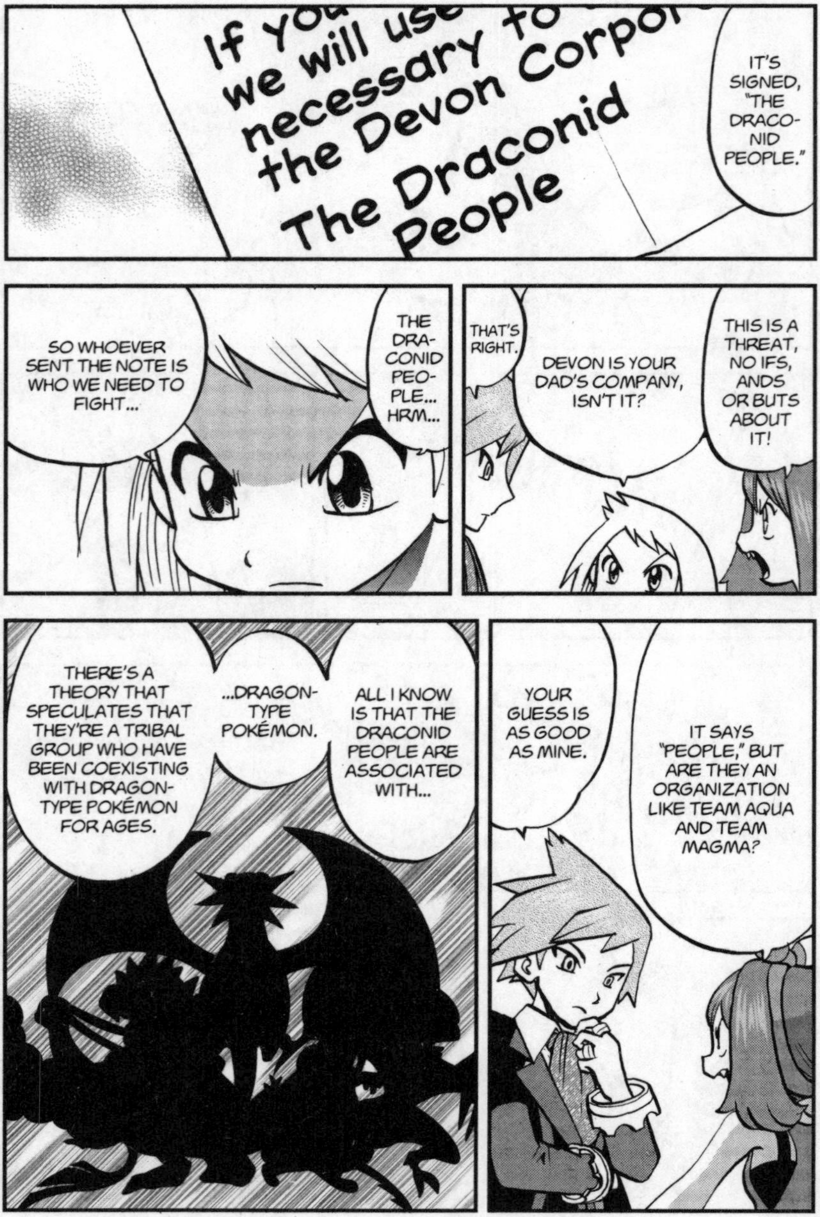
If you
we will use
necessary to
the Devon Corpor
The Draconid
People
IT'S SIGNED, "THE DRACONID PEOPLE."
THIS IS A THREAT, NO IFS, ANDS OR BUTS ABOUT IT!
DEVON IS YOUR DAD'S COMPANY, ISN'T IT?
THAT'S RIGHT.
THE DRACONID PEOPLE... HRM...
SO WHOEVER SENT THE NOTE IS WHO WE NEED TO FIGHT...
IT SAYS "PEOPLE," BUT ARE THEY AN ORGANIZATION LIKE TEAM AQUA AND TEAM MAGMA?
YOUR GUESS IS AS GOOD AS MINE.
ALL I KNOW IS THAT THE DRACONID PEOPLE ARE ASSOCIATED WITH...
...DRAGON-TYPE POKÉMON.
THERE'S A THEORY THAT SPECULATES THAT THEY'RE A TRIBAL GROUP WHO HAVE BEEN COEXISTING WITH DRAGON-TYPE POKÉMON FOR AGES.

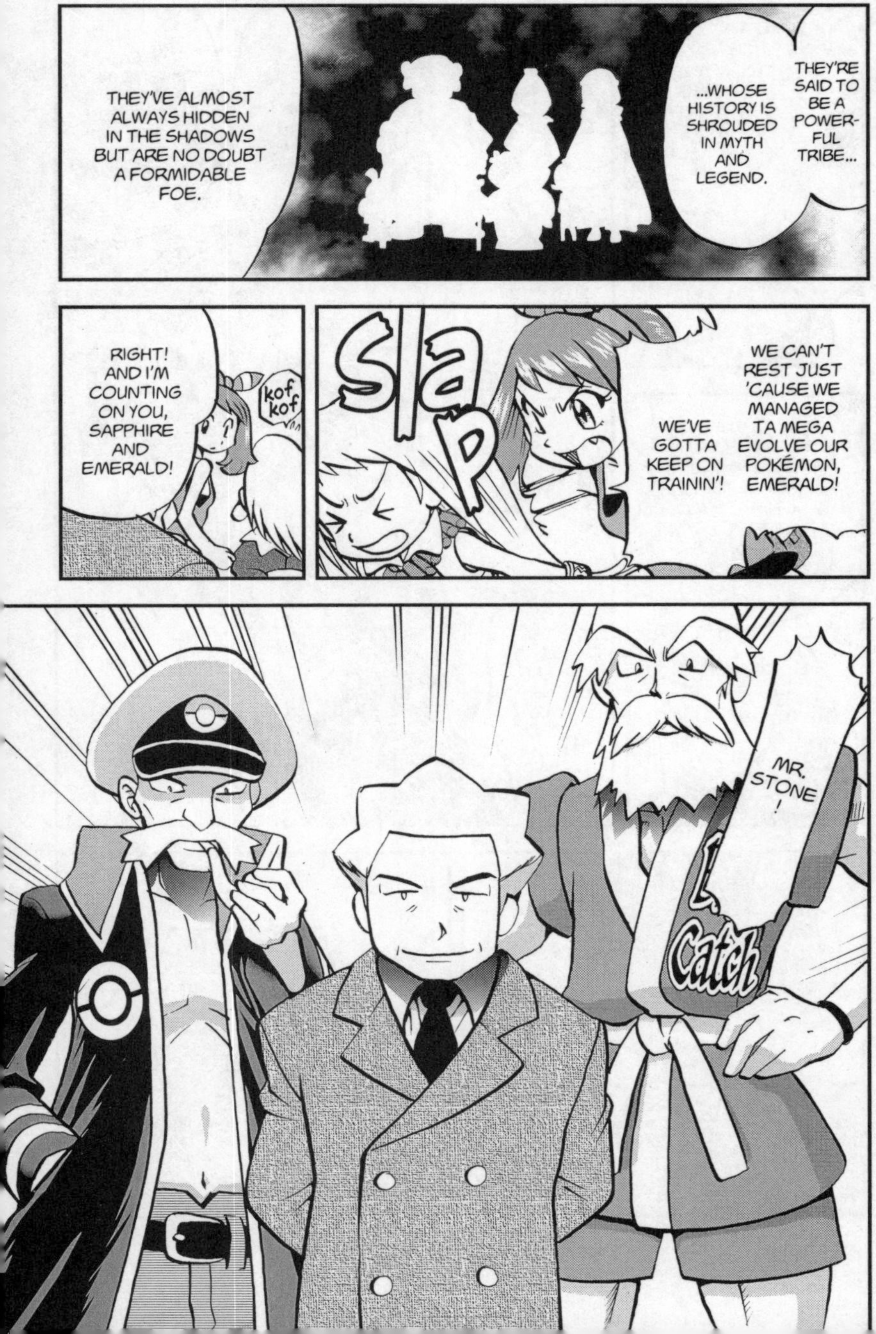
THEY'RE SAID TO BE A POWER-FUL TRIBE...
...WHOSE HISTORY IS SHROUDED IN MYTH AND LEGEND.
THEY'VE ALMOST ALWAYS HIDDEN IN THE SHADOWS BUT ARE NO DOUBT A FORMIDABLE FOE.
WE CAN'T REST JUST 'CAUSE WE MANAGED TA MEGA EVOLVE OUR POKÉMON, EMERALD!
WE'VE GOTTA KEEP ON TRAININ'!
slap
kof kof
RIGHT! AND I'M COUNTING ON YOU, SAPPHIRE AND EMERALD!
MR. STONE!
Catch

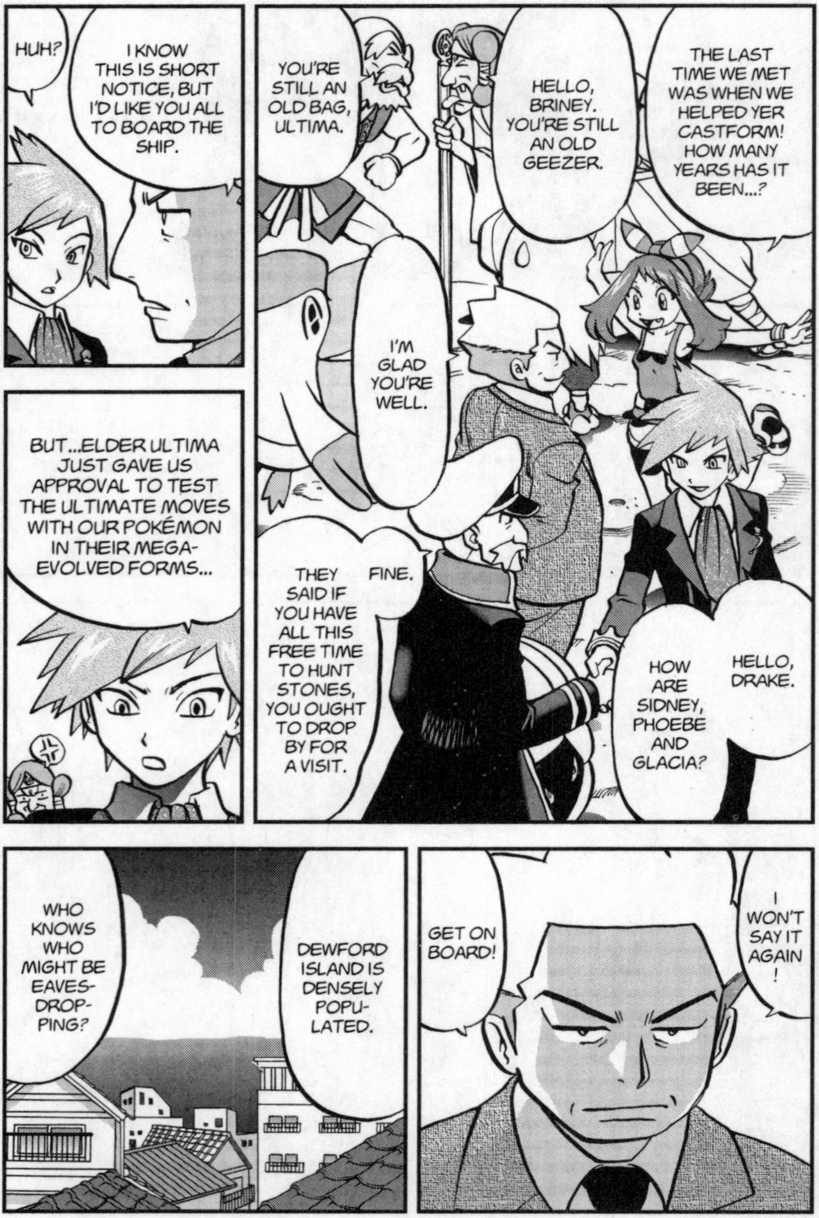
THE LAST TIME WE MET WAS WHEN WE HELPED YER CASTFORM! HOW MANY YEARS HAS IT BEEN...?
HELLO, BRINEY. YOU'RE STILL AN OLD GEEZER.
YOU'RE STILL AN OLD BAG, ULTIMA.
I'M GLAD YOU'RE WELL.
HELLO, DRAKE.
HOW ARE SIDNEY, PHOEBE AND GLACIA?
FINE.
THEY SAID IF YOU HAVE ALL THIS FREE TIME TO HUNT STONES, YOU OUGHT TO DROP BY FOR A VISIT.
I KNOW THIS IS SHORT NOTICE, BUT I'D LIKE YOU ALL TO BOARD THE SHIP.
HUH?
BUT...ELDER ULTIMA JUST GAVE US APPROVAL TO TEST THE ULTIMATE MOVES WITH OUR POKÉMON IN THEIR MEGA-EVOLVED FORMS...
I WON'T SAY IT AGAIN!
GET ON BOARD!
DEWFORD ISLAND IS DENSELY POPU-LATED.
WHO KNOWS WHO MIGHT BE EAVES-DROP-PING?

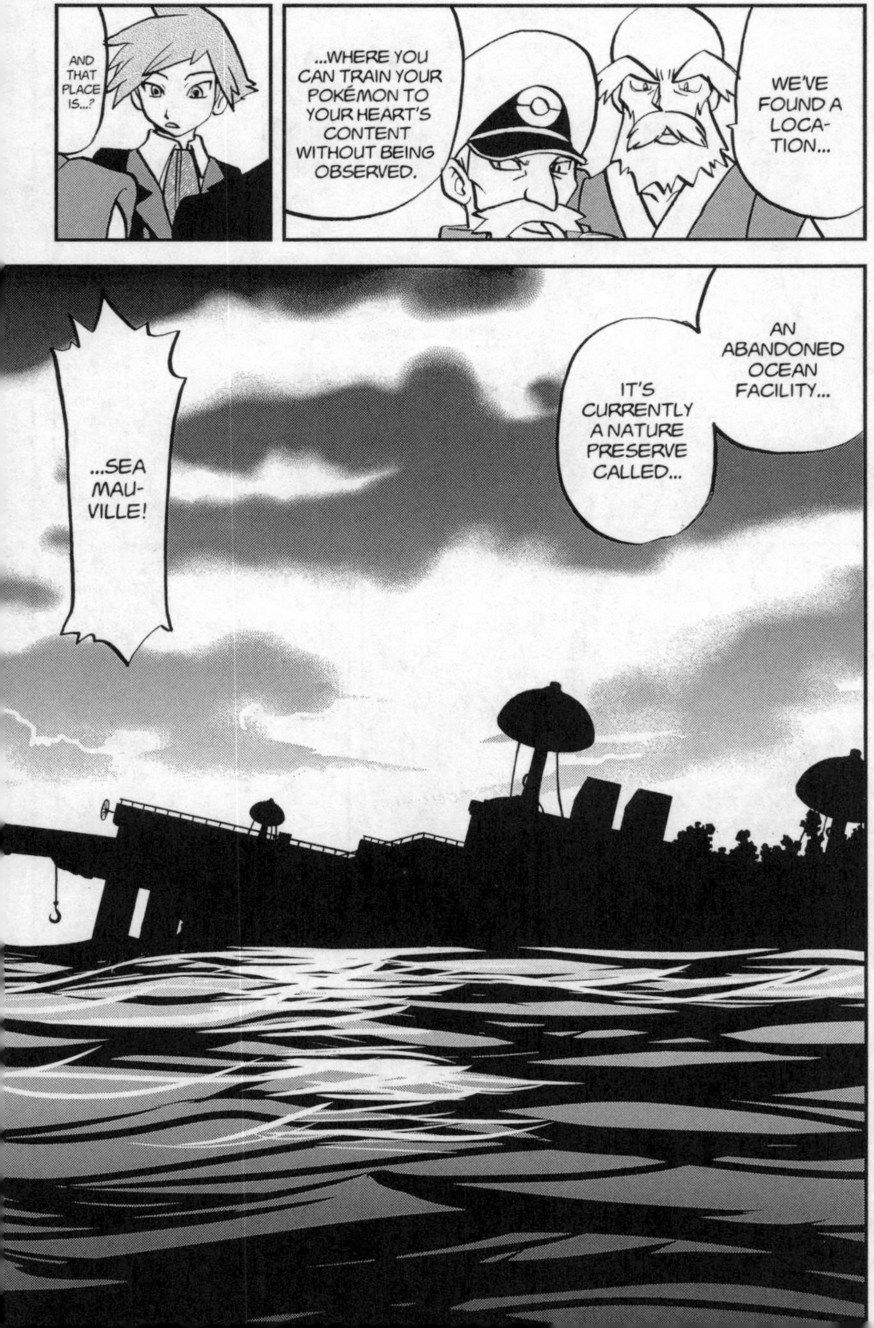
WE'VE FOUND A LOCATION...
...WHERE YOU CAN TRAIN YOUR POKÉMON TO YOUR HEART'S CONTENT WITHOUT BEING OBSERVED.
AND THAT PLACE IS...?
AN ABANDONED OCEAN FACILITY...
IT'S CURRENTLY A NATURE PRESERVE CALLED...
...SEA MAUVILLE!

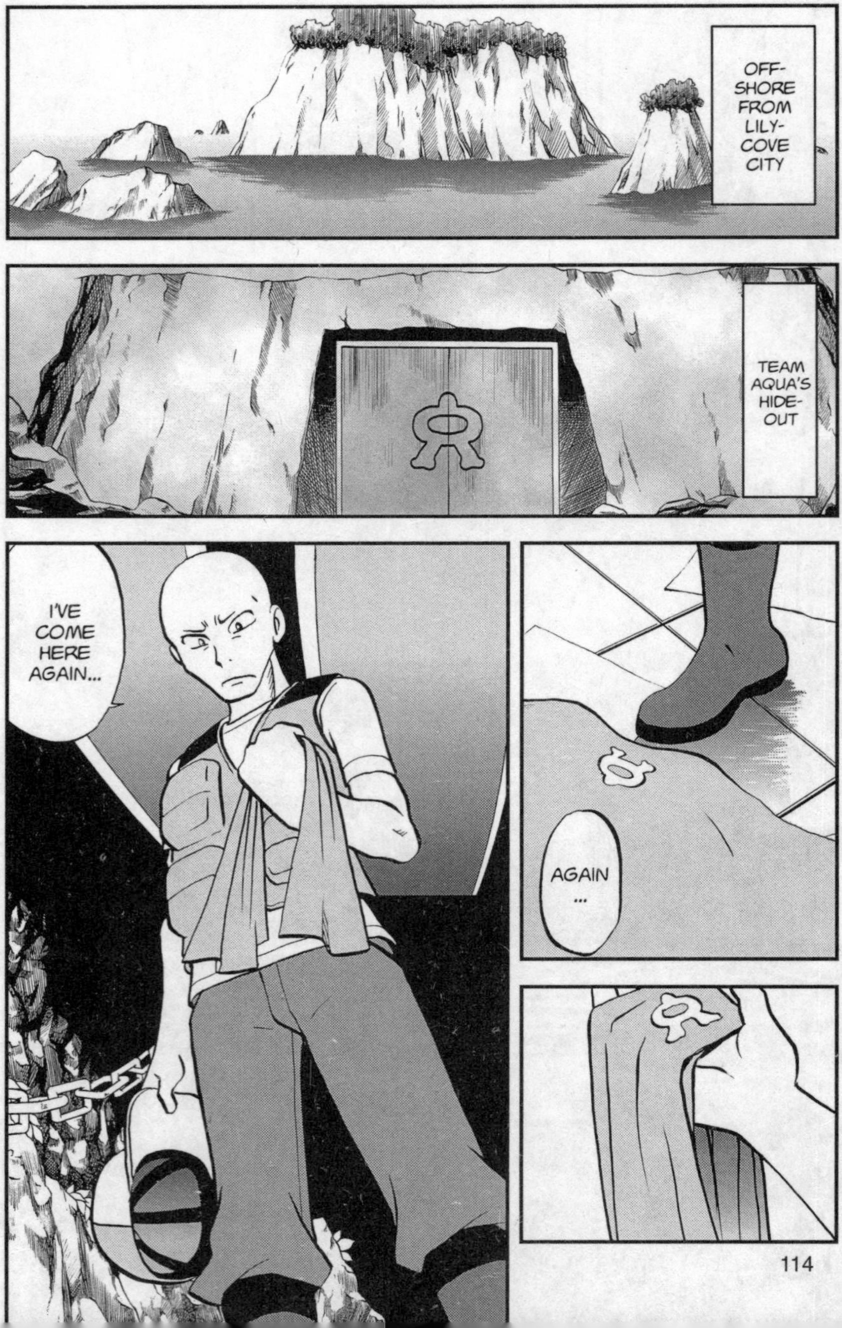
OFF-SHORE FROM LILY-COVE CITY
TEAM AQUA'S HIDE-OUT
AGAIN ...
I'VE COME HERE AGAIN...

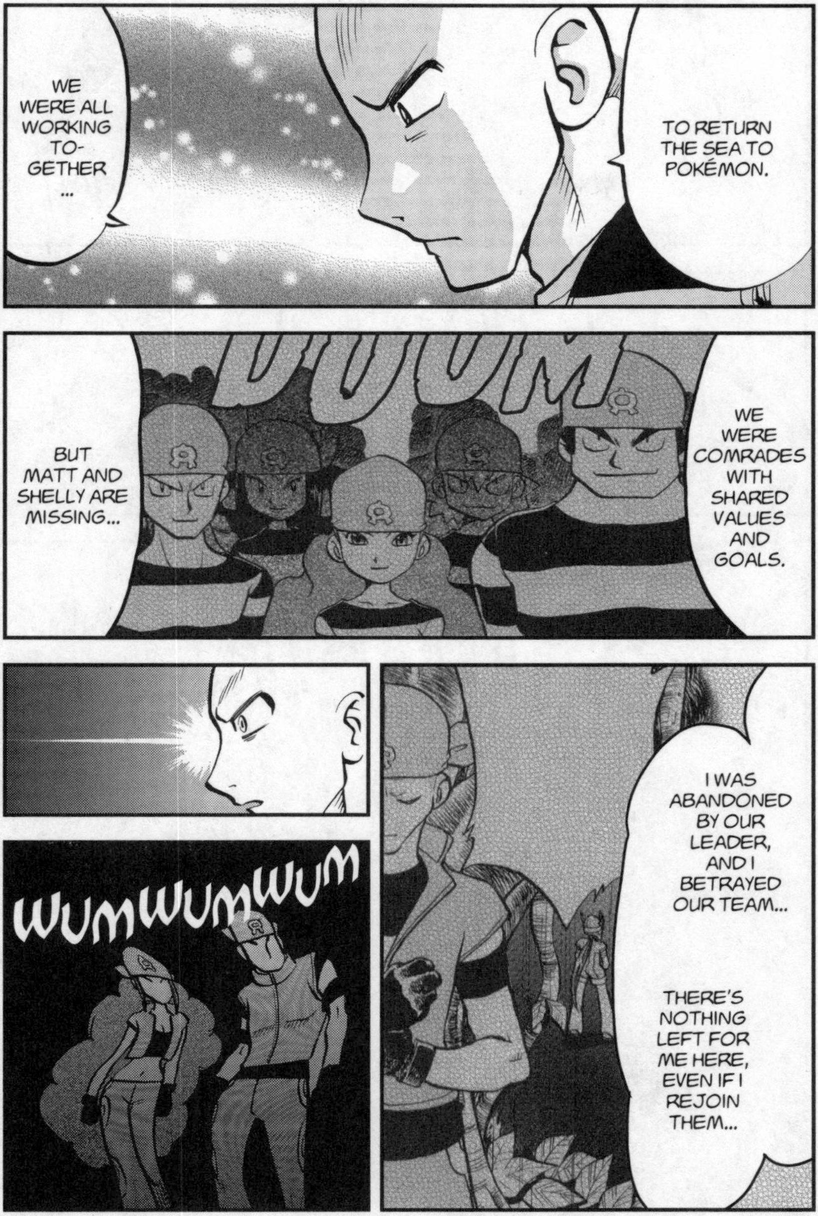
WE WERE ALL WORKING TO-GETHER ...
TO RETURN THE SEA TO POKÉMON.
DOOM
WE WERE COMRADES WITH SHARED VALUES AND GOALS.
BUT MATT AND SHELLY ARE MISSING...
I WAS ABANDONED BY OUR LEADER, AND I BETRAYED OUR TEAM...
THERE'S NOTHING LEFT FOR ME HERE, EVEN IF I REJOIN THEM...
WUMWUMWUM

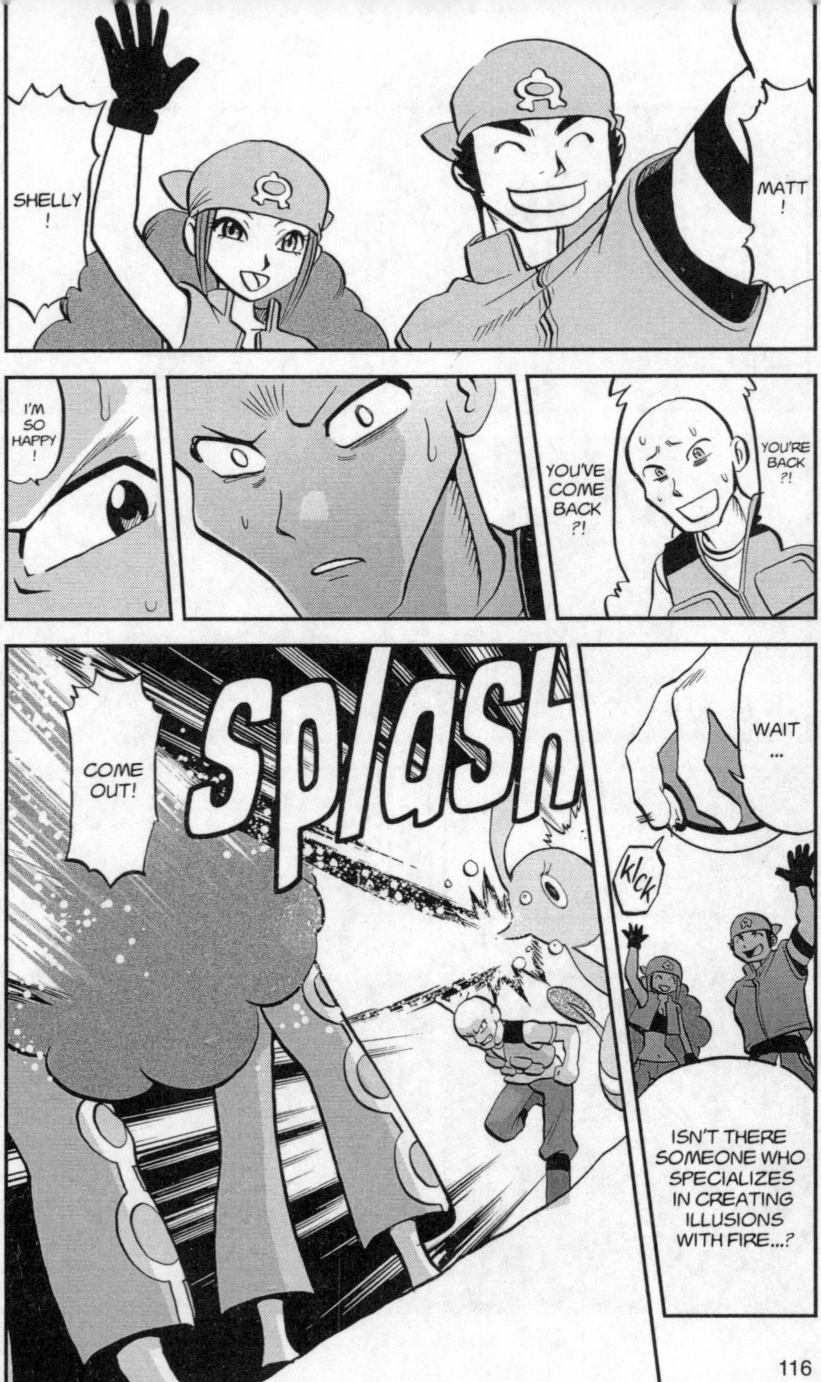
MATT !
SHELLY !
YOU'RE BACK ?!
YOU'VE COME BACK ?!
I'M SO HAPPY !
WAIT ...
KICK
ISN'T THERE SOMEONE WHO SPECIALIZES IN CREATING ILLUSIONS WITH FIRE...?
SPLASH
COME OUT!

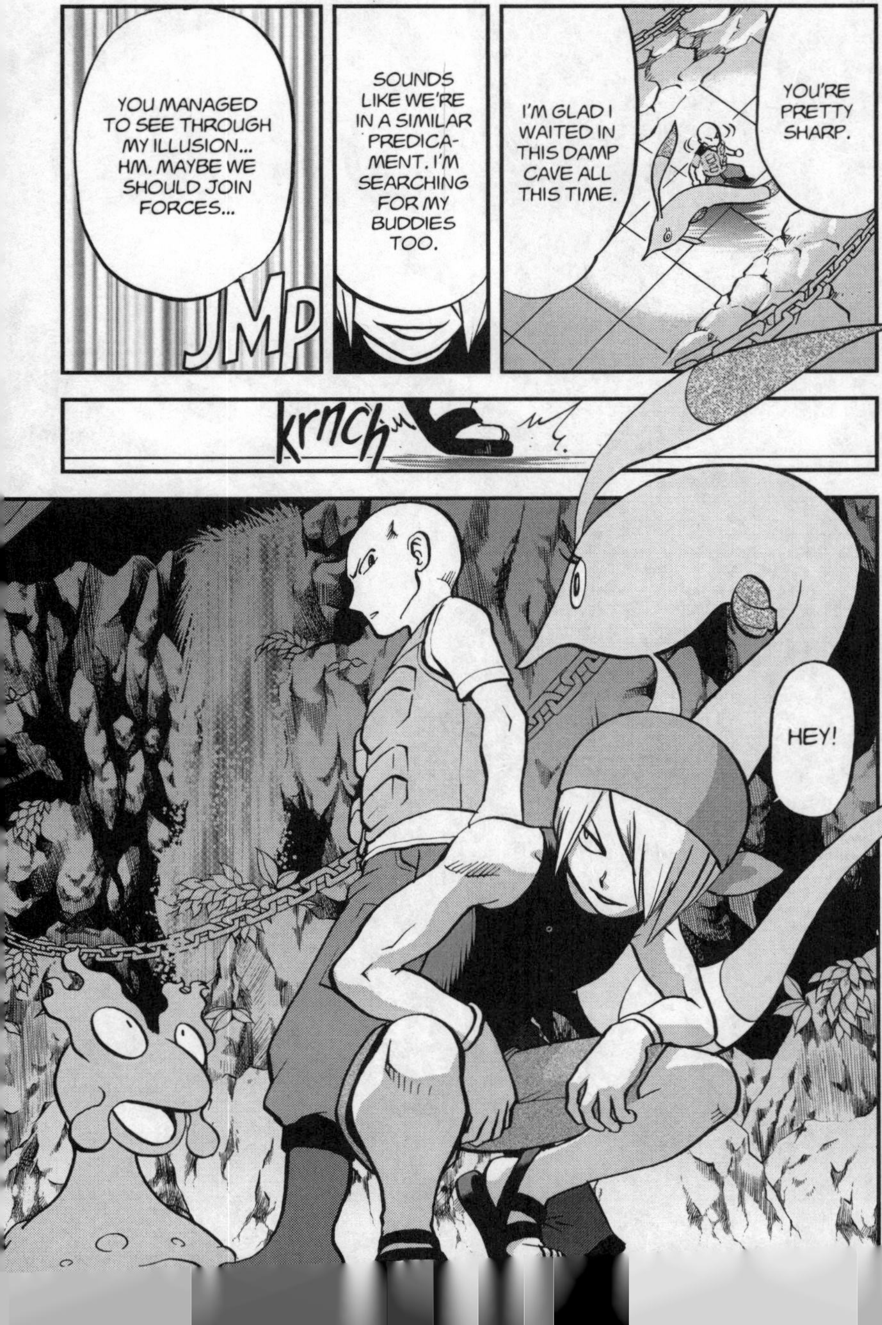

YOU'RE PRETTY SHARP.
I'M GLAD I WAITED IN THIS DAMP CAVE ALL THIS TIME.
SOUNDS LIKE WE'RE IN A SIMILAR PREDICAMENT. I'M SEARCHING FOR MY BUDDIES TOO.
YOU MANAGED TO SEE THROUGH MY ILLUSION... HM. MAYBE WE SHOULD JOIN FORCES...
JMP
KRNCH
HEY!

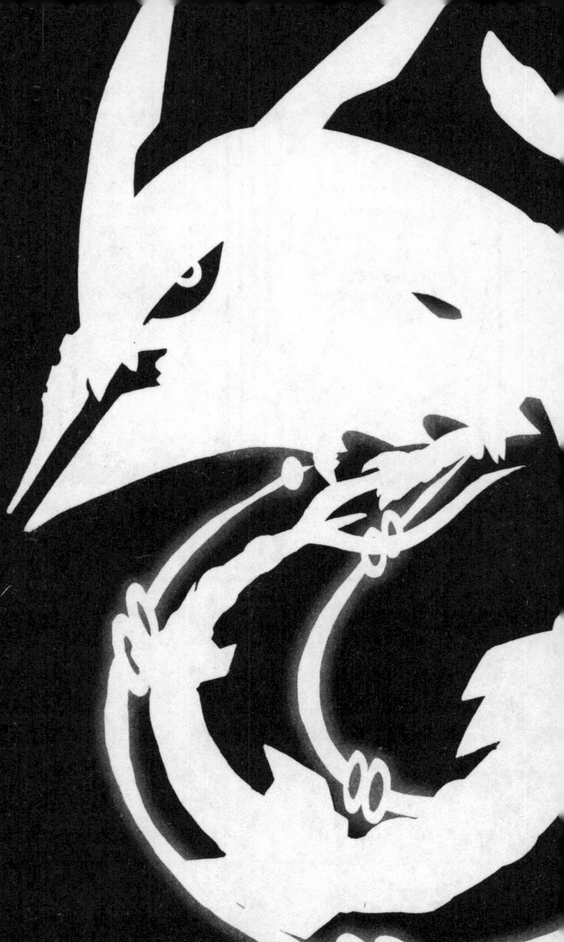

ADVENTURE #6

Beedrill Prepares

POKÉMON™ ADVENTURES
OMEGA RUBY • ALPHA SAPPHIRE

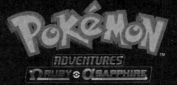

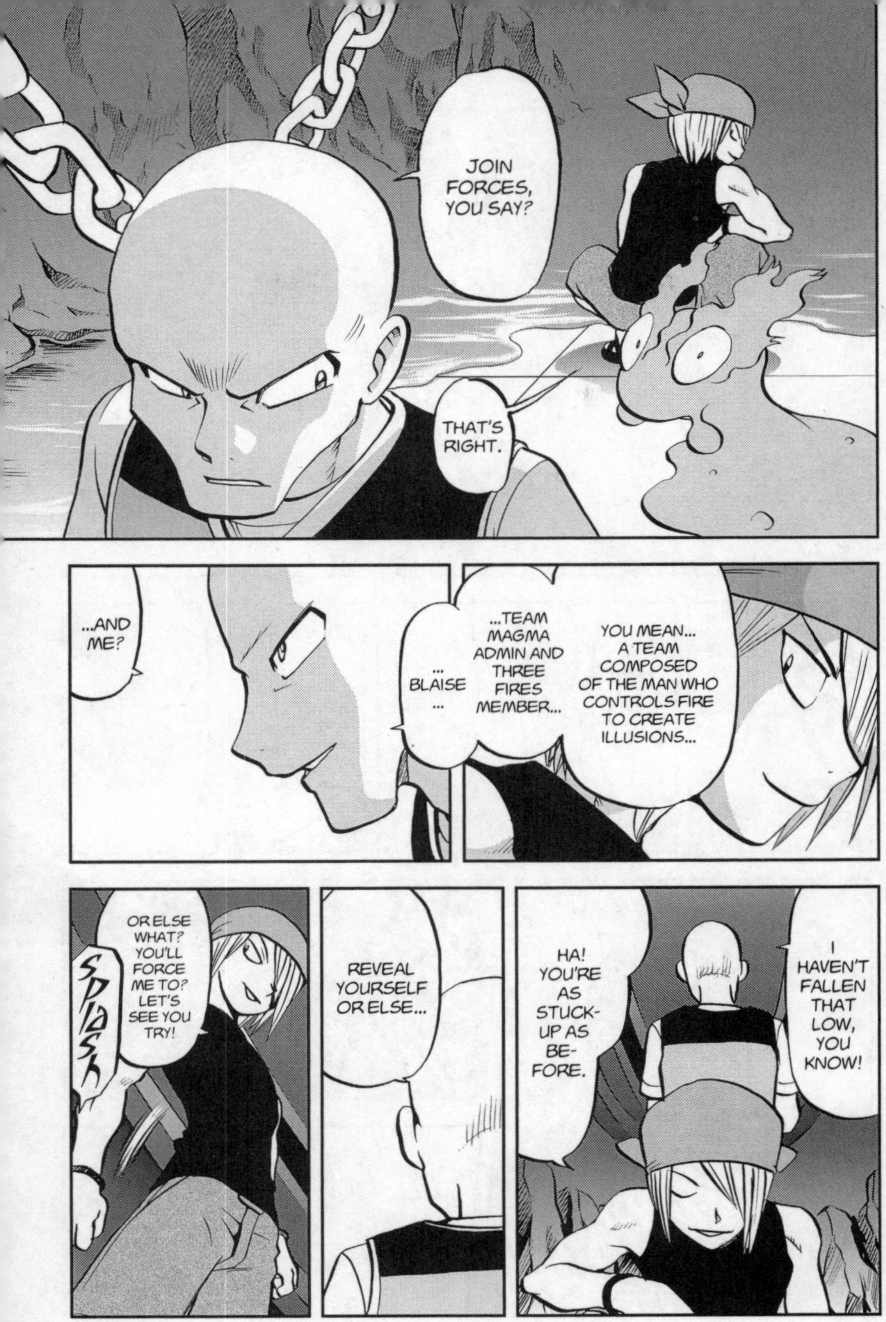
JOIN FORCES, YOU SAY?
THAT'S RIGHT.
YOU MEAN... A TEAM COMPOSED OF THE MAN WHO CONTROLS FIRE TO CREATE ILLUSIONS...
...TEAM MAGMA ADMIN AND THREE FIRES MEMBER...
... BLAISE ...
...AND ME?
I HAVEN'T FALLEN THAT LOW, YOU KNOW!
HA! YOU'RE AS STUCK-UP AS BE-FORE.
REVEAL YOURSELF OR ELSE...
OR ELSE WHAT? YOU'LL FORCE ME TO? LET'S SEE YOU TRY!
SPLASH

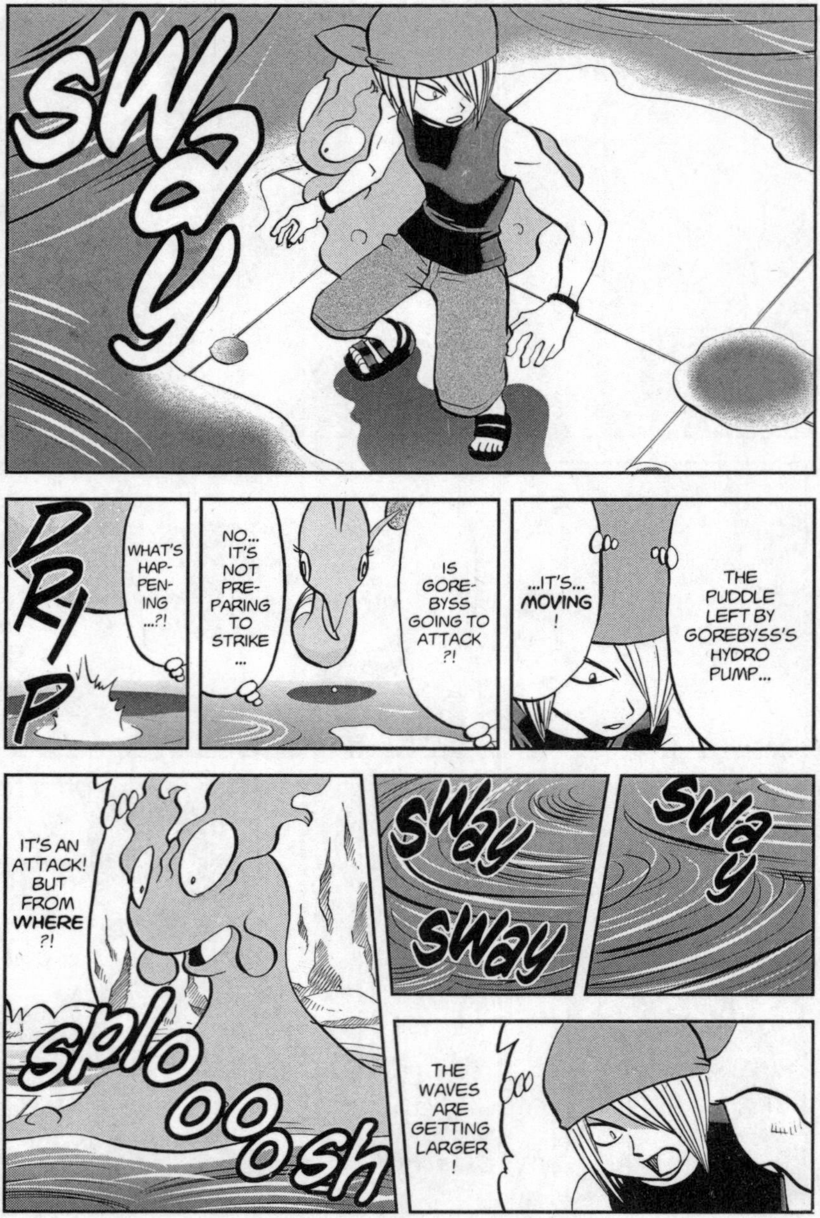
sway
THE PUDDLE LEFT BY GOREBYSS'S HYDRO PUMP...
...IT'S... MOVING!
IS GOREBYSS GOING TO ATTACK?!
NO... IT'S NOT PREPARING TO STRIKE...
WHAT'S HAPPENING...?!
DRIP
sway
sway
sway
THE WAVES ARE GETTING LARGER!
IT'S AN ATTACK! BUT FROM WHERE?!
splooooosh

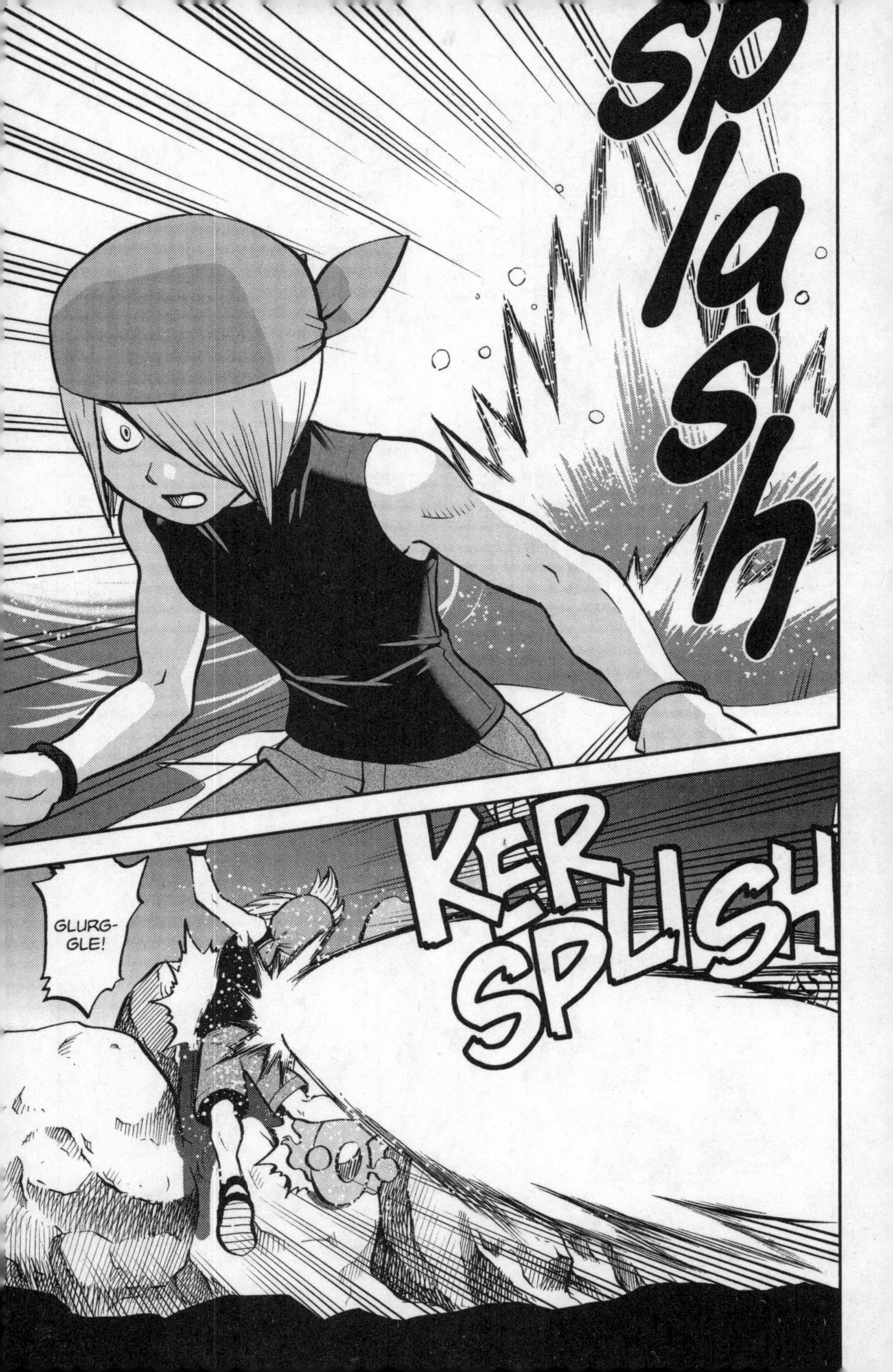
SPLASH
KER SPLISH
GLURG-GLE!

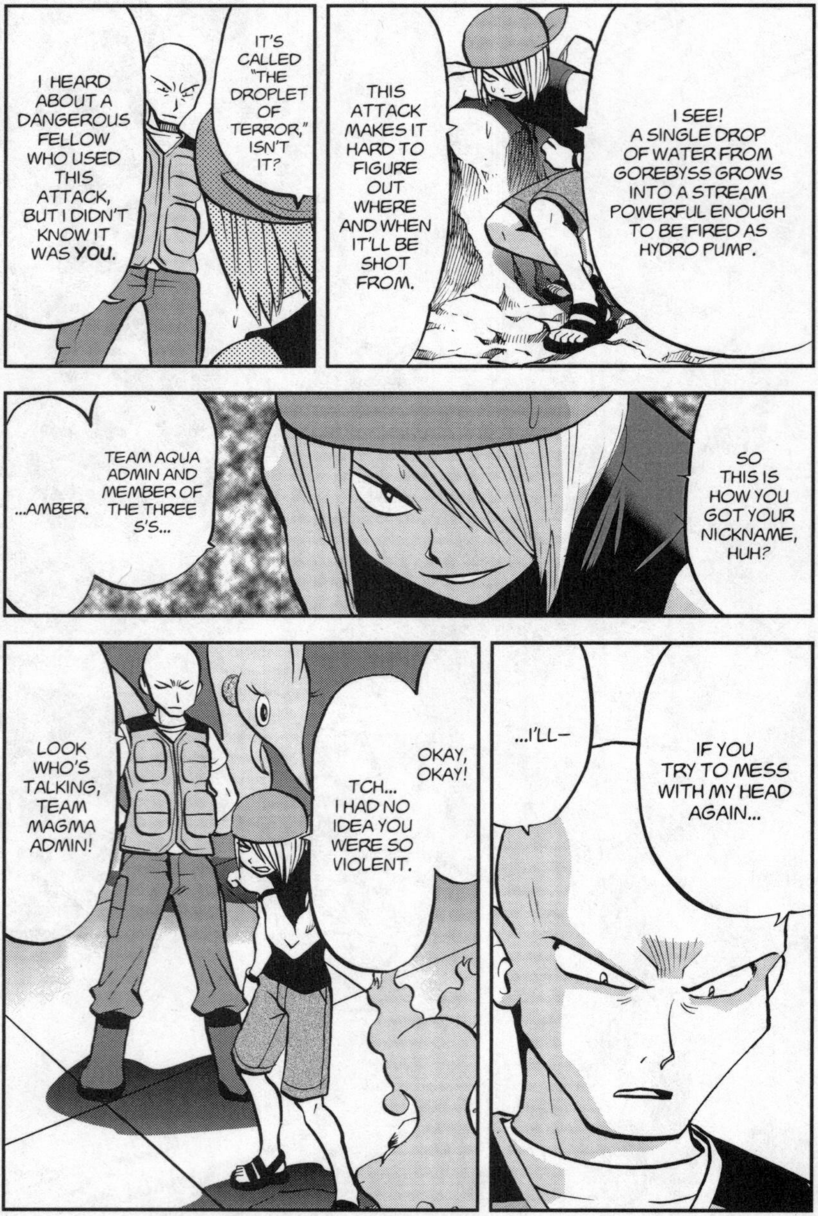
I SEE! A SINGLE DROP OF WATER FROM GOREBYSS GROWS INTO A STREAM POWERFUL ENOUGH TO BE FIRED AS HYDRO PUMP.
THIS ATTACK MAKES IT HARD TO FIGURE OUT WHERE AND WHEN IT'LL BE SHOT FROM.
IT'S CALLED "THE DROPLET OF TERROR," ISN'T IT?
I HEARD ABOUT A DANGEROUS FELLOW WHO USED THIS ATTACK, BUT I DIDN'T KNOW IT WAS **YOU**.
SO THIS IS HOW YOU GOT YOUR NICKNAME, HUH?
TEAM AQUA ADMIN AND MEMBER OF THE THREE S'S...
...AMBER.
IF YOU TRY TO MESS WITH MY HEAD AGAIN...
...I'LL–
OKAY, OKAY!
TCH... I HAD NO IDEA YOU WERE SO VIOLENT.
LOOK WHO'S TALKING, TEAM MAGMA ADMIN!

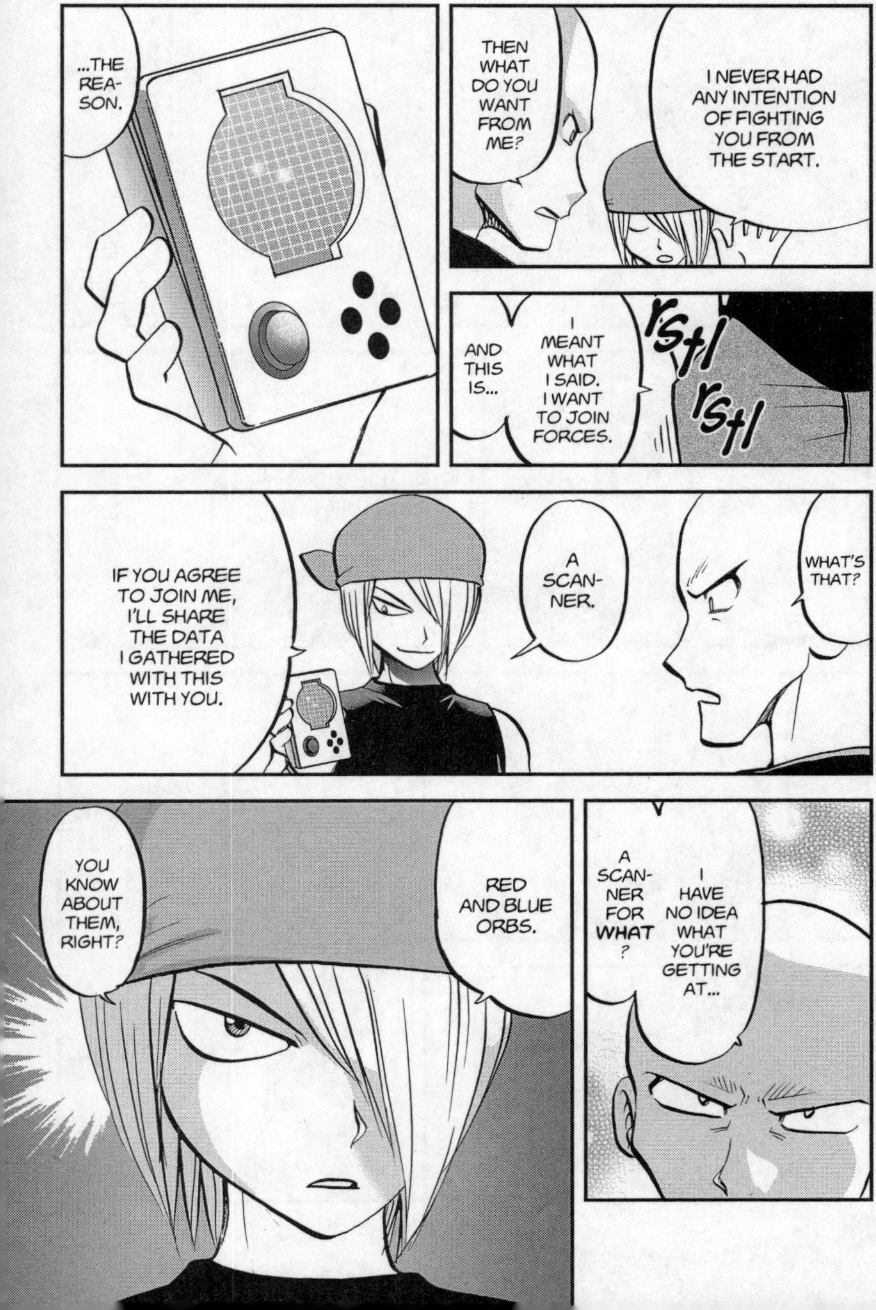
I NEVER HAD ANY INTENTION OF FIGHTING YOU FROM THE START.
THEN WHAT DO YOU WANT FROM ME?
rstl rstl
I MEANT WHAT I SAID. I WANT TO JOIN FORCES.
AND THIS IS...
...THE REASON.
WHAT'S THAT?
A SCANNER.
IF YOU AGREE TO JOIN ME, I'LL SHARE THE DATA I GATHERED WITH THIS WITH YOU.
I HAVE NO IDEA WHAT YOU'RE GETTING AT...
A SCANNER FOR **WHAT**?
RED AND BLUE ORBS.
YOU KNOW ABOUT THEM, RIGHT?

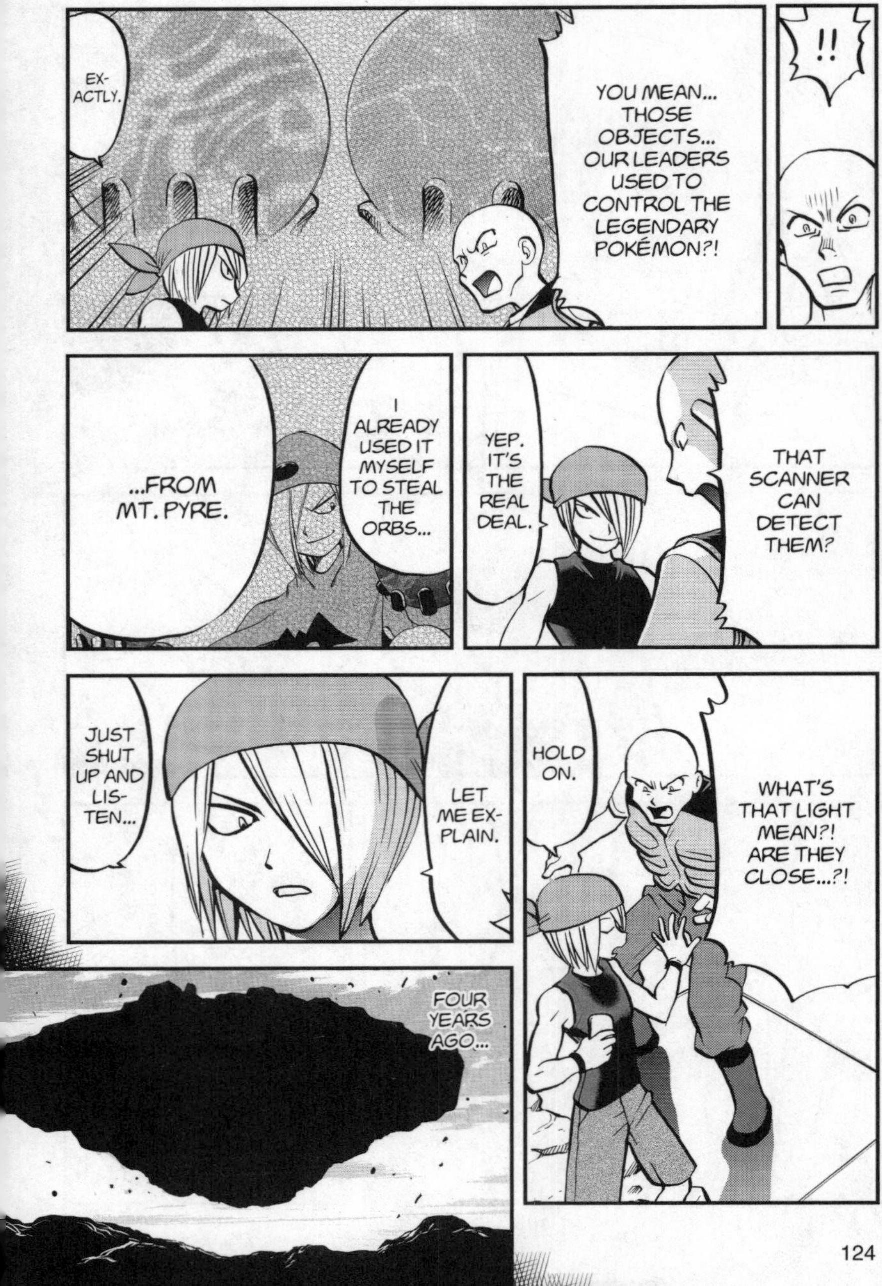
!!
YOU MEAN... THOSE OBJECTS... OUR LEADERS USED TO CONTROL THE LEGENDARY POKÉMON?!
EX-ACTLY.
THAT SCANNER CAN DETECT THEM?
YEP. IT'S THE REAL DEAL.
I ALREADY USED IT MYSELF TO STEAL THE ORBS...
...FROM MT. PYRE.
WHAT'S THAT LIGHT MEAN?! ARE THEY CLOSE...?!
HOLD ON.
LET ME EX-PLAIN.
JUST SHUT UP AND LIS-TEN...
FOUR YEARS AGO...

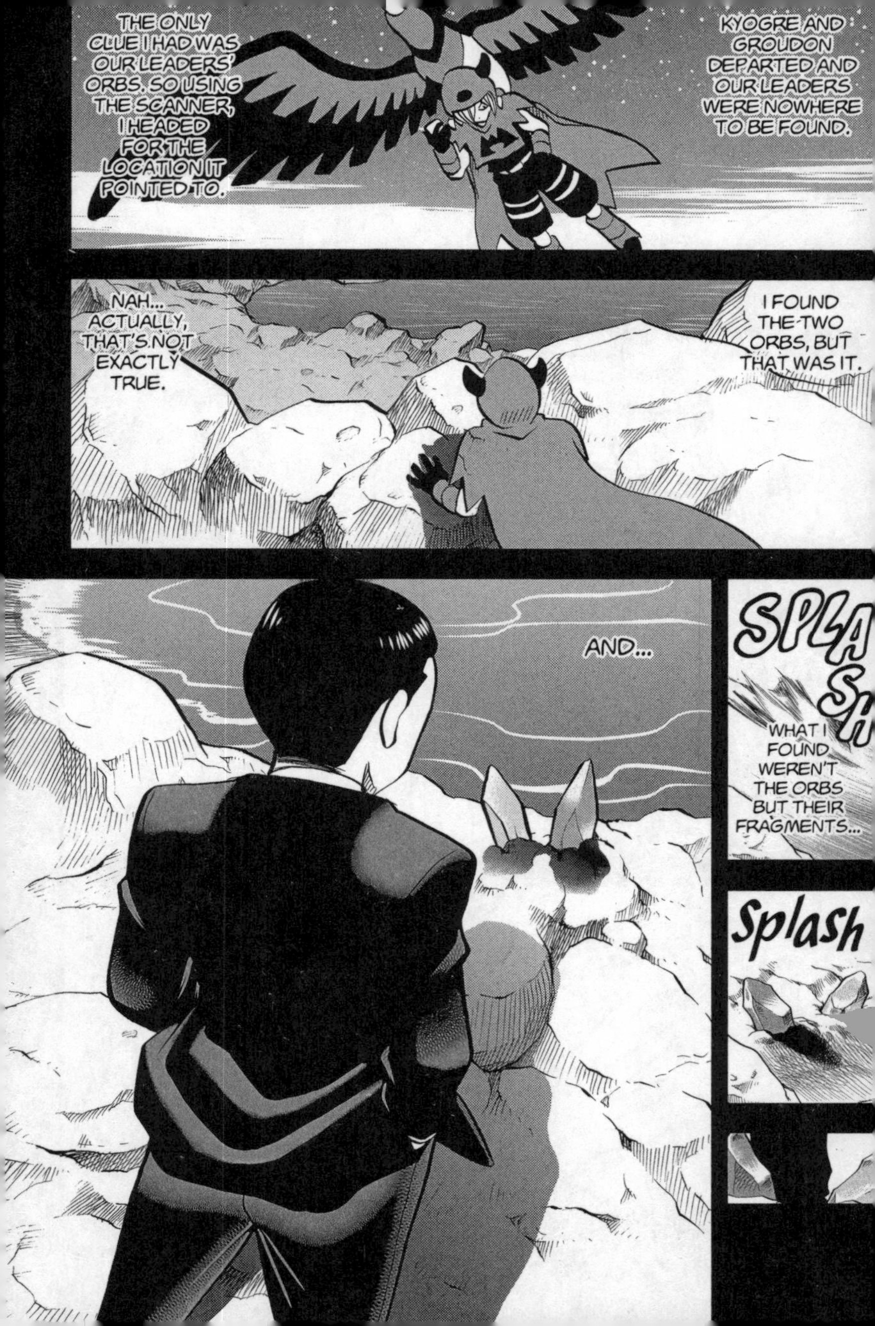
KYOGRE AND GROUDON DEPARTED AND OUR LEADERS WERE NOWHERE TO BE FOUND.
THE ONLY CLUE I HAD WAS OUR LEADERS' ORBS. SO USING THE SCANNER, I HEADED FOR THE LOCATION IT POINTED TO.
I FOUND THE TWO ORBS, BUT THAT WAS IT.
NAH... ACTUALLY, THAT'S NOT EXACTLY TRUE.
SPLA SH
WHAT I FOUND WEREN'T THE ORBS BUT THEIR FRAGMENTS...
Splash
AND...

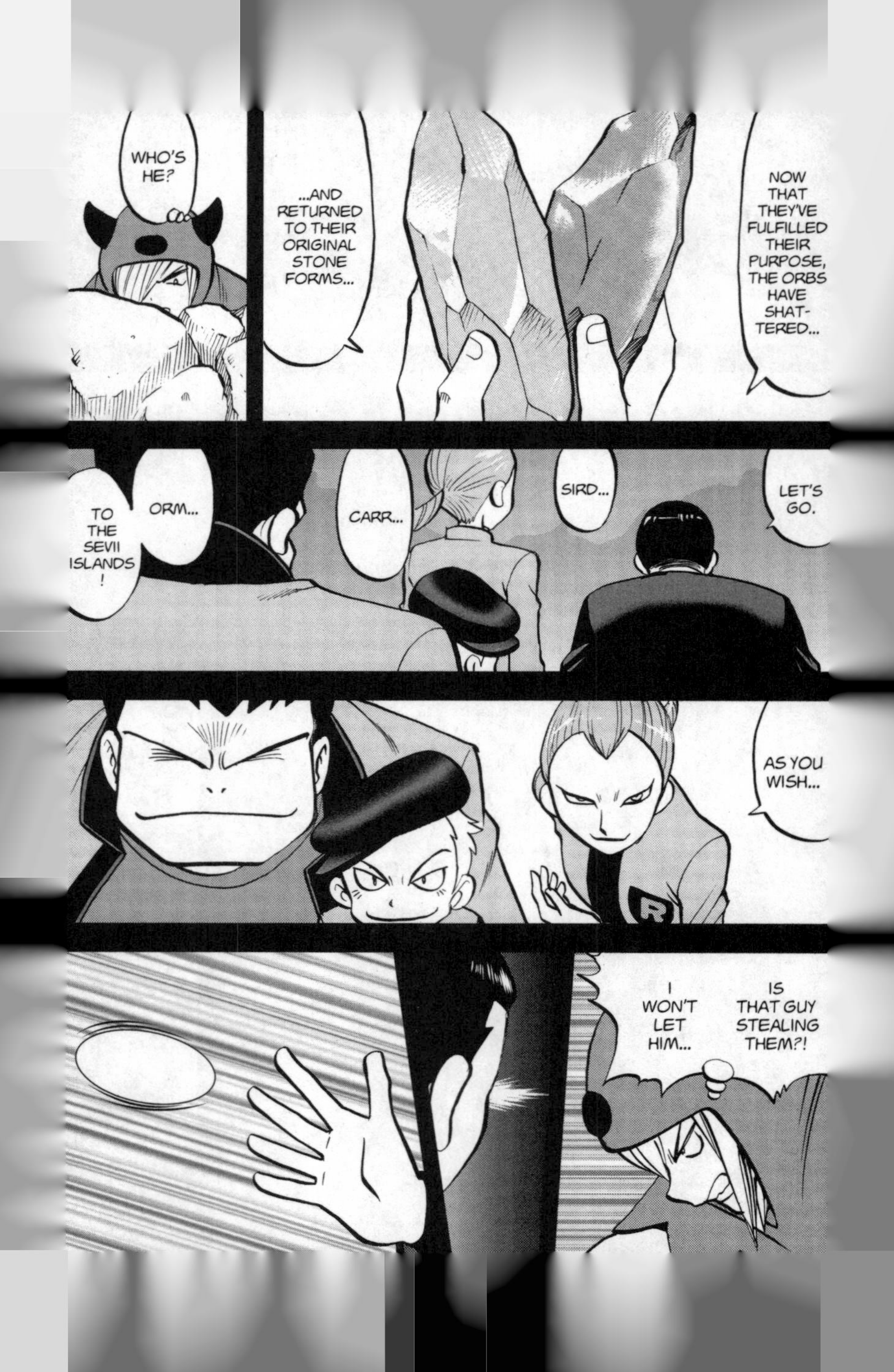
NOW THAT THEY'VE FULFILLED THEIR PURPOSE, THE ORBS HAVE SHAT-TERED...
...AND RETURNED TO THEIR ORIGINAL STONE FORMS...
WHO'S HE?
LET'S GO.
SIRD...
CARR...
ORM...
TO THE SEVII ISLANDS!
AS YOU WISH...
IS THAT GUY STEALING THEM?!
I WON'T LET HIM...

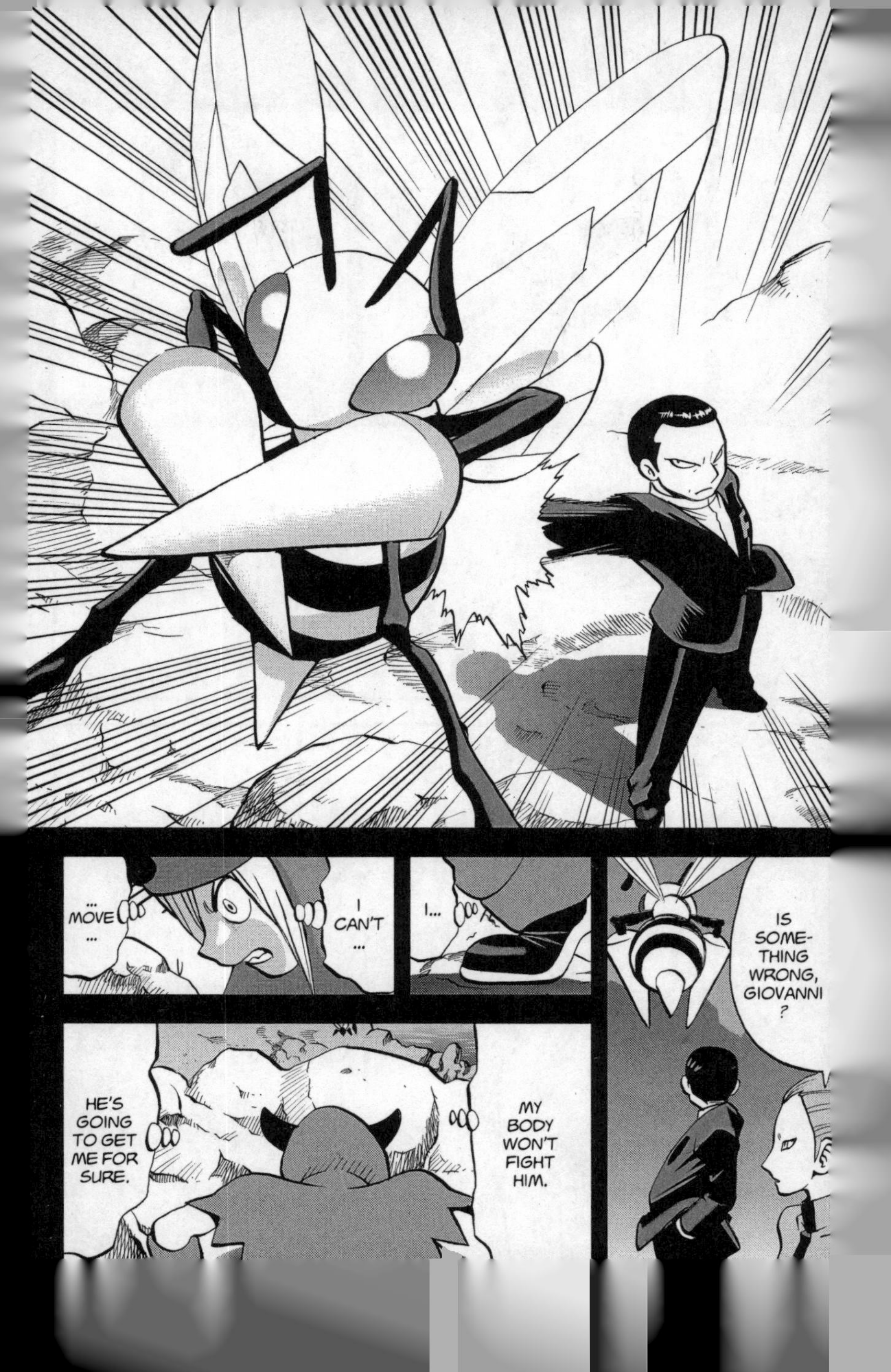
IS SOME-THING WRONG, GIOVANNI?
I...
I CAN'T ...
... MOVE ...
MY BODY WON'T FIGHT HIM.
HE'S GOING TO GET ME FOR SURE.

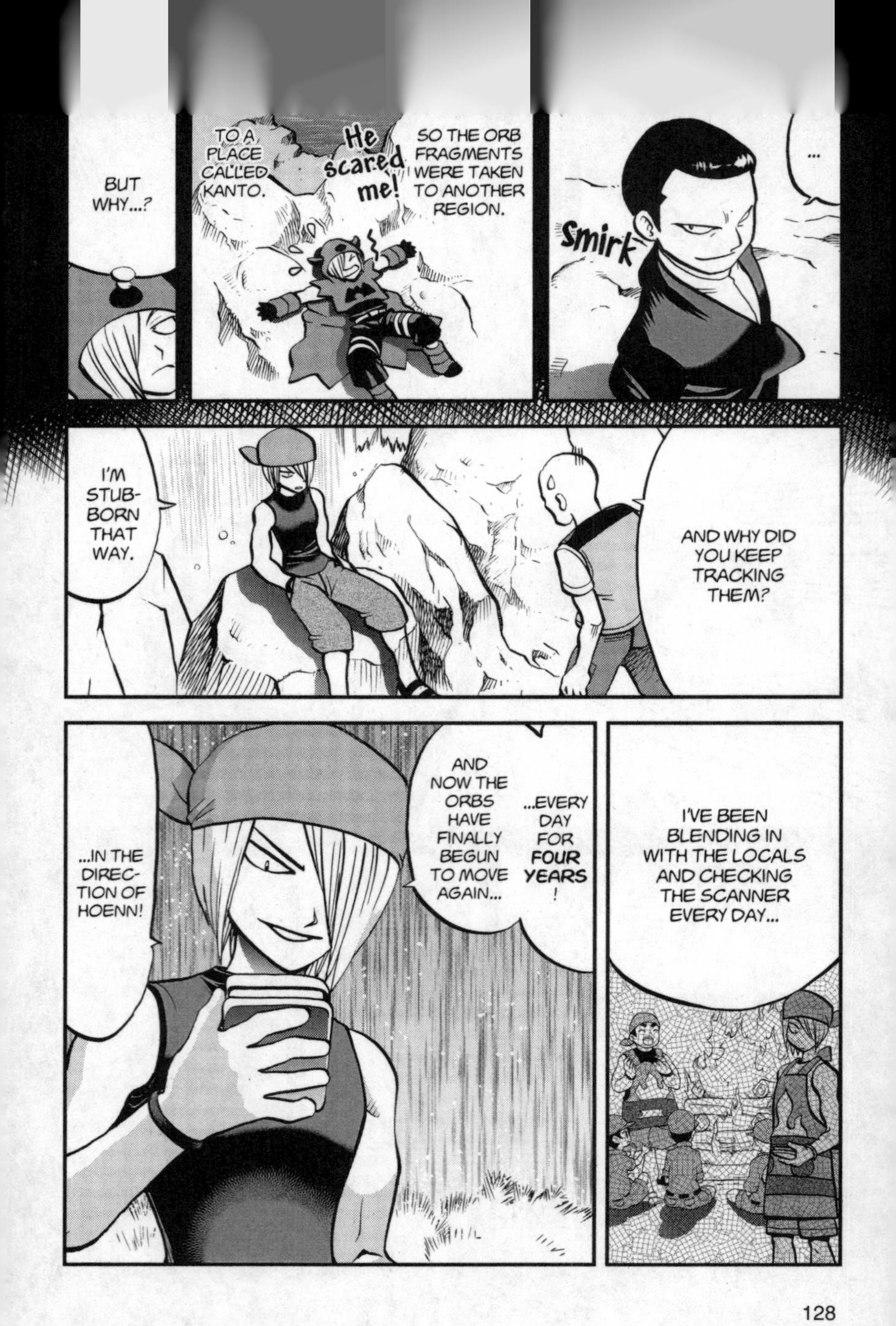
...
Smirk
SO THE ORB FRAGMENTS WERE TAKEN TO ANOTHER REGION.
He scared me!
TO A PLACE CALLED KANTO.
BUT WHY...?
AND WHY DID YOU KEEP TRACKING THEM?
I'M STUB-BORN THAT WAY.
I'VE BEEN BLENDING IN WITH THE LOCALS AND CHECKING THE SCANNER EVERY DAY...
...EVERY DAY FOR **FOUR YEARS**!
AND NOW THE ORBS HAVE FINALLY BEGUN TO MOVE AGAIN...
...IN THE DIREC-TION OF HOENN!

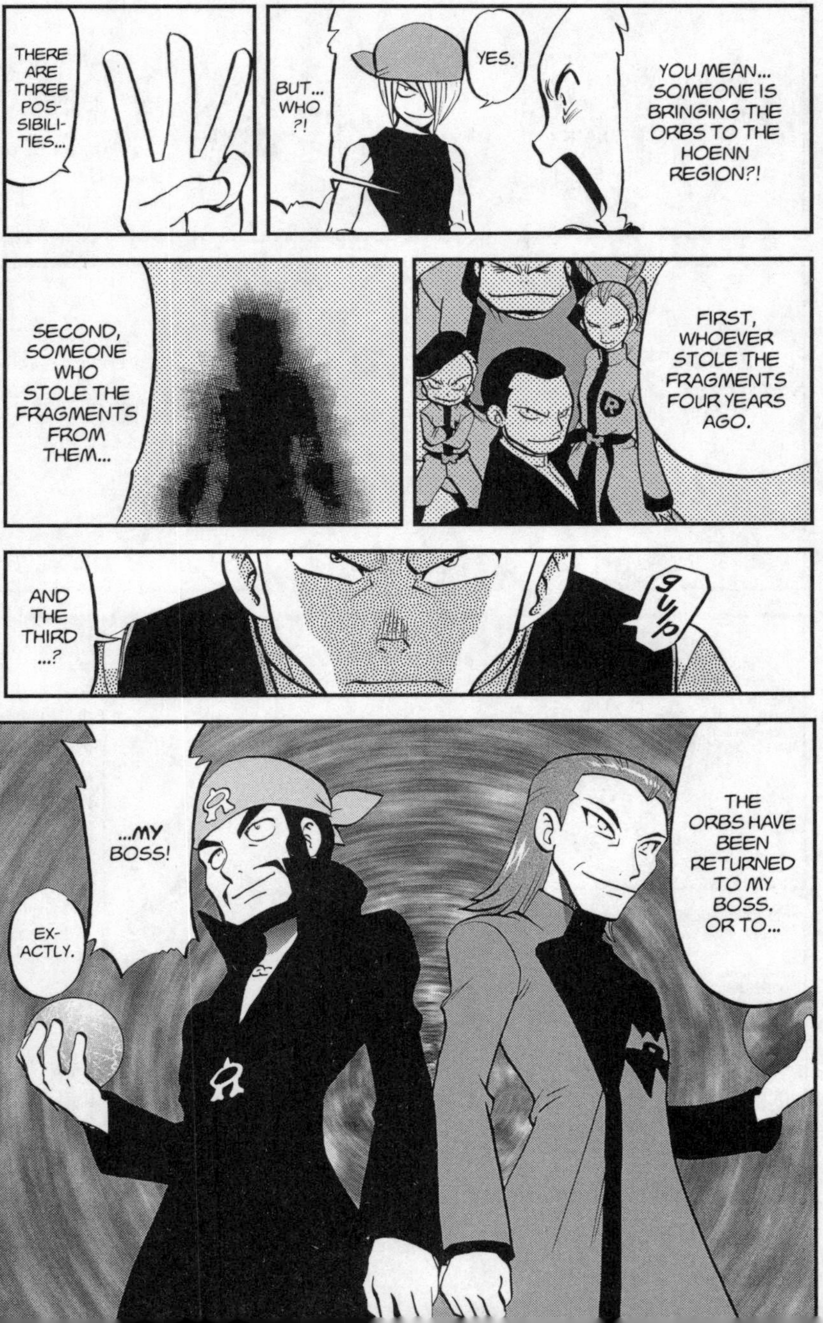
YOU MEAN... SOMEONE IS BRINGING THE ORBS TO THE HOENN REGION?!
YES.
BUT... WHO ?!
THERE ARE THREE POS-SIBILI-TIES...
FIRST, WHOEVER STOLE THE FRAGMENTS FOUR YEARS AGO.
SECOND, SOMEONE WHO STOLE THE FRAGMENTS FROM THEM...
gulp
AND THE THIRD ...?
THE ORBS HAVE BEEN RETURNED TO MY BOSS. OR TO...
...MY BOSS!
EX-ACTLY.

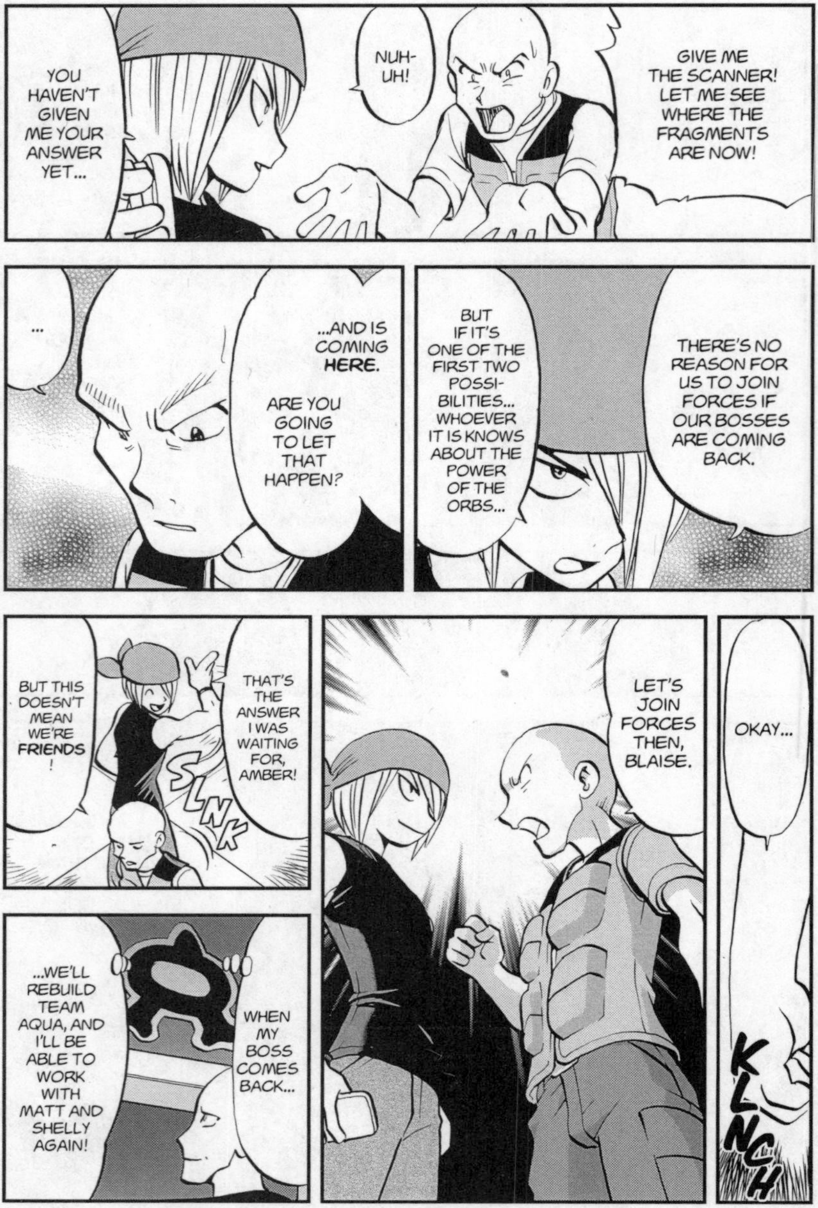
GIVE ME THE SCANNER! LET ME SEE WHERE THE FRAGMENTS ARE NOW!
NUH-UH!
YOU HAVEN'T GIVEN ME YOUR ANSWER YET...
THERE'S NO REASON FOR US TO JOIN FORCES IF OUR BOSSES ARE COMING BACK.
BUT IF IT'S ONE OF THE FIRST TWO POSSI-BILITIES... WHOEVER IT IS KNOWS ABOUT THE POWER OF THE ORBS...
...AND IS COMING **HERE**.
ARE YOU GOING TO LET THAT HAPPEN?
...
OKAY...
KLNCH
LET'S JOIN FORCES THEN, BLAISE.
THAT'S THE ANSWER I WAS WAITING FOR, AMBER!
BUT THIS DOESN'T MEAN WE'RE **FRIENDS**!
SLNK
WHEN MY BOSS COMES BACK...
...WE'LL REBUILD TEAM AQUA, AND I'LL BE ABLE TO WORK WITH MATT AND SHELLY AGAIN!

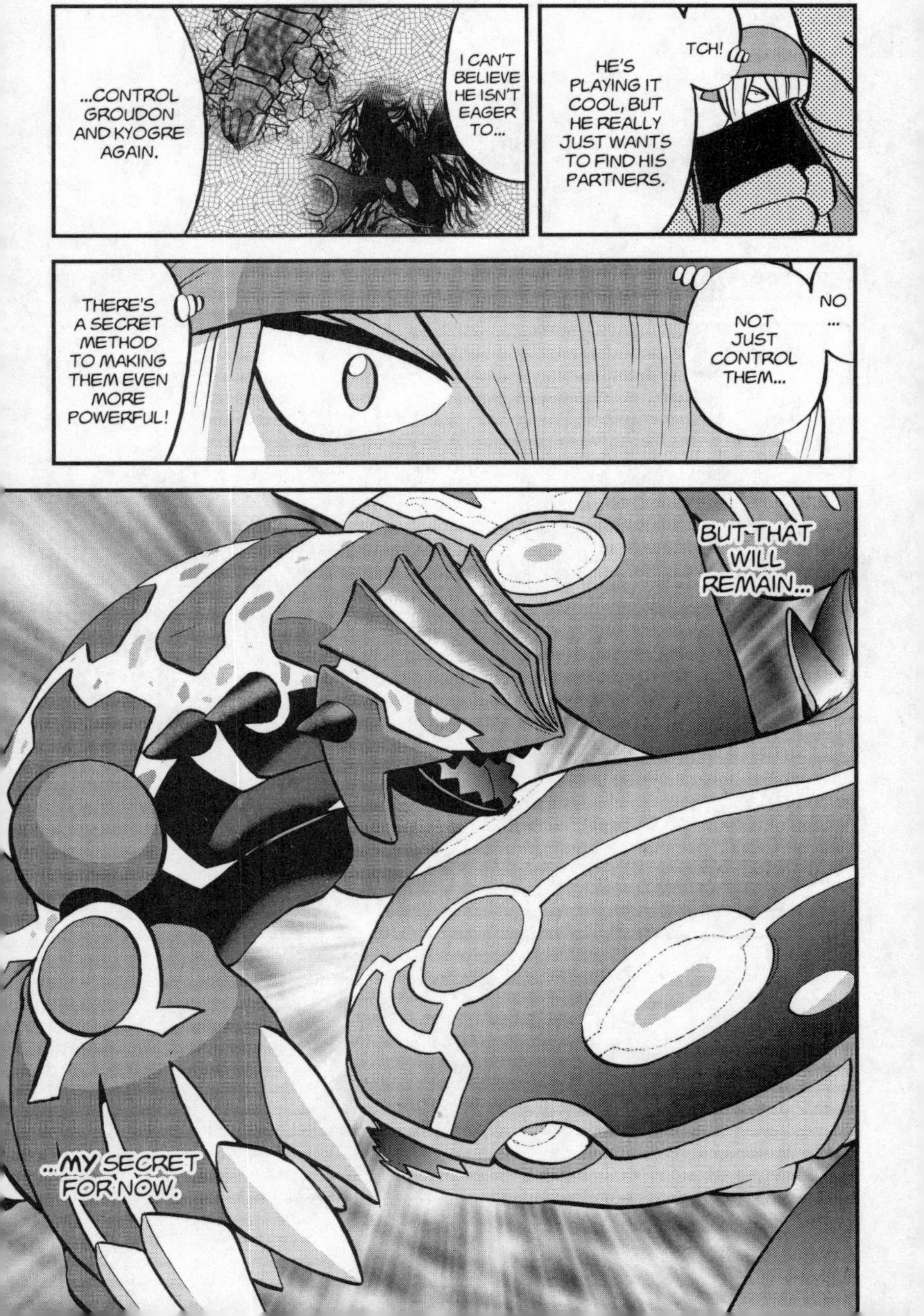
TCH!
HE'S PLAYING IT COOL, BUT HE REALLY JUST WANTS TO FIND HIS PARTNERS.
I CAN'T BELIEVE HE ISN'T EAGER TO...
...CONTROL GROUDON AND KYOGRE AGAIN.
NO ...
NOT JUST CONTROL THEM...
THERE'S A SECRET METHOD TO MAKING THEM EVEN MORE POWERFUL!
BUT THAT WILL REMAIN...
...MY SECRET FOR NOW.

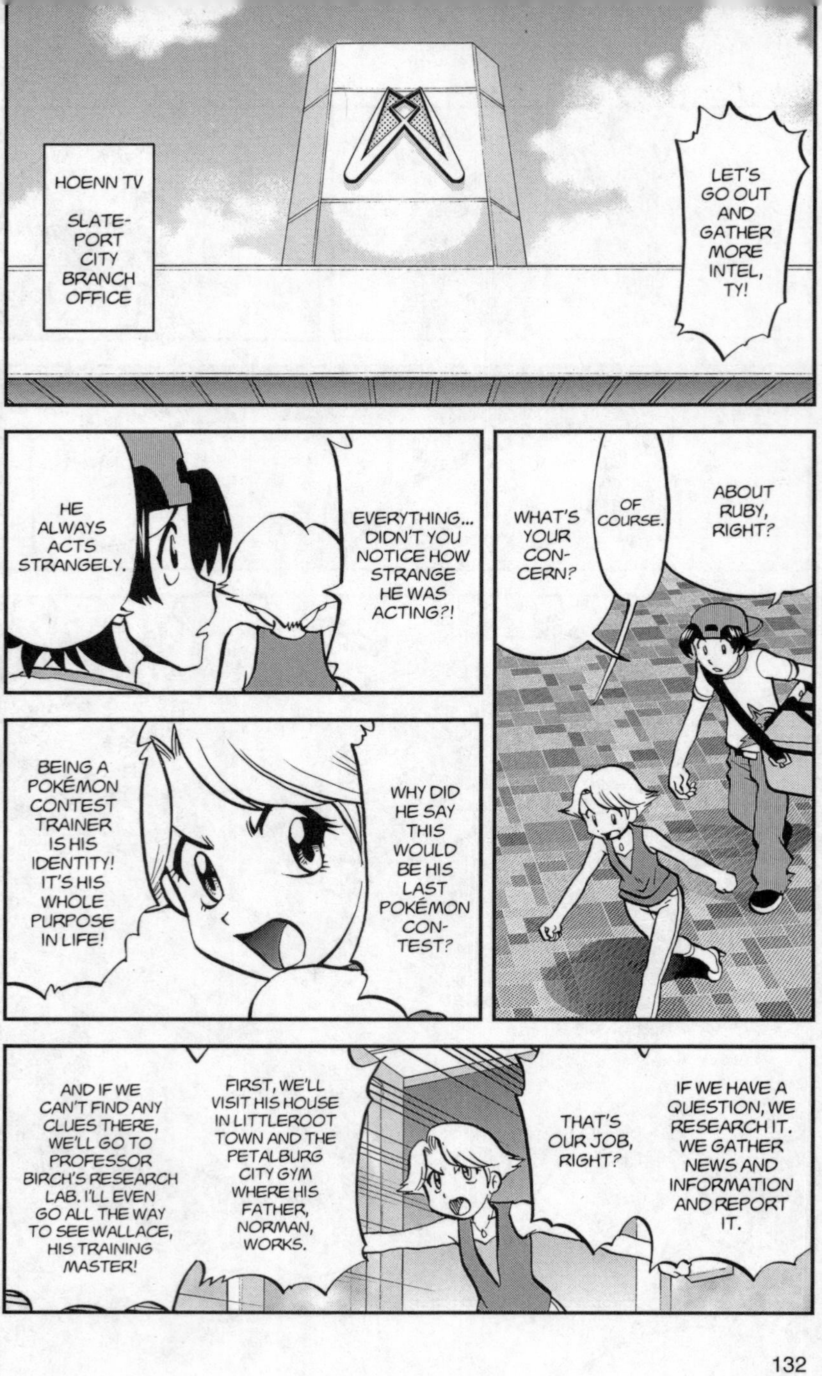
LET'S GO OUT AND GATHER MORE INTEL, TY!
HOENN TV
SLATEPORT CITY BRANCH OFFICE
ABOUT RUBY, RIGHT?
OF COURSE.
WHAT'S YOUR CONCERN?
EVERYTHING... DIDN'T YOU NOTICE HOW STRANGE HE WAS ACTING?!
HE ALWAYS ACTS STRANGELY.
WHY DID HE SAY THIS WOULD BE HIS LAST POKÉMON CONTEST?
BEING A POKÉMON CONTEST TRAINER IS HIS IDENTITY! IT'S HIS WHOLE PURPOSE IN LIFE!
IF WE HAVE A QUESTION, WE RESEARCH IT. WE GATHER NEWS AND INFORMATION AND REPORT IT.
THAT'S OUR JOB, RIGHT?
FIRST, WE'LL VISIT HIS HOUSE IN LITTLEROOT TOWN AND THE PETALBURG CITY GYM WHERE HIS FATHER, NORMAN, WORKS.
AND IF WE CAN'T FIND ANY CLUES THERE, WE'LL GO TO PROFESSOR BIRCH'S RESEARCH LAB. I'LL EVEN GO ALL THE WAY TO SEE WALLACE, HIS TRAINING MASTER!

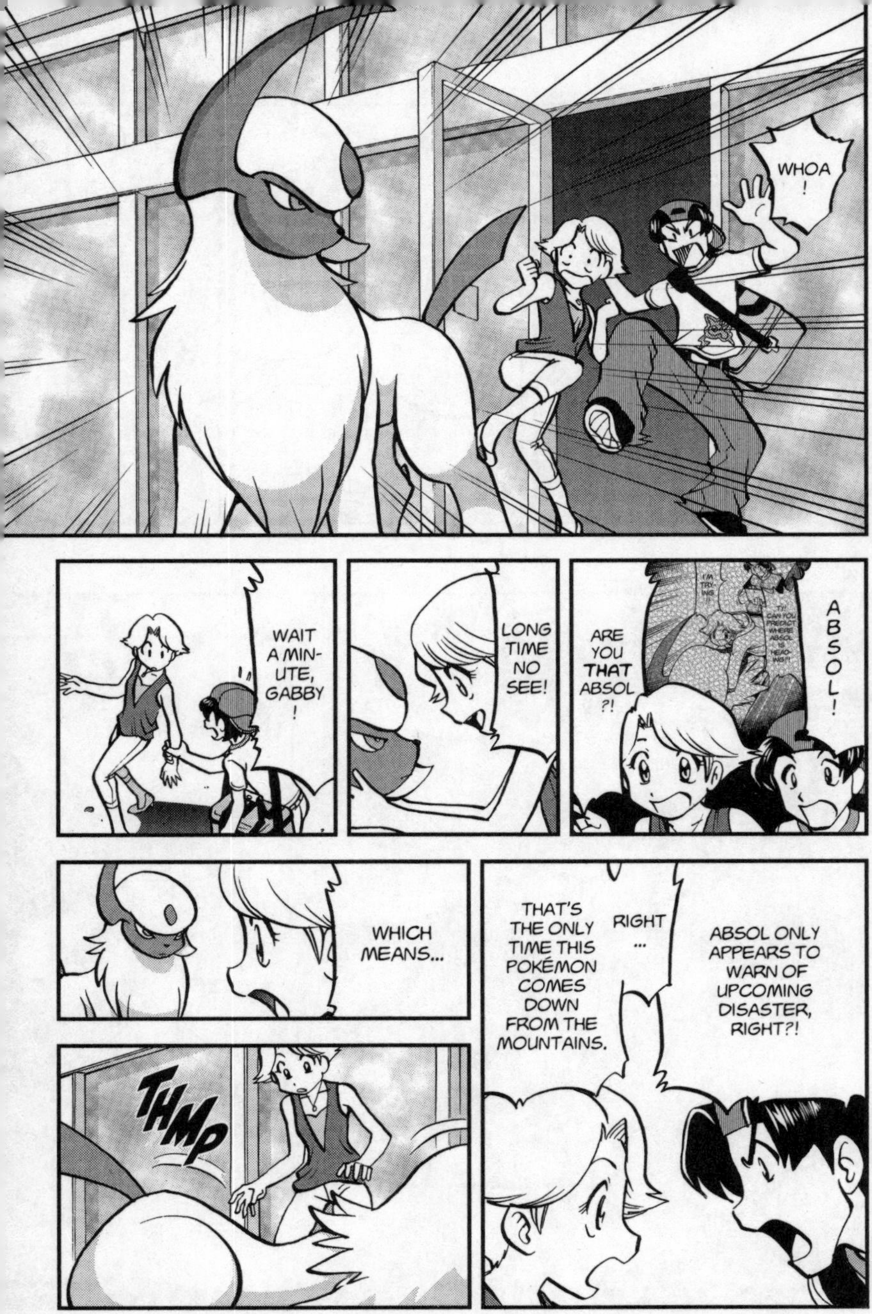
WHOA!
ABSOL!
ARE YOU THAT ABSOL?!
TY! CAN YOU PREDICT WHERE ABSOL IS HEADING!?
I'M TRYING!!
LONG TIME NO SEE!
WAIT A MINUTE, GABBY!
ABSOL ONLY APPEARS TO WARN OF UPCOMING DISASTER, RIGHT?!
RIGHT...
THAT'S THE ONLY TIME THIS POKÉMON COMES DOWN FROM THE MOUNTAINS.
WHICH MEANS...
THMP

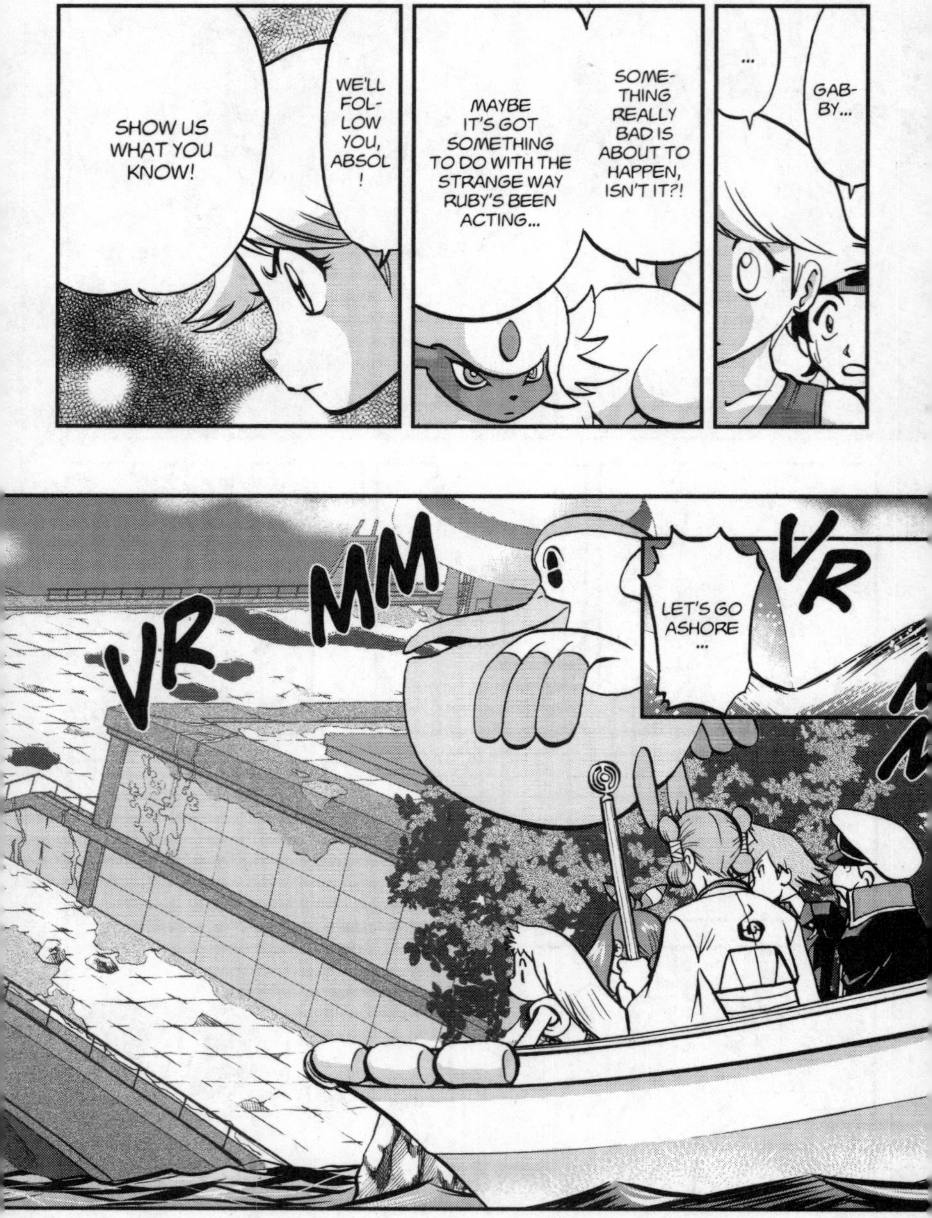
GAB-BY...
...
SOMETHING REALLY BAD IS ABOUT TO HAPPEN, ISN'T IT?!
MAYBE IT'S GOT SOMETHING TO DO WITH THE STRANGE WAY RUBY'S BEEN ACTING...
WE'LL FOLLOW YOU, ABSOL!
SHOW US WHAT YOU KNOW!
VR
LET'S GO ASHORE...
VR
MM

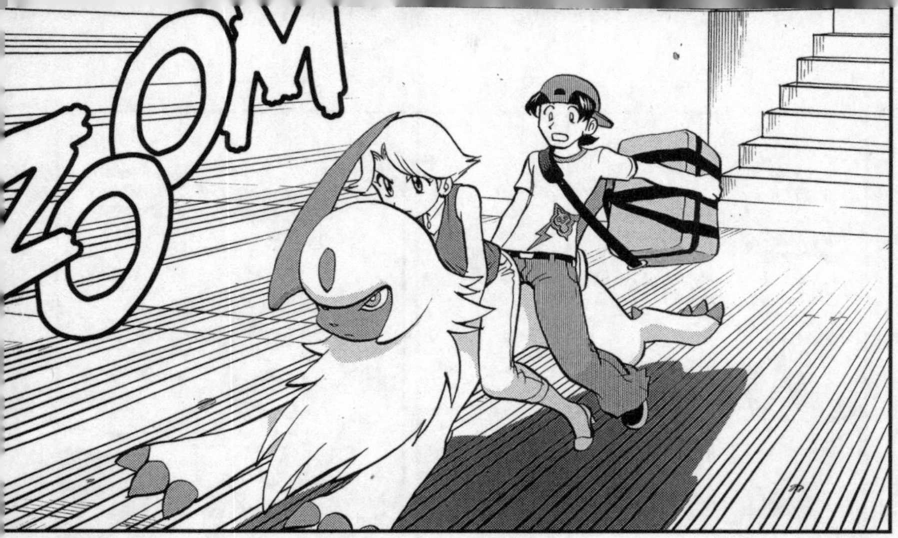
ZOOM
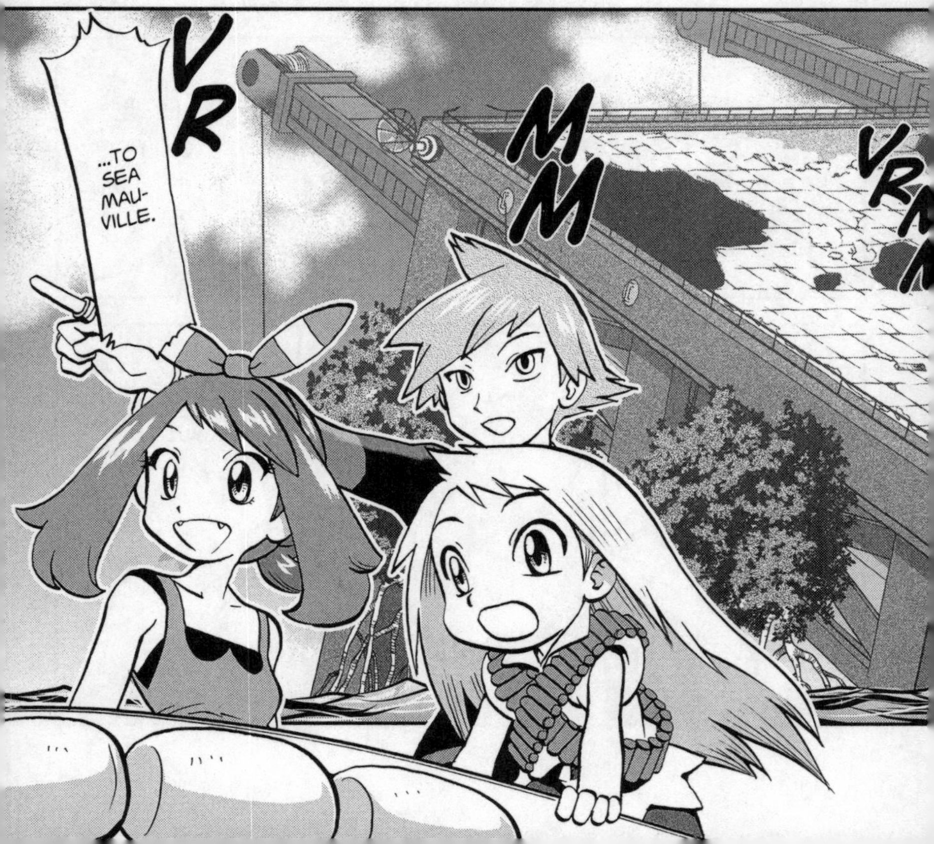
VRMM
...TO SEA MAUVILLE.

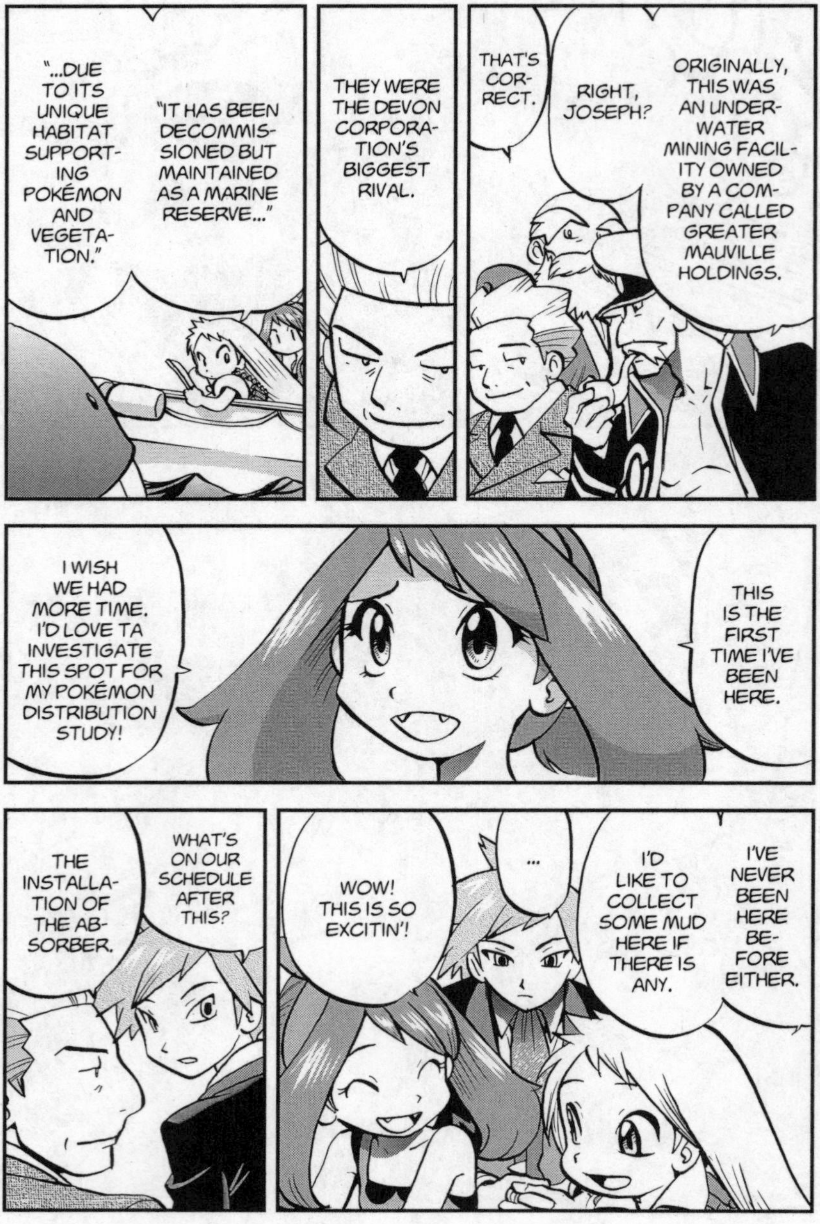
ORIGINALLY, THIS WAS AN UNDERWATER MINING FACILITY OWNED BY A COMPANY CALLED GREATER MAUVILLE HOLDINGS.
RIGHT, JOSEPH?
THAT'S CORRECT.
THEY WERE THE DEVON CORPORATION'S BIGGEST RIVAL.
"IT HAS BEEN DECOMMISSIONED BUT MAINTAINED AS A MARINE RESERVE..."
"...DUE TO ITS UNIQUE HABITAT SUPPORTING POKÉMON AND VEGETATION."
THIS IS THE FIRST TIME I'VE BEEN HERE.
I WISH WE HAD MORE TIME. I'D LOVE TA INVESTIGATE THIS SPOT FOR MY POKÉMON DISTRIBUTION STUDY!
I'VE NEVER BEEN HERE BEFORE EITHER.
I'D LIKE TO COLLECT SOME MUD HERE IF THERE IS ANY.
...
WOW! THIS IS SO EXCITIN'!
WHAT'S ON OUR SCHEDULE AFTER THIS?
THE INSTALLATION OF THE ABSORBER.

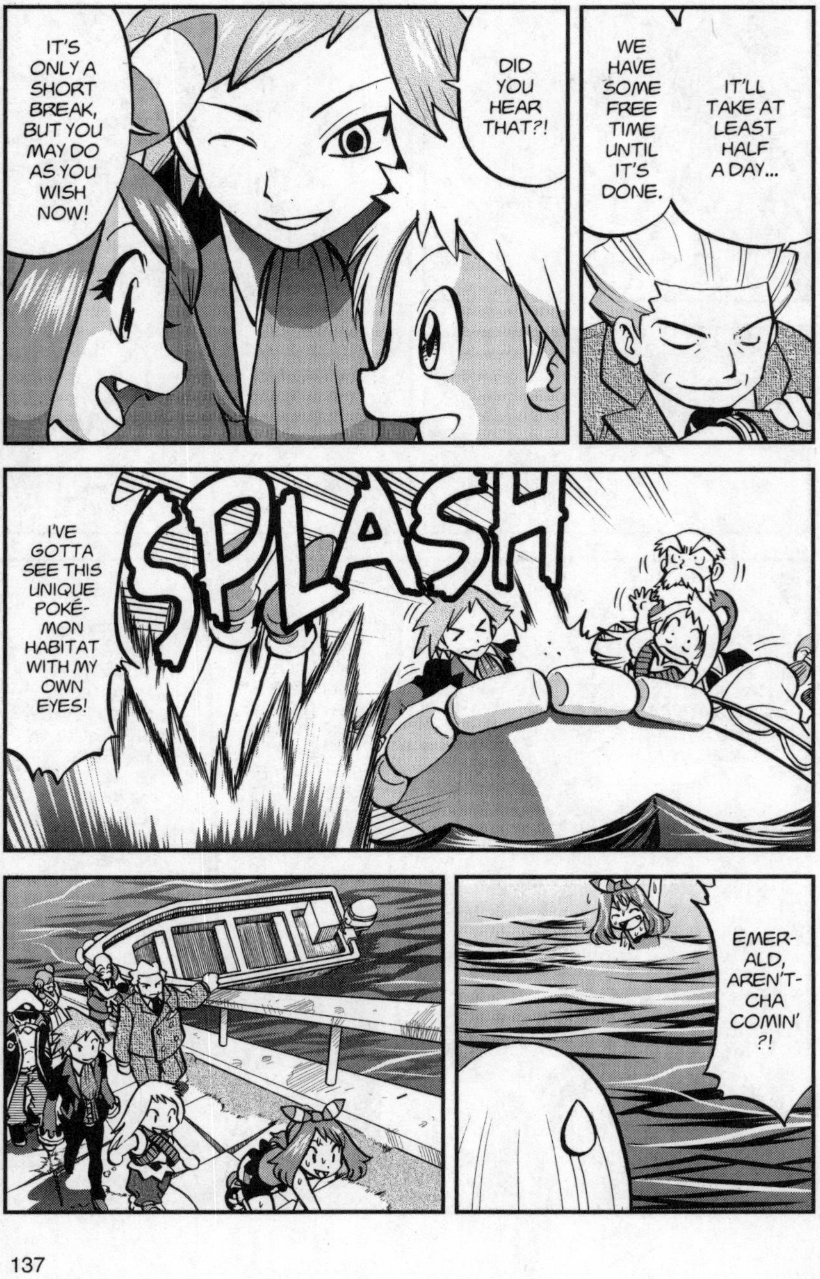
IT'LL TAKE AT LEAST HALF A DAY...
WE HAVE SOME FREE TIME UNTIL IT'S DONE.
DID YOU HEAR THAT?!
IT'S ONLY A SHORT BREAK, BUT YOU MAY DO AS YOU WISH NOW!
SPLASH
I'VE GOTTA SEE THIS UNIQUE POKÉMON HABITAT WITH MY OWN EYES!
EMERALD, AREN'T-CHA COMIN'?!

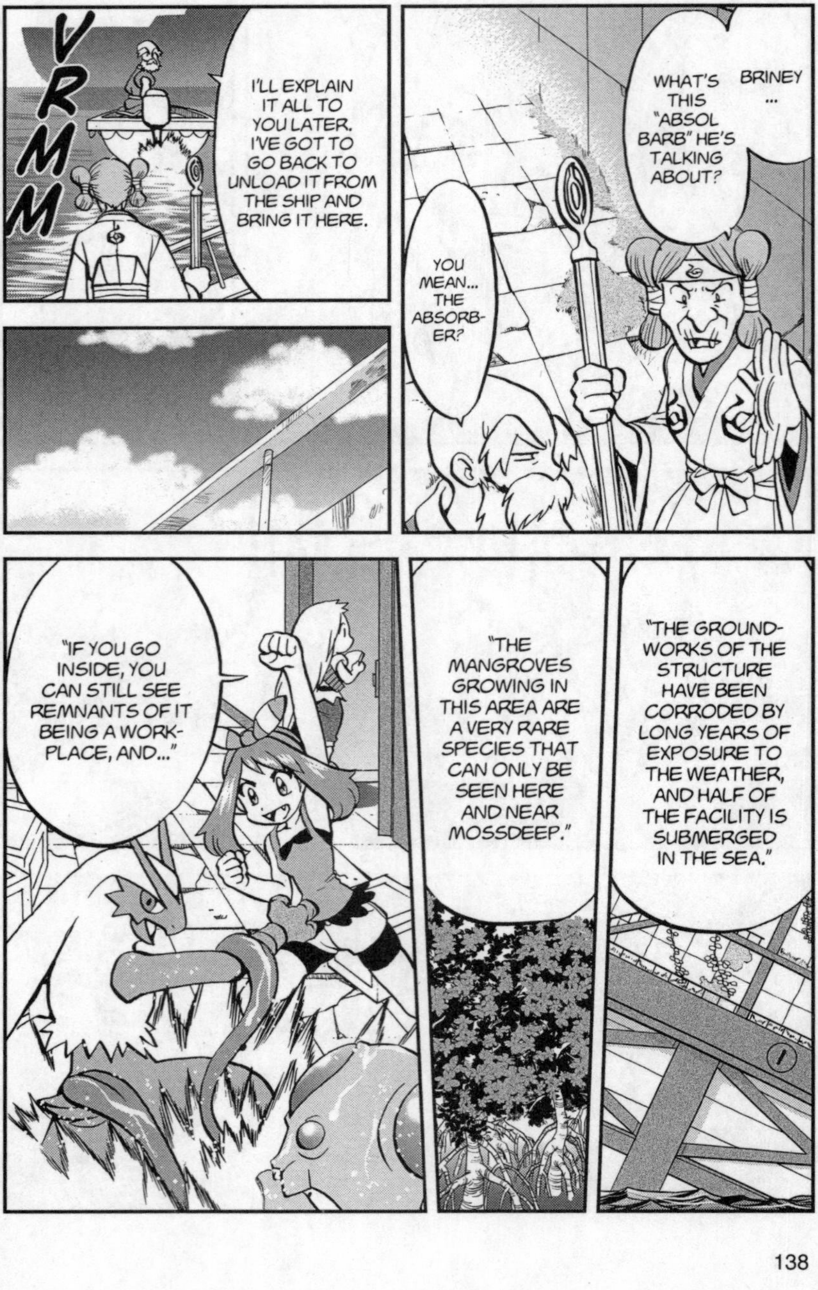
BRINEY ...
WHAT'S THIS "ABSOL BARB" HE'S TALKING ABOUT?
YOU MEAN... THE ABSORB-ER?
VRMM
I'LL EXPLAIN IT ALL TO YOU LATER. I'VE GOT TO GO BACK TO UNLOAD IT FROM THE SHIP AND BRING IT HERE.
"THE GROUND-WORKS OF THE STRUCTURE HAVE BEEN CORRODED BY LONG YEARS OF EXPOSURE TO THE WEATHER, AND HALF OF THE FACILITY IS SUBMERGED IN THE SEA."
"THE MANGROVES GROWING IN THIS AREA ARE A VERY RARE SPECIES THAT CAN ONLY BE SEEN HERE AND NEAR MOSSDEEP."
"IF YOU GO INSIDE, YOU CAN STILL SEE REMNANTS OF IT BEING A WORK-PLACE, AND..."

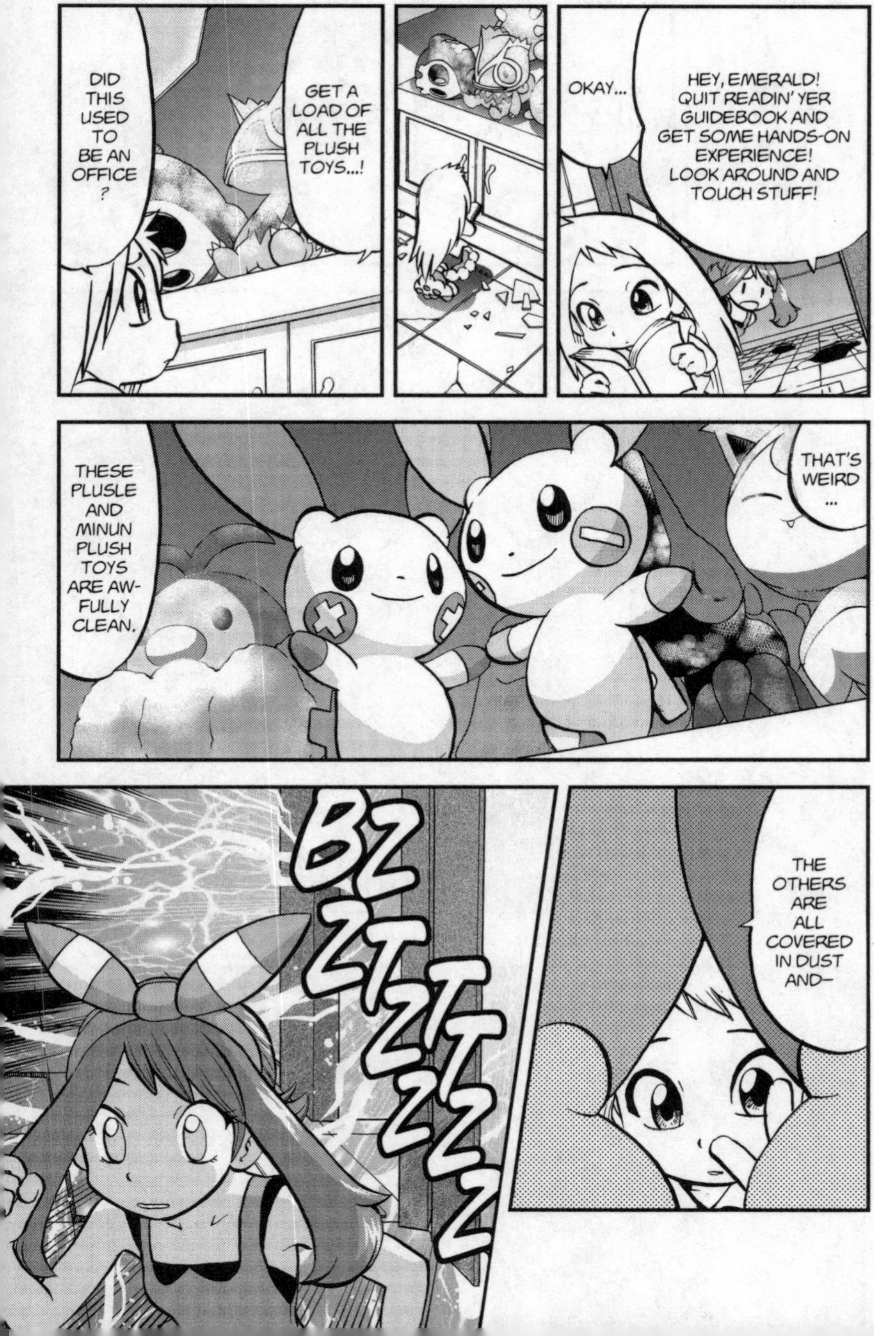
HEY, EMERALD! QUIT READIN' YER GUIDEBOOK AND GET SOME HANDS-ON EXPERIENCE! LOOK AROUND AND TOUCH STUFF!
OKAY...
GET A LOAD OF ALL THE PLUSH TOYS...!
DID THIS USED TO BE AN OFFICE?
THAT'S WEIRD...
THESE PLUSLE AND MINUN PLUSH TOYS ARE AW-FULLY CLEAN.
THE OTHERS ARE ALL COVERED IN DUST AND—
BZZTTZZZZ

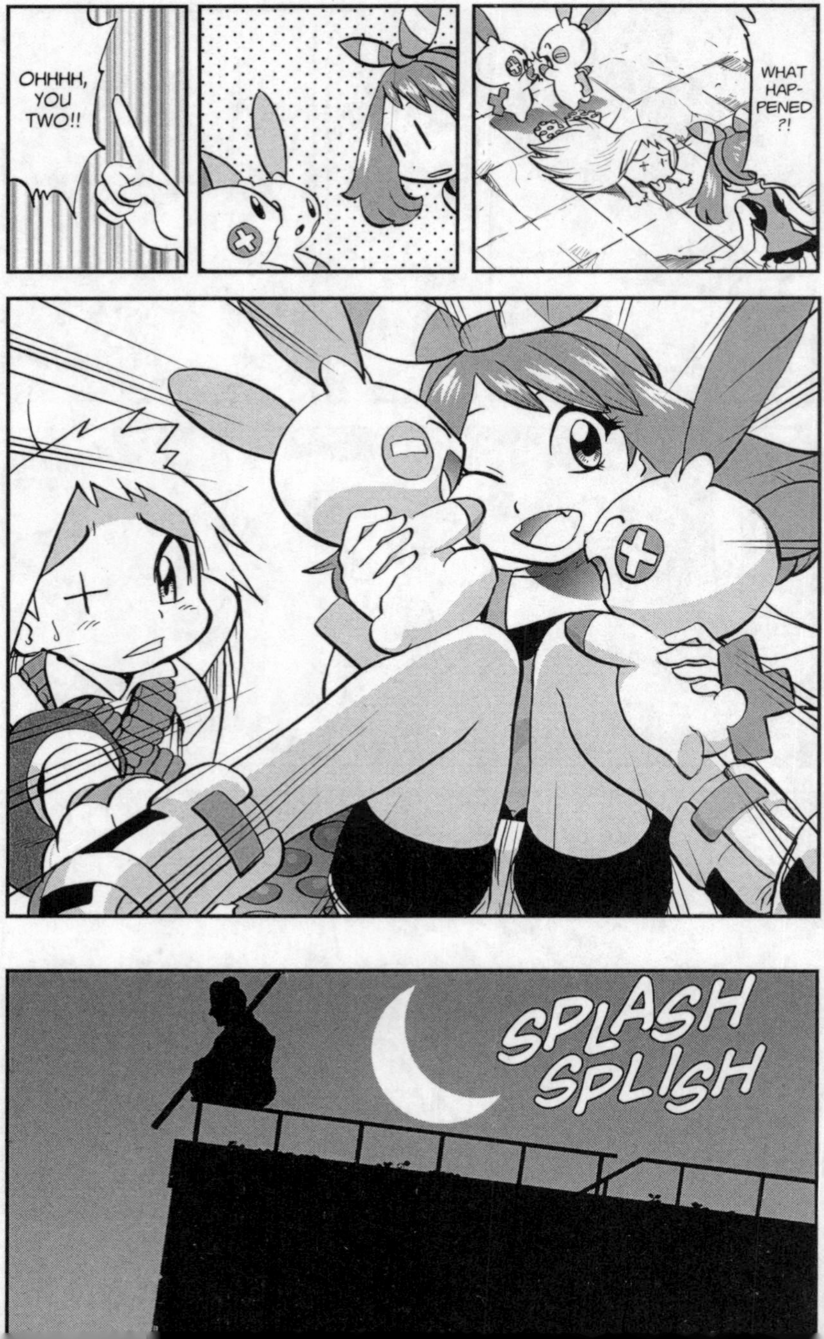
WHAT HAP-PENED ?!
OHHHH, YOU TWO!!
SPLASH SPLISH

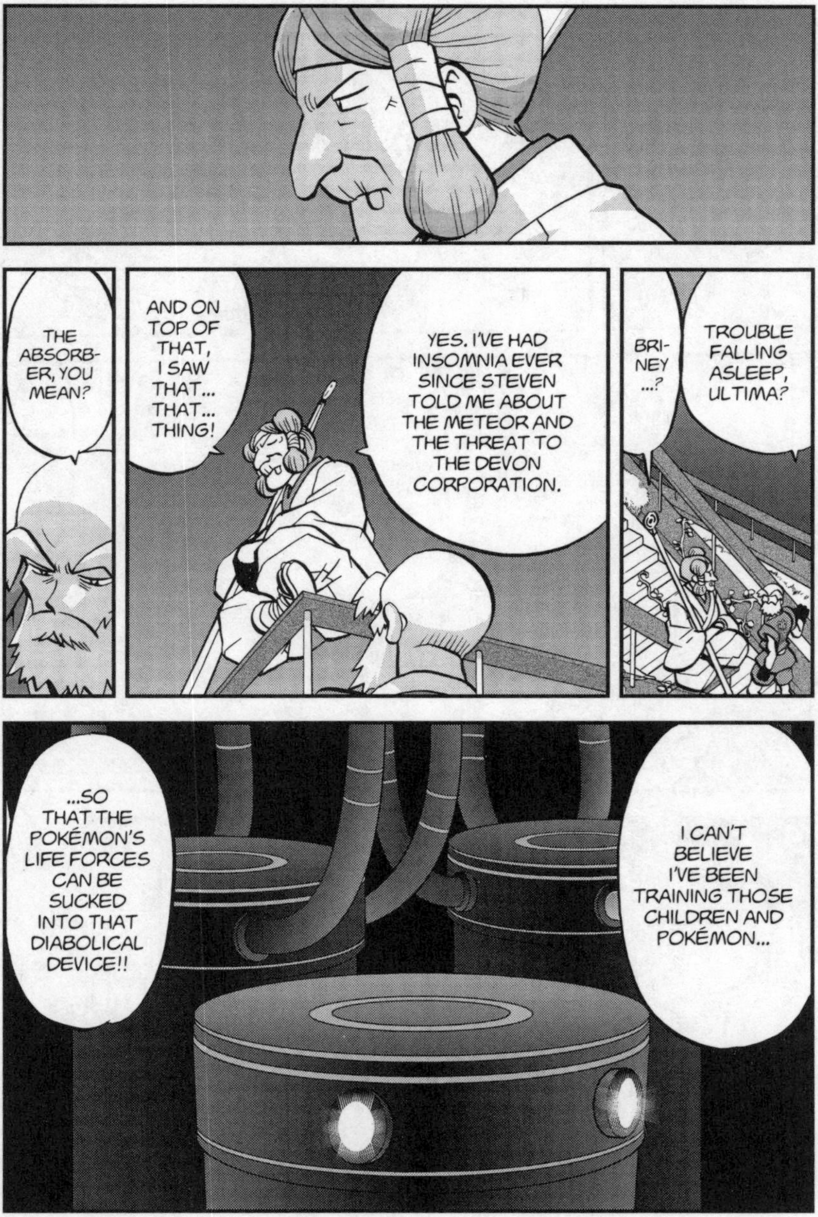
TROUBLE FALLING ASLEEP, ULTIMA?
BRI-NEY ...?
YES. I'VE HAD INSOMNIA EVER SINCE STEVEN TOLD ME ABOUT THE METEOR AND THE THREAT TO THE DEVON CORPORATION.
AND ON TOP OF THAT, I SAW THAT... THAT... THING!
THE ABSORB-ER, YOU MEAN?
I CAN'T BELIEVE I'VE BEEN TRAINING THOSE CHILDREN AND POKÉMON...
...SO THAT THE POKÉMON'S LIFE FORCES CAN BE SUCKED INTO THAT DIABOLICAL DEVICE!!

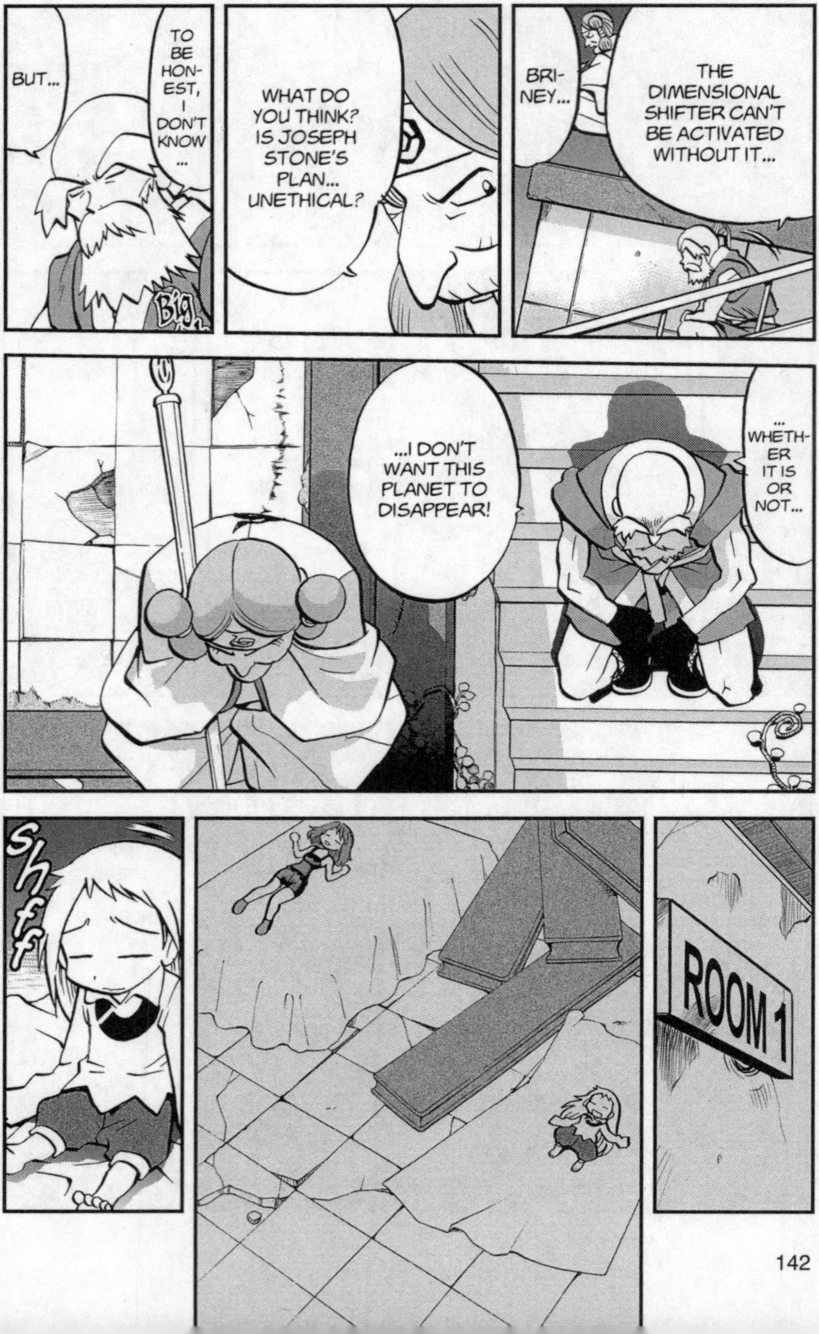

THE DIMENSIONAL SHIFTER CAN'T BE ACTIVATED WITHOUT IT...
BRI-NEY...
WHAT DO YOU THINK? IS JOSEPH STONE'S PLAN... UNETHICAL?
TO BE HON-EST, I DON'T KNOW ...
BUT...
... WHETH-ER IT IS OR NOT...
...I DON'T WANT THIS PLANET TO DISAPPEAR!
ROOM 1
shff

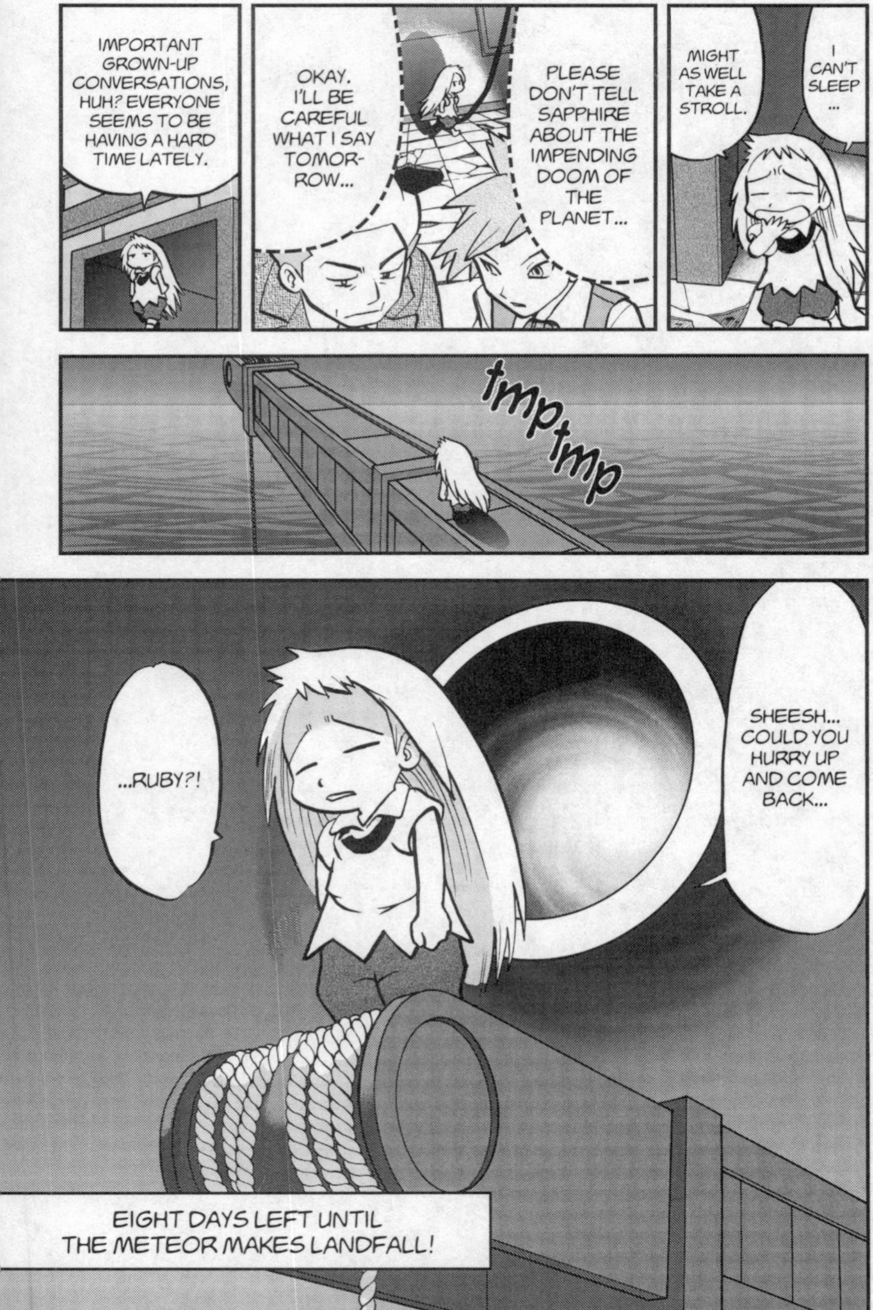
I CAN'T SLEEP ...
MIGHT AS WELL TAKE A STROLL.
PLEASE DON'T TELL SAPPHIRE ABOUT THE IMPENDING DOOM OF THE PLANET...
OKAY. I'LL BE CAREFUL WHAT I SAY TOMORROW...
IMPORTANT GROWN-UP CONVERSATIONS, HUH? EVERYONE SEEMS TO BE HAVING A HARD TIME LATELY.
tmp tmp
SHEESH... COULD YOU HURRY UP AND COME BACK...
...RUBY?!
EIGHT DAYS LEFT UNTIL THE METEOR MAKES LANDFALL!

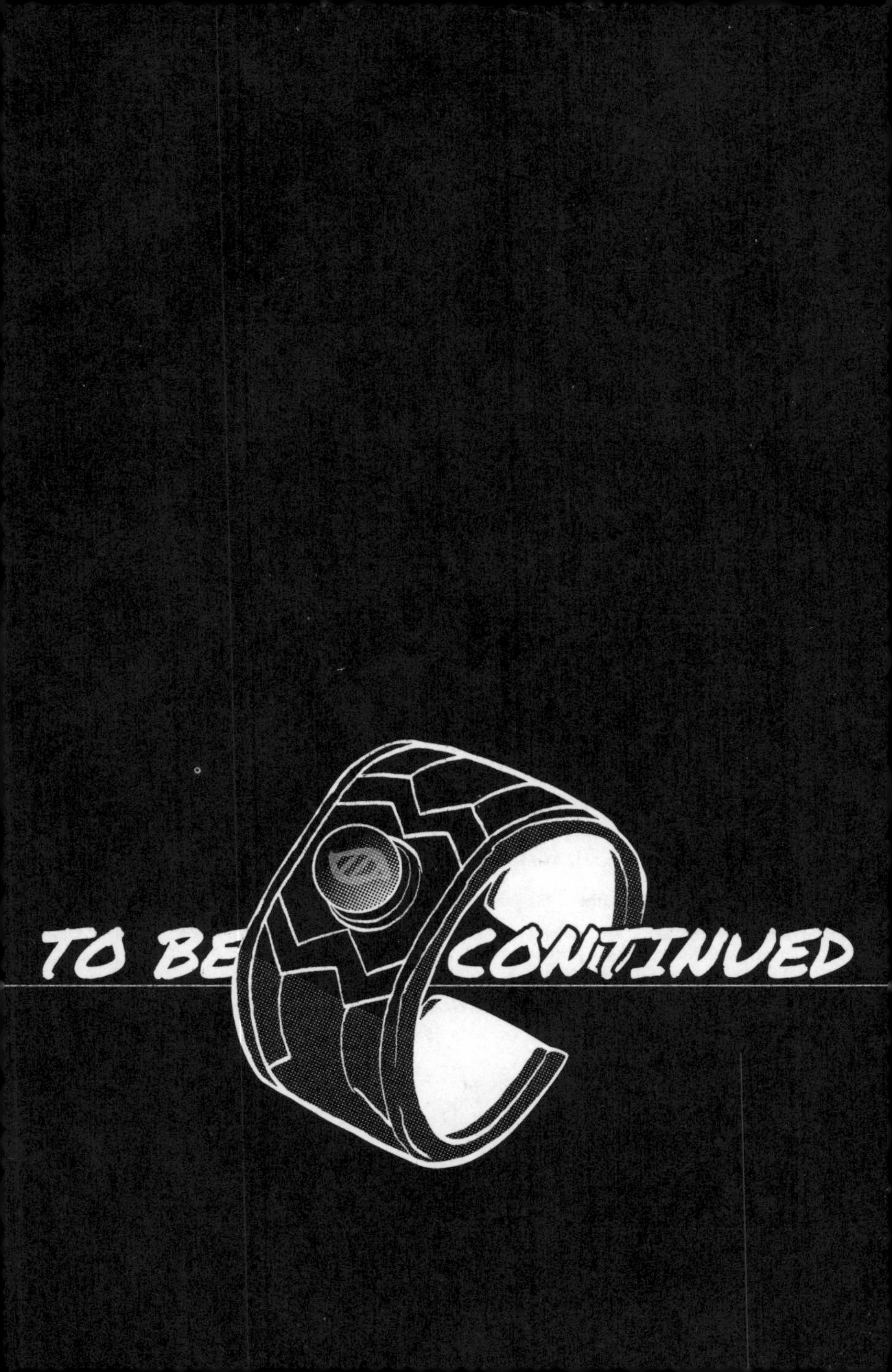
TO BE CONTINUED

Pokémon ADVENTURES: ΩRUBY · αSAPPHIRE
Volume 1
VIZ Media Edition

Story by HIDENORI KUSAKA
Art by SATOSHI YAMAMOTO

©2024 Pokémon.
©1995–2022 Nintendo / Creatures Inc. / GAME FREAK inc.
TM, ®, and character names are trademarks of Nintendo.
© 1997 Hidenori KUSAKA, Satoshi YAMAMOTO
All rights reserved.
Original Japanese edition published by SHOGAKUKAN.
English translation rights in the United States of America,
Canada, the United Kingdom, Ireland, Australia and New Zealand
arranged with SHOGAKUKAN.

Translation/Tetsuichiro Miyaki
English Adaptation/Bryant Turnage
Touch-Up & Lettering/Susan Daigle-Leach
Original Series Design/Shawn Carrico
Original Series Editor/Annette Roman
Graphic Novel Design/Alice Lewis
Graphic Novel Editor/Joel Enos

Original Cover Design/Hiroyuki KAWASOME (grafio)

Special thanks to Trish Ledoux at The Pokémon Company International.

The stories, characters, and incidents mentioned
in this publication are entirely fictional.

Printed in the U.S.A.

Published by VIZ Media, LLC
P.O. Box 77010
San Francisco, CA 94107

10 9 8 7 6 5 4 3 2
First printing, January 2024
Second printing, January 2024

PARENTAL ADVISORY
POKÉMON ADVENTURES
is rated A and is suitable
for readers of all ages.

viz.com

POKÉMON ADVENTURES 20TH ANNIVERSARY ILLUSTRATION BOOK

THE ART OF POKÉMON™ ADVENTURES

THE ART OF
POKéMON
ADVENTURES
SATOSHI YAMAMOTO

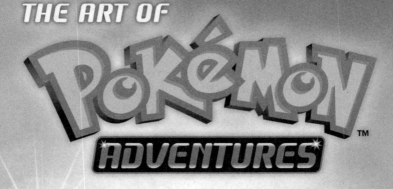

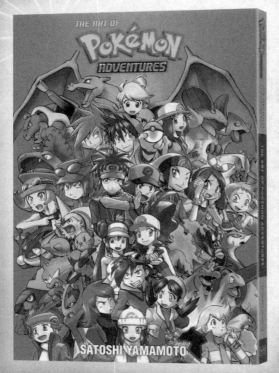

STORY AND ART BY
Satoshi Yamamoto

A collection of beautiful full-color art from the artist of the Pokémon Adventures graphic novel series! In addition to illustrations of your favorite Pokémon, this vibrant volume includes exclusive sketches and storyboards, four pull-out posters, and an exclusive manga side story!

VIZ
viz.com

POKÉMON™
SWORD & SHIELD

Story by
Hidenori Kusaka

Art by
Satoshi Yamamoto

Awesome adventures inspired by the best-selling
Pokémon Sword & Shield video games
set in the Galar region!

Pokémon
ADVENTURES
X·Y

Story by
HIDENORI KUSAKA

Art by
SATOSHI YAMAMOTO

Awesome Pokémon adventures inspired by the best-selling Pokémon X and Y video games!

X was a Pokémon Trainer child prodigy. He hated being in the spotlight, so he took to hiding in his room and avoiding everyone—including his best friend Y. But now a surprise attack has brought X out of hiding!

Pokémon
HORIZON
SUN & MOON

Akira's summer vacation in the Alola region heats up when he befriends a Rockruff with a mysterious gemstone. Together, Akira hopes they can achieve his newfound dream of becoming a Pokémon Trainer and master the amazing Z-Move. But first, Akira needs to pass a test to earn a Trainer Passport. This becomes more difficult when Rockruff gets kidnapped! And then Team Kings shows up with—you guessed it—evil plans for world domination!

Story & Art
TENYA YABUNO

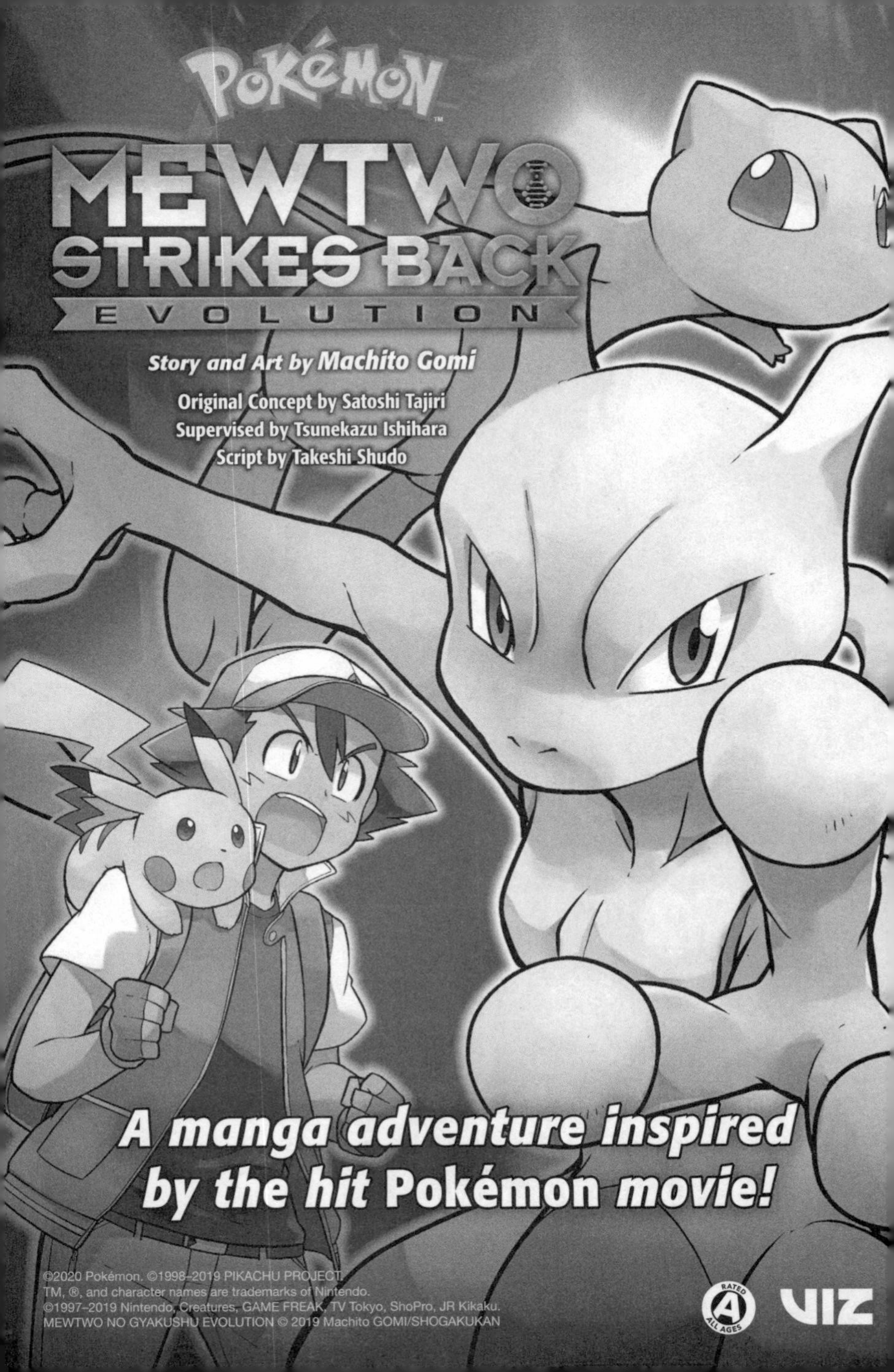

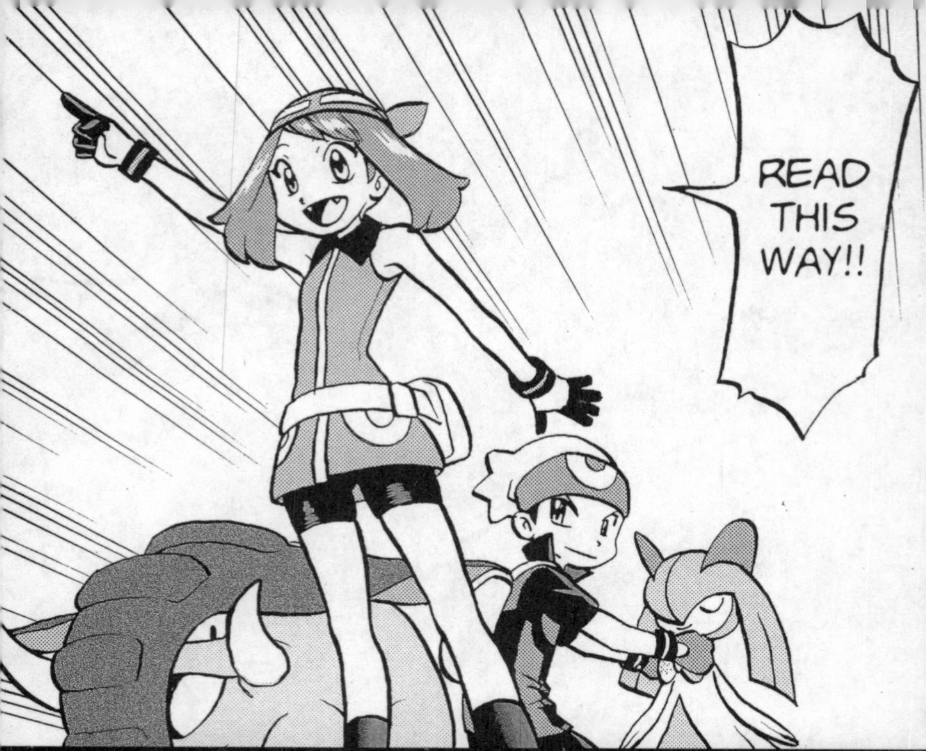
READ THIS WAY!!

THIS IS THE END OF THIS GRAPHIC NOVEL!

To properly enjoy this VIZ Media graphic novel, please turn it around and begin reading from right to left.

This book has been printed in the original Japanese format in order to preserve the orientation of the original artwork.

Have fun with it!

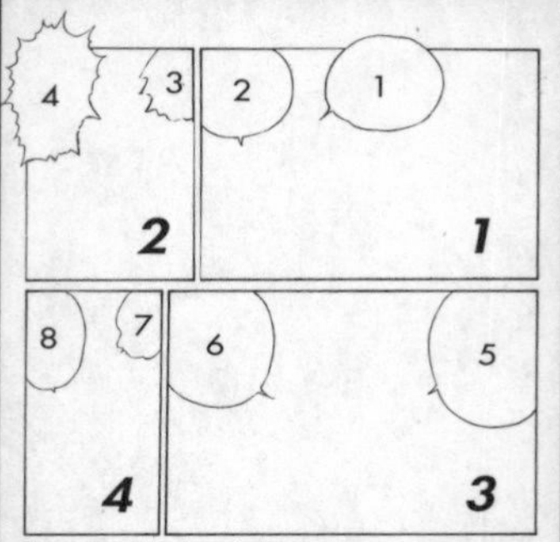

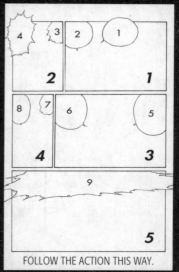

FOLLOW THE ACTION THIS WAY.